"YOU GET AWAY FROM ME," SUSAN CRIED. *"YOU LEAVE ME ALONE!"*

Her face contorted into a mask of fear. She turned and fled into the swirling gray mists. Relentlessly, Michelle started after her.

"Stay here," the voice whispered. "Let me do it. I *want* to do it."

Michelle stood still, listening, waiting. The scream, when it came, was muffled, floating. Then she felt the strange child close to her once more, almost inside her.

"I did it," the voice whispered. "I told you I would, and I did."

The words echoing in her head, Michelle started slowly homeward. By the time she reached the old house, the sun was shining brightly again from a clear early-autumn sky. The only sound was the crying of the gulls. . . .

* COMES THE BLIND FURY *

JOHN SAUL

A DELL BOOK

To Michael

Published by
Dell Publishing Co., Inc.
1 Dag Hammarskjold Plaza
New York, New York 10017

Dell ® TM 681510, Dell Publishing Co., Inc.

ISBN: 0-440-11475-6

Printed in the United States of America

First printing—June 1980
Ninth printing—April 1983

* COMES THE BLIND FURY *

PROLOGUE

She moved slowly along the path, her step careful, yet not hesitant. The path was familiar to her, and she knew almost by instinct when to move to the left, when to veer to the right, when to stay close to the middle of the trail. From a distance, in her black dress and her bonnet, she looked more like an old woman than a child of twelve, and the walking stick she always carried with her did nothing to lessen the impression of age.

Only her face was young, serene and unlined, her sightless eyes often seeming to see that which was invisible to those around her.

She was a solitary child; her blindness set her apart and placed her in a dark world from which she knew there would be no escape. Yet she had accepted her affliction as she accepted everything—quietly, peacefully—gifts from a God whose motives might seem clouded, but whose wisdom was not to be questioned.

It had been difficult at first, but when it had come

upon her she had still been young enough that her adjustment was almost natural. What had been seen was now only dimly remembered, and her dependence on her eyes was completely forgotten. Her other senses had sharpened. Now she heard things no one else heard, smelled perfumes in the sea air that would have been strange to anyone but her, and knew the flowers and the trees by how they felt.

The path she walked today was one of her favorites, winding along the edge of a bluff above the sea. On this path, her cane was almost unnecessary, for she knew it as well as she knew her parents' home a few hundred yards to the south. She counted her steps automatically, and her pace never varied. There were no surprises on the path, but her cane still went before her, waving from side to side, its white tip like a probing finger, eternally searching for anything that might block her way.

The sound of the ocean filled her ears, and the black-clad child paused for a moment, her face turning seaward, a picture of wheeling gulls forming dimly in the far reaches of her memory. Then, from behind her, she heard another sound—a sound that to any ears but hers would have been lost in the roar of pounding surf.

It was the sound of laughter.

She had heard it all day today, and knew what it meant.

It meant her schoolmates had become bored with their games, and were going to focus their attention on her for a while.

It happened every year during the fall. It seemed to her that each summer, when school was out and she seldom ventured beyond the beach and the bluff, the children forgot about her. Then, come September, she would become for a while an oddity to be stared at, wondered about, talked about.

And tormented.

The first day of school she would hear the whispering in class as she came slowly in, tapping along, familiarizing herself once more with the steps, the halls, the doors, the rows of desks. Then there would be the terrible moment, the moment she always hoped would never come, when the teacher would ask her where she would like to sit, and arrange the classroom for her convenience.

That was when her torment would begin.

It never lasted long—in a week, sometimes two, they would forget her, going on to more interesting things, but the damage would have been done. She would spend the rest of the year in solitude, making her lonely way to and from school.

Often there would be a time during the year when she would have a companion for a while. One of the other children would break an arm or a leg, and for some weeks, while the injury mended itself, the girl would have company, someone to talk to, someone who would become suddenly interested in her problems. But then the wound would heal, and she would be left alone once more.

Now, as the sound of laughter floated to her ears, she knew this was the day they had chosen to follow her home, commenting in whispers that one of these days—a day that had never come—they would put a log in the path, and see if she could find her way around it.

She tried to block out the mocking sounds, tried to concentrate on the soothing roar of the surf, but behind her the laughter grew. Finally she turned to face them.

"Leave me alone," she said softly. "Please?"

There was no reply, only a giggle from somewhere to her right. In relief, she turned south, and began moving slowly homeward. But then a voice came from ahead of her.

"Look out! There's a rock in the path!"

The girl stopped, and prodded at the path with her cane. She found nothing and took a step forward, pausing again to read the trail with her stick. Still nothing. She had let herself fall into their trap.

She began moving forward again, but when the same voice came at her out of the blackness, telling her she was about to stumble, she stopped again, and again examined the path with the tip of her cane.

This time, as she prodded at the trail, their laughter burst around her, and she knew she was in trouble.

There were four of them, and they had positioned themselves carefully, one ahead of her, one behind, and two more preventing her from leaving the trail to make her way across the field to the road.

She stood still, waiting.

"You can't stand there forever," a voice said to her. "Sooner or later you have to move, and when you do, you're going to trip, and fall off the bluff."

"Leave me alone!" the girl said. "Just leave me alone!"

She started to take a step, but again was stopped by a voice, warning her, mocking her.

"Not there—that's the wrong way."

It wasn't the wrong way, she was sure of it. But how *could* she be sure? She was confused now, and beginning to be frightened.

The sea. If she could be sure which way the sea lay, she would know in which direction to go. She began turning, listening carefully. If the wind were blowing, it would be easy, but the air was still today, and the sound of the sea seemed to surround her, coming from every direction, mixing with the childish laughter of her tormentors, confusing her .

She would have to try. As long as she stood here, listening to them, letting them upset her, they would remain, enjoying their game.

Ignore them.

That's what she must do. Simply ignore them.

The cane made an arc in front of her, then another. The nerves in her fingers read the smoothness of the trail, and the unevenness where the edge of the path blended into the field.

The girl made her decision and began walking.

Immediately the cries began.

"Watch out! There's a rock right in front of you!"

"You're going the wrong way. If you want to get home, you'd better turn around!"

"Not that way! You'll fall off the edge."

"So what if she does? She won't even see what's going to happen to her!"

"Put something in the path! Let's see if she can figure out what it is!"

The girl ignored them and moved steadfastly along the path, her cane reading the way for her, assuring her she was making no mistake. Around her, the disembodied voices kept pace with her, taunting her, challenging her. She forced herself not to respond to them, telling herself that they would stop soon, give up, leave her alone.

And then one of the voices, a boy's voice, cut through to her.

"Better not go home! Your mama might be having company!"

The girl froze. She stopped waving the stick in her hand, and it hung in the air, quivering uncertainly.

"Don't say that." The girl spoke quietly. "Don't ever say that."

The laughter stopped, and the girl wondered if perhaps the children had gone away.

They hadn't. Instead, their laughter grew uglier.

"Going home to see the whore?"

"Hurry home, and maybe your mother will teach you how to do it."

"My mother says she should be run out of town!"

"My daddy says next time he has two dollars he's coming to your house!"

"Stop it!" the girl screamed. "Don't you say that! It isn't true! *It isn't true!*" Suddenly she raised the cane, took it in both hands, and began swinging it. As it whistled in the air, the children's taunts jabbed at her.

"Your mama's a whore!"

"Your papa doesn't care!"

"I heard he collects the money!"

"When I'm sixteen, can I visit your mother?"

The girl, her black dress swirling around her, the ribbons on her bonnet flying about her head, began moving toward the voices, the cane in her hands whipping back and forth, trying to silence their taunts. She stumbled, began to fall, then caught herself. All around her the voices sounded in her ears, ignoring her blindness now, and concentrating on the sins of her mother.

It wasn't true.

She *knew* it. Her mother wouldn't do what they were saying she did. Why would they say it? Why? Why did they hate her? Why did they hate her mother and her father?

The cane moved more and more wildly, thrashing the air harmlessly as the children danced out of range, their laughter increasing at the specter of the unseeing victim, flailing at nothing, helpless, unable either to defend herself or to flee.

They began closing in around her as she backed away from them, holding the cane in front of her as if to fend them off.

The ground leveled under her feet, and she knew she was back on the trail. She tried to turn, but without the help of her cane she had no idea in which direction she was going.

Around her the four children came closer, their taunts growing more vicious, their laughter more hideous, enjoying their game.

The girl kept backing away. Then she felt something under her right foot. A rock. She started to move her foot, but suddenly the obstruction fell away from her. Unsure of what had happened, she put her foot where the rock had been.

Now there was nothing there.

Too late she realized where she was.

She remained balanced for a second, a look of terror on her face.

The cane in her hands moved wildly as she tried to find some leverage.

Then, as her balance left her and she began to feel herself falling, she let go of the cane. It dropped to the path. The four children stared at each other for a moment, then their eyes went to the cane that lay on the trail. At first none of them moved. Then the oldest among them stepped forward, picked up the cane, and threw it into the sea. As far as they were concerned, she had simply disappeared. . . .

She knew what was happening, knew she was going to die. Time seemed to slow down for her, and she heard the surf, its crashing coming ever closer to her. She was going to die! Why? What had she done? What had her mother done? None of it was right. None of it should have happened.

The roar in her ears was no longer the surf. Instead, she heard the voices of the children, taunting her, screaming at her, echoing through her mind, crashing in her head.

For the first time in her life, anger entered her soul. It was wrong, all of it. She shouldn't have been blind. She shouldn't have had to listen to what the children told her. She should have been able to see everything for herself.

See it, and make it right.

And avenge it.

Her fury grew as she tumbled toward the sea, and by the time the waters closed around her, she was no longer aware of what was happening to her, no longer aware that her life was ending.

All she knew was her anger.

Her anger, and her hatred. . . .

BOOK ONE

PARADISE POINT

*

CHAPTER 1

The August sun was shining brightly when the Pendletons arrived at Paradise Point, and as they drove slowly through the village, all the Pendletons found themselves looking at it with new eyes. Always before, it had been merely a remarkably pretty village. Now it was home, and June Pendleton, her bright blue eyes glistening with eagerness, found herself suddenly more interested in the location of the supermarket and the drugstore than in the carefully restored façades of the inn and the galleries that surrounded the square.

Paradise Point was aptly named, and it seemed to the casual visitor that its setting was its primary reason for being. The village nestled high above the Atlantic, perched on the northern arm of twin outcroppings of land that cradled a small cove. Too small to serve as more than a temporary anchorage for small boats, the cove lay nearly hidden from the sea. The arms that guarded it had a selfish quality to them: they embraced the cove, cuddling it close into the surrounding forest, leaving only a narrow gap of surging water as a lifeline to the ocean. As long as there had been men to watch the roiling waters of Devil's Passage, there had been a village of one kind or another on the Point.

The present village had overlooked the cove and the sea for nearly two hundred years, and by common consent of all who lived there, it remained a village. There was no industry to speak of, no fishing fleet, and only a handful of farms carved out of the inland forests. But Paradise Point survived, supporting itself by the mysterious means of tiny villages everywhere, its modest production of services surviving in large part on the summer people who flooded in each year to bask in its beauty and "get away from it all." Scattered through the village were a handful of artists and craftsmen, sustaining themselves by the sale of a trickle of quilts, moccasins, pottery, sculpture, and paintings that drifted out of Paradise Point in the backseats and luggage compartments of those not fortunate enough to live there.

Dr. and Mrs. Calvin Pendleton were about to become part of Paradise Point, and they counted themselves very much among the fortunate. So did their daughter, Michelle.

Not that they had ever planned to move to Paradise Point. Indeed, until a few months before they arrived, it had never occurred to anyone in the family that they might live anywhere but Boston. Paradise Point, to the Pendletons, had been a beautiful spot to go to for an afternoon, just a couple of hours northeast of the city, a place where Cal could relax, June could paint, and Michelle could entertain herself with the forest and the seashore. Then, at the end of the day, they could drive back to Boston, and their well-ordered lives.

Except that their lives had not stayed well ordered.

Now, as Cal turned right to leave the square and start along the road that would take them out of the village and around the cove toward their new home, he saw several people stare at the car, smile suddenly, then wave.

"Looks like we're expected," he observed. In the seat next to him, June moved heavily. She was in the last weeks of pregnancy, and it seemed to her that it would never end.

"No more impersonality of the big city," she replied. "I suppose Dr. Carson has the welcome wagon all lined up to greet us."

"What's a welcome wagon?" Michelle asked from the backseat. Twelve years old, Michelle presented a sharp contrast to her parents, who were both blue-eyed blondes, with a nordic handsomeness to their features. Michelle was just the opposite. She was dark, her hair nearly black, and her deep brown eyes had a slight tilt to them, giving her a gamin look. She was leaning forward, arms propped on the front seat, her shiny hair cascading over her shoulders, her eyes devouring every detail of Paradise Point. It was all so different from Boston, and, she thought, all perfectly wonderful.

June moved to face her daughter, but the effort was too much for her distended body. As she sank back into her seat she reflected that it might be difficult to explain the old small-town custom of welcome wagons to a twelve-year-old city child anyway. Instead, as they passed the Paradise Point school, she touched her daughter's hand.

"Doesn't look much like Harrison, does it?" she asked.

Michelle stared at the small white clapboard build-

ing, surrounded by a grassy playfield, then grinned,
her elfin face reflecting her pleasure at what she saw.
"I always thought they automatically paved the playfield," she said. "And *trees*. You can actually sit under
trees while you eat lunch!"

Two blocks past the school, Cal slowed the car
nearly to a stop. "I wonder if I should stop in and
speak to Carson?" he mused.

"Is that the clinic?" Michelle asked. Her voice re-
vealed that she didn't think much of it.

"Compared to Boston General, it isn't much, is it?"
Cal said. Then, barely audibly, he added, "But maybe
it's where I belong."

June glanced quickly at her husband, then reached
out to squeeze his hand. "It's just right," she assured
him. The car came to a full stop, and the three Pendletons looked at the one-story building, no larger than a
small house, that contained the Paradise Point Clinic.
On the weatherbeaten sign in front, they could barely
read the name of Josiah Carson, but Cal's own name,
in freshly painted black letters, stood out clearly.

"Maybe I'll just pop in and let him know we got
here all right," Cal suggested. He was about to get out
of the car when June's voice stopped him.

"Can't you go later? The van's already at the house,
and there's so much to do. Dr. Carson won't be expecting you to stop. Not today."

She's right, Cal told himself, though he felt a twinge
of guilt. He owed Carson so much. But still, tomorrow
would be soon enough. He closed the door and put the
car in gear. A moment later the clinic disappeared
from sight, the village was suddenly behind them,
and they were on the road that paralleled the cove.

June let herself relax. Today, at least, she wouldn't

have to see the old doctor who had suddenly become such a major force in her life, a force she neither liked, nor trusted. A bond had sprung up between her husband and Josiah Carson, and it seemed to be growing stronger each day. She wished she understood it better —all she knew, really, was that it had to do with that boy.

That boy who had died.

Resolutely, she put it out of her mind. For now, she would concentrate on Paradise Point.

It was a pretty drive, deep forests on the inland side, and a narrow expanse of grass and bracken separating the road from the crest of the bluffs that dropped precipitously to the tiny bay below.

"Is that our house?" Michelle asked. Silhouetted against the horizon, a house stood out starkly from the landscape, its mansard roofline and widow's walk etched against the blue sky.

"That's it," June replied. "What do you think?"

"It looks great from here. But what's the inside like?"

Cal chuckled. "About the same as the outside. You'll love it."

As they approached the house that was to be their new home, Michelle let her eyes wander over the landscape. It was beautiful, but, in a way, strange. She found it difficult to imagine actually living with all this space. And the neighbors—instead of being right through the wall, they were going to be almost a quarter of a mile away. And, she noticed excitedly, with a graveyard between them. An actual, for-real, old-fashioned, broken-down cemetery. As the car passed the graveyard, Michelle pointed it out to her mother. June looked at it with interest, then asked Cal if he knew anything about it. He shrugged.

"Josiah told me it's his old family plot, but that they don't use it anymore. Or, I guess, *he* doesn't plan to use it. Says he's going to be buried in Florida, and doesn't give a damn if he never sees Paradise Point again."

June laughed out loud. "That's what he says now. But wait'll he gets there. Bet you a nickel he hotfoots it right back up here again."

"And tries to buy the practice back from me? And the house? No, I think he's really looking forward to getting away from here." He paused a moment, then: "I think that accident shook him up more than he's let on."

Suddenly the laughter left June's voice. "It shook us all up, didn't it?" she said quietly. "And we didn't even know the boy. But here we are. Strange, isn't it?"

Cal made no reply.

Their new home—Josiah Carson's old home.

His new life—Josiah Carson's old life.

Who, Cal silently wondered, was fleeing from what?

As the car came to a stop in front of the house, Michelle leaped out and stared up in rapture at the Victorian ornateness of the place, ignoring the peeling paint and worn woodwork that gave the house a curiously foreboding look.

"It's like a dream," she breathed. "Are we really going to live in this?"

Standing beside her, Cal put his arm around his daughter's shoulders and squeezed her affectionately. "Like it, princess?"

"Like it? How could anyone not like it? It looks like something out of a storybook."

"You mean it looks like something out of Charles Addams," June said, emerging from her side of the car.

She peered up to the high roof of the three-story house and shook her head. "I keep getting the feeling that there must be bats up there."

Michelle frowned at her mother. "If you don't like it, why did we buy it?"

"I didn't say I didn't like it," June added quickly. "Actually, I love it. But you have to admit, it's a far cry from a condominium in Boston." She paused a moment, then: "I hope we've done the right thing."

"We have," Michelle said. "I know we have." Leaving her parents standing next to the car, she bounded up onto the porch and disappeared through the front door. Cal reached out and took his wife's hand.

"It's going to be fine," he said, the first acknowledgment either of them had made to the fears they had shared about the move. "Come on, let's go look around."

They had bought the house furnished, and after very little discussion had decided not to try to sell the furniture that came with it. Instead, they had sold their own. Their furniture had been simple and low, and though it had fit perfectly into their Boston apartment, June's artistic eye had told her immediately that it was wrong for the high ceilings and ornate decor of the Victorian. They had decided that a change of lifestyle might as well involve a change of taste, and now they explored the house together, wondering how long it would take them to get used to their new environment.

The living room, set carefully behind a small reception room to the right of the front door, was piled high with the boxes containing their lives. One quick look was enough to shake June's confidence about the wisdom of their project, but Cal, reading his wife's mind, assured her that she could relax—he and Michelle would take care of the unpacking; all she had to do was to tell them where to put things. June smiled at him in relief, and they went on to the dining room.

"What on earth are we going to put into all those china cupboards?" June asked, not really expecting an answer.

"China, of course," Cal said easily. "I've always heard that possessions expand to fill space. Now we'll find out. Are we going to have to eat in here?" The doleful look on his face as he surveyed the formal dining table with its twelve chairs made June laugh out loud.

"I've already got it figured out. We'll convert the butler's pantry into another dining room." She led him through a swinging door, and Cal shook his head.

"How the hell could people live like this? It's obscene." The butler's pantry, containing a sink and a refrigerator, was larger than their dining room had been in Boston.

"It's particularly obscene when you consider this place was built by a minister," June observed archly.

Cal's brows rose in surprise. "Who told you that?"

"Dr. Carson, of course. Who else?" Before Cal could make any reply, June had proceeded into the kitchen. This, she had already decided, was where the family would live.

It was a huge room, a fireplace dominating one wall, with two large stoves, and a walk-in refrigerator, which had been disconnected years earlier. When he had taken them through the house, Josiah Carson had suggested that they tear it out, but Cal had thought the old refrigerator would make an ideal wine cellar: perfectly insulated, though prohibitively expensive to use for its original purpose.

June walked over to the sink and tried the tap. The pipes rattled for a few seconds, coughed twice, then produced a gushing stream of clear, unchlorinated water.

"Lovely," June murmured. Her eyes went to the window, and her face lit up with a smile.

Beyond the window, some fifty feet from the house, there was an old brick building with a slate roof that had once been used as a potting-shed. It was the potting-shed that had convinced June that the house would be perfect for them. One look had told her that it could easily be changed into a studio—a studio where she could spend endless blissful hours with her canvases, developing a style that would be truly her own, something she had never been able to accomplish in Boston.

Seeing the smile on her face, Cal once more read his wife's mind.

"Let's see," he said thoughtfully, brushing his hair back from his brow. "There's the butler's pantry to change into a dining room, and the potting-shed to change into a studio. Then I suppose I could change the barn into a workshop, the front parlor into a sauna, and the study into a surgery. Once that's finished—"

"Oh, stop it!" June cried. "I promise you, I'll do everything in the studio myself, and most of the butler's pantry, too. All you have to do is unpack—and then get on with your country doctor act!"

"Promise?"

"Promise," June said softly, coming into his arms and hugging him close. "Everything will be all right now. I'm sure it will." She wished she truly believed her own words.

Cal kissed his wife, then let his hand rest for a second on her rounded belly. Under his fingers, he could feel the baby move. "We'd better get upstairs and figure out where the nursery is going to be. Seems to me like this little critter is about to make its debut."

"Not for six weeks yet, at least," June replied. But she happily followed her husband upstairs, eager to decide which room could best be changed into a nursery. *There's that word again*, she thought. *This seems to be our year to change.*

They found Michelle on the second floor, in a corner bedroom commanding a sweeping view of the bay, Devil's Passage, and the ocean beyond. To the northeast, the village of Paradise Point stood in silhouette, the spires of its three tiny churches thrusting upward, while its neat white frame buildings huddled close together, as if to protect each other from the furies that raged constantly in the waters around them. June and Cal joined their daughter, and for a moment the small family stood together, examining their new world. Their arms slipped around each other, and for a long moment, they reveled in a closeness and warmth they hadn't felt for a long time. It was June who finally brought them back to reality.

"We'd thought this might be the nursery," she said tentatively. Michelle, seeming to come out of a trance, turned to them.

"Oh, no," she said. "I want this room. Please?"

"But there's a much bigger room on the other side of the house," June objected. "This one's so small . . ."

"But all I need is my bed and a chair," Michelle

pleaded. "Can't I have this one? I could sit on the window seat forever, just looking out."

June and Cal looked at each other uncertainly, neither of them able to think of a reasonable objection. Then Michelle went to the closet, and the question was settled. Michelle reached up and groped around at the back of the closet shelf.

"There *is* something here," she said triumphantly. "I had a feeling there was something in this closet, and I was right. Look!"

In her hand, Michelle held a doll. Old and dusty, it had a porcelain face framed by hair almost as dark as her own and a little lace bonnet. Its gray dress, faded and torn, must once have been covered with ruffles, and on its feet were a tiny pair of cracked patent leather shoes. June and Cal stared at it in surprise.

"Where do you suppose it came from?" June wondered aloud.

"I'll bet it's been there for centuries," Michelle said. "But it must have belonged to a little girl once, and this must have been her room. May I have it? Please?"

"The doll, or the room?" Cal asked.

"Both!" Michelle cried, sure her parents were about to give in.

"Well, I don't see why not," Cal said. "We'd probably do better to have the nursery right next to our room anyway. We can convert one of the dressing rooms, I suppose," he added with an amused glance at June. Then he took the doll from Michelle and inspected it carefully. "It looks just like you," he observed. "Same brown hair, same brown eyes. Same raggedy clothes!"

Michelle snatched the doll away from her father,

and stuck her tongue out at him. "If my clothes are raggedy, it's your fault. If you couldn't afford to dress me, you should have left me in the orphanage!"

"Michelle!" June gasped. "What a thing to say. You didn't come from an orphanage . . ."

It wasn't until her husband and her daughter began laughing that she realized it was a joke between them, and relaxed. Then the child inside her moved, and June suddenly found herself wondering what would happen when the baby arrived. Michelle had been an only child for so long. What would it be like for her? Would she feel threatened? June remembered everything she had read lately about sibling rivalry. What if Michelle hated the new baby? June put the thought out of her mind. Her eyes fell on the sea outside the window, the gulls wheeling overhead, the sun shining brightly. On the spur of the moment, she determined to spend as much time as she could enjoying the sun. It wouldn't, after all, last forever. Fall was coming, and after that, winter. But for now, there was a warmth to the air. Impulsively, she left Cal and Michelle to begin unpacking while she went out to explore what was to be her studio.

They worked as quickly as they could, but the mountain of boxes seemed to remain as high as ever.

"Want to knock off a while, princess?" Cal finally asked. "There's a couple of Cokes in the refrigerator." Michelle promptly left the carton she was struggling with and preceded her father through the dining room, the butler's pantry, and into the kitchen. She threw herself into a chair and grinned happily.

"Imagine—a butler's pantry! Did Dr. Carson have a butler when he lived here?"

"I don't think so," Cal replied, expertly flipping the caps off two bottles and handing one to Michelle. "I think he lived here all by himself."

Michelle's eyes widened. "Really? That'd be creepy."

"Place getting to you already?" There was a teasing tone to Cal's voice that made Michelle grin.

"Not yet. But if anything comes creeping at me through the door tonight, things might change." Her gaze went to the window, and she fell silent for a moment.

"Something on your mind, princess?" her father asked.

Michelle nodded, and when she faced her father, there was a seriousness in her eyes that struck Cal as being beyond her years.

"I'm glad we came here, Daddy," she said finally. "I don't want you to be unhappy anymore."

"I haven't been unhappy—" Cal began, but Michelle didn't let him finish.

"Yes, you have," she insisted. "I could always tell. For a while I thought you were mad at me, because you never came home from the hospital—"

"I was busy—"

Again she interrupted him. "But then you started coming home again, and you were still unhappy. It wasn't until we decided to move out here that you started being happy again. Didn't you like Boston?"

"It wasn't Boston," Cal began, unsure how to explain to his daughter what had happened. The image of a little boy flashed through his mind, but Cal forced it away immediately. "It was just me, I guess. I—I can't really explain it." He smiled suddenly. "I guess I just want to know the people I'm treating."

Michelle turned the matter over in her mind and eventually nodded. "I think I know what you mean. Boston General was weird."

"Weird? What do you mean?"

Michelle shrugged, searching for the right words. "I don't know. It was like they never knew who you were. And when Mom and I went there, they never even knew we were your family. That snotty one in the main lobby always wanted to know why we wanted to see you. You'd think that after this many years, she'd have recognized us. . . ." Michelle's voice trailed off, and she gazed at her father, wondering if he understood. Cal nodded.

"That's it," he said, relieved that he wouldn't have to tell her the truth. "That's it, exactly. And it was the same way with the people I treated. If I saw them three days later, *I* wouldn't recognize *them*. If I'm going to be a doctor, I think I ought to have the fun of knowing who I'm helping." He grinned at Michelle and decided to change the subject. "What about you? Any regrets?"

"About what?" Michelle asked.

"Coming out here. Leaving your friends. Changing schools. All the sorts of things girls your age are supposed to worry about."

Michelle sipped on her Coke, then looked around the kitchen. "Harrison wasn't such a great school," she said at last. "The one in Paradise Point is much prettier."

"And a lot smaller," Cal pointed out.

"And it probably doesn't have a bunch of kids wrecking it all the time, either," Michelle added. "And as for friends, I'd have had to make new friends next year, anyway, wouldn't I?"

Cal looked at her in surprise. "What do you mean?"

Michelle stared guiltily into her glass. "I heard you and Mom talking. Were you really going to send me to boarding school?"

"It wasn't really decided yet—" he began lamely, but when he looked at Michelle's eyes, he gave up the lie. "We thought it would be better for you," he said. "Harrison was just getting too rough. You told us yourself you weren't learning anything anymore. And anyway, it wasn't boarding school. You'd have been home every day."

"Well, this is better," Michelle said. "I'll make friends here, and I won't have to make new friends next year. Will I?" There was a sudden anxiety in her eyes that made Cal want to reassure her.

"Of course not. Unless you hate it. Come to think of it, you'd better not hate it, because I'm not sure we'd be able to send you to private school on what I'm going to be making out here. But I want you to be happy, Princess. That's very important to me."

Michelle suddenly grinned, breaking the seriousness of the moment. "How could I not be happy? Everybody I know would do anything to be living here. We've got the ocean, and the forest, and this wonderful house. What more could I want?"

In a sudden burst of affection, Michelle threw herself into her father's arms and kissed him.

"I love you, Daddy, really I do."

"And I love you, too, princess," Cal replied, his eyes moistening with affection. "I love you, too." Then he disengaged himself from Michelle's arms and stood up. "Come on. Let's get back to those boxes before your mother sends both of us back to the orphanage!"

* * *

"I found it!" Michelle cried triumphantly. It was a
big box, marked on every side with Michelle's name.
"Let's take it up now, Daddy, please?" Michelle
begged. "Everything I own is in it. Everything! Can't
I unpack it next? I mean, we don't know where Mom
wants everything anyway, and I could put all this
stuff away myself. Please?"

Cal nodded his assent and helped her drag the
immense box upstairs to the corner room that Michelle
had claimed as her own.

"Want some help unpacking it?" he offered. Michelle
shook her head vehemently. "And let you see what's
inside? If you knew what was in here, you'd make me
throw half of it away." In her mind's eye, Michelle saw
the jumble of old movie magazines—just the sort of
thing her parents didn't approve of—and the assorted
souvenirs of her departing childhood that she had not
been able to give up. "And don't you dare tell Mom I
said that," she added, enlisting her father in a collab-
oration of silence to help her preserve her childish
treasures.

Then, as Cal left her alone in the room, Michelle
began ripping the carton open to unpack all her
things, first onto the bed, then carefully hidden away
in the closet and dresser.

It wasn't until she'd put the last old toy away that
she noticed the doll, still propped up on the window
seat where she'd left it a few hours earlier. She went
over to the window and picked it up, holding it level
with her eyes.

"I'll have to think of a name for you," she said out
loud. "Something old-fashioned, as old-fashioned as
you." She thought a moment, then smiled.

"Amanda!" she said. "That's it. I'll call you Amanda. Mandy, for short."

Then, pleased with her choice of a name, Michelle put the antique doll back on the window seat and went downstairs to see what her father was doing.

As the afternoon light faded from the corner room, the doll seemed to be staring out the window, its sightless glass eyes fixed on the potting-shed below.

CHAPTER 2

The potting-shed had a solid feel to it, a sturdiness that made June wonder what, exactly, its builder had in mind. It seemed to her, as she went over it for the fourth time, that it must have been intended as more than a simple storage and workroom—the windows overlooking the ocean were too carefully spaced; the floor, its oak planks barely worn after a century of use, too well laid; and its proportions too perfect for it to have been used merely by a gardener. No, she decided, whoever had designed this room had planned to use it himself. It was almost as though it had been designed as a studio. The windows overlooking the sea faced as nearly north as the bluff would allow, and beneath them a long counter with beautifully crafted storage cabinets ran the length of the room. Near one end of the counter, a large sink had been installed. The brick walls, streaked with the grime of years, had once been whitewashed, and the wood trim around the doors and windows, peeling now, were painted a soft green, as if someone had tried to match the shade of the foliage outside. One end of the room held a large closet. For the moment, June chose to leave its door closed, and imagine, instead, what might be hidden there. Relics, she thought deliciously. Relics of the past, just waiting to be discovered.

She lowered her body onto a stool and automatically counted the days until the baby would be born. Thirty-seven, she reflected, was a silly age at which to be having a baby. Not only silly, but possibly dangerous for both her and the child. *Be careful*, she reminded herself. But the thought wouldn't stay with her—instead, she felt a compulsive urge to begin cleaning out the years of disuse that filled the little room.

She got to her feet, ignoring the heaviness of her body, and wondered how it was that a building that had been abandoned for so many years could have become so filled with junk.

In one corner she spotted a trash barrel, which was, miraculously, empty. Minutes later it was filled, and June considered the wisdom of climbing into it herself to compact its contents.

Congratulating herself on her restraint, she put the idea aside, knowing that if Cal caught her at it, he would be outraged at her carelessness. Besides, it would be just like her to break a leg and bring on a premature birth at the same time. Just now, she had entirely too much to do to risk such a thing. She settled instead for pushing the mess in the barrel as far down as it would go, then adding more until it was in danger of bursting. Then she began looking for something to clean the floor with.

Just inside the closet, disappointingly empty of long-secreted treasures, she found a broom, a pail, and a

mop. Opening the window a crack in hope of freshening the stale air, June began sweeping the dust into
a pile.

She was nearly halfway across the floor when the
broom suddenly dragged against something. She poked
at the caked dirt. When it didn't break up, she stopped
to look at it more closely.

It was a stain of some sort that covered a couple of
square feet of the floor. Whatever had been spilled
there had apparently been left to dry on its own, and,
as it dried, dust had settled on it, worked its way in
until now the mess lay, perhaps a quarter of an inch
thick, impervious to the broom.

June stood up and reached for the mop, wondering
what the chances were of finding the old plumbing
still in working order. But before she had a chance to
experiment, Cal and Michelle appeared in the doorway.

Cal gazed around the potting-shed and shook his
head. "I thought you were just going to look around
and make some plans."

"I couldn't resist," June said ruefully. "It's such a
pretty room, and it was such a mess. I think I feel
sorry for it."

Michelle stared around the cluttered room, and her
arms involuntarily hugged her body as if she had been
seized by a sudden chill. Still standing by the door, an
expression of distaste on her face, she spoke. "This
place is creepy—what did they use it for?"

"It's a potting-shed," her mother explained. "The
gardener's headquarters, where he kept all his tools,
and raised seedlings, and that sort of thing." She
paused for a moment, as if thinking something over,

then went on. "But I have the strangest feeling they used this for something else, too."

Cal's brow arched. "Playing detective?"

"Not really," June replied. "But look at it. The floor's solid oak. And those cabinets! Who would build something like this just for the gardener?"

"Until about fifty years ago, a lot of people would have," Cal said, chuckling. "They used to build things to last, remember?"

June shook her head. "I don't know. It just seems too nice to be a potting-shed. There must have been something more to it . . ."

"What's that?" Michelle asked. She was pointing to the stain that June had been working on when they came in.

"I wish I knew. I think someone must have spilled some paint. I was just going to try to mop it up."

Michelle went over to the stain and knelt beside it, examining it carefully. She started to reach out and touch it, but suddenly drew her hand away.

"It looks like blood," she said. She stood up and faced her parents. "I'll bet somebody got murdered in here."

"Murdered?" June gasped. "What on earth would put such a morbid thought into your head?"

Michelle ignored her mother and appealed to her father instead. "Look at it, Daddy. Doesn't it look like blood?"

A small smile playing around his mouth, Cal joined Michelle and examined the stain even more carefully than she had. When he stood up, his face was serious. "Definitely blood," he said solemnly. "No question about it." Then his smile got the best of him. "Of course, it could be paint, or some kind of clay, or God knows what. But if it's blood you want, I'll go along with it."

"That's disgusting," June said, wanting to dismiss the idea. "It's a beautiful room, and it's going to make a wonderful studio, and please don't try to tell me horrible things happened in here. I won't believe it!"

Michelle shrugged, glanced around once more, and shook her head. "Well, you can *have* this place—I hate it." She made a move toward the door. "Is it all right if I go down to the beach?"

"What time is it?" June asked doubtfully.

"Still plenty of time before dark," Cal assured her. "But be careful, princess. I don't want you taking a fall the first day here—I need paying patients, not my own family."

As Michelle started toward the path that would take her down to the cove, her father's words rang in her head: *I don't want you taking a fall.* But why should she? She had never fallen in her life. Then it came to her. It was that boy. Her father was still thinking about that boy. But that hadn't been his fault, and even if it had, it didn't have anything to do with her. Happily, she started down the trail.

Cal waited until Michelle was out of sight, then took his wife in his arms and kissed her. A moment later, when he had released her, June peered up into his face with a quizzical look.

"What was that all about?"

"Nothing in particular, and everything in general," Cal said. "I'm just happy to be here, happy to be married to you, happy to have Michelle for a daughter, and happy to have whatever this is on the way." He patted June's belly affectionately. "But I do wish," he

added, "that you'd be a little more careful about what
you do. Let's not have anything happen to you or the
baby."

"I'm being good," June replied. "I'll have you know
that in the name of propriety, I didn't get into that
barrel to tamp the trash down."

Cal groaned. "That's supposed to make me happy?"

"Oh, stop worrying. I'm going to be fine, and the
baby's going to be fine. In fact, the only one I worry
about is Michelle."

"Michelle?"

June nodded. "I just wonder how the baby's going
to affect her. I mean, she's had all our attention for so
long, don't you think she might resent the competi-
tion?"

"Any other child might, I suppose," Cal mused. "But
not Michelle. She's the most repulsively well-adjusted
child I know. It must be genetic—Lord knows it can't
be the home we've provided."

"Oh, stop it," June protested, a hint of seriousness
hiding behind her bantering tone. "You're too hard on
yourself. You always have been." Then the banter was
dropped, and her voice grew quiet. "I'm just afraid
she might feel threatened by a natural child. It
wouldn't be unusual, you know."

Cal sat heavily on the stool, and crossed his arms
over his chest in a manner that June associated with
his talking to a patient.

"Now look," he said. "Michelle takes things in stride.
My God, just look at the way she's reacted to moving
out here. Any other kid would have squawked like
hell, threatened to run away, done all kinds of things.
But not Michelle. For her, it's just a new adventure."

"So?"

"So that's the way it'll be with the baby. Just a new member of the family to get to know, and take care of, and enjoy. She's just the right age to become a baby-sitter. If I know Michelle, she'll take over the mothering, and leave you to your painting."

June smiled, feeling a little better. "I reserve the right to mother my own child. Michelle can wait till she has one of her own."

Suddenly her eyes fell to the strange stain on the floor, and she frowned. "What do you suppose it is?" she asked Cal as his gaze followed her own.

"Blood," he said cheerfully. "Just as Michelle said."

"Oh, Cal, be serious," June said. "It isn't blood, and you know it."

"Then what are you worried about?"

"I'd just like to know what it is, so I'll know what to use to get it off," June said.

"Well, I'll tell you what," Cal offered. "I'll see what I can do with a putty knife, and then we'll try some turpentine. Chances are it's just paint, and turpentine will cut right through it."

"Do you have a putty knife?" June asked anxiously.

"On me? Not a chance. But there's one in with the tools, if I ever find them."

"Let's go find them," June said decisively.

"Now?"

"Right now."

Deciding that the best thing to do was to humor his pregnant wife, Cal followed as June led him into the house. Confronted with the jumble of boxes in the living room, he was sure June would give it up as a hopeless cause, but instead she scanned the mound expertly and suddenly pointed.

"That one," she said.

"How can you tell?" Cal asked, baffled. The label on the box clearly said Miscellaneous.

"Trust me," June said sweetly.

Cal hauled the box down from its perch near the top of the pile and ripped the tape off it. There, right under the lid, was his toolbox.

"Incredible!"

"Precision labeling," June replied, a bit smugly. "Come on."

She led him back to the studio, and settled herself on the stool while Cal began chipping at the offending stain. A few minutes later, he looked up.

"I don't know," he said.

"Won't it come off?" June asked.

"Oh, it'll come off all right," Cal replied. "I'm just not sure what it is."

"What do you mean?" June got off the stool and lowered herself next to her husband. What had been the body of the stain on the floor was now a pile of crumbling brownish dust scattered around her feet. She reached out and, hesitating, picked up a little of it, rubbing the dust between her fingers, feeling its texture.

"What is it?" she asked Cal.

"It might be paint," he said slowly. "But it looks more like dried blood."

His eyes met his wife's.

"Michelle might have been right after all," he said. He stood up and helped June to her feet.

"Whatever it is," he added, "it's been there for years and years and years. It certainly doesn't have anything to do with us, and it won't take long to get that stain out. Once it's out, you can forget all about it."

But as they left the studio, June turned and looked once more at the brownish mess on the floor.

She wished she were as sure as Cal that she would forget all about it.

Michelle paused on the trail and tried to guess how far down it was to the beach. Hundreds of feet. For a moment she toyed with the idea of trying to find another route down. No, for now, at least, she should stick to the path. There would be plenty of time later to scramble her way through the rocks and brush that clung to the face of the bluff.

The trail was an easy walk, cut in switchbacks, worn smooth by years of use. Here and there it narrowed where winter storms had eaten it away, and there were occasional rocks in her path, which Michelle kicked over the edge, then watched while they gathered force in their plunge to the beach below, disappearing from her line of sight before she heard them crash at the bottom.

The trail ended very close to the high tide line, but this afternoon the tide was out, and a rocky expanse of beach, broken irregularly by a series of low granite outcroppings, lay before her, curving outward in both directions toward the arms of Devil's Passage. The water, trapped in the tight cove, boiled and eddied, its swirling currents twisting the surface into angry patterns that even to Michelle's inexpert eyes looked dangerous. She began walking north, intent on discovering if it might be possible to follow the beach all the way to the foot of Paradise Point. It would be a neat way to go to school—along the beach, then up the bluff and through the village. Much nicer than taking the crowded MTA to Harrison in Boston!

She had gone perhaps a quarter of a mile when she noticed she wasn't alone on the beach. Someone was crouched over a tidepool, oblivious of her presence. She approached the figure warily, unsure whether she should speak, go on by, or maybe even turn back. But before she could make up her mind, the person looked up, saw her, and waved.

"Hi!" The voice seemed friendly, and when he stood up, Michelle saw that it was a boy, about her own age, with dark curly hair, startlingly blue eyes, and a wide smile. Tentatively, she waved back, and called out a hello.

The boy bounded across the rocks toward her.

"Are you the girl that moved into the Carson house?" he asked.

Michelle nodded. "Only it's our house, now," she corrected him. "We bought it from Dr. Carson."

"Oh," the boy said. "I'm Jeff Benson. I live up there." He gestured vaguely toward the bluff, and Michelle's eyes followed his gesture, though there was nothing to be seen.

"You can't see our house from here," Jeff explained. "It sits too far back from the cliff. Mom says the bluff's going to fall into the sea sooner or later anyway, but I don't think so. What's your name?"

"Michelle."

"What do people call you?" Jeff asked.

Michelle frowned, puzzled. "Michelle," she repeated. "What else would they call me?"

Jeff shrugged. "I dunno. It just seems like kind of a fancy name, that's all. Sounds like you must be from Boston."

"I am," Michelle replied.

Jeff regarded her curiously for a moment, then

shrugged again, dismissing the matter. "Did you come down to look at the tidepools?"

"I just came down to look around," she said. "What's in them?"

"All kinds of things," Jeff told her eagerly. "And the tide's way out now, so you can get to the best ones. Haven't you ever seen a tidepool before?"

Michelle shook her head. "Only the ones at the beach," she said. "We used to go there for picnics."

"Those aren't any good," Jeff scoffed. "All the good stuff got taken out of them ages ago, but hardly anybody ever comes down here. Come on—I'll show you."

He began leading Michelle across the rocks, stopping every few minutes to wait for her to catch up. "You should wear tennis shoes," he suggested. "They don't slip on the rocks so much."

"I didn't know it would be this slippery," Michelle said, suddenly feeling clumsy but unsure just why. A moment later they had come to the edge of a large pool, and Jeff was kneeling beside it. Michelle crouched down beside him and stared into the shallow water.

The pool lay clear and still before her, and Michelle realized that it was like looking through a window into another world. The bottom was alive with strange creatures— starfish and sea urchins, anemones waving softly in the currents, and hermit crabs scurrying around in their borrowed homes. On an impulse, Michelle reached into the water and picked one up.

The crab's tiny claw snapped ineffectually at her finger, then the little animal retreated into its shell, only a whisker poking tentatively out.

"Hold your hand real flat, and turn him so he can't

see you," Jeff told her. "Then just wait, and in a couple of minutes he'll come out."

Michelle followed his instructions. A moment later the animal began emerging from its shell, legs first.

"It tickles," Michelle said, her fist involuntarily closing. When she opened it again, the animal had retreated once more.

"Drop it into one of the sea anemones," Jeff told her.

Michelle obeyed, and watched the strange plantlike animal tighten its tentacles around the panicked crab. A moment later the anemone was closed, and the crab had disappeared.

"What'll happen to it?" Michelle asked.

"The anemone will eat it, then open up and dump out the shell," Jeff explained.

"You mean I killed it?" Michelle asked, upset by the thought.

"Something would've eaten it anyway," Jeff said. "As long as you don't take anything away, or put in something that shouldn't be here, you aren't really hurting anything."

Michelle had never thought of such a thing before, but Jeff's words made sense to her. Some things belong, and some things don't. And you have to be careful what you put with what. Yes, it made sense.

Together the two children began making their way around the tidepool, examining the strange world beneath the water. Jeff pried a starfish loose from its hold on the rocks, and showed Michelle the thousands of tiny suction cups that formed its feet and the odd pentangular mouth in the middle of its stomach.

"How come you know so much about all this?" Michelle finally asked.

"I grew up here," Jeff said. He hesitated a moment,

then continued. "Besides, I want to be a marine biologist someday. What are you going to be?"

"I don't know," Michelle said. "I never thought about it."

"Your dad's a doctor, isn't he?" Jeff asked.

"How'd you know that?"

"Everybody knows," Jeff said amiably. "Paradise Point's a small town. Everybody knows everything."

"Boy, it sure wasn't like that in Boston," Michelle replied. "Nobody knew who anybody was. We hated it."

"Is that why you moved here?"

"I guess," Michelle said slowly. "That was part of the reason, anyway." Suddenly she wanted to change the subject. "Did somebody get murdered in our house?"

Jeff looked at her sharply, as if he hadn't heard her quite right. Then, almost too quickly, he stood up and shook his head. "Not that I ever heard of," he said. Turning, he started picking his way back across the rocky beach. When Michelle made no move to follow him, he called out to her.

"Come on! The tide's coming in. It's getting dangerous!"

As Michelle stood up, an odd sensation swept over her. She was suddenly dizzy, and her vision seemed to be fading. It was as if a heavy fog was settling over her. Quickly, she dropped back to her knees.

Ahead, Jeff turned and stared at her.

"Are you all right?" he called back.

Michelle nodded, then stood up again, more slowly this time. "I guess I just stood up too fast. I got dizzy, and it seemed like it was getting dark."

"Well, it's *going* to get dark pretty soon," Jeff said.

"We'd better get back up to the top." He started north, and Michelle asked him where he was going.

"Home," Jeff replied. "We have a path up to our house just like you do." He paused a moment, then asked her if she wanted to come with him.

"I'd better not," Michelle replied. "I told my parents I wouldn't be gone long."

"Okay," Jeff said. "See you."

"See you," Michelle echoed. She turned away from Jeff and started up the beach. When she was at the foot of the trail that would take her home, she stopped and looked back the way she had come. Jeff Benson was no longer in sight. The beach was empty, and fog was closing in.

CHAPTER 3

"Next week we convert the butler's pantry."

June's voice contained a note of determination that let Cal know that his grace period was over. And yet, during the two weeks they had been in the house, he had come to love it the way it was, and found himself less and less willing to change it at all. He had even come to appreciate the cavernous dining room, though there was something impersonal about the huge table that made their small family gather together at the end nearest the kitchen door. Michelle seemed totally unaffected by the size of the room. Indeed, as her mother spoke, she looked around appreciatively.

"I like it," she declared. "I pretend we're in the hall of a castle, and the servants are coming in to wait on us."

"That'll be the day," Cal said. "At the rate we're going, I'm going to have to start hiring *you* out as a maid." He winked at his daughter, who winked back.

"Things will get better," June said, though the

strain in her voice belied the optimistic words. "You can't expect everybody in town to start coming to you." Her voice bitter, she faced her husband. "Not as long as Carson's still around." She put her fork down. "I wish he'd just give up and go away. How long will it be before he turns the whole practice over to you?"

"A long time, I hope," Cal replied. Then, reading June's face, he tried to reassure her. "Don't look like that—he's not taking any of the money anymore. He says I own the practice now, and he's officially retired. Says he's just 'keeping his hand in.' And thank God he is. Without him, I'd probably have been run out of town by now!"

"Oh, come on—" June protested, but Cal held up his hand to stop her.

"It's true. You should have seen me yesterday. Mrs. Parsons came in, and I, being a doctor, was all set to examine her. If Josiah hadn't stopped me, I'd have had her in a gown in nothing flat. But it seems she didn't want to be examined—all she wanted to do was to have a little 'chat.' Josiah listened to her, clucked sympathetically, and told her that if her symptoms persisted, he'd take a look at her next week."

"What was wrong with her?" Michelle asked.

"Nothing. It turns out that her hobby is reading up on various ailments, and she likes to talk about them, but she doesn't think it's right to come into the office just to talk, so she claims she has the symptoms."

"Sounds like a hypochondriac," June commented.

"That's what I thought, too, but Josiah says she isn't. It isn't that she really *feels* the symptoms. She just says she does. And," Cal continued, "it seems Mrs. Parsons not only talks about her own symptoms, she talks about other people's as well. Josiah says that there are at least three people in town who are alive today only because Mrs. Parsons told him things that they wouldn't tell him themselves."

"What does he do?" Michelle interrupted. "Go out and drag them into the office?"

"Not exactly," Cal said, chuckling. "But he does drop in on them and check them out. Apparently Mrs. P. has a particularly good eye for potential heart attacks."

"It doesn't sound very professional," June muttered.

Cal shrugged. "Until a week ago, I'd have agreed with you. But now I'm not so sure." He picked up his wineglass, sipped at the Chablis, then spoke again. "I've been wondering how many people would still be alive if we'd had a Mrs. Parsons at Boston General, where we only had time to look after specific complaints. Josiah says there are lots of things that people don't complain about—instead they just die, thinking things will get better."

"That's creepy," Michelle said, shuddering.

"It is," Cal agreed. "But it doesn't happen so much out here, because Josiah's always had the time to get to know his patients and find out what's wrong with them before it goes too far. He's a great believer in preventive medicine."

"What is he, a witch doctor?" Though she tried to keep her tone light, June was growing tired of Cal's paean to the older doctor. *Josiah says!* Cal seemed to hang on every word Carson uttered. Now, he ignored June's question and turned to Michelle, but before he could go on, the doorbell rang. June, grateful for the chance to end the talk of Josiah Carson, quickly got up to answer it. But when she opened the front door, framed in the entryway was the tall, spare figure of

Josiah Carson, his mane of nearly white hair glowing in the gathering darkness of the evening. June felt herself gasp slightly, then quickly recovered. "Well, speak of the devil . . ."

Carson smiled slightly. "I hope I'm not interrupting your dinner. I'm afraid it really couldn't wait." He stepped into the foyer and closed the door behind him.

Before June could make any reply, Cal appeared in the hall. "Josiah! What are doing out here?"

"Going on a housecall. I'd have phoned, but I was already in the car before I thought of you. Want to come along?"

"I gather it's not an emergency," June observed.

"Well, certainly nothing that would require an ambulance. In fact, I doubt that it's anything much at all. It's Sally Carstairs. She's complaining about a sore arm, and her mother asked me to have a look. And then I had a thought." He paused, and glanced toward the dining room. "Is Michelle here?"

Cal's voice betrayed his curiosity as he repeated his daughter's name. "Michelle?"

"Sally Carstairs is the same age as Michelle, and it occurred to me that your daughter might do her more good than either you or I. Making a new friend often takes a child's mind off the pain."

A look passed between the two doctors, a look that June almost missed. It was as if Carson had asked her husband a question, and Cal had answered. Yet, there was something more, a silent communion between them that worried June. And then Michelle appeared in the foyer, and suddenly everything was settled.

"Want to go on a housecall?" she heard Carson asking her daughter.

"Really?" Michelle glanced at her mother, then turned to her father, her eyes glistening.

"It seems Dr. Carson thinks you might be therapeutic to one of our patients."

"Who?" Michelle asked eagerly.

"Sally Carstairs. She's about your age, and her arm hurts. Dr. Carson wants to use you for a painkiller."

Michelle looked to her mother for permission, but June hesitated for a moment.

"She isn't sick?"

"Sally?" Carson said. "Good Lord, no. Just hurt her arm. But if you want Michelle to stay here—"

"No—take her, by all means. It's time she met a girl her age. In the last two weeks, the only person she's seen is Jeff Benson."

"Who's a very nice boy," Cal pointed out.

"I didn't say he wasn't. But a girl needs girl friends, too."

Michelle started toward the stairs. "I'll be right back." She disappeared up the stairs, and a moment later reappeared with her green bookbag tucked under her arm.

"What's that?" Josiah Carson asked.

"A doll," Michelle explained. "I found it upstairs—in my closet. I thought maybe Sally might like to see it."

"Here?" Carson asked. "You found it here?"

"Uh-huh. It's really old." Suddenly Michelle's face clouded, and she looked up at Carson worriedly. "I guess it must belong to your family, huh?"

"Well, I don't know," Carson replied. "Why don't you let me see it?"

Michelle opened the bookbag and took out the doll.

She offered it to Carson, who glanced at it, but didn't take it.

"Interesting," he said. "I suppose it must have belonged to someone in the family, but I've never seen it before."

"If you want it, you can have it," Michelle said, disappointment plain on her face.

"Now what on earth would I do with it?" Carson replied. "You keep it, and enjoy it. And keep it at home."

June looked at the old doctor sharply. "Keep it at home?" she repeated.

She was sure Carson hesitated, but when he spoke his voice was ingenuous. "It's a beautiful doll, and obviously an antique. I don't think Michelle would want anything to happen to it, would she?"

"She'd be brokenhearted," Cal agreed. "Take it back up to your room, honey, and then we'll get going. Josiah, shall we follow you?"

"Fine. I'll wait in my car." He said good-bye to June, then left the Pendletons alone together.

Cal gave June a quick hug. "Now don't do anything you shouldn't. I don't want to be up all night with you in labor."

"Don't worry. I'll do the dishes, then curl up with a good book." Cal started out the door as Michelle came downstairs once more. "Be careful," she suddenly added, and Cal turned back.

"Be careful? What could happen?"

"I don't know," June replied. "Nothing, I suppose. But be careful, anyway, all right?"

She waited at the open door until they were gone, then slowly started clearing the table. By the time she had finished, she knew what was bothering her.

It was Josiah Carson.

June Pendleton just didn't like him, but she still wasn't sure why.

Josiah Carson drove quickly, so familiar with the streets of Paradise Point that he had no need to concentrate on the road. Instead, he wondered what was going to happen when Cal Pendleton had to examine Sally Carstairs. Cal, he knew, had been avoiding children ever since that day in Boston last spring. But tonight Josiah would find out just how damaged Cal Pendleton was. Would he panic? Would the memories of what had happened in Boston paralyze him? Or had he regained his confidence? Soon, Josiah would know. He pulled up in front of the Carstairs home and waited while Cal parked behind him.

They found Fred and Bertha Carstairs, a comfortable-looking couple in their early forties, sitting nervously at their kitchen table. Carson made the introductions, then briskly rubbed his hands together.

"Well, let's get at it," he said. "Michelle, why don't you keep Mrs. Carstairs company here in the kitchen, just in case we have to take Sally's arm off?" Without waiting for a response, he turned and led Cal into a bedroom at the rear of the house.

Sally Carstairs was sitting up in bed, a book precariously balanced in her lap, her right arm lying limply at her side. When she saw Josiah Carson, she smiled weakly.

"I feel dumb," she began.

"You were dumb the day I delivered you," Carson deadpanned. "Why should today be different?"

Sally ignored his teasing and turned to Cal. "Are you Dr. Pendleton?"

Cal nodded, momentarily unable to speak. His vision seemed to cloud, and in the bed, Sally Carstairs's face was suddenly replaced by another—the face of a boy, the same age, also in a bed, also in pain. Cal felt his stomach churn, and the beginning of panic welled up inside him. But he fought it down, forced himself to be calm, and tried to concentrate on the girl in the bed.

"Maybe you can teach Uncle Joe how to be a doctor," she was saying. "And then make him retire."

"I'll retire you, young lady," Carson growled. "Now what happened?"

The smile left Sally's face, and she seemed thoughtful. "I'm not sure. I tripped out in the backyard, and it felt like I hit my arm on a rock . . ." she began.

"Well, let's have a look at it," Carson said, taking her arm gently in his large hands. He rolled up the sleeve of the child's pajama top and peered at her arm carefully. There was no trace of a bruise. "Couldn't have been much of a rock," he observed.

"That's why I feel dumb," Sally said. "There wasn't any rock. I was on the lawn."

Carson stepped back, and Cal bent over to examine the arm. He prodded tentatively, feeling Carson's eyes watching him.

"Does it hurt there?"

Sally nodded.

"How about there?"

Again, Sally nodded.

Cal continued his probing. Sally's entire arm, from the elbow to the shoulder, was in pain at his touch. He finally straightened up, and made himself look at Carson.

"It could be a sprain," he said slowly.

Carson's brows rose noncommittally. He carefully rolled Sally's sleeve down again. "How bad does it hurt?" he asked.

Sally scowled at him. "Well, I'm not going to die," she said. "But I can't do anything with it."

Carson smiled at her and squeezed her good hand. "I'll tell you what. Dr. Pendleton and I are going to talk to your parents for a while, and we brought a surprise for you."

Sally suddenly looked eager. "You did? What?"

"Not what—who. It seems Dr. Pendleton brought his assistant with him, and she happens to be just your age." He moved to the bedroom door and called to Michelle. A moment later, Michelle came hesitantly into the room. She stopped just inside the door, and looked shyly at Sally. Her father introduced the two girls, then the adults left them alone together to get acquainted.

"Hi," Michelle said, a little uncertainly.

"Hi," Sally replied. There was a silence, then: "You can sit on the bed if you want to."

Michelle moved away from the door, but before she got to the bed, she suddenly stopped, her eyes fixed on the window.

"What's wrong?" Sally asked.

Michelle shook her head. "I don't know. I thought I saw something."

"Outside?"

"Uh-huh."

Sally tried to turn in bed, but the pain stopped her. "What was it?"

"I don't know." Then she shrugged. "It was like a shadow."

"Oh, that's the elm tree. It scares me all the time."
Sally patted the bed, and Michelle settled herself
gingerly at its foot. But her eyes remained fixed on the
window.

"You must look like your mother," Sally said.

"Huh?" Michelle, surprised at the observation,
finally tore her gaze from the window, and met Sally's
eyes.

"I said you must look like your mother. You sure
don't look like your father."

"I don't look like Mom, either," Michelle replied.
"I'm adopted."

Sally's mouth opened. "You are?" There was a note
of awe in her voice that almost made Michelle giggle.

"Well, it's no big deal."

"I think it is," Sally said. "I think it's neat."

"Why?"

"Well, I mean, you could be anybody, couldn't you?
Who do you think your real parents were?"

It was a conversation Michelle had been though
before with her friends in Boston, and she had never
been able to understand their interest in the subject.
As far as she was concerned, her parents were the
Pendletons, and that was that. But rather than try to
explain it all to Sally, she changed the subject.

"What's wrong with your arm?"

Sally, easily diverted from the subject of Michelle's
ancestors, rolled her eyes up in an expression of disgust. "I tripped, and twisted it or something, and now
everybody's making a big deal out of it."

"But doesn't it hurt?" Michelle asked.

"A little bit," Sally conceded, unwilling to let her
pain show. "Are you really your father's assistant?"

Michelle shook her head. "Dr. Carson asked him to bring me along." She smiled. "I'm glad he did."

"So am I," Sally agreed. "Uncle Joe's neat that way."

"He's your uncle?"

"Not really. But all the kids call him Uncle Joe. He delivered almost all of us." There was a pause, then Sally looked at Michelle shyly. "Could I come out to your house sometime?"

"Sure. Haven't you ever been in it?"

Sally shook her head. "Uncle Joe never had anybody over there. He was really weird about that house —always saying he was going to tear it down but never doing it. And then, after what happened last spring, everyone was *sure* he'd tear it down. But I guess you know all about that, don't you?"

"Know about what?" Michelle asked.

Sally's eyes widened. "You mean nobody told you? About Alan Hanley?"

Alan Hanley. That was the name of the boy in the hospital in Boston. "What about him?"

"Uncle Joe hired him to do something to the roof— fix some slates or something, I guess. And he fell off. They took him to Boston, but he died anyway."

"I know," Michelle said slowly. Then: "It was *our* house he fell off of?"

Sally nodded.

"Nobody told me that."

"Nobody ever tells kids anything," Sally remarked. "But we always find out anyway." She shrugged the matter aside, eager to get back to the subject of the Pendletons' house. "What's it like inside?"

Michelle did her best to describe the house to Sally, who listened in fascination. When Michelle was finished, Sally lay back against her pillow, and sighed.

"It sounds like it's just the way I always thought it would be. I think it's the most romantic house I've ever seen."

"I know," Michelle agreed. "I like to pretend it's just my house, and I live there all alone, and—and. . . ." Her voice trailed off, and she blushed in embarrassment.

"And what?" Sally urged her. "Do you have . . . love affairs?"

Michelle nodded guiltily. "Isn't that terrible? To imagine things like that?"

"I don't know. I do the same thing."

"You do? What's the boy like, when you pretend?"

"Jeff Benson," Sally said immediately. "He lives right next door to you."

"I know," Michelle said. "I met him the day we moved out here, down on the beach. He's really cute, isn't he?" A thought suddenly occurred to her: "Is he your boyfriend?"

Sally shook her head. "I like him, but I guess he's Susan Peterson's boyfriend. At least that's what *she* says."

"Who's Susan Peterson?"

"One of the kids at school. She's really kind of stuck-up. Thinks she's special." Sally paused. Then: "Hey, I have a neat idea." Her voice dropped into a whisper, and Michelle leaned closer so she could hear what Sally was saying. The two of them began giggling as each of them added details to Sally's plan. When Bertha Carstairs came into the room a half hour later, they exchanged a conspiratorial glance.

"You two behaving yourselves?" Bertha asked.

"We're just talking, Mom," Sally answered with

exaggerated innocence. "Would it be all right if I go over to Michelle's tomorrow?"

Bertha looked at her daughter doubtfully. "Well, that depends on how your arm is. Doctor thinks you might have sprained it—"

"Oh, it'll be fine by morning," Sally cut in. "It doesn't hurt much at all. Really it doesn't." There was a pleading tone to her voice that Bertha Carstairs chose to ignore.

"That's not what you said when you made me call the doctor away from his dinner," she said severely.

"Well, it's gotten better," Sally announced.

"Let's see how it is in the morning." She turned to Michelle. "Your dad says it's time to go home."

Michelle got up from the bed, said good-bye to Sally, and went to the kitchen to find her father.

"Have a nice visit?"

Michelle nodded. "If she's better, Sally's coming out to our house tomorrow."

"Great," Cal replied. Then he turned to Carson. "See you in the morning?" The old doctor nodded, and a moment later Cal and Michelle left the Carstairses. But as he opened the car door, Cal had an odd feeling, and glanced back toward the Carstairses' front door. There, like a dark shadow against the lights inside, stood the tall figure of Josiah Carson. Though he couldn't see the old man's eyes in the darkness, Cal knew they were fixed on him. He could feel them, boring into him, examining him. Feeling a sudden chill, he quickly got into the car, and slammed the door.

He started the engine, then impulsively reached over and patted Michelle on the leg. "Don't be too disappointed if Sally doesn't make it tomorrow, princess," he said gently.

"Why?" Michelle asked, her face filled with concern. "Is something really wrong with her?"

"I don't know," Cal replied. "Neither of us could find anything particularly wrong."

"Maybe she sprained it like you said," Michelle offered.

"That would hurt either the elbow or the shoulder, depending on which she sprained. But the pain seems to be *between* the joints, not *in* them."

"What are you going to do?"

"Wait until morning," Cal said. "If she isn't much better, and I don't think she will be, we'll take some X rays. I suppose there could be a hairline fracture." He gunned the engine and pulled away. Michelle turned to look back at the house.

Something caught her eye—a movement, or a shadow, very close to the house. She had a feeling— the same feeling that she had had earlier in Sally's room. A feeling of someone being there. Nothing she could see, or hear, but something she could sense. And it wasn't, she was sure, an elm tree.

"Daddy! Stop the car!"

Reflexively, Cal's foot moved to the brake. The car came to a quick halt. "What's wrong?"

Michelle was still staring back at the Carstairses'. Cal's gaze followed his daughter's. In the darkness he could see nothing.

"What's wrong?" he said again.

"I'm not sure," Michelle said. "I thought I saw something."

"What?"

"I don't know," Michelle said hesitantly. "I thought there was somebody there—"

"Where?"

"At the window. At Sally's window. At least I think it was Sally's window."

Cal pulled the car over and shut off the engine. "Stay here. I'll go take a look." He got out of the car, shut the door, and started to walk the few steps back to the Carstairses', then returned to the car.

"Princess? Lock the doors, will you. And stay in the car."

Michelle looked at him with disgust. "Oh, for Pete's sake, Daddy. This is Paradise Point, not Boston."

"But you thought you saw something."

"Oh, all right," Michelle said reluctantly. She reached across and locked the driver's door, then her own.

Cal tapped on the glass, pointing toward the back door.

Making a face at him, Michelle stretched over the seat and pressed the buttons locking the other two doors of the car.

Only then did Cal go to investigate the Carstairses' yard.

A few seconds later he was back, and Michelle dutifully unlocked the door for him.

"What was it?"

"Nothing. It must have been a shadow."

He restarted the car and began driving home. Michelle sat quietly beside him. Finally, he asked her if anything was wrong.

"Not really," Michelle said. "I was just thinking about Sally—I really want her to come over tomorrow."

"Well, as I said, don't count on it, princess." Once again, Cal affectionately patted his daughter. "You like it out here, don't you?" he asked.

"I love it," Michelle said softly.

She snuggled close to her father, the strange shadow she had seen outside Sally's window quickly forgotten.

And I like it out here, too, Cal told himself silently. *I like it just fine.* The housecall had gone all right. He hadn't done much, but at least he hadn't done anything wrong. And that, he reflected, was a step in the right direction.

The next morning, Sally Carstairs appeared at the Pendletons' front door. She explained that the pain in her arm had completely disappeared overnight, but Cal looked the arm over anyway and questioned Sally carefully.

"It doesn't hurt at all?"

"It's fine, Dr. Pendleton," Sally insisted. "Really it is."

"Okay," Cal sighed, reluctantly giving in to her. "Run along and have a good time." As Sally left the front parlor, Cal scratched his head, then went to the phone.

"Josiah? Have you talked to Bertha Carstairs this morning?"

"No, I was just going to call her."

"Don't bother," Cal said. "Sally's here, and she's fine. The pain's completely cleared up."

"Well, that's fine," Josiah Carson replied.

"But it doesn't make sense," Cal said. "If it was a bruise, a sprain, or a fracture, it would still hurt. It just doesn't make sense."

There was a long silence at the other end. For a

moment Cal wasn't sure Josiah Carson was still there. Then the old doctor spoke.

"Sometimes things don't make sense, Cal," he said quietly. "That's just something you're going to have to accept. *Sometimes things just don't make sense.*"

CHAPTER 4

Michelle's eyes devoured every detail of the Paradise Point school as she waited for Sally Carstairs to arrive. It was nothing like Harrison had been—nothing at all. There was no trace of Harrison's dingy paint, no graffiti in the halls, and the trash containers, neatly spaced along the length of the corridor, were not chained to the walls. Instead, Michelle found herself in a brightly lit corridor, painted an immaculate white with green trim, filled with happily chattering children—children who seemed eager for a new school year to begin. She searched the crowd for Sally's familiar face, spotted her, and waved. Sally waved back, then beckoned to Michelle.

"Down here," Sally called. "We're in Miss Hatcher's room!"

Michelle felt curious eyes watching her as she moved toward Sally, but when she met the glances of one or two or her new schoolmates, she saw only friendliness in their faces—none of the suspicious hostility that had hung like a dark cloud over the old school in Boston. By the time she reached Sally, Michelle was sure everything was going to be fine.

"Now, you remember what to do?" Sally asked. Michelle nodded. "Okay. Let's go in. Jeff's already here, but I haven't seen Susan—she's *always* late." She started inside the classroom, but Michelle stopped her.

"What's Miss Hatcher like?"

Sally glanced at her, then grinned at the sudden uncertainty in Michelle's face.

"She's neat. She tries to pretend to be an old-maid schoolteacher, but she has a boyfriend and everything. And she lets us sit wherever we want. Come on."

Sally led Michelle into the classroom as they had planned. They moved directly up to the front row where Jeff Benson had seated himself in the center of the room. Making a great show of innocence, Sally took the seat on Jeff's left, and Michelle took the one on his right. Jeff greeted both of them, then began talking with Sally while Michelle tried to look surreptitiously at her new teacher.

Corinne Hatcher seemed to be the image of a small-town schoolteacher. She wore her light brown hair in a tight chignon, and on a chain around her neck, a pair of glasses dangled. Though Michelle did not yet know it, no one had ever seen her wear the glasses— they simply hung there. But Michelle did notice that there was something behind the spinsterish appearance of Miss Hatcher. Her face was pretty, and her eyes had a warmth to them that softened her severe appearance. Michelle was sure she knew why Miss Hatcher was a great favorite with her students.

At her desk, Corinne Hatcher was aware of Michelle's curious gaze, but made no move to acknowledge it. Better to let the new girl size things up for herself. Instead, she fixed her eyes on Sally Carstairs and tried to figure out what Sally was up to. Obviously, Sally and the new girl, whose name she knew, but not much else, were already friends. But why weren't they sitting together?

It wasn't until Susan Peterson came in that Corinne realized what the game was: Susan started toward the front of the room, her eyes on Jeff Benson. Michelle and Sally exchanged a glance, Sally nodded, and the two of them began giggling. As she heard the giggling, Susan stopped, realizing that the seats on both sides of Jeff were already taken, and that it wasn't a coincidence. Susan glared at Sally, glanced contemptuously at the stranger in the room, then took the seat directly behind Jeff.

And Michelle, seeing Susan's quick anger, immediately began to regret having fallen in with Sally's plan. It had seemed funny at the time, to keep Susan away from the boy she wanted to sit next to, but now Michelle realized that she had made a mistake. And Susan didn't look like the kind of girl who would forget about it, either. Michelle began to wonder what she could do to make things right.

As the bell rang, Corinne rose and faced the class. "We have a new student with us this year," she said. "Michelle, would you stand up?" She smiled encouragingly at Michelle, who blushed a deep red, hesitated for a moment, then haltingly stood up next to her seat. "Michelle is from Boston, and I imagine this school must look very strange to her."

"It's nice," Michelle said. "It isn't like the schools in Boston at all."

"You mean they aren't nice?" Sally teased.

Michelle's blush deepened. "That's not what I meant—" she began. "Miss Hatcher," she appealed, "I didn't mean to say I didn't like the school in Boston . . ."

"I'm sure you didn't," Corinne said quickly. "Why don't you sit down, and we'll let everyone introduce himself to you."

Gratefully, Michelle sank back into her seat, and leaned over to glare at Sally, who was grinning back at her mischievously. Her sense of humor overcoming her embarrassment, Michelle began to giggle, but quickly stopped when she heard the voice behind her.

"I said, my name is Susan Peterson," the voice repeated loudly. Michelle turned, and met Susan's glare, then felt herself turning red again. She quickly faced the front of the classroom, sure that she had accidentally made an enemy, and wishing again she hadn't let herself get caught up in Sally's scheme.

But I didn't mean any harm, she told herself. She tried to concentrate on what Miss Hatcher was saying, but for the first hour all she was conscious of was the memory of Susan Peterson's eyes, wrathful, staring at her. When the first recess bell finally rang, Michelle hesitated, then approached the teacher's desk.

"Miss Hatcher?" she said hesitantly. Corinne looked up at her, and smiled.

"Is something wrong?" she asked, concerned by Michelle's troubled expression.

"I was wondering—could I change my seat?"

"Already? But you've only had it two hours."

"I know," Michelle said. She shuffled her feet uncomfortably, wondering how to tell the teacher what had happened. Then she blurted the story out.

"It was supposed to be a joke. I mean, Sally told me

that Susan Peterson likes Jeff Benson, and she thought it would be fun if we took the seats beside Jeff so Susan couldn't sit next to him. And I went along with her." Michelle seemed to be on the verge of tears as she continued. "I didn't mean for Susan to be mad at me—I mean, I don't even know her, and—and. . . ." Her voice trailed off helplessly.

"It's all right," Corinne told her gently. "I know how things like that can happen, particularly when everything is new and strange. Go on outside, and when you come back, I'll change everybody's seats." She paused a moment, then: "Whom would you like to sit with?"

"Well—Sally, I guess. Or Jeff. They're the only people I know."

"I'll see what I can do," Corinne promised. "Run along now—there's only ten minutes left."

Michelle, unsure whether she had done the right thing, walked slowly out to the schoolyard. In a group under a large maple, Sally Carstairs, Susan Peterson, and Jeff Benson seemed to be arguing about something. Feeling terribly self-conscious, Michelle approached the group, and wasn't surprised when they stopped talking as she drew near. Sally smiled and called out to her, but Susan Peterson ignored her, quickly moving off in the opposite direction.

"Is Susan mad at me?" Michelle asked anxiously. Sally shrugged.

"So what if she is? She'll get over it." Then, before Michelle could say anything more about it, Sally changed the subject. "Isn't Miss Hatcher neat? And wait till you see her boyfriend! He's too dreamy for words."

"Who is he?"

"Mr. Hartwick. He's a psychologist," Sally told her. "He's only here once a week, but he lives in town. His daughter's in the sixth grade. Her name's Lisa, and she's awful."

Michelle didn't hear the comment about Lisa; she was more interested in the father. She groaned, remembering the batteries of tests she and her classmates had been forced to endure each year in Boston. "Are we all going to have to take tests?"

"Nah," Jeff replied. "Mr. Hartwick doesn't do anything unless someone gets in trouble. Then they have to talk to him. Mom says you used to talk to the principal when you were in trouble. Now you talk to Mr. Hartwick. Mom says it was better when you talked to the principal, and got a licking." He shrugged eloquently to let anyone who was interested know that the matter was of supreme indifference to him.

When the bell summoning them back to class rang a few minutes later, Michelle had all but forgotten her embarrassment, but it was quickly brought back to mind when Miss Hatcher held up a blank seating chart. There was a startled buzzing among the students, which Corinne quickly silenced.

"I'm going to try something new with this class," she said smoothly. "As you know, I've always felt that seventh-graders were old enough to decide for themselves where they want to sit." Michelle squirmed, sure that everyone was watching her, and that they knew whatever Miss Hatcher was about to do was her fault. "Unfortunately, it doesn't seem fair to the last people into the room. So I'm going to pass out slips of paper, and I want you all to write down whom you'd like to sit next to. Maybe we can make everyone happy."

Unable to resist, Michelle glanced over her shoulder. Susan Peterson had a smug smile on her face.

Corinne began passing out paper, and for the next few minutes the room was quiet. Corinne gathered up the papers and studied them briefly. Then she began working on her seating chart while the children whispered among themselves, predicting the results.

The rearranging began. When it was over, Michelle found herself seated between Sally and Jeff, with Susan on Jeff's other side. Silently, Michelle sent a message of thanks to Miss Hatcher.

As the last bell sounded, Tim Hartwick stepped out of the office that was reserved for his use at the Paradise Point school. He leaned comfortably against the corridor wall and watched the children swirl past him in their rush to escape into the warm late-summer afternoon. It didn't take him long to spot the face he had been looking for. Michelle Pendleton hurried down the hall with another girl, whom he recognized as Sally Carstairs, and glanced at him timidly as she passed. As she left the building, he could see her whispering to her friend.

His expression thoughtful, Tim went back into his office, picked up a folder, put it in his filing cabinet, then locked the office door behind him before proceeding down to Corinne Hatcher's classroom.

"And so it begins," he intoned. "Another year of young minds to mold, futures to shape . . ."

"Oh, stop it," Corinne laughed. "Help me clean up, so we can get out of here."

Tim started toward the front of the room, then stopped short as he saw the seating chart, still propped against the blackboard.

"What's this?" he said, his voice faintly mocking. "A seating chart in the classroom of Corinne Hatcher, champion of freedom of choice? Another illusion shattered."

Corinne sighed. "There was a problem today. We have a new student this year, and it looked as though she was about to get off on the wrong foot. So I tried to straighten out the situation before things got out of hand." She gave him the details of what had happened that morning.

"I saw her just now," he said when she was finished.

"Did you?" Corinne began stacking the papers on her desk, talking as she worked. "Pretty, isn't she? And she seems to be bright, eager-to-please, and friendly, too. Not what you'd expect to be coming out of Boston these days." Suddenly she frowned, and looked at Tim curiously. "What do you mean, you just saw her? How do you know what she looks like?"

"I found a folder on my desk this morning—Michelle Pendleton's records. Want to take a look?"

"No way," Corinne replied. "I try never to look at the records till there's some reason to."

She thought Tim would drop the subject, but he didn't.

"She's almost too good to be true," he said. "Not a single black mark anywhere."

Corinne wondered what he was getting at.

"Is that so strange? I can think of any number of students here who have spotless records."

Tim nodded. "But this is Paradise Point, not Boston. It's almost as though Michelle Pendleton has been living her life unaware of her surroundings." He paused, then: "Did you know she's adopted?"

Corinne closed her desk drawers. "Should I have?" What was he getting at?

"Not really. But she is. She knows it, too."

"Is that unusual?"

"Somewhat. But what is definitely unusual is that apparently she's never had any reaction to it at all. As far as her teachers could tell, she's always accepted it as a simple fact of life."

"Well, good for her," Corinne said, her voice showing a trace of the annoyance she was beginning to feel. What on earth was Tim trying to get at? The answer came almost immediately.

"I think you should keep an eye on her," Tim said. Before Corinne could protest, he forged ahead. "I'm not saying anything is going to happen. But there's a difference between Paradise Point and Boston—as far as I know, Michelle is the only adoptive child you have here."

"I see," Corinne said slowly. Suddenly it was all becoming clear to her. "You mean the other children?"

"Exactly," Tim said. "You know how kids can be when one of them is different from the rest. If they made up their minds to, they could make life miserable for Michelle."

"I'd like to think they won't," Corinne said softly.

She knew what was in Tim's mind. He was thinking of his own daughter, Lisa, eleven years old, but so different from Michelle Pendleton that comparison was nearly impossible.

Tim liked to believe that Lisa's problems stemmed from the fact that she was "different" from her school friends: her mother had died five years earlier. In all charity, Corinne admitted that was partly true. The death of her mother had been hard on Lisa, even harder than it had been on Tim.

At six, she had been too young to understand what had happened. Until the end, she had refused to believe her mother was dying, and when at last the inevitable had happened, it had been almost too much for her.

She had blamed her father, and Tim, distressed, had begun to spoil her. Lisa, from a happy six-year-old, had grown into a sullen eleven-year-old, uncooperative, listless, a loner.

"Do you have to be home this afternoon?" Corinne asked carefully, hoping Tim wouldn't follow the train of thought that had brought her to what seemed an irrelevant question.

Suddenly, as if Corinne's thoughts had summoned her, Lisa came into the classroom. She glanced quickly at Corinne. Her face, which should have been pretty, was pinched into an expression of suspicion and hostility. Corinne made herself smile at Lisa, but Lisa's dark eyes, nearly hidden under too long bangs, gave no hint of friendliness. She turned quickly to her father. When she spoke, her words sounded to Corinne more like an ultimatum than a request.

"I'm going home with Alison Adams, and having dinner there. Is it all right?"

Tim frowned, but agreed to Lisa's plans. A small smile of satisfaction on her face, Lisa left the room as quickly as she had come in. When she was gone, Tim looked rueful.

"Well, I guess I have the rest of the day," he said. He had wanted to share the afternoon with his daughter, but there was no bitterness in his voice, only sadness and defeat. Then, reading Corinne's expression of disapproval, he tried to make the best of it. "At least she told me what she's up to," he said crookedly. He shook his head. "I'm a pretty good psychologist," he went on, "but as a father, I ain't so terrific, huh?"

Corinne decided to ignore the question. If it wasn't for Lisa, and Lisa's clear dislike of Corinne, she and Tim probably would have been married two years ago. But Lisa ran Tim and had managed, to her own delight, to become a sore spot between Corinne and Tim. "I bought some steaks," she said brightly, linking an arm through Tim's and steering him toward the door. "Just in case you could come over this evening. Come on, let's get out of here."

Together, they left the school building. As they emerged into the soft summer afternoon, Corinne breathed deeply of the warm, sweet air, and looked happily around at the spreading oaks and maples, their leaves still a vibrant green.

"I love it here," she said. "I really do!"

"I love it here—I really do!" Michelle exclaimed, unknowingly echoing the words her teacher had just uttered. Beside her, Sally Carstairs and Jeff Benson exchanged a glance, and rolled their eyes up in disgust.

"It's a tank town," Jeff complained. "Nothing ever happens here."

"Where would you rather live?" Michelle challenged him.

"Wood's Hole," Jeff announced without hesitation.

"Wood's Hole?" Sally repeated. "What's that?"

"I want to go to school there," Jeff said placidly. "At the Institute of Oceanography."

"How boring," Sally said airily. "And it probably isn't any different from the Point. I can hardly wait to get out of here."

"You probably won't," Jeff teased. "You'll probably die here, like everybody else."

"No, I won't," Sally insisted. "You just wait. You'll see."

The three of them were walking along the bluff. As they drew near the Bensons', Michelle asked Jeff if he wanted to come home with her.

Jeff glanced at his house and saw his mother standing at the door, watching him. Then he shifted his gaze, passing over the old cemetery, and coming to rest on the roof of the Pendleton house, just visible beyond the trees. He remembered everything his mother had ever told him about the cemetery and that house. "I don't think so," he decided. "I promised Mom I'd mow the lawn this afternoon."

"Oh, come on," Michelle urged him. "You never come over to my house."

"I will," Jeff said. "But not today. I—I just don't have time."

A glint of mischief came into Sally's eyes. She nudged Michelle with her elbow.

"What's wrong?" she asked, her voice carefully innocent. "Are you afraid of the cemetery?"

"No, I'm not afraid of the cemetery," Jeff snapped. By now they were in front of his house, and he was about to start up the driveway. Sally stopped him with her next words, though she directed them to Michelle.

"There's supposed to be a ghost in the cemetery. Jeff's probably afraid of it."

"A ghost? I never heard that," Michelle said.

"It isn't true, anyway," Jeff told her. "I've lived here all my life, and if there was a ghost, I would have seen it. And I haven't, so there isn't any ghost."

"You saying so doesn't make it so," Sally argued.

"And you saying there *is* a ghost doesn't make it so, either," Jeff shot back. "See you tomorrow." He turned and started up the driveway, then waved back at Michelle when she called a good-bye to him. As he disappeared into his house, the two girls continued their walk, leaving the road at Sally's urging, to follow the path along the edge of the bluff. Suddenly Sally stopped, grabbed Michelle with one arm, while she pointed with the other.

"There's the graveyard! Let's go in!"

Michelle looked over at the tiny cemetery choked with weeds. Until today, she had only glanced at it from the car.

"I don't know," she said, peering uneasily at the overgrown graves.

"Oh, come on," Sally urged. "Let's go in." She started toward a place where the low picket fence surrounding the cemetery had collapsed to the ground.

Michelle started to follow her, then stopped. "Maybe we shouldn't."

"Why not? Maybe we'll see the ghost!"

"There's no such thing as ghosts," Michelle said. "But it just seems like we ought to leave it alone. Who's buried there, anyway?"

"Lots of people. Mostly Uncle Joe's family. All the Carsons are buried out here. Except the last ones—they're buried in town. Come on—the gravestones are neat."

"Not now." Michelle cast around in her mind for some way to distract Sally. She wasn't sure why, but the graveyard frightened her. "I'm hungry. Let's go to my house and get something to eat. Then maybe later we can come back here."

Sally seemed reluctant to give up the expedition, but at Michelle's insistence, she gave in. The two girls continued along the path for a while, in an uneasy silence that Michelle finally broke.

"Is there really supposed to be a ghost?"

"I'm not sure," Sally replied. "Some people say there is, and some people say there isn't."

"Who's the ghost supposed to be?"

"A girl who lived here a long time ago."

"What happened to her? Why is she still here?"

"I don't know. I don't think anybody knows. Nobody's even sure if she's really here or not."

"Have you ever seen her?"

"No," Sally said, with a hesitation so slight that Michelle wasn't certain she'd even heard it.

A few minutes later the two girls slammed through the back door into the immense kitchen, where June was kneading a loaf of bread. "You two hungry?" she asked.

"Uh-huh."

"There're cookies in the jar, and milk's in the refrigerator. Wash your hands first, though. Both of you." June turned back to her dough, ignoring the look of exasperation that passed between Michelle and Sally at the reminder of the childhood they were becoming eager to leave behind. Yet neither of them considered the possibility of ignoring the order. In a moment, June heard the tap running in the kitchen sink.

"We'll be up in my room," Michelle said as she poured two glasses of milk and heaped a plate with cookies.

"Just don't get crumbs all over everything," June said placidly, knowing they were again rolling their eyes at each other.

"Is your mother like that, too?" Michelle asked as they went upstairs.

"Worse," Sally said. "Mine still makes me eat in the kitchen."

"What can you do?" Michelle sighed, not expecting an answer. She led Sally into her room and closed the door. Sally threw herself on the bed.

"I love this house," she exclaimed. "And this room, and the furniture, and—" Her voice stopped suddenly as her eyes fell on the doll that lay on the window seat.

"What's that?" she breathed. "Is it new? How come I haven't seen it before?"

"It was right there last time you were here," Michelle replied. Sally got up and went across the room.

"Michelle, it looks *ancient*!"

"It is, I guess," Michelle agreed. "I found it in the closet when we moved in. It was up on a shelf, way at the back."

Sally picked up the doll, examining it carefully.

"She's beautiful," she said softly. "What's her name?"

"Amanda."

Sally's eyes widened, and she stared at Michelle.

"Amanda? Why did you name her that?"

"I don't know. I just wanted an old-fashioned name, and Amanda sort of—well, came to me, I guess."

"That's weird," Sally said. She could feel goose

bumps forming on her skin. "That's the name of the ghost."

"What?" Michelle asked. It didn't make sense.

"That's the name of the ghost," Sally repeated. "It's on one of the gravestones. Come on, I'll show you."

CHAPTER 5

Sally led the way as the girls left the path and started toward the collapsing fence around the cemetery.

It was a tiny plot, no more than fifty feet square, and the graves had a forgotten look to them. Many of the headstones had been pushed over, or fallen, and most of those still upright had an unstable appearance, as if they were only waiting for a good storm to give up their lonely vigils over the dead. A lightning-scarred oak tree, long dead, stood skeletally in the center of the plot, its branches reaching forlornly toward the sky. It was a grim place, and Michelle was hesitant to enter.

"Be careful," Sally warned Michelle. "There's nails sticking up, and you can't see them through the weeds."

"Doesn't anybody take care of this place?" Michelle asked. "The graveyards in Boston never look like this."

"I don't think anybody cares anymore," Sally answered her. "Uncle Joe says he isn't even going to be buried here—he says being buried's a waste of time and just takes up a lot of ground that could be used for other things. Once he even threatened to take out all the gravestones and let the whole place grow wild."

Michelle paused, and looked around her. "He might as well have," she observed. "This place is creepy."

Sally avoided the tangle of vines and weeds as she moved through the graveyard. "Wait'll you see what's over here."

Michelle was about to follow her when her eyes suddenly fell on one of the headstones. It stood at an odd angle, as if it were about to fall under its own weight. It was the inscription that had caught Michelle's eye. She read it again:

LOUISE CARSON—Born 1850
DIED IN SIN—1880

"Sally?"

Ahead of her, Sally Carstairs paused, and turned back to see what had happened.

"Have you ever seen this?" Michelle was pointing to one of the headstones. Even before she went back to look, Sally knew which one it was. Seconds later she was standing next to Michelle, staring at the strange inscription.

"What does it mean?" Michelle asked.

"How should I know?"

"Does anybody know?"

"Search me," Sally said. "I asked my mother once, but she didn't know either. Whatever it was, it happened a hundred years ago."

"But it's creepy," Michelle said. " 'Died in Sin'! It sounds so—so Puritan!"

"Well, what do you expect? This is New England!"

"But who was she?"

"One of Uncle Joe's ancestors, I guess. All the Carsons were." She took Michelle's arm and pulled at her. "Come on—the one I wanted to show you is over there in the corner."

Reluctantly, Michelle allowed herself to be drawn away from the strange grave, but as she picked her way across the cemetery, her mind stayed on the odd inscription. What could it mean? Did it mean anything? Then Sally stopped and pointed.

"There," she whispered to Michelle. "Look at that."

Michelle's eyes searched out the ground where Sally was pointing. At first she didn't see anything. Then, nearly lost under the brambles, she saw a small slab of stone. She knelt down, and pulled the thorny branches to one side, brushing the dirt off the stone with her free hand.

It was a simple rectangle of granite, unadorned and pitted with age. On it was a single word:

AMANDA

Michelle sucked in her breath, then examined the stone more closely, sure that there must be more to the inscription than just the name. There wasn't.

"I don't understand," she whispered. It doesn't say when she was born, or when she died, or her last name, or anything. Who was she?" Her eyes wide, Michelle stared up at Sally, who quickly knelt down beside her.

"She was a blind girl," Sally said, keeping her voice

low. "She must have been one of the Carsons, and she must have lived here a long time ago. My mother says they think she fell off the cliff one day."

"But why isn't her last name on the stone, or when she was born, and when she died?" Michelle's eyes, reflecting her fascination, were fixed on the pitted granite slab.

"Because she isn't buried here," Sally whispered. "They never found her body. It must have been swept out to sea or something. Anyway, Mom told me they only put this marker here as a temporary thing. But they never found her body, so they never put up a real headstone."

Michelle felt a chill pass through her. "They'll never find the body now," she said.

"I know. That's why they say the ghost will always be around here. The kids say Amanda won't leave until her body's found, and since the body won't ever be found . . ."

Sally's voice trailed off, and Michelle tried to absorb what she had just heard. Almost involuntarily she put her hand out and rested it on the stone for a moment, then pulled it quickly away and stood up.

"There's no such thing as ghosts," she said. "Come on, let's go home."

She started purposefully out of the cemetery, but when she realized Sally wasn't following her she paused and looked back. Sally was still kneeling by the strange memorial, but when Michelle called out to her, she stood up and hurried toward Michelle.

Neither of the girls spoke until they were out of the cemetery and on their way back to the Pendletons'.

"You have to admit, it's weird," Sally said.

"What is?" Michelle said evasively.

"You choosing that name for your doll. I mean, that could have been *her* doll, lying on that shelf all these years, just waiting for you to find it."

"That's dumb," Michelle said flatly, not willing to admit that what Sally had just said was exactly what had been going through her own mind. "I could have named the doll anything."

"But you didn't," Sally insisted. "You named it Amanda. There must have been a reason."

"It was just a coincidence. Besides, Jeff's lived here all his life, and if there were a ghost, he'd have seen it."

"Maybe he has," Sally said thoughtfully. "Maybe that's why he won't go over to your house."

"He doesn't come over because he's busy," Michelle said quickly. "He has to help his mother." Her voice was becoming strident, and she felt herself getting angry. Why was Sally talking like this? "Can't we talk about something else?" she asked.

Sally looked at her curiously, then grinned. "Okay. I'm starting to scare myself, anyway."

Grateful for her friend's understanding, Michelle reached out and gave Sally's arm a friendly squeeze.

"Ouch!" Sally yelped, flinching and pulling away from Michelle.

Her arm, Michelle thought. *Her arm's hurting again, just like it did last week. But nothing happened to her, not today.* A shiver passed through Michelle, but she was careful not to let her sudden feeling of unease show.

"I'm sorry," she said, touching Sally's arm lightly. "I thought it was all better."

"I thought it was, too," Sally replied, glancing back at the cemetery. "But I guess it isn't." Suddenly she wanted to get away from there. "Let's go back to your house," she said. "This place is giving me the creeps."

The two girls hurried toward the old house on the bluff. As they reached the back door, Michelle shivered a little, and watched the afternoon fog gather in the air above the sea. Then she pulled open the door and followed Sally inside.

"Dad?"

The Pendletons were gathered in the front parlor, a room they had quickly adopted as a family den, since the living room was too cavernous to suit them comfortably. Cal was sitting in his big chair, his feet resting on an ottoman, and Michelle was stretched out on the floor near him, a book open in front of her. She was lying on her elbows, her chin propped up in the palms of her hands, and Cal couldn't understand why her neck wasn't hurting her. Flexibility of youth, he decided. In a frightfully hard-looking antique chair next to the fireplace, June was industriously knitting a sweater for the baby, alternating the stripes—blue and pink—just to be on the safe side.

"Um?" Cal replied, his concentration still on the medical journal in his lap.

"Do you believe in ghosts?"

Cal's eyes left the page he had been reading. He glanced at his wife and saw that June had abandoned her knitting. He turned to his daughter, a tentative smile on his face.

"Do I what?" he asked.

"Do you believe in ghosts?"

Cal's smile faded as he realized Michelle was serious. He closed the magazine, wondering what had brought on such a strange question.

"Didn't we talk about this five years ago?" he asked mildly. "About the same time we talked about Santa Claus and the Easter Bunny?"

"Well, maybe not ghosts," Michelle said haltingly. "Not like that, anyway. Spirits, I guess."

"What on earth are you talking about?" June asked.

Michelle began to feel foolish. Now, in the warmth and comfort of the den, the thoughts that had been worrying her all afternoon seemed silly. Maybe she shouldn't have mentioned it at all. She considered for a moment, then decided to tell them what had happened.

"You know that old graveyard between here and the Bensons'?" she began. "Sally showed it to me today."

"Don't tell me you saw a ghost in a graveyard," Cal exclaimed.

"No, I didn't," Michelle said scornfully. "But there's a strange marker there. It—it has the name of my doll on it."

"Amanda?" June said. "That *is* strange."

Michelle nodded. "And Sally says there's no body in the grave. She says Amanda was a blind girl who fell off the bluff a long time ago." She hesitated for a moment, unsure whether to continue. Sensing her indecision, Cal urged her on.

"What else did she say?"

"She said some of the kids think Amanda's ghost is still around here," Michelle said quietly.

"You didn't believe her, did you?" Cal asked.

"No . . ." Michelle said, but her voice made it clear that she wasn't sure.

"Well, you can believe me, princess," Cal declared. "There's no such thing as ghosts, spirits, boogeymen, haunts, poltergeists, or any other such nonsense, and you shouldn't let anyone tell you there is."

"But it's weird, me naming the doll Amanda," Michelle protested. "Sally thinks the doll might even have belonged to her . . ."

"It's just a coincidence, dear." June picked up her knitting, quickly counted her stitches, and resumed her work. "Those things happen all the time. That's how ghost stories start. Something odd happens, purely by coincidence, but people don't want to believe it was just chance. They want to believe there's something else—luck, ghosts, fate, whatever." When Michelle still looked unconvinced, June set her work down once more.

"All right," she said. "How did you happen to choose the name for your doll?"

"Well, I wanted an old-fashioned sounding name—" Michelle began.

"Okay. That lets out a lot of names right there. Yours, and mine, and lots of others that don't sound old-fashioned. The old-fashioned ones, like Agatha, and Sophie, and Prudence—"

"They're all ugly," Michelle protested.

"So that narrows the list down still more," June reasoned. "Now you wanted a name that's 'old-fashioned' but not 'ugly,' and if you start with the A's, as most of us do, about the first one you come to is—"

"—Amanda!" Michelle finished, grinning. "And I thought it had just come to me," she muttered.

"Well, in a way, it did," June said. "The mind works so fast, you didn't even realize you'd gone through all that reasoning. And that, my love, is how ghost stories are born—coincidence! Now off to bed, or you'll fall asleep at school tomorrow."

Michelle pulled herself to her feet, and went to her father. Her arms slid around his neck, and she hugged him.

"I'm really dumb sometimes, aren't I?" she said.

"No more than the rest of us, princess." He kissed her gently, then smacked her bottom. "Off to bed with you."

He listened as Michelle went upstairs, then looked fondly at his wife.

"How do you do it?" he asked admiringly.

"Do what?" June replied absently.

"Think up logical explanations for things that don't seem logical."

"Talent," June replied. "Just talent. Besides, if I'd let you think up an explanation, we'd have been up all night, and wound up all believing in ghosts."

She got to her feet, and poked at the fire, settling it low on the grate, while Cal turned off the lights. Then, hand in hand, they, too, climbed the stairs.

Michello lay in bed, listening to the sounds of the night—the surf pounding on the beach below, the last crickets of summer chirping happily in the darkness, the light breeze soughing in the trees around the house. She thought about what her mother had said. It made sense. And yet—and yet it seemed as though there was something wrong with the explanation. There should be something else. That's silly, she told herself. There isn't anything else. But even as the nightsounds lulled her to sleep, Michelle had the feeling that there *was* something else.

Something ominous.

Maybe she shouldn't have named the doll Amanda at all. . . .

The nightsounds had stopped when Michelle awoke. She lay still in bed, listening. Around her, the silence was almost palpable.

And then she felt it.

Something was watching her.

Something in her room.

She wanted to pull the covers up over her face and hide from whatever had come to her, but she knew she couldn't.

Whatever it was, she had to look at it.

Slowly, Michelle sat up in bed, her eyes, wide and frightened, searching out the dark corners of the bedroom.

By the window.

It was in the corner by the window—a black shape, something standing there, standing still, watching her.

And then, as she watched, it began coming toward her.

It moved out into the room, into the moonlight that was shining silver through the window.

It was a little girl, no older than herself.

Inexplicably, the fear began to drain from Michelle, and was replaced by curiosity. Who was she? What did she want?

The child moved closer to her, and Michelle could see that she was dressed strangely—her dress was black, and fell close to the floor, with large puffed sleeves that ended in tight cuffs at her wrists. On her head, nearly hiding her face, she wore a black bonnet.

Michelle watched, transfixed, as the strange figure approached her. In the moonlight, the girl turned her head, and Michelle saw her face.

It was a soft face, with a cupid's mouth, and a small, upturned nose.

Then Michelle saw the eyes.

Milky white, and shimmering faintly in the moonlight, they gazed sightlessly at Michelle, and as the sightless eyes fixed on her, the little girl raised one arm, and pointed at Michelle.

Her fear flooding over her once again, Michelle began to scream.

Her own screams woke her up.

Terrified, she stared around the empty bedroom, looking for the strange black figure that had been there only a second before.

The room was empty.

Around her, the nightsounds still droned on, the surf pounding steadily below, the breeze still plucking at the pines.

Then the door to her room opened, and her father was there.

"Princess? Princess, are you all right?" He was sitting on her bed, his arms around her, comforting her.

"It was a nightmare, Daddy," Michelle whispered. "It was awful, Daddy, and so real. There was someone here. Right here, in the room . . ."

"No, baby, no," Cal soothed her. "There's nobody here but me. Just you and me, and your mother. It was only a dream, sweetheart."

Cal sat with her for a long time, talking to her, calming her. Finally, near dawn, he kissed her softly and told her to go back to sleep. He left her door open.

Michelle lay still for a while, trying to forget the terrifying dream. Unable to fall asleep, she got out of bed and went to the window seat. Picking up the doll, she sat in the window, staring out into the darkness of the last moments of night. As the fog began to lift, Michelle suddenly thought she saw something—a figure, standing on the bluff to the north, near the old cemetery.

She looked again, straining her eyes, but the mists swirled in the wind, and she could see nothing.

Taking the antique doll with her, Michelle returned to her bed. As the first gray of dawn crept into the sky, she fell asleep once more.

Beside her, its head resting on the pillow, the sightless doll gazed blankly upward.

When he left Michelle's room, Cal did not go straight back to bed. Instead, he put on a robe, fished his pipe and tobacco off the dresser, and went downstairs.

He wandered through the house aimlessly for a while, then settled finally in the little formal parlor at the front of the first floor. He lit his pipe, propped his feet up, and let his mind drift.

He was back in Boston, the night that boy had died —the night his life had changed.

He couldn't even remember the boy's name now.

Couldn't, or wouldn't.

That was part of the problem. There were too many whose names he couldn't remember, and who had died.

How many of them had died because of him?

The last one, the boy from Paradise Point, he was sure of. But there might have been others. How many others? Well, there wouldn't be any more.

His mind kept coming back to that boy.

Alan Hanley. That was his name. Cal could remember the day Alan Hanley had been brought to Boston General.

The ambulance had arrived late in the afternoon, with Alan Hanley unconscious, and Josiah Carson tending him. The boy had fallen from a roof.

This roof, Cal knew now, but at the time it had made no difference.

Josiah Carson had done what he could, but when he realized that the boy's injuries were too serious to be handled in the Paradise Point Clinic, he had brought him to Boston.

And Calvin Pendleton had attended him.

It seemed, at first, like a fairly simple case—a few broken bones, and possible cranial damage. Cal had done his best, setting the breaks, and checking for internal injuries. That was when he had found what he thought was a blood clot building up inside the boy's head. It had seemed to him to be an emergency, and so, with Josiah Carson at his side, looking on, he had operated.

Alan Hanley died on the operating table.

And there had been no blood clot, no reason to operate.

The incident had shaken Cal badly, shaken him more than any other single event of his life.

It was not, he knew, the first time he had misdiagnosed something. Nearly all doctors misdiagnose now and then. But for Cal, Alan Hanley's death was a turning point.

From that moment, he had never stopped wondering if he was going to make another mistake, and if another child was going to die because of him.

Everyone at the hospital told him he was taking it too seriously, but the child's death continued to haunt him.

Finally he had taken a day off, and driven out to Paradise Point to talk to Josiah Carson about Alan Hanley. . . .

Josiah Carson greeted him coolly, and at first Cal thought he was wasting his time. Carson blamed him for Alan Hanley's death; he could see it in the old man's piercing blue eyes. But as they talked, something in Carson began to change. Cal was sure the old doctor was telling him things he had told no one else.

"Have you ever lived by yourself?" Carson suddenly asked him. But before he could make any reply, Carson began talking again. "I've been living alone for years, taking care of the people out here, and keeping pretty much to myself. I guess I should have kept it that way, kept on trying to do all the repairs to the house myself. But I'm getting old, and I thought . . . well, never mind what I thought."

Cal shifted uncomfortably, and wondered what the old man was trying to tell him. "What happened that day?" he asked. "Before you brought Alan Hanley to Boston, I mean."

"It's hard to say," Carson replied, his voice low. "I'd been having trouble with the roof, and some of the slates needed replacing. I was going to do it myself, but then I changed my mind. Thought maybe it would be better to get someone a little younger." His voice faded to little more than a whisper. "But Alan was too young. I should have known—maybe I did know. He was only twelve. . . . Well, anyway, I let him go up there."

"And what happened?"

Carson stared at him, his eyes empty, his face sagging with tiredness.

"What happened in the operating room?" he asked.

Cal squirmed. "I don't know. Everything seemed to be going so well. And then he died. I don't know what happened."

Carson nodded. "And that's what happened on the roof. I was watching him, and everything seemed to be going well. And then he fell." There was a long silence, broken by Carson: "I wish you'd saved him."

Again, Cal squirmed, but suddenly Carson smiled at him.

"It's not your fault," he said. "It's not your fault, and it's not my fault. But I suppose you could say that, together, it's *our* fault. There's a bond between us now, Dr. Pendleton. What do you suggest we do?"

Cal had no answers. Josiah Carson's words had numbed him.

And then, as if understanding the problems that had been plaguing Cal since the day Alan Hanley had died, Josiah had made a suggestion. Perhaps Cal should consider giving up his practice in Boston.

"And do what?" Cal asked hollowly.

"Come out here. Take over a small, undemanding practice from a tired old doctor. Get away from the pressure of Boston General. You're scared now, Dr. Pendleton—"

"My name's Cal."

"Cal, then. At any rate you're scared. You made a

mistake, and you think you'll make more. And if you
stay at Boston General, you will. The fear itself will
force you to. But if you come out here, I can help
you. And you can help me. I want out, Cal. I want out
of my practice, and I want out of my house. And I
want to sell it all to you. Believe me, I'll make it worth
your while."

To Cal, it all made sense. A slow practice, in which
not much happened.

And not much could go wrong.

Not much room to make mistakes.

Plenty of time to think about every case, and make
sure he handled it right.

And no one around to realize that he no longer felt
competent to be a doctor. No one except Josiah Carson, who understood him, and sympathized with him.

So they had come to Paradise Point, though initially
June had been against it. Cal remembered her words
when he had explained the idea to her.

"But why the house? I can understand why he wants
to sell his practice, but why is he insisting we take the
house, too? It's too big for us—we don't need all that
room!"

"I don't know," Cal replied. "But he's selling it to us
cheap, and it's a damned good deal. I think we should
consider ourselves lucky."

"But it doesn't make any sense," June complained.
"In fact, it's almost morbid. I'm sure he wants out of
that house because of what happened to Alan Hanley.
Why is he so anxious to have us in it? All it can do is
constantly remind *you* of that boy, too. It's crazy, Cal.
He wants something from you. I don't know what it is,
but you mark my words. Something is going to happen."

But so far, not much *had* happened.

A bad moment with Sally Carstairs, but he'd gotten through it.

And now, his daughter was starting to have nightmares.

CHAPTER 6

June stood at her easel, trying to concentrate on her work. It was difficult. It wasn't the painting that was bothering her—indeed, she was pleased with what she had accomplished: a seascape was emerging, somewhat abstract, but nevertheless recognizable as the view from her studio. No, it wasn't the work that was the problem.

The problem was Michelle, but she still hadn't quite been able to put her finger on why she was worried. It wasn't as if last night's nightmare had been the first. Michelle certainly had had her normal share of bad dreams. But when Cal had come back to bed just before dawn, and told her about Michelle's dream, she'd had an uneasy feeling. It had stayed with her even when she went back to sleep; it was still with her now.

With a sigh of frustration, June laid her brushes aside, and sank onto the stool, her favorite perch.

Her eyes wandered restlessly over the studio. She

was pleased with what she had accomplished in so short a time—the last of the old debris was gone, the walls had been scrubbed and repainted, and the bright green trim had been restored to its original cheerfulness. Her supplies were stored away neatly under the countertop, and in the closet she had installed a rack to hold her canvases upright and separated. Now all she had to do was stop worrying and start painting.

She was about to make one more stab at it when there was a flicker of movement outside the single small window on the inland side of the building, then a light tap at the door.

"Hello?" The voice was a woman's, tentative, almost timid, as if whoever had come to the door had nearly gone away again without announcing herself at all.

June started to get up to open the door, then changed her mind. "Come in," she called. "It's open."

There was a slight pause, then the door opened and a small woman, her hair wrapped neatly in a bun and her dress covered with a flowered apron, stepped hesitantly into the studio.

"Oh, are you working?" the woman asked, starting to back out the door again. "I'm terribly sorry—I didn't mean to disturb you."

"No, no," June protested, getting to her feet. "Please come in. I'm afraid I was really only daydreaming."

A strange look crossed the woman's face—was it disapproval?—then quickly disappeared. She advanced into the room a foot or two.

"I'm Constance Benson," she said. "Jeff's mother. From next door?"

"Of course!" June replied warmly. "I really should have come over to see you before, but I'm afraid I—"

she broke off her sentence, glancing ruefully down at her pregnant midsection. "But that's really no excuse, is it? I mean, I really should be walking huge numbers of miles every day, and instead I just sit here and daydream. Well, three more weeks and the baby should be here. Won't you sit down?" She gestured toward a chaise longue that had been rescued from the attic of the house, but Mrs. Benson made no move toward it. Instead, she gazed around the studio with unconcealed curiosity.

"You've certainly done wonders with this, haven't you?" she observed.

"Mostly just cleaning, and a little paint," June said. Then she saw Mrs. Benson staring at the floor. "And of course I still have to get that stain out," she added, half-apologetically.

"Don't count on it," Constance Benson told her. "You wouldn't be the first that's tried, and you wouldn't be the last that'll fail, either."

"I beg your pardon?" June said blankly.

"That stain'll be there as long as this building is here," Mrs. Benson said emphatically.

"But it's mostly gone already," June protested. "My husband chipped most of it off, and it seems to be scrubbing up fairly well."

Constance Benson shook her head doubtfully. "I don't know," she said. "Maybe now that there's no Carsons here. . . ." Her voice trailed off, but the frown on her face remained.

"I don't understand," June said lamely. "What is the stain? Is it blood?"

"Maybe," Constance Benson replied. "Don't think anyone can say for sure, not after all these years. But if anybody knows, Doc Carson would be the one to ask."

"I see," June said, not really seeing at all. "I suppose I should ask him, then, shouldn't I?"

"Actually, it's those girls I came to see you about," Mrs. Benson announced. Her eyes were now firmly fixed on June. There was something almost accusatory in them, and June wondered if Michelle and Sally had somehow offended Constance Benson.

"You mean Michelle and Sally Carstairs?" At the expression of concern on June's face, Mrs. Benson smiled slightly, the first warmth she had displayed since coming into the studio. Her face was suddenly almost pretty.

"Oh, don't worry," she said hurriedly. "They haven't done anything wrong. I just wanted to warn you."

"Warn me?" June repeated, now totally baffled.

"It's the cemetery," Constance said. "The old Carson cemetery, between here and my house?"

June nodded.

"I saw the girls playing there yesterday afternoon. Such pretty girls, both of them."

"Thank you."

"I was just about to go out and talk to them myself when they left, so I decided not to bother with it until this morning."

"Bother with what?" June wished she'd get to the point.

"It isn't safe for children to play there," Constance said. "Not safe at all."

June stared at Mrs. Benson. This, she decided, was just a bit too much. Apparently, Constance Benson was the local busybody. It must make life hard for Jeff. She could imagine Constance coming up with an objection to everything Jeff might want to do. For her own part, she could simply ignore the woman. "Well, I'll admit, I don't think playing in a cemetery is the most cheerful thing in the world," she said, "but it couldn't be particularly dangerous . . ."

"Oh, it's not the cemetery," Constance said too quickly. "It's the land the cemetery's on. It's not stable."

"But it's granite, isn't it?" June's voice was smooth, giving no hint that she'd picked up on the other woman's apparent fear. "Just like this?"

"Well, I suppose so," Constance said uncertainly. "I don't know much about things like that. But that part of the bluff is going to wash into the sea one of these days, and I wouldn't want any kids to be there when it happens."

June's voice was cool. "I see. Well, I'll certainly tell the girls not to play there anymore. Would you like a cup of coffee? There's some on the stove."

"Oh, I don't think so." Constance glanced at a watch strapped firmly to her left wrist. "I've got to be getting back to my kitchen. Canning, you know." The way she said it gave June the distinct impression that Constance Benson was quite sure June *didn't* know, but should.

"Well, do come back again, when you have more time," June said weakly. "Or maybe I could drop in on you."

"Now that might be nice." By then the two women were standing at the open door to the studio, and Constance was staring at the house. "Pretty house, isn't it?" she said. Before June could reply, she added, "But I've never really liked it. No, I never have." Then,

without saying good-bye, she began walking purposefully along the path toward her own home.

June waited for a moment, watching her, then slowly
closed the door. She had a distinct feeling that she was
done painting for the day.

The noon sun was warm, and Michelle sat in the
shade of a large maple, eating her lunch with Sally,
Jeff, Susan, and a few of her other classmates. Though
Michelle was trying hard to make friends with Susan,
Susan was having none of it. She ignored Michelle
completely, and when she spoke to Sally, it was usually
to criticize her. But Sally, with her sunny disposition,
seemed unaffected by Susan's apparent grudge.

"We ought to have a picnic," Sally was saying. "Summer's almost gone, and in another month it will be too
late."

"It's already too late." Susan Peterson's voice had a
superior sound to it that annoyed Michelle, but everyone else seemed to ignore it. "My mother says that
once Labor Day's past, you don't have picnics anymore."

"But the weather's still nice," Sally said. "Why don't
we have one this weekend?"

"Where?" Jeff asked. If it was going to be on the
beach, he'd be sure to be there. It was as if Michelle
had heard his thought.

"How about the cove between Jeff's house and
mine?" she said. "It's rocky, but there's never anyone
there, and it's so pretty. Besides, if it rains, we'll be
close to home so we can go inside."

"You mean below the graveyard?" Sally asked. "That
would be creepy. There's a ghost out there."

"There isn't either," Jeff objected.

"Maybe there is," Michelle interjected. Suddenly she was the center of attention; even Susan Peterson turned to look at her curiously. "I dreamed about the ghost last night," she went on, launching into a vivid description of her strange vision. In the brightness of the day her terror had left her, and she wanted to share her dream with her new friends. Caught up in the tale, she didn't notice the others' silent exchange of glances. When she was finished, no one spoke. Jeff Benson concentrated on his sandwich, but the rest of the children were still staring at Michelle. Suddenly she felt worried, and wondered if she should have even mentioned the nightmare.

"Well, it was only a dream," she said, as the silence lengthened.

"Are you sure?" Sally asked her. "Are you sure you weren't awake the whole time?"

"Well, of course I wasn't," Michelle said. "It was a dream." She noticed that some of the girls were exchanging suspicious glances. "What's wrong?"

"Nothing," Susan Peterson said casually. "Except that when Amanda Carson fell off the cliff, she was wearing a black dress and a black bonnet, just like the girl you dreamed about last night."

"How do you know?" Michelle demanded.

"Everybody knows," Susan said complacently. "She always wore black, every day of her life. My grandmother told me, and *her* mother told her. And my great-grandmother knew Amanda Carson," Susan said triumphantly. Her eyes challenged Michelle. Once again a silence fell over the group. Was Susan telling her the truth, or were they all teasing her? Michelle looked from one face to another, trying to see what each of them was thinking. Only Sally met her eyes, and she merely shrugged when Michelle looked to her for help. Jeff Benson continued eating his sandwich, and carefully avoided Michelle's gaze.

"It was a dream!" Michelle exclaimed, gathering her things together, and getting to her feet. "It was only a dream, and if I'd known you were going to make such a big deal about it, I'd never have mentioned it!"

Before any of them could make a reply, Michelle stalked away. Across the playground, she could see a group of younger children playing jump rope. A moment later she had joined them.

"I wonder what's wrong with her?" Susan Peterson said when she was sure Michelle was out of earshot. Now her friends were staring at her.

"What do you mean, 'what's wrong with her'?" Sally Carstairs asked. "Nothing's wrong with her!"

"Really?" Susan said, sounding annoyed at the contradiction. "She tattled on you yesterday, didn't she? Why do you think Miss Hatcher changed the seating around? It was because Michelle told her what you did yesterday morning."

"So what?" Sally countered. "She just didn't want you to be mad at her, that's all."

"I think she's sneaky," Susan said. "And I don't think we should have anything to do with her."

"That's mean."

"No, it's not. There's something really strange about her."

"What?"

Susan's voice dropped to a conspiratorial whisper. "Well, I saw her with her parents the other day, and they're both blond. And everybody knows blonds can't have a dark-haired baby."

"Big deal," Sally said. "If you want to know, she's adopted. She told me so herself. What's so strange about that?"

Susan's eyes narrowed. "Well, that settles it."

"Settles what?" Sally asked.

"Settles *her*, of course. I mean, nobody knows where she really came from, and my mother says if you don't know anything about somebody's family, you don't know anything about the person."

"I know her family," Sally pointed out. "Her mother's very nice, and her father treated my arm, along with Uncle Joe."

"I mean her *real* family," Susan said, looking at Sally contemptuously. "Dr. Pendleton isn't her father. Her father could be anybody!"

"Well, I like her," Sally insisted. Susan glowered at her.

"You would—your father's only a janitor." Susan Peterson's father owned the Paradise Point Bank, and Susan never let her friends forget it.

Hurt by Susan's meanness, Sally Carstairs lapsed into silence. It wasn't fair of Susan to dislike Michelle just because she was adopted, but Sally wasn't sure what she should say. After all, she'd known Susan Peterson all her life, and she'd only just met Michelle Pendleton. *Well*, Sally decided, *I won't say anything. But I won't stop being Michelle's friend, either.*

June finished her lunch, and put the dishes in the sink. For now, she would go back to the studio, and try to finish sketching in the seascape.

She left the house, but as she walked to the studio, she found herself glancing north, and thinking about what Constance Benson had told her that morning. And then something struck her.

If Constance Benson was worried about that part of the bluff collapsing into the sea, why hadn't she told June to keep Michelle off the beach as well? And why didn't she keep Jeff off the beach? Better to be on top of the cliff when it went, than underneath it.

With sudden determination, June started along the path toward the cemetery. As she walked, another thought occurred to her: If it's unsafe, why did Mrs. Benson use the path herself? Why didn't she come down the road? June's pace quickened.

She stood on the path, staring at the old graveyard. It would make a wonderful painting. She could use moody colors, blues and grays, with a leaden sky, and exaggerate the collapsed fence, the dead tree, and the overgrown vines. Done properly, it could be positively frightening. For the life of her, she couldn't see why Michelle and Sally would have wanted to come here.

Curiosity, she decided. Just plain curiosity.

The same curiosity that had drawn the children to the graveyard now drew her. She left the path and picked her way carefully over the collapsed fence.

The old gravestones, with their antiquated inscriptions and their odd names, fascinated her immediately, a succession of markers that told a tale. She began tracing the history of the Carson family as they had lived and died on the bluff. Soon she forgot entirely about the condition of the ground, and was only aware of the headstones.

She came to Louise Carson's grave.

DIED IN SIN—1880

Now what on earth could that mean? If the date had been 1680, she would have assumed the woman had been burned for a witch, or some such thing. But in 1880? One thing was certain: Louise Carson's death could not have been a happy one.

As she stood looking down at the grave, June began to feel sorry for the long-dead woman. She was probably born too soon, June thought. *Died in Sin.* An epitaph for a fallen woman.

June chuckled at her own choice of words. They sounded so old-fashioned. And unfeeling.

Without quite realizing what she was doing, she lowered herself to her hands and knees, and began pulling the weeds from Louise Carson's grave. They were well rooted. She had to tug hard at them before they reluctantly gave way.

She had almost cleared the weed growth from the base of the headstone when the first pain struck her.

It was just a twinge, but the first wrenching contraction followed immediately.

My God, she thought, *it can't be.*

She struggled to her feet, and leaned heavily against the trunk of the dead oak.

She had to get back to the house.

The house was too far.

As the next contraction began, she looked frantically toward the road.

It was empty.

The Bensons'. Maybe she could get to the Bensons'. As soon as the pain let up, she'd start.

June lowered herself carefully to the ground and waited. After what seemed like an eon, she felt her muscles begin to relax, and the pain eased. Once again, she started to get to her feet.

"Stay where you are," a voice called out. June turned, and saw Constance Benson hurrying along the path. Sighing gratefully, June sank back to the ground.

She waited there, lying on Louise Carson's grave, praying that the baby would wait, that her first child would not be born in a cemetery.

Then, as Constance Benson knelt beside her and took her hand, June lay back.

Another overwhelming contraction convulsed her, and she could feel a spreading dampness as her water broke. *Dear God*, she prayed, *not here.*

Not in a graveyard.

CHAPTER 7

The three-ten bell rang. Michelle gathered up her books, shoved them into her green canvas bag, and started out of the room.

"Michelle?" It was Sally Carstairs, and though Michelle tried to ignore her, Sally took her arm and held her back.

"Don't be mad," Sally said plaintively. "Nobody meant to hurt your feelings."

Michelle stared suspiciously at her friend. When she saw the concern in Sally's eyes, she let her guard down a little.

"I don't see why everybody kept insisting I saw something I didn't see," she said. "I was asleep, and I had a nightmare, that's all."

"Let's go out in the hall," Sally said, her eyes shifting to Corinne Hatcher. Understanding Sally's glance, Michelle followed her out into the corridor.

"Well?" Michelle asked expectantly.

Sally avoided her gaze. She shifted uncomfortably

from one foot to the other. Then, staring at the floor, she said so quietly that Michelle could barely hear her, "Maybe you did only have a dream. But I've seen Amanda, too, and I think Susan Peterson has."

"What? You mean you've had the same dream I had?"

"I don't know," Sally said unhappily. "But I've seen her, and it wasn't a dream. That day I hurt my arm? Remember?"

Michelle nodded—how could she forget? That was the day she, too, had seen something. Something Sally had tried to pass off as "just the elm tree."

"How come you didn't tell me before?"

"I guess I didn't think you'd believe me," Sally said by way of an apology. "But, anyway, I saw her. At least, I think I did. I was out in the backyard, and all of a sudden I felt something touch my arm. When I turned to look, I tripped and fell."

"But what did you *see*?" Michelle pressed, suddenly sure that, whatever it might be, it was important.

"I—I'm not sure," Sally replied. "It was just something black. I only got a glimpse, really, and after I fell, whatever it was was gone."

Michelle stood silent, staring at Sally, and remembering that night, when she and her father had been leaving the Carstairses', and she had looked back.

There had been something at the window—something dark, like a shadow. Something black.

Before she could tell Sally what she had seen that night, Jeff Benson appeared at the end of the hall, waving to her.

"Michelle? Michelle! Mom's here, and she needs to talk to you!"

"Just a second—" Michelle began, but Jeff cut her off.

"Now! It's about your mother—"

Without waiting for him to finish, Michelle broke away from Sally and ran down the hall.

"What is it? Has something happened?" she demanded. But Jeff was already leading her out of the building to his mother's car. A battered sedan sat by the curb, its engine running, Constance Benson fidgeting behind the wheel.

"What is it?" Michelle asked again, climbing into the car.

"Your mother," Mrs. Benson said tersely, jamming the old car into gear. "She's at the clinic, having the baby."

"The baby?" Michelle breathed. But the baby wasn't due for three more weeks. "What happened?"

Ignoring her question, Constance Benson let the clutch out, pressed on the accelerator, and moved away from the curb. As they drove toward the clinic, she chewed at her lower lip, concentrated on her driving, and maintained her silence.

Michelle sat on the edge of her chair, holding a magazine in her lap but making no attempt to look at it. Instead, she watched the door through which, sooner or later, her father would come. And then, as she willed it to happen, the door opened, and Cal smiled at her.

"Congratulations," he said. "You have a baby sister."

Michelle leaped to her feet and threw herself into her father's arms.

"But what about Mom? Is she all right? What happened?"

"She's fine," Cal assured her. "And so is the baby. Apparently with your mother and your sister, time is *not* of the essence. Dr. Carson says this was the quickest delivery he's ever seen." Though he was careful to keep his tone light, Cal was worried. The delivery had been too quick. Abnormally quick. He wondered what had brought it on. Then he heard Michelle asking about the baby and put the delivery out of his mind.

"A sister? I have a sister?"

Cal nodded.

"Can I see her? Right now? Please?" She gazed appealingly up at Cal, and he hugged her close to him.

"In a few minutes," he promised. "Right now I'm afraid she isn't too presentable. Don't you want to know what happened?" Cal gently pushed Michelle onto a chair, then sat beside her. "Your sister was almost born in the cemetery," he said. Michelle stared at him uncomprehendingly, and the grin on his face faded a little.

"Your mother decided to take a walk," he went on. "She was in the old graveyard when she went into labor."

"The graveyard?" Michelle's voice was low, faintly worried. "What was she doing there?"

"Who knows?" Cal asked wryly. "You know your mother—you can never tell what she might do."

Now Michelle turned to Mrs. Benson. "But where was she when you found her? What part of the cemetery?"

Constance Benson hesitated, reluctant to tell Michelle where she had found June. But why not? "She was on Louise Carson's grave," she said, her voice quiet.

"On the grave?" Michelle echoed. How creepy, she

thought to herself, clutching her father's hand. "Is the baby all right? I mean, it's sort of like an omen, isn't it? A baby born on a grave?"

Cal squeezed her hand, then slipped an arm around her.

"Don't be silly," he said gently. "Your sister was born right here, not on anybody's grave." He stood up, drawing Michelle with him. "Come on, let's go take a look at the baby, then see how your mother's doing." Without a word to Constance Benson, he led his daughter out of the reception room.

"Oh, Mommy, she's beautiful," Michelle breathed, staring down into the tiny face that nestled next to June. As if in reply, the baby opened one eye, peered vacantly at Michelle for a moment, then went back to sleep.

June smiled at Michelle. "Think we should keep her?"

Michelle's head bobbed enthusiastically. "And name her Jennifer, just like we planned."

"Unless," Cal said, "you want to name her Louise, to commemorate the place of her first fuss."

"No, thanks." June's voice was low, but emphatic. "There'll be no Carsons in this family." Her eyes met Cal's, but he quickly broke the moment. Michelle, however, had seen the odd exchange.

"Mother," she asked, her voice thoughtful, "what were you doing out there?"

"Why shouldn't I be out there?" June replied, forcing her voice to be cheerful. "I was supposed to be walking every day, wasn't I? So I walked to the cemetery, and then I decided to go in. Besides," she added, seeing that neither her husband nor her daughter thought that was all there was to it, "Constance Benson told me the cemetery wasn't safe, and I wanted to see for myself. She claimed it was about to fall into the sea."

"Sounds to me like she's full of a lot of nonsense," Cal chuckled. "Just like this one." He leaned down and stroked Jennifer's brow. The baby opened her eyes, stared blankly at her father for a moment, then began crying.

"When can we take her home?" Michelle asked, reaching out tentatively to touch the baby. She wanted desperately to pick Jennifer up, but didn't dare to ask.

"I'm bringing her home tonight," June said. Michelle's eyes widened in surprise.

"Tonight? Really? But I thought—I mean—"

"You mean you thought I should stay in the hospital? Why? Here I'd only have a night nurse to look after me, and Jennifer, too. But at home, I've got both you and your father to boss around."

Michelle turned to her father for confirmation.

"I don't see why they shouldn't come home."

"But the nursery—it's not ready, is it?"

June smiled at her daughter, her eyes merry. "And guess who's going to get it ready?" she asked. While Michelle listened, she began ticking off a list of things that needed to be done in the nursery before she and the baby were brought home. As the list lengthened, Michelle turned to her father, feigning exasperation.

"Isn't she supposed to be weak, or asleep, or something?"

Cal chuckled. "That's your mother—when she decides to do something, she does it—no muss, no fuss, no bother. I have a feeling even keeping her in bed for a couple of days is going to be a major project."

June finished the list, and held her arms out to her daughter. "Now give me a kiss and run along. Mrs. Benson will take you home, and we'll be there after dinner. You can eat with Jeff and Mrs. Benson—I've already arranged it."

"But you haven't even talked to her—" Michelle began.

"On the way here," June said complacently. "And I'll tell you something—having a baby isn't nearly as hard as I thought." She gave Michelle a quick hug, then sent her on her way. Moments later, as Cal watched, she began nursing Jennifer for the first time. The new parents looked happily at each other.

"Is she an angel, or is she an angel?" June asked.

"She's perfect," Cal agreed.

"Do you want us to stay with you?" Mrs. Benson asked as she pulled to a stop in front of the Pendletons'. She peered doubtfully at the old house, as if it was unimaginable to her that anyone Michelle's age would be willing to venture inside it alone. But Michelle was already getting out of the car.

"No, thanks. I have all kinds of things to do before Mom and Dad bring Jenny home."

"Maybe we could help," Mrs. Benson offered.

"Oh, I don't mind," Michelle said immediately. "It's mostly just straightening up the nursery. It'll be fun." Then, before Mrs. Benson could protest further, Michelle asked what time they expected her for dinner.

"We always eat at six," Jeff told her. "Want me to come over and walk with you? Sometimes it gets foggy around then."

"That's okay." Michelle was just a little annoyed—what did he think she was, a baby? "I'll see you at six, or a little before." Waving good-bye, she ran up the steps and disappeared through the front door.

Michelle closed the front door behind her and went up to her room, dropping her bookbag on her bed, her sweater on a chair. Then she went to the window seat, and picked up her doll.

"We have a sister, Amanda," she whispered. As she uttered the doll's name, her dream of the night before, and the memory of the things her friends had said to her came flooding back. "Maybe I should change your name," she said to the doll, staring into its sightless brown eyes thoughtfully. Then she thought better of it. "No! I named you Amanda, and you *are* Amanda, and that's that! Do you want to help me clean up the nursery?"

Taking the doll with her, she went down the hall to the room next to her parents' that was to be Jennifer's. She went in, wondering what to do first.

All the furniture was there: a crib and a bassinet, a tiny chest of drawers with a top that converted into a changing table. The walls had been freshly painted, and at the windows there were curtains covered with Pooh and his friends. Propped up in the one full-size chair in the room was a stuffed animal—Kanga, with Baby Roo peeping shyly out of her pocket. Michelle propped Amanda up next to the toys, and set to work.

She soon realized that there wasn't all that much to do. She found a pink blanket (edged in blue—just in case) and carefully arranged it in the bassinet. Then, picking up her doll, she went on to her parents' room, where she changed the bed so June would find it fresh and clean.

When she had gone over June's list in her mind

several times, and decided she'd done everything she could remember, she took Amanda and returned to her own room, where she dumped her schoolbooks out of their bag. She stared at them resentfully. It was unfair that she be expected to do her homework on the very day when her baby sister had been born. Deciding that Miss Hatcher would understand, she returned to her window seat, her doll held comfortably in her lap.

As she stared out the window, Michelle's mind began to wander. She wondered what things had been like when she had been born. Had she had a sister who had set up a nursery for her? Probably not. Unhappily, she reflected that she probably hadn't even been taken home from the hospital, at least not until the Pendletons had come for her.

The Pendletons.

She never thought of them as anything but Mom and Dad. But, of course, she realized with a start, they weren't *really* her parents at all.

What had her real mother been like? Why hadn't she wanted Michelle? As she turned the matter over in her mind, she hugged the doll closer, and began to feel lonely. Suddenly she wished she hadn't told Jeff and his mother to leave her alone.

"I'm being silly," she said out loud, the sound of her own voice startling her in the silence of the house. "I have a wonderful mother, and a wonderful father, and now I have a sister, too. Who cares what my real mother was like?"

Resolutely, she left the window seat, and picked up one of her schoolbooks. Better to do her homework than make herself miserable. She settled herself on the bed, tucked Amanda under her arm, and began reading about the War of 1812.

* * *

At five-thirty, Michelle put her books aside and
started out on the path along the bluff. It was still
light, but there was a damp chill in the air. The fog
would roll in off the sea long before she got to the
Bensons'. She wasn't sure she wanted to walk the path
in the fog. Retracing her steps, she went back to the
house, and down the driveway to the road. The trees
around her were beginning to turn, and the tinges of
red and gold among the green seemed to offset the
grayness of the mists that were gathering over the sea.
Then, as she came abreast of the old cemetery, she
glanced eastward. The fog had, indeed, made its silent
way to the bluff and was swirling softly toward her,
its billowing whiteness turning to brilliant gold where
the fading sun still struck it, then giving way to the
chilly gray of the offshore mass behind it.

Michelle stopped walking, and watched the fog as
it crept steadily toward her, flooding across the graveyard whose only visible feature, from where she stood,
was the gnarled oak tree. As she watched, the fog
engulfed the tree, and it faded away into the grayness.

Suddenly, something seemed to move in the fog.

It was indistinct at first, no more than a dark shadow
against the gray of the mist.

Tentatively, Michelle took a step forward, leaving
the road.

The shadow moved toward her, and began to
darken, and take on a shape.

The shape of a young girl, clad in black, her head
covered with a bonnet.

The girl Michelle had seen the night before, in her
dream.

Or had it been a dream?

The beginnings of fear gripped Michelle, and a coldness surrounded her.

The strange figure moved in with the fog, advancing toward her. Michelle stood transfixed, staring, unsure of what she was seeing.

The fog drifted around the black-clad child, and for a moment it disappeared, until the wind shifted, and the mists suddenly parted.

She was still there, silent, completely still now, her empty eyes fixed on Michelle with the same milky pale, sightless stare that Michelle had seen the night before.

The figure raised one black-clad arm, and beckoned. Almost involuntarily, Michelle took a step forward. And the strange vision disappeared.

Michelle stood quite still, terrified.

The fog, very close to her now, was beginning to surround her, soft tendrils of mist, cool and damp, reaching out to her as moments before the dark apparition had beckoned.

Slowly, Michelle began to back away from the mist.

Her foot touched the pavement of the road, and the firm feel of the asphalt beneath her seemed to break the spell. Only seconds before, the fog seemed to have become almost a living thing. Now it was only fog again.

As the fading light of the September afternoon filtered through the mist, Michelle hurried along the road toward the comfort of the Bensons'.

"Hi!" Jeff said as he opened the door. "I was going to come and look for you—you were supposed to be here at six."

"But it can't be six yet!" Michelle protested. "I left

home at five-thirty, and it only took me a few minutes to walk down here."

"It's six-thirty now." Jeff pointed to the grandfather clock that dominated the Bensons' hall. "What did you do, stop in the graveyard?"

Michelle gave Jeff a sharp look, but saw nothing in his eyes except curiosity. She was about to tell him what had happened when once again she remembered the conversation at lunchtime that day. Abruptly, she changed her mind.

"I guess our clock's wrong," she said. "What's for dinner?"

"Pot roast." Jeff made a face and led Michelle to the dining room, where his mother was waiting.

Constance Benson surveyed Michelle critically as she came into the room. "We were getting worried—I was about to send Jeff out looking for you."

"I'm sorry," Michelle said, slipping onto her chair. "I guess our clock must be slow."

"Either that, or you were dawdling," Constance said severely. "I don't approve of dawdling."

"It was the fog," Michelle confessed. "When the fog came in, I stopped to watch it."

Michelle reached out and helped herself to the pot roast, unaware that both Jeff and his mother were staring at her in puzzlement.

Constance's eyes went to the window. If there had been fog, she certainly hadn't seen it. To her, the evening looked perfectly clear.

CHAPTER 8

Cal reached out and squeezed June's hand affectionately. They were nearly home, and he drove slowly,
weaving back and forth to avoid the worst of the pits
in the road, then sighed in relief as he turned into their
driveway.

He parked the car as close to the house as he could,
and took the baby from his wife's arms. "Let me put
Jennifer in the nursery, then I'll come back for you."

"I'm not crippled." June eased herself out of the car
and started toward the front door. " 'A little shaky, but
on our feet.' What's that from?"

"*Who's Afraid of Virginia Woolf?* Except it's not
apropos. The character was drunk."

"I could use a drink," June said halfheartedly. "I
don't suppose I can have one?"

"You suppose right." He cradled Jennifer in one arm
and offered the other to June, who took it gratefully.

"All right, having a baby wasn't as easy as I claimed.
Bed is going to feel good."

They went into the darkened house. June waited at the foot of the stairs while Cal took Jennifer up. A moment later he was back, and, leaning heavily on him, June made her way slowly up the stairs.

"I hope there isn't anything I have to do," she said wearily when they had reached the top. "Is everything all ready?"

"All you have to do is get into the bed, which is all turned back. And Michelle left us a note. She wants us to call her at the Bensons' as soon as we get home."

"As if we wouldn't," June chuckled. "Leave it to Michelle to think of everything."

She took off the robe and hospital gown they'd given her at the clinic. Then, before putting on her own comfortable flannel nightgown, she glanced at herself in the mirror.

"My God, are you sure I'm done? I look like I'm still pregnant!"

"You will for two or three weeks," Cal assured her. "Nothing abnormal. Just a lot of extra tissue that has to go back where it came from. Now go to bed."

"Yes, sir!" June replied, saluting weakly. She eased herself into the bed, and sank back against the pillows. "All right, I'm here." She smiled up at her husband. "Why don't you bring Jennifer in, then call Michelle? I'll bet she saw us go by."

Cal brought the baby from the adjoining nursery, and picked up the telephone. "She even left the Bensons' number in the note," he commented.

"I'd have been surprised if she hadn't." June lowered the top of her nightgown, and nestled the baby against her breast. Hungrily, Jennifer began nursing.

"Mrs. Benson? Is Michelle there?" Cal said into the telephone. His eyes remained fondly on his wife and infant daughter. He reached out to touch Jennifer's tiny head as he waited for Michelle to come to the phone.

"Daddy? Are you home? Is Mom all right?"

"We're home, and everybody's fine. You can come back anytime you want to. And hurry. Your sister's eating and growing, and if you want to see her as a baby, you'd better get here within the next ten minutes."

There was a short silence at the other end. When Michelle spoke again, there was an element in her voice, an uncertainty, that Cal thought was unusual.

"Daddy? Could you come and pick me up?"

Cal frowned and June, noticing the change in his expression, looked at him curiously.

"Pick you up? But you're only a few hundred yards down the road . . ."

"Please?" Michelle begged. "Just this once?"

"Hang on a second," he said. He covered the mouthpiece with his hand, and spoke to June.

"She wants me to pick her up." He sounded puzzled, but June only shrugged.

"So, pick her up."

"I'm not sure I should leave you alone," Cal said.

"I'll be fine. You won't be gone more than five minutes. What can happen? I'll just lie here and feed Jennifer."

Cal removed his hand from the mouthpiece. "Okay, honey. I'll be there in a couple of minutes. Will you be ready?"

"I'll be right by the front door," Michelle replied, her voice sounding much stronger.

Cal said good-bye and put the receiver back on the hook. "I don't get it. She's so self-sufficient, and all of a sudden she wants to be picked up less than a quarter of a mile away."

"I don't think it's so surprising," June said mildly. "It's dark out there, you have to go right by a graveyard, and, let's face it, we've been pretty much ignoring her all day and she probably wants some attention. My God, darling, she's only twelve years old. Sometimes I think we forget that."

"But it's not like her. She knows there are all kinds of things to be done—"

"She already did them," June pointed out. "Now stop stalling, and go get her. By now, you could have been gone and back."

Cal struggled into his coat, kissed his wife and baby, and left the house.

Before Cal could toot the horn, the Bensons' front door opened. A moment later Michelle was in the car next to him.

"Thanks for coming to get me," she said as her father put the car in gear.

Cal glanced at her curiously. "Since when are you afraid of the dark?"

Michelle retreated to the far side of the seat, and Cal was immediately sorry for his implied criticism. "It's all right," he added quickly. "Your mother's in bed feeding the baby, and everything's fine. But what spooked you?"

Mollified, Michelle moved closer to her father. "I don't know," she hedged, not wanting to tell him what she'd seen in the fog that evening. "I guess I just didn't want to walk by the graveyard at night."

"Has Jeff been telling you ghost stories?" Cal inquired. Michelle shook her head.

"He doesn't believe in ghosts. At least that's what he says." She stressed the last word, just slightly. "But it's so dark tonight, I just didn't want to walk by myself. I'm sorry."

"It's all right."

They made the rest of the short trip in silence.

"You were a busy girl this afternoon."

With Jennifer sleeping peacefully in the crook of her arm, June smiled at her older daughter, and gestured for her to come and sit on the edge of the bed. "Everything was perfect. You must have worked all afternoon."

"It didn't take long," Michelle replied, her eyes fastened on the baby. "She's so small!"

"It's the only size they come in. Would you like to hold her?"

"Can I?" Michelle's voice was filled with eagerness.

"Here." June lifted the baby, handed her to Michelle, then rearranged herself against the pillows. "You hold her just like a doll," she instructed. "Tuck her into your elbow, and let her lie on your arm."

As Michelle looked down into the tiny face resting against her chest, Jennifer opened her eyes, and burped.

"Is she all right?"

"She's fine. If she starts crying, I'll take her. As long as she isn't crying, nothing's wrong." As if to prove her mother's point, Jennifer closed her eyes and went back to sleep.

"Tell me everything," Michelle said suddenly, her eyes finally leaving the baby and looking eagerly to her mother.

"Well, there isn't much to tell. I was out taking a walk, and I went into labor. That's all there was to it."

"But in the *graveyard?*" Michelle asked. "Didn't it give you the creeps?"

"Why should it?"

"But Jenny wasn't supposed to come yet. What happened?"

"Nothing happened. Jenny just decided it was time, that's all."

There was a silence as Michelle turned things over in her mind. When she finally spoke again, her voice was hesitant. "Why were you at Louise Carson's grave?"

"I had to be at one of the graves, didn't I? I was in the graveyard, after all." June was careful to keep her voice level, disarming. And she wondered why.

"Did you see her headstone?" Michelle asked.

"Of course I did."

"What do you suppose it means?"

"I'm sure it doesn't mean a thing," June said, holding out her arms to take Jennifer, who was awake again and beginning to cry. Michelle handed the baby back to her mother almost reluctantly. "She needs to be fed," June explained. "Then you can hold her again."

Michelle stood up, uncertain whether she should stay in the room while her mother nursed the baby. "Why don't you make a pot of tea?" June suggested. "And tell your father to come up. Okay?"

June watched Michelle leave the room, as Jennifer eagerly began sucking at her breast. She tried to make herself relax, but it was impossible. Something had happened to Michelle. She couldn't figure out what it was, except she was almost sure that it had to do with the graveyard. But what?

* * *

Michelle lay awake in bed, listening to the silence of the house. It seemed to her that it was too silent.

That, she was sure, was why she wasn't able to sleep.

That, and the fact that she was all alone at her end of the house.

Down the hall.

That's where everybody else was.

Her father, and her mother, and her baby sister. Everyone but her.

She got out of bed, put her robe over her shoulders, and left her room.

She stood outside her parents' room for a moment, listening, then silently opened the door and went in.

"Mommy?"

June turned over and opened her eyes, surprised to find Michelle standing by the bed. "What time is it?"

"It's only eleven," Michelle said defensively. June pulled herself up to a sitting position.

"What's wrong?"

"I—I couldn't sleep."

"You couldn't sleep? Why not?"

"I don't know," Michelle said quietly, sitting down on the bed. "Maybe I drank too much tea?"

"That's coffee, sweetheart." She felt Cal shift next to her, then the baby suddenly began crying. Cal woke abruptly and switched on the light. Then he saw Michelle.

"What are you doing in here? Is that why the baby's crying?"

Seeing Michelle suddenly on the verge of tears, June tried to save the situation. "The baby's hungry, and Michelle couldn't sleep. Why don't you get Jenny for me, and then go down and reheat the tea? Michelle can stay with me while I feed little miss loudmouth." She winked at Michelle, and Michelle suddenly felt better.

"I'll get Jenny," she offered.

Sighing heavily, Cal pulled his robe on and went downstairs. June waited until he was out of earshot, then tried to apologize for him. "He didn't mean that it was your fault Jenny was crying. He was just asleep, that's all."

"It's all right," Michelle said listlessly. "I was just lonely, I guess."

"Well, it's a big house." A thought struck her, and without waiting to think it out, she spoke. "Maybe we should move you down to this end, closer to us," she suggested.

"Oh, no," Michelle replied quickly. "I love my room. I feel like I belong there. Ever since I found Mandy . . ."

"Mandy? I thought her name was Amanda."

"Well, it is. But Mandy's the same thing, just like some people shorten my name to Mickey. Ugh! But Mandy's pretty."

Cal came back into the room, carrying a tray with three steaming cups of tea. "Only this once," he announced. "From now on, just because Jennifer gets hungry it doesn't mean we're going to have a picnic. And you, young lady, are supposed to be in bed. You have to go to school tomorrow."

"I'll be all right. I just got lonely." She took a sip of her tea, then stood up. "Will you tuck me in?"

Cal grinned at her. "I haven't done that for years."

"Just tonight?" Michelle pleaded.

Cal glanced at his wife, then nodded. "All right," he said. "Finish your tea, and let's go."

Michelle drained her cup and leaned over to kiss her mother, then followed her father out of the room and down the hall to her own bedroom.

Climbing into bed, she pulled the covers snugly around her chin, and offered her cheek to her father. Cal bent down, kissed her, then straightened up.

"You'll be asleep in no time," he promised. He was about to turn off the light and return to June and the baby when Michelle suddenly asked him for her doll.

"She's on the window seat. Could you get her for me?"

Cal picked up the ancient doll, and glanced at its porcelain face. "Doesn't look very real, does it?" he commented as he handed the doll to Michelle. She tucked it protectively under the covers, its head resting on her shoulder.

"She's real enough," Michelle told her father. He smiled at her, then turned off the lights. Closing the door quietly behind him, he started down the hall.

Once again, Michelle was alone in her room, listening to the silence of the house. As the darkness gathered oppressively around her, she drew the doll closer, and whispered softly to it.

"It isn't like I thought it was going to be. I was looking forward to having Jenny so much. But now she's here, and everything's so different. They're all in there together, and I'm all by myself. Mommy has Jennifer to take care of now. But who do I have?"

Then a thought came to her.

"I could take care of you, Mandy. Really I could . . ."

She snuggled the doll closer, and a tear trickled down her cheek. "I'll take care of you, just like

Mommy takes care of Jenny. Would you like that? I'll be your mother, Amanda, and give you anything you want. And you'll stay with me, won't you? So I'll never be lonely again?"

Crying quietly, with the doll pressed close against her, Michelle fell asleep.

CHAPTER 9

Michelle awoke on Saturday morning to the soft sound of birds chirping. She lay still in bed, enjoying the knowledge that this morning she didn't have to hurry, this morning she could stay in bed for a few minutes and enjoy the sun flooding her room, its warmth seeping through the blankets and filling her with a sense of well-being. Today was going to be a good day.

Today was the day of the picnic at the cove.

Until this morning, Michelle hadn't been sure she would go to the picnic.

The pain of Susan Peterson's taunting had begun to fade after three days; even the memory of the strange girl who had appeared first in her dream, then in the graveyard on Tuesday, was fading. And since the arrival of Jennifer, Michelle's mind had been too full of other things to dwell on the black-clad image that had seemed to want something from her.

Now, surrounded by sunlight, she wondered why she had been worrying, why, when Sally Carstairs

had called her last night, she had said she might not
be able to go. Of course she would go. If Susan Peterson tried to tease her, she would just refuse to let it
get to her.

The decision made, Michelle scrambled out of bed
and put on a pair of well-worn blue jeans, a sweat
shirt, and her sneakers. As she was about to go downstairs, her eyes suddenly fell on her doll, still resting
on the pillow where she always kept it now at night.
Picking it up, Michelle carefully propped it up on the
window seat.

"There," she said softly. "Now you can spend the
day sitting in the sun. Be a good girl." She bent over
and kissed the doll lightly, as she had seen her mother
kiss her baby sister, then left her room, closing the
door behind her.

"Looks like somebody's planning to help her father,"
June said as Michelle came into the kitchen. She
glanced up from the eggs she was frying, and, seeing
the look on Michelle's face, smiled at her. "Don't look
at me that way—I'm going right back to bed after I
finish breakfast. But I have to start getting up—I need
the exercise, I've been in bed for three days, and I'm
going out of my mind up there!" Then, to prevent
Michelle from protesting, she pointed to the refrigerator. "There's orange juice in there."

Michelle opened the refrigerator and took out the
pitcher of juice. "Help Dad with what?" she asked.

"The butler's pantry. Today's the day the remodel-
ing starts."

"Oh."

"Don't you want to help him?" June was puzzled.
Usually Michelle couldn't be kept away from her

father's side, but this morning she sounded almost disappointed at the prospect.

"It's not that," Michelle replied hesitantly. "It's just that some of us were planning a picnic—"

"A picnic? You didn't say anything about a picnic."

"Well, I wasn't sure I was going. Actually, I only just made up my mind when I got up. I—I can go, can't I?"

"Of course you can," June replied. "What are you supposed to take?"

"Take where?" Cal asked, emerging from the stairway that led to the basement.

"There's a picnic today," Michelle explained. "Me, and Sally, and Jeff and some other kids. Sort of the last day at the beach, I guess."

"You mean you're not going to help me with the pantry?"

"Would you give up a picnic?" June divided the eggs onto three plates, and led her husband and daughter into the dining room. "Maybe I'll take Jenny, and join in."

"But it's just us kids," Michelle protested.

"I was only kidding," June said quickly. "How about if I make some deviled eggs?"

"Would you?"

"Sure. What time's the picnic?"

"We're all meeting down at the cove at ten."

"Oh, great," June moaned. "Really, Michelle, couldn't you have given me just a little more warning? I'll hardly have time to make the eggs, let alone chill them."

"You won't make them at all," Cal announced. He turned to Michelle. "I only let your mother get up to fix breakfast if she promised to go right back to bed again. If you want deviled eggs, you'll have to fix them yourself."

"But I don't know how."

"Then you'll have to learn. You're a big girl now, and your mother has a baby to take care of." At the look of dismay in Michelle's eyes, Cal relented. "Tell you what," he offered. "After breakfast we'll send your mother back to bed, you do the dishes, and I'll see what I can do about the eggs. Okay?"

Michelle's face cleared—everything was going to be all right after all. But everything's different, she thought as she began to clear the table. Now that they have Jenny, it's all different.

She decided she didn't much like it.

Michelle hurried down the trail to the cove. It was already ten-thirty, and she was going to be the last one there. In one hand she clutched the bag containing the deviled eggs. They were still warm, as her mother had predicted. Well, maybe no one would notice.

She could see them, a hundred yards north, scrambling over the rocks, following the ebbing tide, staying close to Jeff as he moved easily over the granite outcroppings. Only one person was still on the beach, but even from the trail, Michelle recognized Sally Carstairs's blond hair. As she reached the beach, Michelle began running.

"Hi!" she called out. Sally looked up and waved to her.

"I'm sorry I'm late. Daddy just finished the eggs. Do you think anybody'll notice that they're not cold?"

"Who cares? I was afraid you weren't coming."

Michelle looked at Sally shyly. "I almost didn't. But it's such a nice day. . . ." Her voice trailed off, and

Sally saw her staring out to the shelf of granite, where Susan Peterson was kneeling down next to Jeff. "Don't worry about her," Sally said. "If she starts teasing you again, just ignore it. She teases everybody."

"How'd you know that's what I was worried about?"

Sally shrugged. "I used to worry about her, too. Just because her father's a big shot, she thinks she is, too."

"Don't you like her?"

"I don't know," Sally said thoughtfully. "I guess I don't think about it, really. I mean, I've known her all my life, and she's always been my friend."

"That's neat," Michelle said. She sat down on a blanket next to Sally and picked up a Coke. "Can I have a sip of this?"

"Take the whole thing," Sally said. "I can't drink any more of it. What's neat?"

"Knowing somebody all your life. There isn't anybody I've known all my life." Her voice dropped almost to a whisper. "Sometimes I wonder who I really am."

"You're Michelle Pendleton. Who else would you be?"

"But I'm adopted," Michelle said slowly.

"Well, so what? You're still you."

Suddenly wanting to change the subject, Michelle got to her feet. "Come on, let's go see what they found." Far out on the rocks, everyone was clustered around Jeff, who was holding something in his hand.

It was a tiny octopus, only three inches across, and it was wriggling helplessly in Jeff's palm. As Michelle and Sally approached, Jeff held it out to them, grinning.

"Want to hold it?" It was a dare. Sally shrank back,

but Michelle put her hand out, tentatively at first, and touched the slippery surface of the octopus's skin.

"It doesn't bite," Jeff assured her, casting a disdainful glance at Sally.

Hesitating, Michelle took the little sea creature in her hand, and carefully turned it over. It put out a tentacle, braced itself against her finger, and righted itself.

"Won't it die out of the water?" Michelle asked.

"Not for a while," Jeff said. "Is it holding on to you?"

Michelle took hold of one of the tentacles and pulled gently. There was a slight tingling sensation as its suction cups pulled loose from her skin.

"Ooh! How can you *do* that!" It was Susan. She stood back from Michelle, her hands protectively behind her back, her face screwed up in revulsion. Grinning mischievously, Michelle tossed the squirming creature at Susan, who screamed and ducked. The octopus fell back into the water, and immediately disappeared, leaving only a trail of disrupted sand swirling behind as it fled.

"Don't do that!" Susan glared at Michelle.

"It's only a baby octopus," Michelle laughed. "Who can be afraid of a little tiny octopus?"

"It's horrible," Susan declared. She turned, and started back toward the beach. Michelle, suddenly sorry for what she'd done, tried to apologize, but Susan ignored her. The rest of the children looked first at Susan, then at Michelle, as if trying to make up their minds what to do. Then, as Susan continued picking her way across the rocks, they all began following her. Ony Sally Carstairs hung back.

"Maybe you shouldn't do things like that," Sally said softly. "It makes her mad."

"I'm sorry," Michelle replied. "It was only supposed to be a joke. Can't she take a joke?"

"She doesn't think things are funny when they're on her. Only when they're on someone else. She'll probably start teasing you now."

"So what if she does?" Michelle asked. Suddenly she felt very brave. "I can take it. Come on—we might as well go back to the beach."

The sun was high in the sky, and the children were scattered over the beach, munching sandwiches and washing them down with an apparently endless supply of Cokes. Michelle was sitting with Sally Carstairs, but she was uncomfortably aware of Susan Peterson, a few feet away, sharing a blanket with Jeff Benson. Susan hadn't spoken to her, but had kept watching her, as if sizing her up. Now she put her soda down, and stared at Michelle maliciously.

"Seen the ghost lately?" she asked.

"There isn't any ghost," Michelle said, her voice barely audible.

"But you saw it the other night, didn't you?" Susan's voice was louder now, insistent.

"It was a dream," Michelle said. "Only a dream."

"Was it? Are you sure?"

Michelle glared at Susan, but Susan returned her gaze unwaveringly. Michelle could feel anger begin to well up inside her. *What is it?* she asked herself. *Why do I always make her mad at me?*

"Can't we talk about something else?" she asked.

"I like to talk about the ghost," Susan said serenely.

"Well, I don't!" Sally Carstairs exclaimed. "I think talking about the ghost is dumb! I want to hear about Michelle's little sister."

Michelle smiled gratefully at Sally. "She's beautiful, and she looks just like my mother," she said.

"How would you know?" Susan Peterson's voice was icy; her eyes flashed with a gleeful malice.

"What do you mean?" Michelle asked. "Jennifer looks just like my mother. Everybody says so."

"But you don't even know who your mother is," Susan said. "You're adopted."

Suddenly Michelle could feel all the children watching her, wondering what she would say next.

"That doesn't make my parents any less my parents," she said carefully.

"Who said it did?" Susan replied. "Except the Pendletons aren't really your parents, are they? You don't know who your parents are, do you?"

"They are too my parents," Michelle shot back. She stood up, facing Susan. "They adopted me when I was just a little baby, and they've always been my parents."

"That was before," Susan said. She was grinning now as she watched Michelle's anger grow.

"What do you mean, before?"

"Before they had their own baby. The only reason people adopt babies is because they can't have one of their own. So what do your parents need you for anymore?"

"Don't say that, Susan Peterson," Michelle shouted. "Don't you ever say that. My parents love me as much as your parents love you."

"Do they?" There was a sweetness in Susan's voice that belied the expression on her face. "Do they really?"

"What's that supposed to mean?" As soon as the words came out of her mouth, Michelle wished she hadn't said them. She should just ignore Susan—just

get her stuff, and walk away. But it was too late. All
the other children were listening to Susan, but they
were watching Michelle.

"Don't they spend more time with the baby than
they do with you? Don't they really love her more?
Why shouldn't they? Jenny's their real child. All you
are is some orphan they took in when they thought
they couldn't have any kids of their own!"

"That isn't true," Michelle cried. But even as she
spoke, she knew she wasn't as certain as she was trying
to sound. Things *were* different now. They had been
ever since Jenny was born. But that was only because
Jenny was a baby, and needed more than she did. It
didn't mean her parents didn't love her. Did it? Of
course it didn't. They loved her. *Her parents loved
her!*

Suddenly Michelle wanted to be home—home with
her mother and her father—home, where she would
be close to them, part of them. She was still their
daughter. They still loved her—they still wanted her.
Of course they did! Without bothering to pick up her
things, Michelle turned and started running down the
beach toward the trail.

Sally Carstairs jumped to her feet and started to run
after Michelle, but Susan Peterson's voice stopped her.

"Oh, let her go," Susan said. "If she can't take a little
teasing, who needs her?"

"But that was mean, Susan," Sally declared. "It was
just plain mean."

"So?" Susan replied carelessly. "It wasn't very nice
of her to throw that octopus at me, either."

"But she didn't know it would scare you."

"She did too," Susan replied. "And even if she didn't,
she shouldn't have done it. I was just paying her back."

Sally sank back on her blanket, wondering what to do. She wanted to go after Michelle, and bring her back, but it probably wouldn't do any good. Susan wouldn't quit—now that she knew how to get to Michelle, she'd just keep at it. And if Sally kept being friends with Michelle, Susan would start in on her, too. Sally knew she couldn't take that.

"She sure can run, can't she?" Sally heard the rest of the kids laugh at Susan's question, and looked up. Michelle was almost at the foot of the trail. Sally decided that even if the rest of the kids were going to watch, she wouldn't. Besides, she couldn't. If she did, she knew she would start crying, and she didn't want to do that. Not in front of Susan.

Susan Peterson's words pounded in Michelle's ears as she ran down the beach.

What do they need you for?

Don't they really love her more?

It wasn't true, she told herself. None of it was true. But as she ran, the words seemed to follow her, swept on the wind, poking at her, prodding her.

She reached the trail and started upward.

Her breathing, already labored from her anger and running, came harder and harder. Soon she was gasping, and she could feel her heart pounding.

She wanted to stop, wanted to rest, wanted to sit down, just for a minute, to catch her breath, but she knew she couldn't.

They would be back there, on the beach, watching her. She could almost hear Susan's voice, sweet and vicious:

She can't even make it up the trail.

She forced herself to look up, to see how far she had

to go before she would be safely at the top, out of
sight of the beach.

Far.

Too far.

And now the fog was coming in.

It was just a grayness at first, a slight mistiness that
blurred her vision.

But then, as she forced her feet one after the other
up the trail, it gathered around her, cold and damp,
closing her off, isolating her, leaving her alone, no
longer within sight of her tormentors on the beach, but
far from home as well.

She must be close to the top. She had to be!

It was like a bad dream, a dream in which you have
to run, but your feet, mired in some kind of mud,
refuse to move. Michelle could feel panic closing in on
her.

It was then that she slipped.

It seemed like nothing for a split second—just a
slight wrenching as her right foot hit a loose rock and
twisted outward.

Suddenly there was nothing beneath her foot to
support her. It was as if the trail had vanished.

She felt herself starting to fall through the terrifying
gray mist.

She screamed, just once, and then the fog seemed to
tighten itself around her, and the gray turned into
black. . . .

"Dr. Pendleton! Dr. Pendleton!"

Cal heard the voice calling to him. The terror it
conveyed made him drop his hammer and dash into
the kitchen. He reached the back door just as Jeff
Benson leaped up onto the porch.

"What is it? What's happened?"

"It's Michelle," Jeff cried, his chest heaving, his breath coming in heavy pants. "We were on the beach, and she was coming home, and—and—" His voice broke off, and he sank to the top step, trying to catch his breath.

"What happened?" Cal tried to keep from shouting as he stood over Jeff. "Is she all right?"

Jeff shook his head in despair.

"She was on the trail. We were all watching her, and all of a sudden she slipped, and—oh, Dr. Pendleton, come quick."

Cal felt the first rush of panic, the same panic he had felt when he'd seen Sally Carstairs, the panic that was rooted in Alan Hanley. And now it was Michelle.

She'd fallen, as Alan Hanley had fallen.

Through his sudden terror he could hear Jeff Benson's voice, pleading with him: "Dr. Pendleton, please —Dr. Pendleton?—"

He forced himself to move, off the porch, across the lawn, to the edge of the bluff. He looked down, but could see nothing on the beach except a cluster of children, gathered together below him.

Dear God, let her be all right.

He started down the trail, slowly at first, then recklessly, though every step seemed to take an eternity. He could hear Jeff behind him, trying to tell him what had happened, but the boy's words made no sense to him. All he could think of was Michelle, her lithe body lying on the rocks at the base of the cliff, broken and twisted.

At last he was on the beach, elbowing his way through the group of children who stood, helpless, around Michelle.

Cal knelt beside his daughter, touched her face.

But it was not her face he saw. As had happened with Sally Carstairs, he saw instead the face of Alan Hanley, dying, staring at him, accusing him.

His mind reeled. *It wasn't his fault. None of it was his fault.* Then why did he feel so guilty? Guilty—and angry. Angry at these children who made him feel incompetent, ineffectual. And guilty. Always guilty.

Almost unaware of what he was doing, he placed his fingers on Michelle's wrist.

Her pulse beat steadily.

Then, as he bent over her, her eyes fluttered, and opened. She looked up at him, her immense brown eyes frightened and filled with tears.

"Daddy? Daddy? Am I all right?"

"You're fine, baby, just fine. You're going to be all right." But even as he spoke the words, he knew they were a lie.

Without pausing to think, Cal picked Michelle up in his arms. She moaned softly, then closed her eyes.

Cal started up the trail, his daughter cradled against his chest.

She'll be all right, he told himself. *She's going to be just fine.*

But as he climbed the trail, the memories came back to him, the memories of Alan Hanley.

Alan Hanley had fallen, and had been put in his care. And he had failed Alan—the boy had died.

He couldn't fail Michelle. Not his own daughter. But even as he carried her to the house, he knew it was too late.

He had already failed her.

BOOK TWO
MANIFESTATIONS

CHAPTER 10

The darkness was almost like a living thing, curling around her, grasping her, strangling her.

She reached out, tried to struggle with it, but it was like trying to struggle with water: no matter how she tried, the darkness slipped through, flooded back over her, made it difficult to breathe.

She was alone, drowning in the darkness.

And then, as if a tiny glimmer of light had appeared in the blackness, she knew she was not alone.

Something else was there, reaching out to her, trying to find her in the darkness, trying to help her.

She could feel it brush against her, just a faint tickling sensation, at the edge of her consciousness.

And a voice.

A soft voice, calling to her as if from a great distance.

She wanted to answer that voice, to cry out to it, but her own voice failed her; her words died in her throat.

She concentrated on feeling the presence, tried to draw it close, tried to reach out and pull it to her.

Then the voice again, clearer now, though still far away.

"Help me . . . please help me . . ."

But it was she who needed help, she who was sinking into the black void. How could she help? How could she do anything?

The voice faded away; the darkness began to brighten.

Michelle opened her eyes.

She lay very still, uncertain where she was. Above her there was a ceiling.

She examined it carefully, looking for the familiar patterns she had identified in the cracked paint.

Yes, there was the giraffe. Well, not *really* a giraffe, but if you used your imagination, it could almost be a giraffe. To the left, just a little bit, should be the bird, one wing stretched in flight, the other bent strangely, as if it was broken.

She moved her eyes, just slightly. She was in her own bed, in her room. But it didn't make sense. It was at the cove. She remembered. She was having a picnic at the cove with Sally and Jeff, and Susan. Susan Peterson. There were some others, but it was Susan she remembered as the morning came flooding back to her. Susan had been teasing her, saying horrible things to her, telling her that her parents didn't love her anymore.

She had decided to go home. She was on the trail, and she could hear Susan's voice echoing in her mind.

And then—and then? Nothing.

Except that now she was home, and she was in bed.

And there had been a dream.

There had been a voice in the dream, calling to her.

"Mom?" Her own voice seemed to echo oddly in the room, and for a second she wished she hadn't called out. But the door opened, and her mother was there. Everything was going to be all right.

"Michelle?" June hurried to the bed, bent over Michelle, kissed her gently. "Michelle, are you awake?"

Her eyes wide and puzzled, Michelle stared up at her mother, seeing the fear that lay like a haunting mask over June's face.

"What happened? Why am I in bed?"

Michelle started to sit up, but a stab of pain shot through her left side, and she gasped. At the same time, June put her hands on Michelle's shoulders and gently pushed her back down.

"Don't try to move," she said. "Just lie very still, and I'll get Daddy."

"But what happened?" Michelle pleaded. "What happened to me?"

"You tripped on the trail and fell," June told her. "Now just lie still, and let me call Daddy. Then we'll tell you all about it."

June left the bed and went to the door. "Cal?" she called. "Cal, she's awake!" Without waiting for him to respond, she came back into the room to hover once more over Michelle's bed.

"How do you feel, darling?"

"I—I don't know," Michelle stammered. "I feel sort of—" She hesitated, searching for the right word. "Numb, I guess. How did I get here?"

"Your father brought you," June told her. "Jeff Benson came up and got him, then—"

Cal appeared in the doorway, and as Michelle's eyes met her father's, she knew something had changed.

It was the way he looked at her, as if she had done something—something bad. But all she had done was have an accident. Could he be mad at her about that? "Daddy?" As she whispered the word, it seemed to echo in the room, and she saw her father step back slightly. But then he came toward her, took her wrist in his hand, counted her pulse, and tried to smile.

"How bad does it hurt?" he asked softly.

"If I lie still, it's only sort of an ache," Michelle replied. She wanted to reach up to him, put her arms around him, and be held by him. But she knew she couldn't.

"Try not to move," he instructed her. "Just lie perfectly still, and I'll give you something for the pain."

"What happened?" Michelle asked again. "How far did I fall?"

"Everything's going to be fine, honey," Cal told her, avoiding her questions.

Very gently, he eased the covers back and began examining Michelle carefully, his fingers moving slowly over her body, pausing every few inches, prodding, pressing. As he moved close to her left hip, Michelle suddenly cried out in pain. Instantly, Cal withdrew his hands.

"Get my bag, will you, darling?" He kept his eyes on Michelle as he spoke, and tried not let his voice betray the fears that were building inside him. June slipped from the room, and as he waited for her to return, Cal talked quietly to Michelle, trying to calm her fears, and his own as well.

"You gave us quite a scare. Do you remember what happened? Any of it?"

"I was coming home," Michelle began. "I was coming up the trail, sort of running, I guess, and—and I must have slipped."

His blue eyes clouded with worry, Cal watched Michelle intently. "But why were you coming home? Was the picnic over?"

"N-no . . ." Michelle faltered. "I—I just didn't want to stay any longer. Some of the kids were teasing me."

"Teasing you? Teasing you about what?"

About you, she wanted to cry out. *About you and Mom not loving me anymore*. But instead of speaking her thoughts, Michelle only shook her head uncertainly. "I don't remember," she whispered. "I don't remember at all." She closed her eyes and tried to force the sound of Susan Peterson's mocking voice out of her mind. But it stayed there, crashing around in her brain, nearly as painful as the dull ache that permeated her body.

She opened her eyes as June came back into the room, and watched as her father took a vial out of his bag, filled a hypodermic needle from it, then swabbed her arm with alcohol.

"This won't hurt," he promised. He forced a grin. "At least, not next to what you've already been through." He administered the injection, then straightened up. "Now, I want you to go to sleep. The shot will make the pain go away, but I want you to lie still, and try to sleep."

"But I've already been sleeping," Michelle protested.

"You've been unconscious," Cal corrected her, a smile softening the worry lines that seemed etched into his face. "One hour unconscious doesn't count as a nap. So take a nap." Winking at her, he turned and started out of the room.

"Daddy?" Michelle's voice, sharp in the sudden quiet of the room, stopped him. He turned back to her, his face questioning. Michelle gazed at him, pain clouding her eyes. "Daddy," she said, her voice now little more than a whisper, "Do you love me *very* much?"

Cal stood silent for a moment, then went back to his daughter. He leaned over her, and kissed her gently on the cheek. "Of course I do, sweetheart. Why wouldn't I?"

Michelle smiled at him gratefully. "No reason," she said. "I just wondered."

As Cal left the room, June came over and very carefully sat down on the edge of the bed. She took Michelle's hand in her own. "We both love you very much," she said. "Did something make you think we didn't?"

Michelle shook her head, but her eyes, moist with tears now, remained fixed on June's face, as though asking for something. June bent forward and kissed Michelle, her lips lingering on her daughter's cheek.

"I'll be all right, Mommy," Michelle said suddenly. "Really, I will!"

"Of course you will, darling." June stood up and tucked the covers over Michelle. "Is there anything I can get you?"

Michelle shook her head, then, a thought occurring to her, changed her mind. "My doll," she said. "Could you get Mandy for me? She's on the window seat."

June picked up the doll, brought it to the bed, and placed it on the pillow next to Michelle. Though her face twisted in pain at the effort, Michelle turned Mandy around, tucked her under the covers, then lay back, the porcelain figure nestled like a baby against her shoulder. She closed her eyes.

June stood watching Michelle for a moment, then, thinking that her daughter had already fallen asleep, she tiptoed out of the room, easing the door closed behind her.

Cal sat at the kitchen table, staring out the window, his unseeing eyes fixed on the horizon.

It was all going to happen again.

Only this time, the victim of his incompetence was not going to be a stranger, someone he barely knew. This time it was going to be his own daughter.

And this time, there were going to be no easy excuses, no salving of his conscience by telling himself that anybody could have made such a mistake.

Without realizing quite what he was doing, Cal got up and poured himself a tumbler of whiskey.

June came into the kitchen just as he had taken his first swallow of the liquor. For a moment she wasn't sure he was aware of her presence. Then he spoke.

"It's my fault."

June knew instantly that he was thinking of Alan Hanley, and connecting his death to Michelle's accident.

"It's not your fault," she said. "What happened to Michelle was an accident, and though I know you don't believe it, Alan Hanley's death was an accident, too. You didn't kill him, Cal, and you didn't push Michelle off the bluff."

It was as if he didn't hear her. "I shouldn't have brought her up." His voice was dull, lifeless. "I should have left her on the beach until I could get a stretcher."

She stared at him. "What are you talking about? Cal, what are you saying? She's not that badly hurt!" She waited for an answer. When none was forthcoming, she began to feel the fear that had subsided as Michelle came out of her unconsciousness surge through her once more, clutching at her stomach, choking her. "Is she?" she demanded, her voice rising sharply.

"I don't know." Cal's empty eyes met hers, then shifted to the bottle. He refilled the tumbler, then stared at it, as if realizing for the first time what he was drinking. "She shouldn't be hurting as much as she is. She should be bruised, and she should be aching, but she shouldn't have those sharp pains when she moves."

"Is something broken?"

"Not as far as I can tell."

"Then what's causing the pain?"

Cal's hand crashed down on the table. "I don't know, damn it! I just don't know!"

June reeled at his outburst, then, seeing that he was on the edge of some kind of breakdown, forced herself to stay calm.

"What do you *think*?" she asked when she felt she could trust her voice.

His eyes took on a wildness that June had never seen before, and his hand began to quiver. "I don't know. I don't even want to guess. But there could be all kinds of damage, and it'll all be my fault."

"You can't know that," June objected. "You don't even know that anything serious is wrong."

It was as if he didn't hear her. "I shouldn't have moved her. I should have waited."

He was about to pour some more whiskey into his

glass when there was a rapping at the back door, and Sally Carstairs stuck her head in.

"May I come in?"

"Sally!" June said. She'd thought the children had left long ago. She glanced at Cal. He appeared to have calmed down slightly—enough, anyway, that she was able to shift her concentration to Sally. "Are you all out there? Come in."

"There's only me," Sally said half-apologetically as she let herself into the kitchen. "Everybody else went home." She stopped uncertainly, then: "Is Michelle all right?"

"She will be," June said with an assurance she didn't feel. She offered Sally a glass of lemonade, and invited her to sit down. "Sally," she began as she poured the lemonade, "what happened down on the beach? Why was Michelle coming home early?"

Sally fidgeted at the table, decided there was no reason not to tell what had happened.

"Some of the kids were teasing her. Susan Peterson, mostly."

"Teasing her?" June kept her voice level, curious but not condemning. "What about?"

"About her being adopted. Susan said that—that—" She fell silent with embarrassment.

"That what? That we wouldn't love her anymore, now that we have Jennifer?"

Sally's eyes widened in surprise. "How did you know?"

June sat down at the table, her eyes meeting Sally's. "It's the first thing everyone thinks of," she said quietly. "But it's not true. Now we have two daughters, and we love both of them."

Sally's eyes fell to her glass, and she seemed intent

on its contents. "I know," she whispered. "I never said anything to her at all, Mrs. Pendleton. Really, I didn't."

June could feel herself slipping. She wanted to cry, wanted to lay her head on the table, and weep. But she couldn't let herself. Not now. Not yet. She stood up, struggling to maintain her self-control, and made herself smile at Sally.

"Maybe you should come back tomorrow," she said. "I'm sure by tomorrow, Michelle will want to see you."

Sally Carstairs finished her lemonade, and left.

June sank back onto her chair and stared at the bottle, wishing she dared have a drink, wishing there was some way she could make Cal see that whatever had happened to Michelle wasn't his fault. She watched him refill his glass, started to say something to him. But as she was about to speak, she suddenly had the feeling that she was being watched. She turned quickly.

Josiah Carson was standing in the kitchen door. How long had he been there? June didn't know. He nodded at her, then he stepped into the room and placed his hand on Cal's shoulder.

"Want to tell me what happened?" he asked.

Cal stirred slightly, as though Carson's touch had brought him back to some kind of reality.

"I hurt her," he said, his voice almost childish. "I tried to help her, but I hurt her."

June stood up, deliberately shoving the table against Cal. The sudden movement distracted him from what he was saying. June spoke quickly.

"She's in pain, Dr. Carson," she said, keeping her voice neutral. "Cal says she hurts more than she should."

"She fell off a cliff," Josiah said bluntly. "Of course she hurts." His eyes moved from June to Cal. "Trying to drown her pain in alcohol, Cal?"

Cal ignored the question. "I may have injured her myself, Josiah," he said.

"Perhaps so. Or perhaps not. Suppose I go up and have a look at her. And just what is it you think you did to her?"

"I brought her home. I didn't wait for a stretcher."

Carson nodded curtly and turned away, but just as his face disappeared from her line of sight, June thought she saw something.

She thought she saw him smile.

Michelle lay awake in bed, listening to the voices below. She had heard Sally a while ago, and now she could hear Dr. Carson.

She was glad Sally hadn't come up, and she hoped Dr. Carson wouldn't either. She didn't want to see anybody, not right now.

Maybe not ever.

Then the door to her room opened, and Dr. Carson stepped in. He closed the door and came close to the bed, leaned over her.

"Want to tell me what happened?" he asked. Michelle looked up at him, and shrugged.

"I don't remember."

"You don't remember anything?"

"Not much. Just—" She hesitated, but Dr. Carson was smiling at her, not forcing himself to, as her father had, but really smiling. "I don't know what happened. I was running up the trail, and then all of a sudden it was foggy. I couldn't see, and—and I tripped, I guess."

"So it was the fog, was it?" There had been fog the day Alan Hanley fell, too. He could remember it clearly. It had come on suddenly, the way it did sometimes with sudden changes in temperature.

Michelle nodded.

"Your father thinks he hurt you. Do you think so?"

Michelle shook her head. "Why would he?"

"I don't know," Carson said softly. His eyes moved to the doll on the pillow next to Michelle. "Does she have a name?"

"Amanda—Mandy."

Josiah paused, then smiled, more to himself than to Michelle. "Well, I'll tell you what. You lie here, and let Amanda take care of you. All right?" He patted Michelle's hand, then stood up. A second later he was gone, and Michelle was alone once more.

She pulled her doll closer to her.

"You're going to have to be my friend now, Mandy," she whispered into the empty room. "I wish you were a real baby. I could take care of you, and we could be friends, and show each other things, and do things together. And you'd never say bad things to me, like Susan did. You'd just love me, and I'd just love you, and we'd take care of each other."

Fighting against the pain, she moved the doll around until it lay on her chest, its face only inches from her own.

"I'm glad you have brown eyes," she said softly. "Brown eyes, like mine. Not blue, like Jenny's and Mom's and Dad's. I'll bet my mother—my real mother —had brown eyes, and I'll bet yours did, too. Did your mama love you, Mandy?"

She fell silent again, and tried to listen, tried to hear whatever voices might be talking in the house.

Then she began wishing that Jenny were in the room with her. Jenny couldn't talk to her, but at least Jenny was alive, was breathing, was—real.

That was the trouble with Mandy. She wasn't real. Try as she would, Michelle couldn't make her be anything but a doll. And now, as she lay alone, her whole body throbbing with pain, Michelle wanted somebody—somebody who would be hers alone, belong to her, be a part of her.

Somebody who would never betray her.

Slowly, the drug began to take effect. In a little while, Michelle drifted back to the darkness.

The darkness, and the voice.

The voice that was out there, calling to her.

Now, as she slept, the darkness no longer frightened her. Now she only wanted to find the voice, or have the voice find her.

CHAPTER 11

For the Pendletons, there was a sense of waiting for something—something unforeseen and unknowable, something that would bring them all back to the real world, and tell them that life was going to be again what it had been before. It had been that way for ten days now, ever since Michelle had been brought back from the hospital in Boston, riding into town in an ambulance, making the kind of entrance she would have loved only a month ago.

But something inside her had changed. It was more than the accident—it had to be.

At first she had refused to get out of bed at all. When June, backed up by the doctors, had insisted that it was time for her to begin taking care of herself, they had discovered that she could no longer walk by herself.

She had been given every examination possible, and as far as the doctors could tell, there was nothing

wrong with her except for some bruises that had long since begun to heal.

Her left hip hurt her, and her left leg was nearly useless.

They had given her more tests—X-rayed her brain and spinal column again and again, injected dyes into her bloodstream, tapped her spine, checked her reflexes—gone over her until she wished she could simply die. Still unable to determine the cause of her lameness, they had brought in a physical therapist, who had worked with Michelle until, ten days ago, she had finally been able to walk by herself, though painfully, and only by leaning heavily on a cane.

So they had brought her home. June told herself that time would make the difference.

In time, Michelle would regain herself, would begin to recover from the shocks and indignities of the hospital, would begin dismissing her lameness with the same humor with which she had always dismissed whatever problems she had faced.

Michelle was taken up to her room and put in her bed.

She asked for her doll.

And there, for ten days, she lay, the doll tucked in the crook of her arm, staring idly at the ceiling. She responded when she was spoken to, called for help when she needed to go to the bathroom, and sat uncomplainingly on a chair for the few minutes it took June to change her bed each day.

But for the most part, she simply stayed in bed, silent and staring.

June was sure there was more to it than even the accident, the pain, or the crippling. No, it was something else, and June was sure it had to do with Cal.

Now, on Saturday morning, June glanced across the breakfast table at Cal, who was staring into his coffee cup, his face expressionless. She knew what he was thinking about, though he hadn't told her. He was thinking about Michelle, and the recovery he claimed she was making.

It had started the day after they had brought her home, when Cal had announced that he thought Michelle was getting better. And each day, while June was horribly aware that nothing was changing for Michelle, Cal had talked of how well she was doing.

June knew the cause of it—Cal was convinced that whatever was wrong with Michelle was his fault. For him to live with himself, Michelle had to get better. And so he insisted that she was.

But she wasn't.

As June watched him, she found herself becoming angry.

"When are you going to stop this charade?" she heard herself saying. As Cal's head came up and his eyes narrowed, she knew she had chosen the wrong words.

"Would you like to tell me what you're talking about?"

"I'm talking about Michelle," June replied. "I'm talking about the fact that every day you say she's better, when it's obvious that she's not."

"She's doing fine." Cal's voice was low, and June was sure she could hear a desperation in his words.

"If she's doing fine, why is she still in bed?"

Cal shifted, and his eyes avoided June's. "She needs to get her strength back. She needs to rest—"

"She needs to get out of bed, and face life! And you need to stop kidding yourself! It doesn't matter what happened, or whose fault it is. The fact is she's crippled, and she's going to stay that way, and both of you have to face up to it and get on with things!"

Cal rose from his chair, his eyes wild, and for a split second, June was afraid he might hit her. Instead, he moved toward the hall.

"Where are you going?"

He turned back to face her.

"I'm going to talk to Josiah Carson. Do you mind?"

She minded. She minded very much. She wished he would stay home, and if he did nothing else, at least finish the reconstruction of the butler's pantry. But Cal was spending more and more time with Josiah, hanging on to him, and she knew there was no way to stop him.

"If you need to talk to him, talk to him," she said. "What time will you be back?"

"I don't know," Cal replied. A moment later, she heard the front door slam as he left the house.

June sat alone at the table, wondering what to do. And then it came to her. Today she was going to get through to Michelle, make her see that her life was *not* over.

As she was about to start upstairs, there was a soft rapping at the kitchen door. She opened it to find Sally Carstairs and Jeff Benson standing on the porch.

"We came over to see Michelle," Sally announced. She seemed slightly uncertain, as if she wasn't sure they should have come. "Is it all right?"

June smiled, and some of the tension left her. Every day she had hoped Michelle's friends would come. For a while she had toyed with the idea of calling Mrs. Carstairs, or Constance Benson, but each time had rejected it—visitors forced to come would be worse than no visitors at all. "Of course it's all right," she said. "You should have come a long time ago."

She settled the children at the kitchen table, gave them each a cinnamon roll, then went upstairs.

"Michelle?" She kept her voice soft, but Michelle was awake, her eyes, as usual, fixed on the ceiling.

"Um?"

"You have visitors—Sally and Jeff are here to see you. Shall I bring them up?"

"I—I don't think so." Michelle's voice was dull.

"Why not? Don't you feel well?" June tried to keep her irritation out of her voice, but failed. Michelle peered at her mother.

"Why did they come?" she asked. She sounded frightened.

"Because they want to see you. They're your friends." When Michelle didn't respond, June pressed the issue. "Aren't they?"

"I guess," Michelle replied.

"Then I'll bring them up." Not giving Michelle time to protest, she went to the head of the stairs and called down to the children below. A moment later she ushered them into Michelle's room. Michelle was struggling to sit up in bed. When Sally made a move to help her, Michelle looked at her angrily.

"I can do it," she said. Summoning all her strength, she heaved herself up, then flopped against the pillows, wincing at the strain.

"Are you all right?" Sally asked, her eyes wide as she realized the extent of Michelle's injuries.

"I will be," Michelle said. There was a pause. "But it hurts," she added. She looked from Sally to Jeff, an unspoken accusation in her eyes.

June hesitated in the doorway, watching the interplay among the three children. Perhaps it was a mistake—perhaps she shouldn't have brought Sally and Jeff upstairs. But Michelle had to face them, had to talk to them; they were her friends. Without a word, she slipped out of the room, pulling the door closed behind her.

There was an awkward silence after June left, as each of the children waited for someone else to speak first. Jeff shuffled restlessly, and avoided Michelle's eyes.

"Well, I'm not dead, anyway," Michelle said at last.

"Can you walk?" Sally asked.

Michelle nodded. "But not very well. It hurts, and I limp something awful."

"It'll get better, won't it?" Sally sat carefully on the edge of the bed, trying not to shake Michelle.

Michelle didn't answer.

Sally's eyes filled with tears. It just didn't seem fair. Michelle hadn't done anything. If anybody should have gotten hurt, it should have been Susan Peterson. "I'm sorry," she said aloud. "Nobody meant for anything to happen to you. Susan was only teasing . . ."

"I slipped," Michelle said suddenly. "It wasn't anybody's fault. I just slipped. And I'll be all right—you'll see! I'll be fine!" She turned her head away from Sally, but not before Sally saw the bitter tears beginning to form.

"Do you hate us all?" Sally asked. "I hate Susan . . ."

Michelle looked at Sally curiously. "Then why didn't you make her shut up? Why didn't you help me?"

The tears welled over and ran down her cheeks, and Sally quietly began crying too. Jeff tried to ignore the girls, and wished he hadn't come. He hated it when girls cried—it always made him feel as though he'd done something wrong. He decided to change the subject.

"When are you coming back to school? Do you want us to bring you your work?"

Michelle sniffled. "I don't feel like studying."

"But you'll get so far behind," Sally protested.

"Maybe I won't come back to school."

"You have to," Jeff said. "Everybody has to go to school."

"Maybe my parents will send me to another school."

"But why?" Sally's tears had disappeared.

"Because I'm crippled."

"But you can walk. You said so."

"I limp. Everybody will laugh at me."

"No, they won't," Sally assured her. "We won't let them, will we, Jeff?" Jeff nodded in agreement, though his expression was uncertain.

"Susan Peterson will," Michelle said lifelessly, as if she didn't care.

Sally made a face. "Susan Peterson laughs at everybody. Just ignore her."

"Like everybody did at the picnic?" Michelle's voice was bitter now, and her face turned angry. "Why don't you leave me alone? Why don't all of you just leave me alone!"

Abashed at Michelle's outburst, Sally stood up quickly. "I—I'm sorry," she stammered, her face reddening. "We were just trying to help . . ."

"Nobody can help," Michelle said, her voice quivering. "I have to do it myself. All of it!"

She turned her face away and closed her eyes. Jeff and Sally stared at her for a moment, then started toward the door.

"I'll come back again," Sally offered, but when there

was no response from Michelle, she followed Jeff out into the hall.

June was waiting for them downstairs. She knew immediately that something had gone wrong.

"Did she talk to you?"

"Sort of." Sally's voice was unsteady. June saw that she was on the verge of tears. She put an arm around the girl and hugged her gently.

"Try not to let her worry you," she urged. "It's been terrible for her, and she's been in pain all the time. But she'll be all right. It'll just take time."

Sally nodded mutely. Then her tears overflowed, and she buried her face in June's shoulder.

"Oh, Mrs. Pendleton, I feel like it's our fault. All our fault."

June drew the girl to her. "It's not your fault, or anyone's fault, and I'm sure Michelle doesn't think it is."

"Are you really going to send her away to school?" Jeff asked suddenly. June looked at him blankly.

"Away? What do you mean?"

"Michelle said she might be going to another school. I guess a school for—cripples," he finished, stumbling on the word as if he hated to use it.

"Is it true?" Sally searched June's face, but June carefully remained expressionless.

"Well, we've talked about it . . ." she lied, wondering where Michelle had gotten such an idea. It had never even been mentioned.

"I hope she can stay here." Sally's voice was eager. "Nobody will laugh at her—really they won't!"

"Why, whatever put such an idea into your heads?" June exclaimed. She began to wonder exactly what

had transpired upstairs, but knew better than to try
to pry it out of Jeff and Sally. "Now why don't you
two run along and come back in a couple of days. I'm
sure Michelle will be feeling much better then."

June watched the two children retreat along the
bluff. She could see them talking animatedly together.
When Jeff glanced back at the house, June waved to
him, but he ignored her, turning almost guiltily away.

June's spirits, buoyed by the appearance of Sally and
Jeff, sank again. She started upstairs to have a talk
with Michelle. But as she was about to go into her
daughter's room, Jennifer suddenly began crying. June
stood indecisively at Michelle's door for a moment. As
Jennifer's howls increased, she decided to see to the
baby first. Then she would face Michelle, and have a
talk with her. A real talk.

Michelle lay in bed, her eyes open, staring sightlessly at the ceiling, listening to the voice.

It was closer now, closer than it had ever been before. She still had to listen carefully to make out the
words, but she was getting better at it.

It was a pleasant voice, almost musical. Michelle
was almost sure she knew where it came from.

It was the girl.

The girl in the black dress, the one she had seen
first in her dreams, then that day at the graveyard. The
day Jennifer had been born.

At first, the girl had only called out to her, calling
for help. But now she was saying other things. Michelle lay in bed, and she listened.

"*They're not your friends,*" the voice crooned. "*None
of them are.*

"Don't believe Sally. She's Susan's friend, and Susan hates you.

"All of them hate you.

"They pushed you.

"They pushed you off the trail.

"They want to kill you.

"But it won't happen. I won't let it happen.

"I'm your friend, and I'll take care of you. I'll help you.

"We'll help each other . . ."

The voice faded away, and Michelle became aware of a soft tapping at her door. The door opened, and her mother came in, smiling at her, Jennifer in her arms.

"Hi! How's everything?"

"All right, I guess."

"Did you have a nice visit with Sally and Jeff?"

"I guess."

"I thought you might like to say hello to your sister."

Michelle stared at the baby, her face expressionless.

"What did Sally and Jeff have to say?" June was beginning to feel desperate. Michelle was barely answering her questions.

"Nothing much. They just wanted to say hi."

"But you must have talked with them."

"Not really."

A heavy silence fell over the room. June began fiddling with Jennifer's blanket while she tried to decide what tactic to take with Michelle. Finally, reluctantly, she made up her mind.

"Well, I think it's time you got out of bed," she said flatly. At last there was a reaction from Michelle. Her eyes flickered, and for a moment June thought they filled with fear. She shrank further down under the covers.

"But I can't . . ." she began. June quietly interrupted her.

"Of course you can," she said smoothly. "You get out of bed every day. And it's good for you—the sooner you get out of bed and start exercising, the sooner you can go back to school."

"But I don't want to go back to school," Michelle said. Now, suddenly, she was sitting up straight, staring intensely at her mother. "I never want to go back to that school. They all hate me there."

"Don't be silly," June said. "Who told you that?"

Michelle glanced wildly around the room, as if searching for something. Her eyes came to rest on her doll, sitting in its usual place on the window seat.

"Mandy," she said. "Amanda told me!"

June's mouth fell open in surprise. She stared first at Michelle, then at the doll. Surely she didn't think it was real! No, she couldn't. Then June realized what had happened. An imaginary friend. Michelle had made up an imaginary friend to keep her company. And yet, there was the doll: its glass eyes, large and dark as Michelle's, seemed to see right through her. June closed her mouth, and stood up.

"I see," she said hollowly. "Well." *Dear God, what's happening to her?* she thought. *What's happening to all of us?* Trying to keep her confusion from her voice, and forcing herself to smile at Michelle as if nothing were wrong, she got to her feet.

"We'll talk about it later." She bent over and kissed Michelle lightly on the cheek. Michelle's only response was to lower herself, so she was once more lying on the bed. As June watched, all expression seemed to fade from Michelle's face. Had her eyes not remained open, June would have sworn she had fallen asleep.

Hugging Jennifer close to her, June backed slowly out of the room.

Cal came home in the middle of the afternoon, and spent the rest of the day reading and playing with Jennifer. He spoke only briefly to June, and didn't go up to Michelle's room at all.

As June finished setting the table for dinner, and was about to call Cal into the kitchen, an idea came to her. Without pausing to think about it, she went into the living room where Cal sat with Jennifer in his lap.

"I'm going to have Michelle come down for dinner," she said. She saw Cal flinch, but he quickly recovered himself.

"Tonight? What brought this on?" His voice was guarded, and June prepared herself for another argument.

"She's spending too much time by herself. You never go up there—"

"That's not true," Cal started to protest, but June didn't let him finish.

"Whether it's true or not isn't the point. The point is that she's spending too much time alone, feeling sorry for herself. And I won't let it continue. I'm going to go up and tell her to put on her robe and come downstairs. And I'm not going to take 'no' for an answer."

As soon as she left the room, Cal put Jennifer in the extra bassinet they had installed in the living room, and fixed himself a drink. By the time June returned, he had finished it and begun on a second, which he brought with him when June called him to the table.

They sat silently, waiting for Michelle. As the hall clock ticked hollowly, Cal began twisting his napkin.

"How long are you going to wait?" he asked.

"Until Michelle comes down."

"What if she doesn't?"

"She will," June said firmly. "I know she will." But inside she did not feel the assurance of her own words.

The minutes dragged. June had to force herself to stay at the table, not to go upstairs, not to give in at all. And then it hit her.

Maybe Michelle *couldn't* come down. She got up from the table and hurried into the hall.

At the top of the stairs, Michelle, her robe tied tightly around her waist, was clutching the bannister with one hand, while with the other she tested the top step with her cane.

"Can I help?" June offered. Michelle glanced at her, then shook her head.

"I'll do it," she said. "I'll do it by myself."

June felt the tension that had been building up in her suddenly release itself. But then, as Michelle spoke once more, the knot of fear that had been clutching at her all afternoon regained its grip, more tightly than ever.

"Mandy will help me," Michelle said quietly. "She told me she would."

Very carefully, Michelle started down the stairs.

CHAPTER 12

The morning sun, crackling with an autumnal brightness, flooded through the windows of the studio, its rays seeking out every corner, its brightness lending a new mood to the canvas on the easel. June had begun it several days ago. It depicted the view from the studio, but it was moody, somber, cast in heavy blues and grays that reflected all too well her own mood over the past few weeks. But this morning, bathed in the sunlight, its colors seemed to have changed, brightened, capturing the excitement of a suddenly gusting wind churning the cove on a dark day. Dipping her brush in white paint, June began adding whitecaps to the boiling sea that erupted over her canvas.

In one corner of the studio, Jennifer lay in her bassinet, cooing and gurgling in her sleep, her tiny hands contentedly clutching at her blanket. June tore herself away from her work long enough to smile at Jenny. As she was about to return to the canvas, a movement outside caught her eye.

Putting her palette and brush aside, she went to the window and looked out.

Michelle, leaning heavily on a cane, was making her way toward the studio.

As she watched, June fought to control her emotions, struggled against an almost overpowering impulse to go to Michelle, to help her.

Michelle's pain was written boldly on her face: her features, even and delicate, were screwed into a mask of concentration as she made herself keep moving steadily forward, her good right leg moving easily, almost eagerly, while her left leg dragged reluctantly behind as if mired in mud, being moved by sheer strength of will.

June felt tears well up in her eyes. The contrast between this fragile child bravely limping toward her, and the robust, agile Michelle of only a few weeks ago tore at her.

I won't cry, she told herself. *If Michelle can take it, so can I.* In a strange way, June drew strength from the pain-contorted body that drew steadily nearer, then, suddenly feeling self-conscious about watching Michelle, she turned back to her easel. When, a few minutes later, Michelle appeared at the door, she was able to feign surprise.

"Well, look who's here!" she exclaimed, forcing her voice to a level of cheerfulness she didn't feel. Reflexively, she took a step toward Michelle, but Michelle shook her head.

"I made it," she said triumphantly, lowering herself on June's stool so that her left leg hung nearly straight to the floor. She sighed heavily, then grinned at her mother, a trace of her old humor briefly illuminating her face. "If I hurried, I bet I could have made it twice as fast."

"Does it hurt terribly?" June asked, letting her mask of cheerfulness fall away. Michelle seemed to consider her answer carefully, and June wondered whether she was going to hear the truth, or some evasion Michelle thought she might like to hear.

"Not as much as yesterday," Michelle said.

"I'm not sure you should have tried coming all the way out here . . ."

"I needed to talk to you." Michelle's face turned serious, and she shifted her weight on the stool. Even that slight movement sent stabs of pain through her. She winced slightly, and waited for the spasm to pass before she spoke again.

"What is it?" June asked finally.

"I—I'm not sure. It's—" She floundered for a moment, then her eyes moistened, and a tear began running slowly down her cheek. June quickly put her arms around Michelle and hugged her close.

"What is it, darling? Tell me. Please?"

Michelle buried her face against her mother, her body suddenly wracked with sobs. With each sob, June could feel Michelle's body tighten with the pain in her hip. For several minutes June held her, until Michelle's agony slowly passed.

"Is it that bad? Does it hurt that much?" June wished there were some way she could take the pain upon herself. But Michelle was shaking her head.

"It's Daddy," she said finally.

"Daddy? What about him?"

"He's—he's changed," Michelle said softly, so softly June had to strain to hear her.

"Changed?" June echoed. "How?" But even as she asked the question, she knew the answer.

"Ever since I fell," Michelle began, but then another storm of tears broke over her. "He doesn't love me anymore," she wailed. "Ever since I fell, he doesn't love me!"

June rocked her gently, trying to comfort her. "No, darling, that isn't true. You know that isn't true. He loves you very much. Very, very much."

"Well, he doesn't act like it," Michelle sobbed. "He —he never plays with me anymore, and he doesn't talk to me, and when I try to talk to him he—he goes somewhere else."

"Oh, now that isn't true," June said, though she knew it was. She had been afraid of this moment, sure that sooner or later Michelle was going to realize that something had happened to Cal, and that it had to do with her. She could feel Michelle shivering in her arms, though the studio was warm.

"It *is* true," Michelle was saying, her voice muffled in the folds of June's blouse. "This morning I asked him if I could go to the office with him. I only wanted to sit in the waiting room and read the magazines! But he wouldn't let me."

"I'm sure it wasn't that he didn't want you with him," June lied. "He probably had a busy day, and didn't think he'd have much time for you."

"He *never* has time for me. Not anymore!"

June pulled her handkerchief out of her pocket, and dried Michelle's eyes. "I'll tell you what," she said. "I'll have a talk with him tonight, and explain to him that it's important for you to get out of the house. Then maybe he'll take you along tomorrow. Okay?"

Michelle sniffled a little, blew her nose into the

handkerchief, and shrugged. "I guess," she replied, straightening up and trying to smile. "He does still love me, doesn't he?"

"Of course he does," June assured her once again. "I'm sure there's nothing wrong at all. Now, let's talk about something else." She cast about in her mind quickly. "Like school, for instance. Don't you think it's about time you thought about going back?"

Michelle shook her head uncertainly. "I don't want to go back to school. Everybody will laugh at me. They always laugh at cripples."

"Maybe they will at first," June conceded. "But you just turn the other cheek, and ignore it. Besides, you're not crippled. You just limp a little. And soon you won't even limp anymore."

"Yes, I will," Michelle said evenly. "I'll limp for the rest of my life."

"No," June protested. "You'll get well. You'll be fine."

Michelle shook her head. "No I won't. I'll get used to it, but I won't be fine." Painfully, she got to her feet. "Is it all right if I go for a walk?"

"A walk?" June asked doubtfully. "Where?"

"Along the bluff. I won't go very far." Her eyes searched her mother's face. "If I'm going to go back to school, I'd better practice, hadn't I?"

Go back to school? A minute ago she said she didn't want to go back to school. In confusion, June nodded her agreement. "Of course. But be careful, sweetheart. And please, don't try to go down to the beach, all right?"

"I won't," Michelle promised. She started toward the studio door but suddenly stopped, her eyes fixed on the stain on the floor. "I thought that was gone."

June shook her head. "We tried, but it wouldn't come out. Maybe if I knew what it was . . ."

"Why don't you ask Dr. Carson? He probably knows."

"Maybe I will," June said. Then: "How long will you be gone?"

"However long it takes," Michelle said. Leaning on her cane, she slowly went out into the sunlight.

Josiah Carson stared up at the ceiling, ran one hand through his thick mane of nearly white hair, and drummed the fingers of his other hand on the desk top in front of him. As always when he was alone, he was thinking about Alan Hanley. Things had been going well until that day when Alan had fallen from the roof. Or *had* he fallen?

Josiah was sure he hadn't. Over the years, too many things had happened in his house, too many people had died.

His mind drifted back to his wife, Sarah, and the days when life had seemed to him to be perfect. He and Sarah were going to have a family—a big family— but it hadn't worked out that way. Sarah had died giving birth to his daughter. She shouldn't have died— there was no reason for it. She had been healthy, the pregnancy had been easy, but as his daughter was born, Sarah had died. Josiah had survived the loss, pouring his love out to his daughter, little Sarah.

And then, when Sarah was just twelve, it had happened.

He still didn't know how it had happened.

He came downstairs one morning and opened the huge walk-in refrigerator in the kitchen.

On the floor, holding a doll that Josiah had never seen before, he found his daughter, dead.

Why had she gone into the refrigerator? Josiah never knew.

He buried little Sarah and with her, he buried the doll.

After that, he had lived alone, and as the years, more than forty of them, passed, he had begun to believe that he was safe, that nothing more was going to happen.

And then, Alan Hanley had fallen.

In his own mind he was convinced that Alan hadn't simply lost his footing. No, there was more to it than that, and the doll was the proof.

The doll he had buried with his daughter.

The doll he had found under Alan's broken body.

The doll Michelle Pendleton had shown him.

Josiah had wanted to talk to Alan about the doll, but the boy had never regained consciousness: Cal Pendleton had let him die.

Had killed him, really.

If Cal hadn't killed him, Josiah could have found out what had actually happened on the roof that day —what Alan had seen, and felt, and heard. He could have found out what was happening in his house, what had happened to his family. Now he'd never know. Cal Pendleton had ruined it for him.

But he'd get even.

He was already starting to get even.

It had been so easy, once he'd found out how guilty Cal felt about Alan. From there it was easy. Sell him the practice. Sell him the house. It had worked.

He'd gotten Cal into the house, and the doll was back.

Cal's daughter had the doll now.

And whatever was happening, it was no longer happening to the Carsons.

Now it was happening to the Pendletons.

His thoughts were interrupted by the sound of voices from the examining room next to the office, where Cal was examining Lisa Hartwick.

Cal had tried to beg off examining Lisa, but Josiah hadn't let him. He knew how frightened Cal was of children now, how he had a feeling—reasonable or not—that whatever he did with a child, it was going to be wrong, and he was going to hurt the child.

Josiah Carson understood those feelings.

In the examining room, Lisa Hartwick stared at Cal, her light brown bangs nearly hiding her suspicious eyes. When he asked her to open her mouth, she pouted.

"Why should I?"

"So I can look at your throat," Cal told her. "If I can't see it, I can't tell you why it's sore, can I?"

"It isn't sore. I just told Daddy that so I wouldn't have to go to school."

Cal put down his tongue depressor, a feeling of relief flooding through him. With this child, at least, there was no immediate threat. Still, she wasn't the nicest child he'd ever run across. In fact, he found himself disliking her intensely. "I see," he replied. "Don't you like school?"

Lisa shrugged. "It's okay. I just can't stand the snotty kids around here. If you weren't born here, they never want to be your friends."

"Oh, I don't know," Cal replied. "Michelle's made some friends."

"That's what *she* thinks," Lisa said. "Wait'll she goes back to school." Then she cocked her head, and stared impudently at Cal. "Is it true that she can't walk?"

Cal felt himself flush. When he answered, his voice was gruff. "She can walk just fine. There's nothing wrong with her, and pretty soon she'll be as good as new. She just got banged up a little." He knew he was lying, but he couldn't help himself—it made things easier if he pretended Michelle was going to be all right. And maybe—just maybe—she would be.

"Well, that's not what I heard," Lisa said, hopping off the examining table. Her expression changed suddenly, and her face took on a vulnerability Cal hadn't seen since she showed up in the office. "I don't have a mother, either," she said softly.

For a moment Cal wasn't sure what she meant, but then it came to him. "But Michelle has a mother," he said. "We adopted her when she was just a baby."

"Oh," said Lisa, and Cal thought he could see disappointment in her eyes.

"Still," Cal went on smoothly, "I suppose the two of you do have some things in common. Neither one of you was born here, and even though Michelle's a full-fledged orphan, you're half a one, aren't you? Maybe you should come out and see Michelle sometime. . . ." He deliberately left the question hanging in the air. For a moment he thought Lisa was going to pick it up. But she didn't, not quite.

"Maybe I will," she said halfheartedly. "But maybe I won't, either." Before Cal could reply to her rudeness, she was gone.

* * *

When Cal came into the office they were sharing, Josiah Carson pretended to be engrossed in a medical journal. Only when Cal had seated himself at his makeshift desk did Carson glance up.

"Everything all right?" he asked.

Cal shrugged. "She's a difficult child."

"She's a brat," Carson stated.

"Well, life isn't easy for her."

"Life isn't easy for any of us," Josiah said pointedly.

Cal flinched visibly, then met Carson's eyes. "What's that supposed to mean?"

The old doctor shrugged elaborately. "Make of it what you will."

It was as if he'd pulled a plug. Cal sagged in his chair, his eyes as lifeless as his posture. He looked bleakly at Carson.

"Josiah, what am I going to do? I can't face Michelle, I can't talk to her, I can't even touch her. I keep thinking about Alan Hanley, and wondering what I did wrong. And what I did wrong with Michelle."

"We all make mistakes, Cal," Josiah said. "We can't blame ourselves for showing bad judgment under pressure. We just have to accept our limitations, and live with them."

He paused, trying to assess Cal's reaction. Maybe he'd pushed him too far. But Cal was watching him, concentrating on what he was saying. Josiah smiled and took another tack. "Maybe it's all my fault. Certainly what happened to Michelle is my fault. If I hadn't sold you that damned house—"

Cal glanced at Josiah sharply. " 'Damned house'? Why did you say that?"

Josiah shifted in his chair. "I probably shouldn't have. Call it a slip of the tongue."

But Cal was not to be put off.

"Is there something about that house I should know?"

"Not really," Carson said carefully. "I guess I just think it's an unlucky house. First Alan Hanley. Now Michelle. . . ." His voice trailed off.

Cal stared at him, feeling cheated. He loved the house, more every day, and wanted to hear nothing bad about it. "I'm sorry you feel that way," he said. "For me, it's a good house."

He took off his white jacket, ready to go home for lunch. He was at the door when he suddenly turned back.

"Josiah?"

Carson looked at him inquiringly.

"Josiah, I just want you to know—I appreciate everything you've done for me. I don't know how I'd have gotten through all of this without you. I consider myself very lucky to have a friend like you." Then, embarrassed by his own words, Cal hurried out of the office.

Alone once more, Carson's mind went back to the words that had caught Cal's attention.

Damned house.

And that's what it is, he thought. An image came to his mind, an image of a stain, spread thickly on the floor of the potting-shed.

A stain that no one had ever been able to get rid of.

A stain that had haunted his life. Irrationally, he was convinced that it was somehow connected to Michelle Pendleton's doll.

Now, he was sure, it would haunt the Pendletons.

Indeed, it was already beginning.

Josiah Carson didn't pretend to know exactly what it was about the house that made things happen to the people who lived there, but he had his suspicions. And it was beginning to look like his suspicions were correct. For Michelle, it had already begun. And it would go on, and on, and on. . . .

Michelle stood in the cemetery, staring at the tiny stone with the single word on it:

AMANDA

She tried to make her mind blank, as if by closing out her thoughts, she would be able to hear the voice better. It worked.

She could hear the voice, far away, but coming closer.

As the voice approached, the bright sunlight faded, and the sea fog closed around her.

Soon Michelle felt as though she were alone in the world.

Then, as if something had reached out and touched her, she knew she was not alone.

She turned. Standing behind her she saw the girl.

Her black dress fell nearly to the ground, and her head was covered by her bonnet. Her sightless, milky eyes were fixed on Michelle. She was smiling.

"You're Amanda," Michelle whispered. Her words hung in the fog, muffled. Then the girl nodded her head.

"I've been waiting for you." The voice was soft, musical, and soothing to Michelle. "I've been waiting for you for a long time. I'm going to be your friend."

"I—I don't have any friends," Michelle murmured.

"I know. I don't have any friends, either. But now we'll have each other, and everything will be fine."

Michelle stood still, staring at the strange apparition in the fog, vaguely frightened. But Amanda's words appealed to her, and comforted her. And she wanted a friend.

Silently, she accepted Amanda.

CHAPTER 13

"Now, you're sure you'll be all right?"

"If I need help, I'll call you, or Miss Hatcher will, or *someone* will," Michelle replied. She opened the car door, put her right foot on the sidewalk, braced herself with her cane, and pulled herself upright. June watched anxiously as she teetered, but Michelle quickly gained her balance, and slammed the door. Without waving or saying good-bye, she began limping slowly up the walk to the school building. June stayed where she was, watching, unable to drive away until Michelle was inside the building.

Carefully, her left hand holding on to the railing, her right hand maneuvering the cane, Michelle mounted the steps, leading with her right foot, then dragging her left leg after her. The process was slow, but steady. Only when she had reached the top of the seven steps did she turn, wave to her mother, then disappear into the school. Sighing, June put the car in gear and pulled away from the curb. As she drove home, she prayed that everything would be all right. And, feeling a pang of guilt, she began to look forward to spending a day—a whole day—with her baby and her work.

Corinne Hatcher had already begun the lesson when the door opened and Michelle appeared, leaning on her cane, her expression uncertain, as if she might be in the wrong room. The class fell silent. The students shifted in their seats to stare at her.

Trying to ignore them, Michelle limped down the aisle, keeping her eyes fixed on her goal—the vacant seat in the front row, between Sally and Jeff, that had apparently been saved for her. As she reached the seat, and carefully lowered herself into it, she allowed herself to look at Miss Hatcher and smile.

"I'm sorry I'm late," she said shyly.

"It's all right," Corinne assured her. "We haven't even begun. I'm so glad you're back. Doesn't anyone want to say hello to Michelle?"

She looked at the class expectantly. After a moment, a murmuring began as each of the children, unsure of what was expected of him, muttered a greeting. Sally Carstairs, reaching across the aisle, squeezed Michelle's hand, but Michelle quickly withdrew it. From the other side, she heard Jeff speaking to her, but when she turned to him, she saw Susan Peterson nudging him, and he looked quickly away. Michelle felt her face reddening with embarrassment.

She couldn't concentrate on her lessons. Instead, she was terribly aware of the other children, feeling their eyes boring into her back, hearing their whisperings, kept so low she couldn't make out the words.

For a while, Corinne Hatcher thought of stopping

the lesson, of facing the issue of Michelle's accident head on, but she discarded the idea: it would be too embarrassing for Michelle. So she pressed ahead, trying to keep the children's minds on their work and off their classmate. As the first recess bell rang, Corinne gratefully released the class. All except Michelle.

When the room was empty except for the two of them, she pulled her chair over near Michelle's desk.

"It wasn't too bad, was it?" she asked in as conversational a tone as she could muster. Michelle looked at her blankly, as though she didn't understand the ques. 1.

"What wasn't?"

"Why—why your first morning back at school."

"It's fine," Michelle said. "Why shouldn't it be?" There was a challenging note in her voice that threw Corinne off. It was as if Michelle were daring her to talk about the whisperings that had pervaded the room for the last two hours.

"Perhaps we should go over some of the work you've missed," she offered, taking her lead from Michelle: if Michelle didn't want to talk about the class's reaction to her, then it wouldn't be talked about.

"I can catch up by myself," Michelle said. "Is it all right if I go to the restroom?"

Corinne stared at the girl, so composed, so seemingly sure of herself. But she shouldn't be—she should be nervous, she should be feeling insecure, she should even be crying. But she should *not* be calmly asking if she could go to the restroom. Suppressing the questions that were in her mind, and wishing that Tim Hartwick were here today, Corinne watched Michelle make her way toward the door. Corinne Hatcher was very worried.

* * *

Michelle was pleased to find the hall deserted—at least there would be no one to watch her as she made her slow progress toward the girls' room, her cane tapping hollowly on the wood floors.

She wished she could disappear.

They were laughing at her, just like she thought they would.

Sally had barely spoken to her, and the rest of them hadn't known what to say.

Well, she wouldn't give in to them.

She pushed the door open and went into the restroom, where she stared at herself in the mirror, wondering if the pain was showing in her face.

It was important that it not show, that nobody know how she felt, how much she hurt.

How angry she was.

Especially at Susan Peterson.

Susan had said something to Jeff.

Said something that made him stop talking to Michelle.

Amanda was right—they weren't her friends, not anymore. Michelle washed her face, then looked once more in the mirror. "It doesn't matter," she said out loud. "I don't need them. Amanda's my friend. The *hell* with them!" Then, surprised at her use of the swearword, she took a step backward and nearly fell. She caught herself on the edge of the sink, steadied herself. A wave of frustration swept over her, and she wanted to cry, but she wouldn't give in. *I'll show them,* she vowed silently. *I'll show them all.*

Painfully, she started back to the classroom.

* * *

After recess, something in the classroom changed. The whispering stopped, and the children seemed to be keeping their minds on their work.

Except that every now and then, one of the children would glance surreptitiously first at Michelle, then at Susan Peterson. If the girls were aware of what was happening, they gave no sign.

Sally Carstairs was having a very bad time of it. Every few minutes she looked up from her work, glanced at Michelle, then quickly glanced across both Michelle and Jeff Benson to Susan Peterson. When their eyes met, Susan's lips tightened and her head shook almost imperceptibly. Sally went back to her work, her face flushing guiltily.

When the lunch bell rang, not even Sally Carstairs waited for Michelle. Instead, within seconds the room was empty except for Michelle and Corinne. Michelle reached under her desk for her bookbag and got out her lunch. Then she stood up and started out of the room.

"Why don't you stay and eat with me?" Corinne suggested.

For a brief instant Michelle hesitated, then shook her head. "I'll go outside," she said.

"Are you sure?" Corinne pressed.

Michelle nodded. "I'll just sit at the top of the steps where I can see everything." She was almost out of the room when she stopped suddenly, and turned to face Corinne. "It's important to be able to see. Did you know that, Miss Hatcher?" Without waiting for an answer, Michelle left the room.

Michelle sat on the top step, her left leg stretched stiffly away from her, her right drawn up against her chest. She rested her chin on her right knee and watched the children in the schoolyard.

Under the big maple she could see her own classmates, Susan and Jeff and Sally—all of them—clustered together in a group.

They were talking about her, and she knew it.

Susan Peterson, particularly. Michelle could see her, leaning over to whisper something in someone's ear, then the two of them—Susan and whomever she had spoken to—glancing at Michelle, and giggling.

Once Susan started to say something to Sally, but Sally only shook her head and immediately started to talk to someone else.

Michelle made herself stop watching them. Her eyes wandered over the playground. Out near the back fence, some of the fourth-graders were playing softball, and Michelle felt a twinge of envy as she watched them run. She used to play softball. She had been one of the fastest runners in her school.

But that had been before.

Across the schoolyard, near the gate, Michelle saw Lisa Hartwick sitting by herself. For a second, she wished Lisa would come over and sit on the steps with her, but then she remembered—the other kids didn't like Lisa, and even if they weren't talking to her, she wouldn't make things worse by being friendly with Lisa.

Close by her, at the foot of the steps, three girls—perhaps eight years old—were engrossed in a game of jacks, oblivious to Michelle above them. She watched the game for a while, and remembered when she had been their age. She'd never been good at jacks—the little pieces had always somehow slipped through her fingers. And yet, the game didn't involve running, or jumping, or any of the things Michelle couldn't do anymore. Maybe she should ask them—

The bell rang. Lunchtime was over.

Michelle stood up and went back into the building. She made sure she was the first to arrive in the classroom. As soon as she was inside the door, she slipped into a seat at the back of the room.

A seat where none of them would be able to see her unless they turned around and openly stared at her.

But she would be able to see them.

Watch them.

Know who was laughing at her. . . .

When the three-ten bell rang, Corinne Hatcher again asked Michelle to wait, and beckoned Michelle to her desk at the front of the empty room.

"I want to apologize for the class."

Michelle stood before her expressionlessly, her face a blank mask of indifference.

"Apologize? For what?"

"Why, for the way they treated you today. It was very rude."

"Was it? I didn't notice anything," Michelle said tonelessly.

Corinne leaned back in her chair, and tapped her desk with a pencil. "I noticed you weren't having lunch with your friends."

"I told you—it was easier not to try to get down the steps. Is it all right if I go now? It's a long walk home."

"You're walking?" Corinne was aghast. She couldn't walk—it was much too far. But Michelle was nodding calmly.

"It's good for me," she said affably. Corinne noticed that now that the subject had nothing to do with her classmates, Michelle seemed to relax. "Besides, I like to walk. And now that I can't walk as fast as I used to, I see a lot more. You'd be amazed."

In Corinne's mind, Michelle's own words rang out: *It's important to be able to see.*

"What do you see?" Corinne asked.

"Oh, all kinds of things. Flowers, and trees, and rocks—things like that." Her voice dropped a little. "When you're by yourself, you really look around."

Corinne felt very sad for Michelle. When she spoke, her voice reflected her emotions. "Yes," she said, "I'm sure you do." She stood up and began gathering her things together. Walking very slowly, so Michelle could keep up, she left the room and locked the door behind her.

"You're sure I couldn't give you a lift home?" Corinne offered when they reached the front steps.

"No, thanks. Really, I'll be fine." Michelle sounded distracted, and her eyes were searching the schoolyard, as if she were looking for someone.

"Was someone going to walk with you?"

"No—no, I just thought. . . ." Michelle's voice trailed off, and she started down the steps. "See you tomorrow, Miss Hatcher," she called over her shoulder. Reaching the bottom of the steps, she slung her bookbag over her shoulder, and limped toward the sidewalk.

Corinne Hatcher watched her until she disappeared around the corner, then started toward her car.

He could have waited for me, Michelle thought bitterly.

She walked as quickly as she could, but within a few blocks her hip began hurting her, and she slowed her pace.

She tried to force her mind off Jeff Benson, but as she walked, every sight she saw reminded her of the days they had walked home together. Now he probably walked Susan Peterson home, she thought.

She left the village behind and made her way along the road, staying well off the pavement. Even though the path was rough, and it was easier to walk on the asphalt, she knew she wouldn't be able to get out of the way of an oncoming car—the path was much safer.

She stopped every few yards, partly to rest, but also to look around, to examine everything carefully, as if she were seeing it for the first, or maybe the last, time. Once or twice, she stood perfectly still, closed her eyes tightly, and tried to imagine what it would be like to be blind. With the cane, she poked at things around her, seeing if she could identify them by the way they felt.

Most of the time, she couldn't.

It would be awful, she thought. Being blind would be the most awful thing in the world.

She was almost halfway home when she heard a voice calling to her.

"Michelle? Hey, Michelle, wait up!"

Stoically, ignoring the voice, Michelle kept walking.

A minute later, Jeff Benson caught up with her.

"Why didn't you wait?" he demanded. "Didn't you hear me?"

"I heard you."

"Well, why didn't you stop?"

"Why didn't you wait for me after school?" Michelle countered.

"I promised Susan I'd walk her home."

"And you knew you could catch up with me?"

Jeff blushed. "I didn't say that."

"You didn't have to." There was a silence, and Michelle continued on her way, Jeff keeping pace with her. "If you want to go home, you don't have to wait for me," she said.

"I don't mind."

They continued walking. Michelle wished Jeff would go away. Finally, she told him so.

"You make me feel like a freak!" she exclaimed. "Why don't you just go on home, and leave me alone?"

Jeff stopped in his tracks and stared at her. His mouth opened, then closed again. His face reddened and his fists clenched. "Well, if that's the way you feel, maybe I will," he said at last.

"Good!" Michelle could feel tears welling up in her eyes, and for a moment she was afraid she was going to cry. But then Jeff turned away from her, and began loping down the road. When he was a few yards away, he suddenly looked back, waved, and broke into a run. To Michelle, it was like a slap in the face.

Jeff slammed into his house, and called out to let his mother know he was home. He tossed his books on a table and went into the living room, where he flopped down on the sofa and put his feet on the coffee table. Girls! What a pain!

First Susan Peterson, telling him that he shouldn't talk to Michelle anymore, then Michelle, telling him that she didn't want him to walk with her anymore.

It was crazy, that's what it was. He glanced out the window.

There she was, all by herself. Jeff watched as Michelle passed his house and started past the cemetery. Suddenly she stopped, and stared into the graveyard, as if she were watching something. But there was nothing to watch. To Jeff, the cemetery looked the same as it always did—choked with weeds, gravestones collapsing, deserted. What was Michelle looking at?

As Michelle drew abreast of the cemetery, the bright afternoon sun faded. Fog began to form around her. She had grown used to it now, and was no longer surprised when the damp coldness suddenly closed in around her, blotting out the rest of the world, leaving her alone in the mist. She knew she wouldn't be alone long: when the fog came, so did Amanda. Michelle was beginning to look forward to the fog, look forward to seeing her friend.

There she was, coming toward her out of the cemetery, smiling to her, and waving.

"Hi," Michelle called.

"I've been waiting for you," Amanda said as she came through the broken fence. "Was it as bad as we thought it would be?"

"Yes. They laughed at me, and kept whispering to each other."

"It's all right," Amanda said. "I'll walk with you and you can show me things."

"Can't you see things yourself?"

Amanda's milky white eyes fixed on Michelle's face. "I can't see anything," she said, "unless I'm with you." Michelle took Amanda's hand and started along the path. For some reason, she noticed, it was easier to walk with Amanda next to her. Her hip didn't hurt nearly as much, and she hardly limped at all.

Amanda led her across the cemetery and along the bluff trail. Soon they arrived at the Pendletons', and Michelle instinctively started toward the house.

"No," Amanda said. Michelle felt Amanda's grip on her hand tighten. "The potting-shed. What I want to see is in the potting-shed." Michelle hesitated, then, her curiosity aroused, allowed Amanda to lead her toward her mother's studio.

Amanda led Michelle around the corner of the little building, and stopped at the window.

"Look inside," she whispered to Michelle.

Obediently, Michelle peered through the window. The fog, thick around her, seemed to have permeated the studio as well. There was a mistiness inside; everything was indistinct.

And nothing looked quite right.

Her mother's easel was there, but the painting propped up on it was not her mother's.

Michelle stared at the painting for a second, then a movement caught her eye, and her glance shifted. There were people in the studio, but she couldn't see them clearly. The mists swirled around them, and their faces were invisible to her.

Then Michelle heard the sounds.

It was Amanda, next to her.

"It's true," Amanda whispered, her voice constricted into a hiss. "She's a whore . . . a *whore!*"

Michelle's eyes widened in fright at the anger in her friend's voice. She tried to pull her hand from Amanda's grip, but Amanda hung on.

"Don't!" she begged. "Don't pull away! Let me see! I have to *see!*"

Her face twisted in fury, and her grip on Michelle's hand became painful.

Suddenly Michelle wrenched free. She backed away from Amanda, and as their hands parted, Amanda's sightless gaze fixed on her.

"Don't," she repeated. "Please? Don't go away. Let me see. I'm your friend, and I'm going to help you. Won't you help me, too?"

But Michelle had already turned away. She started toward the house. The fog seemed to lift a little.

By the time she reached the house the mist had cleared.

But her limp had slowed her nearly to a stop, and her hip was once more throbbing with pain.

CHAPTER 14

Michelle let the kitchen door slam noisily behind her, dumped her bookbag on the table, and went to the refrigerator. She was terribly conscious of her mother watching her, and struggled to control the trembling of her hands. It wasn't until she had poured herself a glass of milk that June spoke to her.

"Michelle? Are you all right?"

"I'm fine," Michelle replied. She put the milk back into the refrigerator, and smiled at her mother.

June regarded her daughter cautiously. Something was wrong. She looked frightened. But what could have frightened her? June had watched her come along the path, hesitate for a moment, then continue on to the studio, where she had paused briefly at the window. When she had started toward the house, it was as if she had seen something.

"What were you looking at?"

"Looking at?" June was almost sure Michelle was stalling for time.

"In the studio. I saw you looking through the studio window."

"But you couldn't—" Michelle began. Then she caught herself, and glanced out the window.

The sun was shining brightly.

The fog was gone.

"Nothing," Michelle said. "I was just looking to see if you were working."

"Mmm," June said noncommittally. Then: "How did it go at school?"

"All right." Michelle finished her glass of milk and struggled to her feet, her hip throbbing. She picked up her bookbag and started toward the butler's pantry.

"I thought you might bring Sally home with you this afternoon," June suggested.

"She—she had some things she had to do," Michelle lied. "Besides, I wanted to walk by myself."

"You mean Jeff didn't even walk with you?"

"He did for a while. He walked Susan Peterson home, then caught up with me."

June looked sharply at Michelle. There was something her daughter wasn't telling her. Michelle's face was guileless. And yet June was positive she was hiding something, holding something back. "You're sure nothing went wrong?" she pressed.

"It was *fine*, Mother." There was a hint of irritation in Michelle's voice, so June decided to drop the subject.

"Want to help me with the bread?"

Michelle considered it for a moment, then shook her head. "I've got a lot to catch up on. I think I'd better go up to my room."

June let her go, then returned to her bread dough. As she worked, her eyes drifted outside to the studio.

What was it? What did she see in there? Something that frightened her, I'm sure of it. She pulled her fingers loose from the dough, wiped them off on her apron, then left the house. Whatever Michelle had seen, it must still be in the studio. . . .

Michelle closed her bedroom door, and sank onto the bed. She wondered if she should have told her mother about the people in the studio. But something had told her not to. What she had seen was a secret. A secret between her and Amanda. But it had been scary. Even as she remembered it, a shiver went through her body.

She got up from the bed and went to the window seat, picking up the doll that was propped there. She raised the doll to eye level, and gazed into its china face.

"What do you want, Amanda?" she asked softly. "What do you want me to do?"

"I want you to show me things," the voice whispered in her ear. "I want you to show me things, and be my friend."

"But what do you want to see? How can I show you things if I don't know what you want to see?"

"I want to see things that happened a long time ago. Things I could never see then . . . I've been waiting for you for so long—for a while I didn't think I'd ever be able to see. I tried. I tried to get other people to show me, but they never could. And then you came . . ."

The whispering was interrupted by a sound.

"What's that?" the voice whispered.

"Just Jenny. She's crying." From the nursery down the hall, the wails of the baby increased. Michelle waited a moment, sure she would hear her mother's tread on the stairs. Then the voice whispered to her again.

"Show her to me."

"The baby?"

"I want to see her."

Jennifer's cries had turned into a squalling sob. Michelle went to the door.

"Mom?" There was no response.

"Mom, Jenny's crying!" When there was still no response, Michelle started down the hall toward the nursery. She was sure Amanda was with her, beside her: though she could see nothing, she could feel a presence. She decided she liked that feeling.

She opened the door to the nursery. Jennifer's cries were suddenly louder. Michelle picked up the crying baby, cradling it against her chest as she had been taught by her mother.

"Isn't she beautiful?" she whispered to Amanda.

"Do something to her," Amanda whispered back.

"Do something? Why?"

"She's like the others . . . she's not your friend . . ."

"She's my sister," Michelle protested uncertainly.

"No, she isn't," Amanda told her. "She's *their* daughter, not *your* sister. They love her, not you."

"That isn't true."

"It is true. You know it's true. You have to do something." The whisper became intense, urging Michelle, commanding her.

She looked down into the face of the baby, saw Jenny's tiny features, grimacing with unhappiness, and suddenly, unreasonably, she wanted to squeeze her, wanted to make her stop crying, wanted to punish her.

Her arms tightened, and she pressed Jennifer against her chest.

Jennifer's screams took on a note of pain.

Michelle squeezed harder. Jenny's cries seemed to fade away, and the sound of Amanda's voice grew louder.

"That's right," the voice crooned in her ear. "Harder. Squeeze her harder . . ."

Jenny's eyes began to bulge in her head, and her little arms flailed as she tried to breathe. The wailing was growing softer, turning into a whimper.

"Just a little more . . ." the voice whispered.

And then June appeared at the nursery door. "Michelle? Michelle, what's happening?"

It was as if a switch had been turned. The voice in Michelle's head was gone. She stared first at her mother, then down into Jennifer's face. She realized she was squeezing the baby, squeezing it so hard, she was hurting it. She relaxed the pressure. Jennifer suddenly stopped crying and gasped a little. The slight bluish cast to her skin faded, and her eyes seemed to ease back to a normal position. "I—I heard her crying," Michelle said. "When you didn't come up, I came in to see what was wrong. All I did was pick her up . . ."

June took Jenny, who had once more begun to sob, and cuddled her against her breast.

"I was out in the studio. I couldn't hear her. But it's all right now." She stroked the crying Jennifer, and made soothing noises. "I'll take care of her," she told Michelle. "You go on back to your room. Okay?"

For a moment, Michelle hesitated. She didn't want to go back to her room. She wanted to stay here, with her mother and her sister.

Amanda's voice came back to her, reminding her that Jennifer was not her sister. And this woman was not her mother. Not *really*. Her mind filled with confused images and thoughts, Michelle limped out of the nursery, made her way down the hall to her room.

She lay on the bed, cradling her doll in her arms, staring at the ceiling.

It was all starting to make sense to her now. . . .

Amanda was right.

She was alone.

Except for Amanda.

Amanda was her friend.

"I love you," she whispered to the doll. "I love you more than anything in the world."

When Cal came home that afternoon June was sitting in the kitchen, holding Jennifer on her lap, gazing out at the sea. He paused at the kitchen door, and watched them. The indirect light of the afternoon cast a soft glow over them, and for a moment Cal was overwhelmed by the beauty of the scene—the mother and child, *his* wife and daughter, with the window and the cove beyond framing them almost like a halo. But when June turned to face him, his feeling of well-being was shattered.

"Sit down, Cal. I have to talk to you." He didn't need to be told that she wanted to talk about Michelle.

"Something's wrong," June began. "It's more than her limp, and God knows that's bad enough. Something happened at school today, or after school. She wouldn't tell me what, but it frightened her."

"Well, it was her first day back—" Cal began, but June didn't let him finish.

"There's more. I was out in the studio this afternoon,

working. I heard Jenny crying, and when I went up to take care of her, Michelle was there. She was holding Jenny, and she had the strangest look on her face. As if she wasn't aware of what was going on. And she was squeezing Jenny. . . ." Her voice trailed off, the memory of the afternoon still vivid in her mind.

Cal remained silent for a moment. When he finally spoke, his voice was strained.

"What are you trying to say? You think something's wrong with Michelle?"

"We know something's wrong with her," June began, but this time Cal didn't let her finish.

"She fell, and she got bruised, and she's missed some school. But she's getting better every day."

"She's not getting better. You wish she were, but if you'd spend some time with her, you'd see that she's not the same girl she used to be." Against her will, June's voice began to rise. "Something's happening to her, Cal. She's turning into a recluse, spending all her time by herself with that damned doll, and I want to know why. And as for you, you're going to spend some time with her, Cal. You're going to go with me when I take her to school tomorrow, and you're going to go with me when I pick her up. And in the evenings, you're going to stop burying yourself in Jenny and your journals, and start paying some attention to Michelle. Is that clear?"

Cal stood up, his face dark, his eyes brooding. "Let me handle my life my own way, all right?"

"It's not your life," June shot back. "It's my life, and Michelle's life, and Jenny's life, too! I'm sorry about everything that's happened, and I wish I could help you. But my God, Cal, what about Michelle? She's a little girl and she needs us. We have to be there for her. Both of us!"

But Cal didn't hear her last words. He had already left the kitchen, hurrying down the hall to the living room, where he closed the door behind him, poured himself a drink, and tried to shut out his wife's words, accusing him, forever accusing him.

But the words would not be shut out.

He would have to prove her wrong.

Prove to her, and to himself, that everything was fine, that Michelle was all right. That *he* was all right.

That evening, after dinner, Michelle appeared in the living room, her chess set tucked under her arm.

"Daddy?"

Cal was sitting in his chair, reading a journal, while June sat opposite him, knitting. He made himself smile at his daughter. "Hmmm?"

"Want to play a game?" She rattled the box of chessmen.

Cal was about to beg off, when June shot him a look of warning. "Okay," he said without enthusiasm. "Set it up while I get a drink."

Michelle carefully lowered herself to the floor, her left leg sticking out awkwardly, and began setting up the chessboard. By the time her father returned, she had already made her first move. Cal settled himself on the floor.

Michelle waited.

He seemed to be studying the board, but Michelle wasn't sure. Finally, she spoke.

"It's your move, Daddy."

"Oh. Sorry." Automatically, Cal reached out to counter Michelle's opening. She frowned slightly and wondered what was wrong with her father's game. Tentatively, she began setting him up for a fool's mate.

Again, Cal sat silently staring at the board, sipping his drink, until Michelle reminded him that it was his move. When he made his play, Michelle looked up at him in astonishment. Didn't he see what she was up to? He'd never let her get away with this before. She advanced her queen.

June put her knitting aside, and came to look at the board. Seeing Michelle's strategy, she winked at her daughter, then waited for Cal to spoil the gambit. But Cal didn't seem aware of what was happening.

"Cal? It's your move."

He made no response.

"I don't think he cares," Michelle said quietly. Cal didn't appear to hear her. "Daddy," she said, "if you don't want to play, you don't have to."

"What?" Cal came out of his reverie, and reached out to make a move. Michelle, tempted by his lack of concentration, quickly set her trap and waited for her father to slip out of it. He'd been baiting her, she was sure of it. Now he'd come up with something smart, and the real fight would begin. She began to look forward to the rest of the game.

But Cal only drained his drink, listlessly made a useless move, and shrugged as Michelle slid her queen into position and announced the checkmate. "Set 'em up, and we'll do it again," he offered.

"Why?" Michelle asked. She stared at her father, her eyes stormy. "It isn't any fun if you aren't even going to try!" Quickly, she tossed the chessmen back in the box, struggled to her feet, and went upstairs.

As soon as she was gone, June spoke. "I suppose I

should give you credit for trying. Even if you didn't look at her, talk to her, or react to her, at least you sat across from her. How did it feel?"

Cal made no reply.

CHAPTER 15

Cal sat in his car for a long time after Michelle had disappeared into the school building. He watched the other children arriving, sturdy, healthy children, skipping through the autumn morning, laughing among themselves.

Or were they laughing at him?

He could see them glancing over at him every now and then. Sally Carstairs even waved to him. But then they would turn away, giggling and whispering among themselves, as if they somehow knew how frightened he was of them. But they couldn't know. They were only children, and he was a doctor. Someone to be trusted, and admired.

It was a sham, all of it. He neither trusted nor admired himself, and he was sure they knew it; he knew all about children's instincts—their ability to pick up the vibrations around them. Even tiny babies, carefully shielded from reality, react to tension between their parents. These children, the children whose health he was supposed to be responsible for—what did they think of him? Did they know what he was really like?

Did they know he was afraid of them?

Did they know that fear was turning to hatred?

He was sure they did.

A car pulled into the parking lot next to the school, and Cal saw Lisa Hartwick get out, glance at him, wave, then follow the last of the stragglers up the steps. He twisted the key in the ignition, put the car in gear, and was about to pull away when he saw a man waving to him. Lisa's father, apparently. Cal put the car in neutral, and waited.

"Dr. Pendleton?" Tim Hartwick was leaning down on the passenger side of Cal's car, his hand poking in through the window. "I'm Tim Hartwick."

Cal forced himself to smile genially and take the outstretched hand. "Of course. Lisa's father. You have a wonderful daughter."

"Even when she lies about being sick?"

"They all do it," Cal replied. "Even Michelle did her best to stay in bed a few extra days."

"But there was something wrong with Michelle," Tim reminded him. "Lisa was out-and-out faking. Thanks for not letting her get away with it."

Cal shrugged. "Actually, she owned up to it herself. I was about to stick a tongue depressor in her mouth, and she decided the truth was better than choking on the lie."

"How's Michelle getting along?" The question caught Cal off guard, and he hesitated for a second. Then, too quickly:

"Fine. She's doing just fine."

Tim Hartwick's brow furrowed. "I'm glad to hear it.

Corinne—Miss Hatcher, Michelle's teacher—was a little worried. Said something about yesterday being hard for Michelle. I thought I might have a chat with her."

"With Michelle? Why?"

"Well, I'm the psychologist for the school, and if one of the kids is having a problem—"

"Your own kid is the problem, Mr. Hartwick. She lies, remember? As for Michelle, she's fine. Just fine. Now, if you don't mind, I have some appointments waiting for me." Without waiting for a reply, he put the car in gear and drove away.

Tim Hartwick stood thoughtfully on the sidewalk, watching Cal's car disappear down the street. Obviously, the man was under strain. Too much strain. If Michelle was, indeed, having problems, Tim was sure he knew where they were rooted. He made a mental note to talk to Corinne about it, and, if necessary, Michelle's mother.

It was even worse today. Michelle felt like an outsider, a freak, and by the time the last bell rang, she was glad that her parents were coming to get her.

She made her way slowly down the hall. When she reached the front steps, all her classmates had disappeared. She halted at the top of the stairs and looked around.

There was still a group of little girls, the third-graders, playing with a jump rope. With her parents nowhere in sight, Michelle settled on the top step to watch them. Suddenly one of the little girls left the group, came to the bottom of the stairs, and looked up at Michelle.

"Do you want to play with us?"

Michelle frowned at the child. "I can't," she said.
"Why not?"

"I can't jump anymore."

The little girl appeared to consider this bit of information. Then she brightened.

"Well, you could turn the rope, couldn't you? That way I'd have more turns."

Michelle thought it over. The little girl didn't seem to be making fun of her. Finally, she stood up. "Okay. But promise me you won't ask me to try to jump."

"I won't. My name's Annie Whitmore. What's yours?"

"Michelle."

Annie waited while Michelle came slowly down the stairs.

"Did you hurt yourself?"

"I fell off the bluff out by the cove," Michelle said. She watched Annie carefully, but the child's eyes held nothing but curiosity.

"Did it hurt?"

"I guess so," Michelle replied. "I don't remember. I fainted."

Now Annie's eyes fairly bulged with excitement. "Really?" she breathed. "What was it like?"

Michelle grinned at the wide-eyed child. "I don't know—I was out cold!"

With that, Annie ran off, skipping ahead of her, and rejoined her group of friends. As Michelle approached the little girls, she could hear Annie saying excitedly:

"Her name's Michelle. She fell off the bluff, and fainted, and she can't jump, but she's going to turn the rope for us. Isn't that neat?"

Now all the little girls stared at Michelle. For a

moment she was afraid they were going to laugh at her.

They didn't.

Instead, they seemed to think she was lucky to have something so exciting happen to her. A few minutes later she was standing with her back braced against a tree, turning the rope, and chanting the rhymes along with the rest of them.

June had let the silence between her husband and herself remain unbroken as they drove into Paradise Point. She could sense Cal's hostility, and didn't need to hear him tell her that he thought she was being foolish. Only when they were in front of the school did he say anything, and when he spoke, his voice was triumphant.

"Take a look at that, will you? And tell me if you think she's a 'recluse.'" He spat the word out as if it was something bitter.

June followed his gaze and saw Michelle, leaning against a tree, merrily swinging the rope for the younger children. They could hear her voice, louder than the others, carrying across the schoolyard:

"Call for the doctor,
 Call for the nurse,
 Call for the lady
 With the alligator purse . . ."

She stared at the scene, almost unable to believe what she was seeing. *I was wrong*, she told herself. *Everything's going to be just fine. I was overreacting.* Today, in the clear sunlight of the fall afternoon, everything seemed perfectly normal.

Michelle saw them, waved, and handed her end of the rope to Annie Whitmore. She started toward them. When she reached the car, she paused, a smile lighting her face.

"Hi! What took you so long? I was getting worried. But not *very* worried." She climbed into the backseat of the car.

"Everything's fine, honey," Cal said. "Nothing for you to worry about."

But as he spoke, June wondered. His voice, though she knew he was trying to control it, was shaking. Not much, but enough so she knew he was lying. Her worries flooded back to her—perhaps Michelle *was* getting better. But was her husband?

Michelle turned restlessly in her sleep, moaned a little, then woke up.

It wasn't a slow waking, the kind that makes you wonder for a few moments if you're still asleep. It was, rather, the instant awakening that comes with a disturbance, an unusual sound in the night.

And yet, there had been no sound.

She lay very still, listening.

She could hear only the steady crashing of the sea against the bluff, and an occasional rustling as the autumn winds brushed branches against the house.

And Amanda's voice.

The sound was comforting to Michelle. She snuggled deeper into the bed, listening.

"Come with me," Mandy whispered.

Then, more urgently: "Come outside with me."

Michelle threw off the covers and got out of bed. She went to the window and looked out.

The moon was nearly full, casting an ethereal glow

on the sea. Michelle let her eyes wander over the scene. Finally they came to rest on the studio, sitting small and lonely on its perch at the edge of the bluff. Then, as her eyes remained fixed on the studio, a cloud seemed to pass over the moon, obscuring her sight.

"Come on," Mandy whispered. "We have to go outside."

Michelle could feel Mandy pulling at her. She pulled on her robe, tying it snugly at the waist, put on her slippers, then left her room, walking slowly, carefully, listening to Amanda's voice.

In her room, her cane was still propped next to her bed.

She moved through the darkened house and went out by the back door. Steadily, Mandy's voice guiding her, she walked across the lawn and let herself into her mother's studio.

A canvas, the seascape her mother had been working on for so long, stood on the easel. Michelle stared at it in the gloom, its colors faded to shades of gray, the whitecaps appearing as strange points of light in the foreboding picture.

She felt herself being drawn away from the easel, and moved toward the closet. "What is it?" she asked, her voice barely audible.

She opened the closet door and stepped inside.

"Make me a picture," Amanda whispered to her.

Obediently, Michelle reached for a canvas and took it to the easel. Setting her mother's painting on the floor, she replaced it with the canvas she had brought from the closet.

"A picture of what?" she asked.

In the darkness there was a silence, then Amanda's voice, suddenly clearer, spoke to her once more.

"What you showed me. Make me a picture of what you showed me."

Michelle picked up a piece of charcoal and began sketching.

She could feel Amanda's presence behind her, watching over her shoulder as she worked.

She drew quickly, as if some unseen force was guiding her hand.

The figures emerged on the canvas.

First the woman, just the bare outlines, her limbs stretched languidly on a studio couch.

Then the man, above her, caressing her.

Michelle began to feel a certain excitement as she drew, an energy flowing into her from the presence at her shoulder.

"Yes," Amanda whispered. "That's the way it was . . . I can see it now. For the first time, I can really see it. . . ."

An hour later Michelle took the canvas off the easel, put it back in the closet, and replaced her mother's picture exactly as it had been before.

When she left the studio, there was no sign that she had ever been there. No sign at all, except the charcoal sketch buried in the jumble at the back of the closet.

When she woke up the next morning, Michelle wondered why she still felt tired.

She had slept well that night.

She was sure she had.

And yet she felt tired, and her hip was throbbing with pain.

CHAPTER 16

June's eyes filled with concern as Michelle came into the kitchen. In silence, she noted the pronounced increase in her daughter's limp. There was a tiredness in the child's eyes that worried her.

"Are you all right this morning?"

"I'm all right," Michelle replied. "My hip hurts, that's all."

"Maybe you shouldn't go to school," June suggested.

"I can go. I'll ride in with Daddy again, and if my hip isn't better this afternoon, I'll call you. Okay?"

"But if you're too tired . . ."

"I'm all right," Michelle insisted.

Cal glanced up from the newspaper he was reading, and gave June a look of warning, as if to say, *If she says she's fine, she's fine—don't push it.* Reading the look, June turned her attention to the eggs she was scrambling. Michelle eased herself into a chair opposite her father.

"When are you going to finish the pantry?"

"When I get to it. There isn't any hurry."

"I could help you," Michelle offered.

"We'll see." Though Cal's voice was noncommittal, Michelle could feel his rejection of her offer. She opened her mouth to protest, then thought better of it. She decided to drop the subject.

Upstairs, Jenny began crying. At the stove, June glanced upward, then turned to her husband and daughter. "Michelle, do you think you could . . . ?"

But Cal was already on his feet, starting toward the stairs. "I'll take care of her. Be back in a minute."

June watched as Michelle's eyes followed her father out of the kitchen, but when her daughter's gaze shifted and she seemed about to speak, June quickly busied herself with the eggs. There just wasn't anything she could do. She felt helpless, and inadequate, and angry—at herself, and at Cal.

"Here's my girl," Cal said as he returned to the kitchen, Jenny cradled in his arm. He seated himself at the table and began bouncing the baby gently, making her laugh and gurgle with pleasure.

"Can I hold her?" Michelle asked.

Cal glanced at her, then shook his head. "She's happy where she is. Isn't she beautiful?"

Without answering, Michelle suddenly rose from the table.

"I forgot something upstairs. Call me when it's time to go, okay?" Cal nodded absently, still engrossed in Jennifer.

"That was cruel," June said when Michelle was gone from the kitchen.

"What was?" Cal looked up from the baby, surprised at the expression on June's face. What had he done?

"Couldn't you have at least let her hold Jenny?"

"I beg your pardon?" Cal's baffled look told her that he hadn't the vaguest idea of what she was talking about.

"Oh, never mind," she said. She began serving the eggs.

As they drove into Paradise Point that morning, neither Cal nor Michelle spoke. It was not a comfortable silence, not the kind of close, companionable silence they had enjoyed back in Boston; instead, it was as if there were a gulf between them. A gulf that was growing wider, which neither of them knew how to bridge.

Sally Carstairs tried not to listen as Susan Peterson's voice droned on.

They were sitting under the maple, eating their lunch, and it seemed to Sally that Susan just wouldn't shut up. It had been going on now for nearly fifteen minutes.

"You'd think she'd go to another school," Susan had begun. They'd all known whom she was talking about, since her eyes were fixed on Michelle, sitting by herself at the top of the steps. "I mean, do we really have to look at her, gimping around like some kind of a freak? Why don't they send her to one of those schools for special children? If you can call retarded special."

"She's not retarded," Sally objected. "She's just lame."

"What's the difference?" Susan said airily. "If you're a freak, you're a freak."

She went on, her voice vibrant with malice, listing her objections to Michelle's being in the some school with the rest of them, let alone the same classroom.

Sally kept trying not to listen, but Susan's voice was like a bee buzzing in her ear. Every few seconds, she glanced over to see if Michelle could hear what Susan was saying, but Michelle seemed to be ignoring them. Then, just as Sally decided she'd heard enough, and was about to get up and go over to Michelle, she saw Annie Whitmore run up to her. She could see the two of them talking, then Annie took Michelle by the hand, and started pulling her to her feet. As the rest of the group under the maple became aware of what was happening, Susan's voice fell silent. They watched as Annie led Michelle down the steps, then walked with her to a spot a few yards away, where the rest of the third-graders were gathered. A moment later Michelle was holding one end of the jump rope, Annie the other, and the littler girls were starting to take their turns in the middle.

"Don't tell *me* she's not retarded," Susan Peterson said. Around her, her group of friends began to giggle.

Michelle tried to ignore the sounds, telling herself that they were laughing at something else. But she knew it wasn't true. She could feel them: looking at her, whispering among themselves, laughing. As the first twinge of anger knotted her stomach, she tightened her grip on the jump rope and forced herself to concentrate on Annie Whitmore, whose feet were lightly skipping in rhythm to the chant as she began her turn.

But as the laughter from Susan Peterson's group increased, Michelle found it more and more difficult to ignore it. Her anger grew; she could feel her face growing hot. She closed her eyes for a moment, hoping that by shutting her classmates out of her vision, she could shut them out of her mind.

When she opened her eyes again, something seemed to have happened. The sun, so bright a moment before, was fading into a gray mist. And yet, it was too early in the day for the fog to be coming in. The fog always came in late afternoon, not lunchtime. . . .

In her ears, Susan Peterson's taunts grew louder, carrying through the mist, tormenting her.

Turn the rope, she told herself. Just turn the rope, and pretend nothing's happening.

Her vision was fading rapidly, and soon she was aware of nothing but the rope in her hand. She increased the tempo of the chant, turning the rope faster to keep up with the rhythm.

The happy grin on Annie's face began to fade as she tried to keep up with Michelle's suddenly furious pace. She skipped faster and faster, and soon gave up using the little intermediate hop that filled the time between the rope's rotations. She was jumping now, facing Michelle, trying to make up her mind whether she should keep going or try to run out. But the rope was going too fast: she couldn't run out, nor could she keep up.

The rope slashed against her ankles, and Annie screamed in pain, tripping, stumbling to the ground.

It was the scream that got through to Michelle.

Drowning out the laughter from Susan Peterson, it cut through the fog, piercing the mist like a shaft of lightning.

The rope, jerked from her hand when it hit Annie, lay at Michelle's feet. She couldn't remember dropping it, couldn't remember what, exactly, had happened.

But there was Annie, rubbing her ankle and looking at Michelle with more reproach than fear.

"Why did you do that?" Annie demanded. "I can't do hot peppers."

"I'm sorry," Michelle said. She took a step forward, but Annie seemed to shrink away from her. "I didn't mean to turn it so fast. Really, I didn't. Are you all right?"

Again she moved toward Annie, and the little girl, seeing nothing but concern in Michelle's face now, let herself be helped up.

"It hurts," she wailed. "It stings!" A welt was rising on her leg, and she rubbed at it once more before getting to her feet. A small crowd had gathered, watching curiously, pointing first to Annie, then to Michelle. As Susan Peterson approached, Michelle hobbled away as quickly as she could. She was at the foot of the steps when she heard Sally Carstairs's voice behind her.

"Michelle? What happened?"

Michelle turned to face Sally. Though there was nothing but curiosity in Sally's eyes, Michelle was distrustful. After all, only a few moments ago Sally had been under the maple with Susan and the rest of them.

"Nothing," she said. "I just turned the rope a little too fast, and Annie tripped."

Sally watched her carefully as she spoke, and wondered if Michelle was telling the truth. But as the bell rang calling them back from lunch, she decided not to press Michelle. "Do you want me to walk back in with you?" she asked.

"No," Michelle replied, her voice sharp. "I just want you to leave me alone!" Hurt, Sally stepped backward, then hurried up the steps. By the time Michelle regretted her words, it was too late—Sally was already inside the building. Slowly, Michelle started up the stairs, relieved to see the rest of the children streaming past her, chattering among themselves, the incident with Annie forgotten.

"I saw what you did," Susan Peterson hissed in her ear.

Startled, Michelle nearly lost her balance and had to grab at the railing to keep from falling.

"What?"

"I saw it," Susan said, her eyes glistening with malice. "I saw you deliberately try to trip Annie, and I'm going to tell Miss Hatcher. You'll probably get expelled!" Without waiting for a reply, she hurried inside. Michelle, suddenly alone in the schoolyard, paused and looked back at the playground, as if she might somehow see what had really happened. She hadn't done it on purpose. She was sure she hadn't. But she couldn't really remember what *had* happened, until Annie Whitmore had screamed. Sighing heavily, she started up the steps once more. *I wish she were dead*, she thought. *I wish Susan Peterson were dead!* As she reached the top of the steps, Michelle paused. In her head, she could hear Amanda's voice, very soft, talking to her.

"I'll kill her," Mandy whispered. "If she tells, I'll kill her. . . ."

June settled Jennifer into her bassinet, carefully tucked a blanket around her, then turned to her easel, and surveyed the seascape. It was nearly finished. Time to start on something else. She opened the closet door, pulled the string that hung from the naked bulb just inside and reached for the closest canvas. Its size didn't suit her, and she went further into the closet, rummaging through the tangle of frames and canvases stacked haphazardly at the back. Finally she saw one that suited her and pulled it loose from the rest.

It wasn't until she had it out in the studio that she realized it wasn't blank.

She stared at the charcoal sketch, frowning. She couldn't remember having done the sketch, and yet she must have. She set the canvas up on the easel, then stepped back and looked at it once more.

It was strange.

The sketch, two nude figures making love, was not bad.

But it was not hers.

The style was wrong, and the subject matter.

Over the years she had sketched dozens of canvases, then, displeased with them, set them aside, intending either to do them over, or clean them off. Invariably, when she came across one of them, she remembered the picture, or at least recognized it as her own—her technique, or a subject that interested her.

But this was different. The strokes were bold, bolder than her own, and more primitive. And yet the figures were good—the proportions were right, and they almost seemed to move on the canvas. But who could have done them?

The work had to be hers. It had to! And yet, she couldn't remember it at all. She was about to clean the canvas, when she changed her mind. Feeling strangely uneasy, she put it back into the closet.

Michelle began gathering her books together, keeping her eyes on the floor as the rest of the class hurried out into the corridor. The afternoon had been miserable for her: she had waited in agony for the recess period. She was sure Miss Hatcher would want to talk to her. But recess had come and gone, and Miss Hatcher had said nothing. Now the day had passed. She got to her feet, picked up her cane, and faced the door.

"Michelle? Would you wait a minute please?"

Slowly she turned to the teacher. Miss Hatcher was looking at her, but she didn't seem angry. Instead, she seemed worried.

"Michelle, what happened at lunchtime today?"

"Y-you mean with Annie?"

Corinne Hatcher nodded. "I understand there was an accident." Her voice sounded concerned, but not angry. Michelle let herself relax a little.

"I turned the rope too fast, I guess. Annie tripped, and the rope hit her leg. But she said she's all right."

"But how did it happen?" Miss Hatcher pressed. Michelle wished she knew what Susan Peterson had told her.

"It—it just happened," Michelle said helplessly. "I guess I just wasn't paying attention." She paused, then hesitantly asked a question. "What did Susan say?"

"Nothing much. Just that she saw Annie get hit by the rope."

"She said I did it on purpose, didn't she?"

"Why would she say that?" Corinne countered. It was exactly what Susan *had* said.

"She said I was going to get expelled for it." Michelle's voice was quavering, and she was struggling to hold back her tears.

"Well, even if you'd done it on purpose, I don't think we'd expel you for it. Maybe make you write 'I won't trip Annie Whitmore' on the blackboard a hundred times. But since it was an accident, it doesn't seem to require punishment, does it?"

"You mean you believe me?" Michelle breathed.

"Of course I do." The last of the tension went out of Michelle. Things were going to be all right after all. Now she looked beseechingly at Miss Hatcher.

"Miss Hatcher, why would Susan say I did that on purpose?" she asked.

Because she's a mean, nasty little liar, Corinne thought to herself. "Sometimes some people see things differently from others," she said evenly. "That's why it's important to find out what other people say about things. For instance, Sally Carstairs said you didn't do anything deliberately. She said it was an accident, too."

Michelle nodded. "It *was* an accident. I wouldn't hurt Annie—I like her. And she likes me."

"Everybody likes you, Michelle." Corinne reached out and patted her shoulder affectionately. "Just give everyone a chance, and you'll see."

Michelle avoided her eyes. "Can I go now?" she asked.

"Of course. Is your mother picking you up?"

"I can walk." The way Michelle said it made Corinne think it was almost a challenge.

"I'm sure you can," she agreed gently. Michelle started toward the door, but again Corinne stopped her.

"Michelle." The child stopped, but didn't turn around, forcing Corinne to talk to her back. "Michelle, what happened to you was an accident, too. You mustn't be angry about it, or blame anybody. It was an accident, just like what happened to Annie today."

"I know." Her voice was dull, the words sounding like an automatic response.

"And the children will get used to you. With the older ones, it will just take a little while, that's all. They'll stop making fun of you."

"Will they?" Michelle asked. But she didn't wait for an answer.

By the time she emerged from the school building, the grounds were deserted. Michelle limped slowly along, half glad there was no one to see her, half disappointed there was no one to talk to. She had almost expected Sally to be waiting for her. But why should she? Michelle reflected. Why should Sally waste her time on a cripple?

She tried to tell herself that what Miss Hatcher had said was true, that soon her classmates would get used to her limp and find something else to talk about, someone else to laugh at. But as she walked, her hip hurting her more with each step, she knew it wasn't true. She wasn't going to get better—she was going to get worse.

She paused when she got to the bluff road and leaned on her cane for a while, looking at the sea, watching the gulls soar effortlessly on the wind.

She wished she were a bird, so she could fly, too, fly high above the sea, fly away, far away, and never see anybody again. But she couldn't fly, she would never even be able to run again.

She started on, her limp more pronounced than ever. As she passed the graveyard, she heard the voice:

"Cripple . . . cripple . . . cripple!"

Even before she looked, she knew who it was. She stood still, then finally turned to face Susan Peterson.

"Stop that."

"Why?" Susan called, her voice mocking. "What are you going to do about it? *Cripple!*"

"You're not supposed to be in the cemetery," Michelle said, trying to put down the anger that was rising in her.

"I can go where I want to, and do what I want," Susan taunted. "I'm not gimpy, like *some* people are!"

The words rang in Michelle's ears, stinging, hurting, cutting into her. Her anger swelled inside her, and once more the fog began closing in around her.

But now, with the fog, came Amanda.

She could feel Amanda before she heard her, feel her presence next to her, supporting her. And then Mandy began whispering to her.

"Don't let her say things like that," Mandy said. "Make her be quiet. Make her keep her mouth shut!"

Michelle started into the cemetery, her feet tangling in the weeds, her cane more a hindrance than a help. But she could feel Mandy beside her, steadying her, urging her on.

And through the fog, she could see Susan Peterson's face, her grin gone, her laughter dying on her lips.

"What are you doing?" she whispered. "Don't you come near me."

Michelle kept going, dragging her lame leg, her pain forgotten, striking out with her cane at the brambles and rocks in her path, ignoring Susan's words, listening only to Mandy's encouragements.

Susan began backing away as Michelle approached.

"Get away from me," she cried. "Leave me alone. *You leave me alone!*" Her face contorted into a mask of fear, she turned suddenly, and began running away across the graveyard, fleeing into the swirling gray mists. Relentlessly, Michelle started after her.

"Stay here," Amanda whispered to her. "You stay here, and let me do it. I *want* to do it . . ."

And then she, too, was gone, and Michelle was suddenly alone, standing in the overgrown cemetery, resting on her cane, the damp grayness of the fog drifting around her.

The scream, when it came, was muffled, floating through the fog almost softly. Then, once more, there was only silence.

Michelle stood still, listening, waiting. When she heard Amanda's voice again, she could feel the strange child close to her once more, almost inside her.

"I did it," Mandy whispered. "I told you I would, and I did."

The words echoing in her head, Michelle started slowly homeward. By the time she reached the old house, the sun was shining brightly again from a clear autumn sky, and the only sound she heard was the crying of the gulls.

CHAPTER 17

It had been a quiet day at the clinic. The last patient had left, and now the two of them were alone. Josiah produced a bottle of bourbon from his desk drawer and poured two glasses. This was one of his favorite rituals—an afternoon drink on quiet days.

"Anything new at home?" he asked casually.

"I'm not sure what you mean," Cal replied.

You're a cool one, Carson thought to himself. *But it's getting to you. I can see it in your eyes.* When he spoke, he kept his voice friendly. "I was thinking about Michelle. Any new ideas about what's causing that lameness?"

Before Cal could answer, the telephone jangled from the outer office. Carson cursed softly.

"Isn't that the way—the nurse takes off, and the phone rings," he commented. He made no move to answer it, so Cal reached over and picked it up.

"Clinic," he said.

"Is Dr. Carson there?" an agitated voice demanded. Cal was sure he recognized the caller.

"This is Dr. Pendleton, Mrs. Benson. Can I help you?"

"I asked for Dr. Carson," Constance Benson snapped, her irritation amplifying her voice. "Is he there?"

Cal covered the mouthpiece as he handed Josiah the phone. "Constance Benson. She's upset, and she'll only talk to you."

Josiah took the phone. "Constance? What's the problem?"

Cal watched Josiah's face as the old doctor listened to Mrs. Benson. As Carson paled, fear began to build in Cal. "We'll be right there," he heard Carson say. "Don't do anything—anything you might try to do could only make things worse." He hung up the phone, and stood up.

"Has something happened to Jeff?"

Carson shook his head. "Susan Peterson. Call an ambulance, and let's get going. I'll tell you about it on the way."

"I hope to God the ambulance gets here in time," Cal said darkly.

They were speeding out of town, and the tires on his car squealed as he turned south onto the cove road.

"I doubt we'll need it," Carson replied, his face set in grim lines. "If what Constance said is true, there won't be much we can do."

"But what happened?" Cal demanded.

"Susan fell off the cliff. Except that from what Con-

stance said, she didn't exactly fall. Constance said she
ran over the edge."

"Ran? You mean—*ran?*" Cal floundered. What
could she have meant?

"That's it. Unless I didn't get the story straight. I
may not have—she's pretty upset."

Before Carson could tell Cal all of what Constance
had said, they arrived at the Bensons'. Constance was
waiting for them on the porch, her face pale, her
hands nervously wringing at her apron.

"She's on the beach," she called as they were getting
out of the car. "Please—hurry! I don't know if—if—"
Her voice trailed off helplessly. Josiah started toward
her, telling Cal to go down to the beach and see what
he could do for Susan Peterson.

"There's a path behind the house. It's the fastest way
down, and Susan should be about a hundred yards
south."

Automatically, Cal's eyes scanned the bluff to the
south. "You mean by the graveyard?" he asked.

Josiah nodded. "Don't be surprised by what you
find—the bluff drops straight down there."

Cal grabbed his bag and started around the house.
Already, he could feel the panic gripping him. He
fought it off, repeating to himself, over and over
again, *She's already dead. I can't hurt her. I can't do
anything to her. She's already dead.* As he drove the
words into his consciousness, the panic began to sub-
side.

The path, very much like the one on his own prop-
erty, was steep and rough, making several switchbacks
as it wound down to the beach. Half running, half
sliding, Cal made his way down the trail, his mind
involuntarily summoning up another afternoon, only

five weeks ago, when he had also run down a path to the beach.

Today he wouldn't make the same mistakes he had made then.

Today, he would do what had to be done, and do it right.

Except that today, there was nothing to be done.

He reached the beach, and finally was able to increase his pace to a run. When he'd covered fifty yards, he saw her, ahead of him, lying still.

Knowing there was no use in hurrying, he slowed to a trot, then walked the last few steps.

Susan Peterson, her neck broken, her head twisted around in a violently unnatural angle, stared blindly up at the sky, her eyes open, an expression of terror still contorting her features. Her arms and legs, spread limply around her, looked grotesque in their uselessness. The incoming tide was lapping hungrily at her, as if the sea were eager to devour the strange piece of wreckage that had only a little while ago been a twelve-year-old child.

Cal knelt beside her, and picked up her wrist, pressed his stethoscope to her chest. It was a useless exercise, merely verifying what he already knew.

He was about to pick her up when something stopped him. His muscles froze, refusing to obey the commands his brain was sending them. He stood up slowly, his eyes fixed on Susan's face, but his mind seeing Michelle's.

I can't move her, he thought. *If I move her, I could hurt her.*

The thought was irrational, and Cal knew it was irrational. And yet, as he stood on the beach, alone with the remains of Susan Peterson, he couldn't bring himself to pick her up, to carry her up the trail as he had carried his own daughter so short a time ago. His mind numb with shame, Cal started back up the beach, leaving Susan alone with the flowing tide.

"She's dead."

Cal uttered the words in a matter-of-fact tone, the sort of voice he might have used to announce the death of a cat to an owner who had brought the animal to him for destruction.

"Dear God," Constance Benson muttered, sinking into a chair in her living room. "Who's going to tell Estelle?"

"I will" was Josiah Carson's automatic response, though his eyes were fixed on Cal. "You didn't bring her up?"

"I thought we'd better wait for the ambulance," he lied, knowing he wasn't fooling the old doctor. "Her neck's broken and it looks like a few other things are, too." His attention shifted to Constance Benson. "What happened? Josiah said she ran off the bluff." He stumbled a little on the word *ran*, as if he still found it difficult to believe such a thing could have happened.

Constance did not answer. Instead, she looked to Josiah Carson, who nodded his head slightly. "I think you'd better tell him," he said. Cal felt a twinge of fear go through him, and knew before Mrs. Benson began that there was going to be something more to the story, something terrible. Even so, he wasn't prepared for what he heard.

"I was at the sink, paring some apples," Constance Benson said. She kept her eyes fixed on a spot on the floor, as if to look at either of the doctors would make it impossible for her to repeat the story. "I was sort of looking out the window, the way you do, and I saw Susan Peterson in the graveyard. I don't know what she was doing—I've told Estelle she should keep Susan away from there, just like I told your wife she should keep Michelle away, but I guess they just don't listen to me. Well, maybe now they will.

"Anyway, I was sort of half watching my apples, and half watching Susan, not really paying much attention. Then all of a sudden Michelle came down the road. Susan must have said something to her, because she stopped, and sort of stared at Susan."

"What did she say?" Cal asked. For the first time since she had begun her recitation, Constance glanced up from the floor.

"I couldn't hear. The window was closed, and it's quite a distance to the cemetery. But they were talking, all right, and Susan must have wanted to show Michelle something, because Michelle started to go into the graveyard. Climbed right over the fence, the weeds almost tripping her—how she did it with that limp of hers is beyond me, but she did. Susan waited for her, at least that's what it looked like. Except for what happened next. That's the part I can't understand at all."

She paused, shaking her head, as if she were trying to fit the pieces of a puzzle together, and they just wouldn't go.

"Well, what happened?" Cal urged her.

"It was the darnedest thing," Constance mused. Then she fixed a cold eye on Cal. "Michelle must have said something to Susan. I couldn't hear it, of course, but whatever it was, it must have been something pretty awful. Because all of a sudden Susan got a look on her face such as I hope I never see again. Fear, that's what it was. Plain old outright fear."

A picture of Susan flashed across Cal's memory. The look Constance Benson had described tallied exactly with the expression Cal had seen on the dead child's face.

"And then she took off running," he heard Mrs. Benson saying. "Just took off, like she was being chased by the devil himself. She ran right over the edge of the bluff."

The last words were whispered, barely audible, but they hung in the living room, chilling the atmosphere.

"She ran off the edge of the bluff?" Cal repeated dully, as if he couldn't believe his ears. "Was she watching where she was going? She couldn't have been."

"She was. She was looking straight ahead, but she didn't even pause."

"My God," Cal said, his eyes closing in a futile effort to blot out the image he was seeing. Then he remembered that his own daughter had also seen what had happened. He opened his eyes again. Almost apprehensively, he faced Constance Benson.

"And what about Michelle? What did she do?"

Constance Benson's face hardened, and she glared at him coldly. "Nothing," she said, spitting the word at him.

"What do you mean, nothing?" Cal asked, ignoring her tone. "She must have done *something*."

"She just stood there. She just stood there, like she didn't even see what happened. And then, when Susan screamed, she waited a minute, then started walking home."

Cal stood rooted to the floor, unable to move, unable to absorb what the woman was saying. "I don't believe it," he said finally.

"You can believe it or not, as you see fit," Constance Benson said. "But it's God's own truth, and that's that. She acted like nothing had happened at all."

Cal turned to Josiah Carson, as if to appeal to him, but Josiah was lost in thought. As Cal spoke his name, he came back to reality. He reached out and squeezed Cal's arm, but when he spoke, his voice was strange, as if he was thinking about something else. "Maybe you'd better go on home," he said. "I can take care of things here. You'd better go see if Michelle is all right. She could be in shock, you know."

Cal nodded mutely and started out of the room. He paused a moment, turned back as if to say something. At the chilly expression on Constance Benson's face, he seemed to change his mind. Then he was gone.

Josiah Carson and Constance Benson waited in silence until the ambulance had arrived. Then, as Carson was about to take his leave, Constance suddenly spoke.

"I don't like that man," she said.

"Now, Constance, you don't even know him."

"And I don't want to. I think he made a mistake, bringing his family out here." She fixed Carson with a look that was very nearly belligerent. "And I don't think you did him any favor either, selling him that house. You should have torn that place down years ago."

Now Carson's own expression hardened. "You're being silly, Constance, and you know it. That house didn't have anything to do with what's happened out here."

"Didn't it?" Constance turned away from Josiah and went to the window, where she stood staring out across the cemetery. In the distance, etched against the sky, were the ornate, Victorian lines of the Pendleton house.

"Don't see how they can live there," Constance muttered. "Even you couldn't live there, after Alan Hanley. It doesn't make sense. If I were June Pendleton, I'd pack up my clothes, take my baby, and get out while I still could."

"Well, I'm sorry you feel that way," Josiah said stiffly. "I happen to think you're wrong, and I'm glad the Pendletons are here. And I hope they'll stay, in spite of what's happened. Now I'd better go see Estelle and Henry Peterson." As he left her house, without saying good-bye, she was still standing at her window, staring into the distance, keeping her own counsel.

Cal ran up the steps onto the front porch, opened the door, then slammed it behind him.

"Cal? Is that you?" June's voice from the living room sounded startled, but not as startled as Cal felt when he found her calmly sitting in a chair, working on a piece of needlepoint.

"My God," he swore. "What are you doing? How can you just sit there? Where's Michelle?"

June gaped at him, surprised by his strangled tone.

"I'm doing needlework," she said uncertainly. "And why shouldn't I be sitting here? Michelle's upstairs in her room."

"I don't believe it," Cal said.

"What don't you believe? Cal, what's going on?"

Cal sank into a chair, trying to put his thoughts in order. Suddenly nothing made any sense.

"When did Michelle come home?" he asked at last.

"About forty-five minutes ago, maybe an hour." June set her needlepoint aside. "Cal, has something happened?"

"I can't believe it," Cal muttered. "I just can't believe it."

"Can't believe *what*?" June demanded. "Will you please tell me?"

"Didn't Michelle tell you what happened today?"

"She didn't say much of anything," June replied. "She came in, had a glass of milk, said school went 'okay'—which I'm not sure I believe—then went upstairs."

"Jesus!" It was crazy, like a nightmare. "Michelle must have said something. She *must* have!"

"Cal, if you don't tell me what's going on, I'm going to start screaming!"

"Susan Peterson is dead!"

For a moment, June simply stared at him, as if the words had no meaning. When she finally spoke, her voice was a whisper.

"What do you mean?"

"Just what I said. Susan Peterson is dead, and Michelle saw it happen. She *really* didn't tell you?" As best he could, Cal recounted exactly what had happened at the Bensons,' and what Constance Benson had told him.

As June listened, she felt an edge of fear begin to grow in her, sharpening with each word. By the time Cal was finished, it was all June could do to keep from shaking. Susan Peterson couldn't be dead, and Michelle couldn't have seen anything. If she had, she would have said something. Of course she would have.

"And Michelle really didn't say anything when she came home this afternoon?"

"Nothing," June said. "Not a word. It's—it's unbelievable."

"That's what I keep telling myself." Cal got to his feet. "I'd better go up and have a talk with her. She can't just pretend nothing happened."

He started out of the room. June rose to follow him. "I'd better go with you. She must be horribly upset."

They found Michelle lying on her bed, a book propped on her chest, her doll tucked in the crook of her left arm. As her parents appeared at the door, she looked up at them curiously.

Cal came directly to the point. "Michelle, I think you'd better tell us what happened this afternoon."

Michelle frowned slightly, then shrugged. "This afternoon? Nothing happened. I just came home."

"Didn't you stop at the graveyard? Didn't you talk to Susan Peterson?"

"Only for a minute," Michelle said. Her expression told June that she clearly didn't think it was worth talking about. When Cal began to demand the details of their conversation, June interrupted him.

"You didn't tell me you'd seen Susan," she said carefully, trying not to betray anything. For some reason, it seemed important to hear Michelle's version of the story from Michelle's point of view, rather than in response to Cal's impatient questioning.

"I only saw her for a minute or two," Michelle said. "She was messing around in the cemetery, and when I asked her what she was doing, she started teasing me. She—she called me a cripple, and said I 'gimped.'"

"And what did you do?" June asked gently. She settled herself on the bed and took Michelle's hand in her own, squeezing it reassuringly.

"Nothing. I started to go into the graveyard, but then Susan ran away."

"She ran away? Where to?"

"I don't know. She just disappeared into the fog."

June's eyes flicked to the window. The sun, as it had all day, was glistening on the sea. "Fog? But there hasn't been any fog today."

Michelle looked at her mother in puzzlement, then shifted her gaze to her father. He seemed to be angry with her. But what had she done? She couldn't understand what they wanted of her. She shrugged helplessly. "All I know is that when I was in the cemetery, the fog suddenly came in. It was really thick, and I couldn't see much of anything. And when Susan ran away, she just disappeared into the fog."

"Did you hear anything?" June asked.

Michelle thought a moment, then nodded. "There was something—sort of a scream. I guess Susan must have tripped or something."

My God, June thought. *She doesn't know. She doesn't even know what happened.*

"I see," she said slowly. "And after you heard Susan scream, what did you do?"

"Do? I—I came home."

"But, darling," June said. "If the fog was so thick, how could you find your way home?"

Michelle smiled at her. "It was easy," she said. "Mandy led me. The fog doesn't bother Mandy at all."

It was only by the sheer force of her will that June kept from screaming.

CHAPTER 18

Supper that evening was nearly intolerable for June. Michelle sat placidly, apparently unbothered by what had happened that afternoon. Cal's silence, a silence that had begun as Michelle told them what had happened that afternoon, hung over the table like a shroud. Throughout the meal, June's eyes flicked from her husband to her elder daughter, constantly wary, constantly vigilant, on the watch for something —anything—that would lend the atmosphere a hint of normality.

And that, she realized as she cleared the table when the meal was finally over, was the problem—the situation appeared *too* normal, and it seemed as though she was the only person aware that it was not. As she stacked the dishes in the sink, she found herself beginning to question her own sanity. Twice, she started to leave the kitchen, and stopped herself. Finally, the tension was too much to bear.

"I think we have to talk," she said to Cal, coming

into the living room. Michelle was nowhere to be seen: June assumed she was in her room. Cal was holding Jennifer in his lap, bouncing her gently and talking to her. As June spoke, he looked up from the baby and regarded his wife cautiously.

"Talk about what?" Cal stared at her, and June could see a wall go up in front of his eyes, a wall that threatened to shut her out entirely. He frowned slightly, the skin around his eyes crinkling into deep lines. When he spoke, his voice was brittle. "I don't know that there's anything to talk about."

June's mouth worked for a moment, then she found her voice. "Don't know!" she exclaimed. Then she repeated the phrase, louder. "*Don't know?* My God, Cal, we have to get help for her." What was he doing? Was he shutting everything out? Ignoring everything that was happening? Of course he was. She could see it in his eyes.

"I don't think anything's so terribly wrong."

And there it was. That was why he'd been so silent since Michelle had told them her version of the afternoon—he was simply blocking it all out. But she had to find a way to get through to him. "How can you say that?" she asked, struggling to keep her voice calm and reasonable. "Today Susan Peterson died, and Michelle was there—she *saw* it, or at least she *should* have seen it. If she really didn't, then we're in more trouble than I even thought. She hasn't got any friends, except Mandy, who's a *doll*, for God's sake. And now there's this thing with the fog. Cal, there *wasn't* any fog today—I know, I was here all day, and the sun was out. Cal, she must be losing her vision! And you say you don't think anything's terribly wrong? Are *you* blind?" June stopped suddenly, realizing her voice had risen and become shrill. But it didn't matter. Cal's eyes were icy now, and she knew what he was going to say before he spoke.

"I won't hear this, June. You want me to believe I've made Michelle crazy. I haven't. She's fine. She had a shock this afternoon, and blocked it. That's a normal reaction. Do you understand? It's *normal!*"

Stunned, June sank into a chair, and tried to gather her thoughts into some kind of coherency. Cal was right: there was nothing left to talk about—something had to be done.

"Now listen to me," she heard Cal saying, his voice calm, his words maniacally reasonable. "You weren't there this afternoon, and I was. I heard what Constance Benson had to say, and I heard what Michelle had to say, and it doesn't make much difference whom you believe—Michelle had nothing to do with what happened to Susan. Even Mrs. Benson didn't say Michelle *did* anything—all she said was that Michelle didn't react to what happened. Well, how could she have? She must have been in a state of shock. So how *could* she react?"

Half of June's mind was listening to what Cal was saying, but the other half was screaming in protest. He was twisting things, forcing things to sound the way he wanted them to sound.

"But what about the fog?" she asked. "Michelle said there was fog, and there wasn't! Damn it, there wasn't."

"I didn't say there was," Cal said patiently. "Maybe Michelle did see what happened to Susan, and her reaction—the reaction Mrs. Benson said wasn't there—was simply to shut it out of her mind. Her mind could have invented the fog, to screen out what she didn't want to see."

"Just like your mind is screening out what you don't want to see?" June regretted her words as soon as they were out, but there was no way to recover them. They seemed to hit Cal with a physical force: his body shrank into his chair, and he raised Jenny just slightly, as if the baby were a shield.

"I'm sorry," June apologized. "I shouldn't have said that."

"If that's what you think, why not say it?" Cal countered. "I'm going up to bed. I don't see much point in going on with this."

June watched him go, made no move to try to stop him, or to continue the conversation. She felt glued to her chair, unable to summon the strength to get up. She listened as Cal climbed the stairs, then waited until his footsteps had faded away toward their bedroom. Then, when the house was quiet, she tried to think, tried to force herself to concentrate on Michelle, and what was to be done for her. Steeling herself for whatever might be about to happen, June made her decision. She would not be dissuaded.

Time seemed to have stopped for Estelle and Henry Peterson. Now, near midnight, Estelle sat quietly with her hands in her lap, saying nothing. She wore a slightly puzzled expression, as if she were wondering where her daughter was. Henry was pacing the floor, his florid face flushed a deep red, his indignation growing every minute. If Susan was really dead, someone was to blame.

"Tell me again, Constance," he said. "Tell me once

more what happened. I just can't believe you haven't left something out."

Constance Benson, perched uncomfortably on one of Estelle's better chairs, shook her head tiredly.

"I've told you everything, Henry. There just isn't anything more to say."

"My daughter would not have run over the edge of a cliff," Henry stated, as if by saying it he could make it true. "That girl must have pushed her. She *must* have."

Constance kept her eyes firmly fixed on her hands as they twisted nervously in her lap, wishing she could tell Henry Peterson what he wanted to hear.

"She didn't, Henry. I suppose she must have said something, but I couldn't hear it from my kitchen. And she wasn't even very close to Susan. It was—well, it was very strange, that's all."

"Too damn strange, if you ask me," Henry muttered. He poured himself a shot of whiskey, bolted it down, then clapped his hat on his head. "I'm going to talk to Joe Carson," he said. "He's a doctor—he should know what happened." He stalked from the room. A moment later the front door slammed, and a car engine raced.

"Oh, dear," Estelle sighed. "I hope he isn't going to do anything rash. You know how he can be. Susan gets so upset with him sometimes. . . ." Her voice faded away as she realized Susan would never get upset with her father again. She looked beseechingly at Constance Benson. "Oh, Constance, what are we going to do? I just can't believe it. I just keep having the feeling that any minute Susan's going to walk through that door, and it will all turn out to be a dream. A horrible dream."

Constance moved over to the sofa and drew Estelle

close to her. Only now, with Constance's large and comforting arm around her, did Estelle give in to her tears. Her body trembled, and she dabbed ineffectually at her eyes with a crumpled handkerchief.

"You just let it out," Constance told her. "You can't keep it all bottled up, and Susan wouldn't want you to. And don't worry about Henry—he'll calm down. He just has to make a fuss, that's all."

Estelle sniffled, and straightened up a little. She tried to smile at Constance, but the effort was too much for her. "Constance, are you sure you told us everything? Wasn't there maybe something you didn't want to say in front of Henry?"

Constance sighed heavily. "I wish there was. I wish there was something that would make sense out of the whole thing. But there isn't. All I know is that I've told people time and time again, don't let the kids play around that cemetery. It's dangerous. But nobody believed me, and now look what's happened."

Estelle's eyes met Constance Benson's. For some time the two women simply gazed at each other, as if there were an unspoken communication going on between them. When at last Estelle spoke, her voice was low, and highly controlled.

"It was that girl, wasn't it? Michelle Pendleton? Susan told me there's something wrong with her."

"She's crippled," Constance said. "She fell down the bluff."

"I know," Estelle said. "I don't mean that. There was something else. Susan told me about it yesterday, but I can't remember what it was."

"Well, I don't see that it matters much," Constance sniffed. "It seems to me that what has to be done is see to it that everybody's warned. I think we should warn everyone to keep their children away from that graveyard, and away from Michelle Pendleton. I don't know what she did, but I know she did something."

Estelle Peterson nodded.

It didn't take long for the word to spread through Paradise Point. Constance Benson called her friends, and her friends called theirs. As the night wore on there were small family groups all over the village, huddled together in kitchens and living rooms, talking quietly to their sleepy children, warning them about Michelle. The older children nodded wisely.

But to the younger ones, it made no sense. . . .

At the Carstairses', it was Bertha who talked briefly to Constance Benson, then murmured a few words of sympathy for Estelle Peterson before hanging up and facing her husband. Fred was watching her.

"A little late for phone calls, isn't it?" he asked, pulling himself to a sitting position. He hated being disturbed in the middle of the night.

"That was Constance Benson," Bertha said matter-of-factly. "She seems to think that Michelle Pendleton had something to do with what happened today."

"Leave it to Constance," Fred grumbled sleepily, but he looked wary, nonetheless. "What does Constance think Michelle did?"

"She didn't say. I don't think she exactly knew. But she said we ought to have a talk with Sally, and warn her to stay away from Michelle."

"I wouldn't warn a man to stay out of a beartrap on Constance Benson's say-so," Fred muttered. "She's always yammering about that graveyard, too, but she hardly ever goes out of the house. Must be tough for that boy of hers."

"Well, that's between him and her, and nothing to do with us."

Bertha was about to snap out the light when there was a soft tap at their door, and Sally came in. She sat down on their bed, apparently wide awake.

"Who was that?" she asked. "On the phone."

"Just Mrs. Benson," Bertha said. "She wanted to talk about Susan. And Michelle," she added.

"Michelle? What about her?"

"Well, Michelle was with Susan today, you know," Bertha pointed out. Sally nodded, but seemed puzzled.

"I know," she agreed. "But it's funny. Susan hated Michelle. Why would Susan have been with someone she hated?"

Bertha ignored the question. Instead, she posed one of her own. "Why did Susan hate Michelle?"

Sally shrugged uncomfortably, then decided that it was time she told someone how she'd been feeling.

"Because she's lame. Susan kept acting like Michelle was some kind of freak—kept calling her retarded, and things like that."

"Oh, no . . ." Bertha murmured. "How terrible for her."

"And—and we all sort of went along with it," Sally said miserably.

"Went along with it? You mean you all agreed with Susan?"

Sally nodded, her eyes filling with tears. "I didn't want to—really I didn't. But then—well, Michelle didn't seem to want to be friends anymore, and Susan. . . . Well, Susan acted like anybody who wanted to be Michelle's friend couldn't be hers. And

I—I've known Susan all my life." She began crying, and Bertha hugged her close.

"Now, honey, don't you cry. Everything's going to be all right . . ."

"But now Susan's *dead*," Sally wailed. A thought struck her, and she pulled away from her mother. "Michelle didn't kill her, did she?"

"Of course not," Bertha said emphatically. "I'm sure it was just an accident."

"Well, what did Jeff's mother say?" Sally asked.

"She said—she said—" Bertha floundered, then looked to her husband for assistance.

"She didn't say anything," he said flatly. "Susan must have tripped and fallen, just like Michelle did a while ago. Michelle was just luckier than Susan, that's all. And if you ask me, I think what Susan and the rest of you kids did to Michelle is rotten. I think you ought to tell her you're sorry, and that you want to be her friend again."

"But I already told her that," Sally said.

"Then tell her again," Fred Carstairs said. "That child has had a bad time, and if Constance Benson is doing what I think she's doing, things are only going to get harder for her. And I don't want anybody to say my daughter was a part of it. Is that clear?"

Sally nodded silently. In a way, what her father had just told her was exactly what she wanted to hear. But what if Michelle really didn't want to be her friend anymore? Then what could she do?

It was very puzzling, and when she went back to bed, Sally was still unable to sleep.

There was something wrong.

Something very wrong.

But she couldn't figure out what it was.

* * *

Although no one had called the Pendletons that evening, Cal could feel a tension in the air. Coming to Paradise Point, he sometimes felt, had been a mistake. What had it gotten him? Up to his ears in debt, a starvation-level practice, a new baby, and a daughter who would be crippled for the rest of her life.

But the problems would be solved, all of them. For as the weeks had gone by, Cal had come to a realization. For some reason, a reason he only vaguely understood, he belonged in Paradise Point. He belonged in this house, and he knew he wouldn't leave it. Not for anything. Not even for his daughter.

But she wasn't his daughter, not really. They'd adopted her. She wasn't a *real* Pendleton.

As the thought struck him, Cal shifted in bed, his guilt at even entertaining such an idea making him even more restless. And yet, it was true, wasn't it?

Of all his probems, why should the worst come from someone who wasn't even his daughter?

He turned over and tried to think about something else.

Anything else.

Images began to flow through his mind, images of children. Alan Hanley was there, and Michelle, and now Susan Peterson as well. Faces. Faces twisted in fear and pain, blending one into the other, all of them staring at him, all of them accusing him.

And there were others. Sally Carstairs, and Jeff Benson, and the little ones, the ones Michelle had been playing with—when? Yesterday? Was it really just yesterday? It didn't matter, not really. They were all there, and they were all looking at him, asking him.

Are you going to hurt us, too?

Sleep began to swirl over him, but it wasn't an easy sleep. Always they were there, helpless, appealing.

And accusing.

During the night, Cal's confusion grew, and his anger grew with it. None of it was his fault. None of it! Then why were they accusing him?

The night, and his emotions, exhausted him.

The moon, going into its last phase, had reached its crest as Michelle awoke, and her room was filled with its ghostly light. She sat up in bed, sure that Amanda was with her.

"Mandy?" She whispered her friend's name, then waited in the stillness of the moonlit night for an answer. When it came, Amanda's voice was faint, far-away, but the words were clear.

"Outside. Come outside, Michelle . . ."

Michelle got out of bed and went to the window. The sea sparkled in the moonlight, but Michelle only glanced at it, then shifted her gaze to the lawn below her, searching the shadows for a flicker of movement that would tell her where Amanda was.

And then it came. A shadow, darker than the rest, suddenly moved out onto the lawn.

Her face tipped back, catching the strange light of the fading moon, Amanda beckoned to her.

Michelle slipped her bathrobe on and crept from her room. She paused in the hall, listening. When she heard no sound from her parents' room, she started down the stairs.

Outside, Amanda waited for her. As Michelle approached she could feel her friend's presence, pulling at her, guiding her.

She moved down the path, then along the bluff to the studio.

Letting herself in, Michelle made no move to turn on a light. Instead, knowing what Amanda wanted, she went to the closet, and took out a canvas.

She set it up on the easel, picked up a piece of her mother's charcoal, and waited.

Whatever Amanda wanted to see, Michelle knew she would be able to draw it.

A moment later, she began.

As before, her strokes were bold, quickly drawn, and sure, as if an unseen hand were guiding her. And as she worked, a change came over her face. Her eyes, her brown eyes that had always seemed so alert, grew hazy, then seemed to glaze over. In contrast, Amanda's milky pale, blind eyes came alive, flickering eagerly over the canvas, darting around the studio, drinking in the sights so long denied her.

The picture emerged rapidly, in the same bold strokes she had used the night before.

Only tonight, Michelle drew Susan Peterson, her face twisted in fear, at the edge of the bluff. Susan seemed to be suspended in mid-air, her body pitched forward, her arms flailing.

And on the bluff, her mouth curving in a mirthless smile, there was another girl, dressed in black, her face all but covered by her bonnet. It was Mandy. She seemed to be suspended in midair, her body pitched arms extended, not in fear, but as if she had just pushed something.

Her smile, though joyless, seemed somehow victorious.

Michelle finished the drawing, then stepped back.

Behind her, she could feel Amanda's presence, peering over her shoulder at the canvas, breathing softly.

"Yes," Amanda's voice whispered in her ear. "That's the way it was."

Almost reluctantly, Michelle put the canvas back into the closet, obeying Amanda's whispered command to hide it deep at the back of the closet, in a far corner, where it wouldn't be found.

Then, leaving the studio as it had been when she came in, Michelle started back toward the house.

As they crossed the lawn, Amanda whispered to her.

"They're going to hate you now. All of them. But it doesn't matter. They hated me, too, and they laughed at me.

"But it's all right, Michelle. I'll take care of you. They won't laugh at you. They'll never laugh at you.

"I won't let them."

And then Amanda disappeared into the night. . . .

BOOK THREE

THE
BLIND
FURY

*

CHAPTER 19

The day had been an ordeal for everyone. Corinne Hatcher glanced at the clock for what must have been at least the sixtieth time. All day, the children had whispered among themselves, their eyes constantly coming to rest, if only briefly, on Michelle Pendleton, then shifting guiltily elsewhere when they realized Miss Hatcher was watching them.

Corinne knew no more than anyone else. She had heard all the speculations. She had been called by several women the night before, all professing their desire to be sure their children's teacher knew "the truth," all eager to tell her that they hoped she would "see to it" that Michelle Pendleton was "separated" from the class immediately. Finally, in desperation, she had called Josiah Carson for the true story of what had happened, then left her phone off the hook.

And now, as three o'clock approached, she was still trying to decide whether or not to mention Susan Peterson. But as the last few minutes of the school

day ticked slowly away, she knew she would not—
there just wasn't anything she could tell them, and
there was certainly nothing she wanted to tell them
with Michelle Pendleton present.

Michelle.

Michelle had arrived that morning, as every morning
recently, just in time to slip unobtrusively into her
seat at the back of the room. Of all the children, she
seemed to be the only one capable of concentrating
on her lessons: while the others exchanged glances
and whispers, Michelle sat calmly—was it stoically?—
at the back of the room, as if unaware of what was
going on around her. Michelle's reaction to the situation had set the example for her own. If Michelle
could act as though nothing had happened, so could
she. God knows, she rationalized to herself, it won't
make any difference to Susan, and maybe, if I ignore
the situation, the children will too.

Corinne heaved a silent sigh of relief as the final
bell rang, and sank into her chair to watch the children scurry out into the hall. None of them, she
noticed, spoke to Michelle, although she thought she
saw Sally Carstairs pause for a second, hesitate as
though she was going to say something, then change
her mind and leave with Jeff Benson.

When no one was left in the room but the two of
them, Corinne smiled at Michelle.

"Well," she said as brightly as she could. "How was
your day?" If Michelle wanted to talk about it,
Corinne had given her the opportunity. But Michelle
didn't want to talk.

"All right," she replied, her voice listless. She had
gotten to her feet and was gathering her books. Just

before she started out of the room, she smiled briefly at Corinne. "See you tomorrow," she said. And she was gone.

As she left the classroom, Michelle glanced down the corridor and, seeing Sally Carstairs and Jeff Benson talking together near the front door, turned the other way.

She emerged onto the back stairs and let herself relax for the first time that day: none of her classmates was in the schoolyard. Annie Whitmore was there, playing with her friends, but today they had given up their jump rope in favor of hopscotch. Michelle watched them for a moment and wondered if perhaps she could do it, jumping on her good leg. Maybe, after the children were gone, she'd try it.

She started down the stairs, intending to leave the schoolyard by the back gate, but as she passed the swings, one of the second grade boys called to her.

"Will you push me?"

Michelle stopped and looked at the little boy.

He was seven years old, and small for his age. He was perched on one of the swings, wistfully watching his friends as they pumped themselves back and forth. His problem was immediately obvious. His legs didn't reach the ground, and he couldn't get the swing started. He watched Michelle with large and trusting brown eyes, the eyes of a puppy.

"Please?" he begged.

Michelle set her bookbag on the ground and, with effort, took up a position behind the little boy. "What's your name?" she asked as she gave him a little push.

"Billy Evans. I know who you are—you're the girl who fell off the bluff. Did it hurt?"

"Not much. I got knocked out."

Billy seemed to accept this as perfectly normal. "Oh," he said. "Push me harder."

Michelle pushed a little harder. Soon Billy was swinging happily, his little legs kicking out, his childish squeals echoing across the playground.

Sally Carstairs and Jeff Benson walked slowly down the front steps, reluctant to start home, prolonging their comfortable companionship. A bond had formed between them—nothing spoken, but something nevertheless there. If asked, neither of them could have explained it—indeed, neither of them would even have been likely to admit to it. Yet, as they reached the front yard, they lingered.

A car pulled up, and the two children watched as June Pendleton got out. Self-consciously, each of them muttered a faint hello as she passed them, but June didn't seem to hear them. They watched her disappear into the school.

"I don't think Michelle had anything to do with it," Sally said suddenly. They had not been talking about Michelle or Susan, but Jeff knew immediately what she meant.

"My mother said she was there," Jeff replied.

"But that doesn't mean she did anything," Sally countered.

"Well, she didn't like Susan, that's for sure."

"Why should she have?" Sally demanded, the first touch of heat coming into her voice. "Susan was mean to her. From the first day of school, Susan was always mean to her."

Jeff shuffled uncomfortably, knowing that what Sally said was true, but not wanting to agree with her.

"Well, all of us sort of went along with it."

"I know. Maybe we shouldn't have."

Jeff looked at Sally sharply. "You mean if we hadn't, Susan wouldn't be dead now?"

"I didn't say that!" But Sally silently wondered if that's what she had meant. "Is it all right if I walk home with you?"

Jeff shrugged. "If you want to. But you'll just have to walk back to town again."

"That's all right." The two of them started along the sidewalk, then turned the corner onto the street that would take them past the playground. "Maybe I'll go see Michelle," Sally said tentatively.

Jeff stopped and looked at her.

"My mother says we shouldn't have anything to do with her. She says it's dangerous."

"That's silly," Sally replied. "My parents told me I should be friends with her again."

"I don't see why. She can't do anything anymore. If you ask me, her leg wasn't the only thing she hurt when she fell. I think she must have landed on her head!"

"Jeff Benson, you stop that," Sally cried. "That's just the kind of thing Susan used to say. And look what happened to her!"

Now Jeff stopped, and his eyes fixed on Sally. "You *do* believe Michelle did something, don't you?" he asked. Sally bit her lip and stared at the ground.

"Well, it's all right if you do," Jeff told her. "Everybody in town thinks she did something to Susan. Except, I guess nobody knows exactly what."

They were near the playground now, and Sally suddenly felt a creepy sensation, as though she were being watched. When she turned around, she drew a sudden and involuntary breath: a few feet away, just inside the fence, Michelle stood, facing her, gently pushing a swing while Billy Evans laughed happily and begged to be pushed harder.

For a split second Sally's eyes met Michelle's. In that instant, she was sure that Michelle had heard what Jeff had said. There was a look in Michelle's eyes, a look that frightened Sally. She reached out and took Jeff's hand.

"Come on," she said, her voice barely louder than a whisper. *"She heard you!"*

Jeff frowned, then glanced around to see why Sally was suddenly whispering.

He saw Michelle staring at him.

His first impulse was to stare her down, and his eyes narrowed. But Michelle's gaze never wavered, and her face remained expressionless. Jeff could feel himself losing control. When he finally gave up, and looked away, he tried to act as if he'd done it on purpose.

"Let's go, Sally," he said loudly, making sure Michelle would hear him. "If Michelle wants to play with the babies, what do we care?" He started down the street, leaving Sally by herself. She waited a few seconds, confused, wanting to catch up with him. Yet part of her held back, wishing she could somehow apologize to Michelle. Unable to sort it out, she ran off down the street after Jeff's retreating figure.

Corinne Hatcher glanced up from the tests she was correcting, her automatic smile of greeting fading to a look of concern when she saw June Pendleton framed in the classroom door. There was a haggardness about

June as she waited uncertainly at the door, her unease writ plain on her from her windblown hair to her somewhat rumpled skirt. Corinne rose from her chair and waved June into the room.

"Are you all right?" She realized only when it was too late that her words couldn't help but amplify June's obvious discomfort. June, however, seemed not to take offense.

"I must look the way I feel," she said. She tried to smile, but failed. "I—I need to talk to someone, and there just doesn't seem to be anybody else."

"I heard about Susan Peterson," Corinne offered. "It must have been terrible for Michelle."

Grateful for the teacher's immediate understanding, June dropped into the chair at one of the undersized desks, then quickly stood up again—the feeling of grossness the tiny desk gave her was more than she could bear.

"That's one of the reasons I came," she said. "Did—well, did you notice anything about Michelle today? I mean, anything unusual?"

"I'm afraid today wasn't one of the better days for any of us," Corinne replied. "The children were all sort of—how shall I say it? Preoccupied? I guess that's the best way to put it."

"Did they say anything? To Michelle?"

Corinne hesitated, then decided there was no reason to keep the truth from June. "Mrs. Pendleton, they didn't say anything to her. Nothing at *all*."

June grasped her meaning immediately.

"I was afraid that would happen," she said, more to herself than to Corinne. "Miss Hatcher—I don't know what to do."

Once again June lowered herself to a seat, suddenly

too tired, too defeated by her whole situation to care how she might have looked. This time it was Corinne who drew her to her feet.

"Come on. Let's go to the teachers' room and have a cup of coffee. You look as though you need something stronger, but I'm afraid the rules are still the rules around here. And I think it's time we started calling each other June and Corinne, don't you?"

Nodding dispiritedly, June let herself be led out of the classroom and down the corridor.

"Do you think your friend can help?" June asked. She had told Corinne what had happened the day before, and how senseless it had all seemed. First Michelle coming home—calm, apparently nothing wrong. And then Cal's return, and the nightmare beginning.

June recounted everything as it had happened, trying to convey to the teacher the sense of unreality it all had for her. It was, she said at last, as if her whole world had been turned into something out of *Alice's Adventures in Wonderland*—the most horrible things happening, and everyone around her acting as though nothing at all was the matter. She wasn't sure, really, whether she was more worried about her husband or her daughter, but she had decided, late last night, that Michelle must come first.

Corinne heard the tale out, not interrupting, not questioning, sensing that June needed simply to tell it, to externalize the chaos that had been churning in her mind. Now, as June finished, she nodded thoughtfully.

"I don't see why Tim couldn't help," she said. She stood up and went to the coffee pot, thinking while she refilled her cup and June's. As she turned back to June, she tried to make her voice sound encouraging.

"Maybe things aren't as bad as they sound." She hesitated a moment, unsure what to say. "I know it all seems frightening," she continued gently, "but I think you're worrying too much."

"No!" It was almost a shriek. June's eyes filled with tears. "My God, if you could hear her, the way she talks about that doll. I swear, I think she really believes that Mandy—she calls her Mandy now—is real!" There was a bleakness in her voice that frightened Corinne.

She took June's hand in her own, and tried to keep her voice confident. "It *is* frightening, but it will be all right. Really it will." Deep inside, she wasn't nearly as certain as she tried to appear. In the depths of her being, Corinne had a feeling—a feeling that whatever had happened to Michelle, it was beyond their understanding. And that feeling terrified her.

Michelle tried to put Jeff's words out of her mind as she watched Sally disappear down the street. But they lingered there, echoing in her head, mocking her, tormenting her. She was vaguely aware of Billy Evans, calling out to her to push him harder, but his words seemed distant, as if they were coming to her through a fog.

She let the swing die down, and, when Billy protested, told him she was tired, that she would push him some more another time. Then she moved painfully over to the maple tree, and lowered herself to the grass. She would wait a while, until Jeff and Sally were long gone, before she started the long walk home.

She stretched out on the grass and stared up into the leaves of the tree, which were changing colors with the coming of fall. When she was like this, by herself, with no one around her, the loneliness wasn't so bad. It was only when she could hear them, or see them, their voices taunting her, their eyes mocking her, that Michelle really hated the children who had been her friends.

Except for Sally. Michelle still wasn't sure about Sally. Sally seemed better than the others, kinder. Michelle decided to talk to Amanda about Sally. Maybe, if Amanda agreed, they could be friends again. Michelle hoped they could—she really liked Sally, deep down. But still, it was up to Amanda. . . .

From her classroom window, Corinne watched June cross the playground. She thought there was a reluctance about June, a reluctance to disturb Michelle, as if, as long as she was asleep under the tree, she was safe from whatever chaos was going on in her mind. But as Corinne watched, June knelt and gently awakened Michelle.

Michelle got to her feet stiffly, the pain in her hip visible in her face, even from across the yard. She seemed surprised to see her mother, but at the same time grateful. Taking her mother's hand, Michelle allowed herself to be led around the corner of the building and out of Corinne's sight.

Even after they had disappeared, Corinne remained at the window, the image of Michelle—her shoulders stooped, her hair hanging limp, her spirit defeated by her crippling accident—imprinted on her mind.

It seemed a long time ago, that first day of school, when Michelle had come bouncing into her classroom, bright-eyed, grinning, eager to begin her new life in Paradise Point.

And now, only a few weeks later, it had all changed. Paradise Point? Well, maybe for some people. But not for Michelle Pendleton.

Not now, and Corinne was suddenly sure, probably not ever again.

CHAPTER 20

It was a crisp afternoon, and Corinne walked swiftly, her mind more on June Pendleton's visit than on the direction she had taken. It wasn't until she saw the building ahead of her, tucked in a small grove of trees, its walls covered with climbing roses, that she realized that the clinic had been her destination all along. She paused for a moment, reading the neatly lettered sign, with Josiah Carson's faded name, and freshly lettered above it, that of Calvin Pendleton. The lettering struck Corinne as sad somehow, and it took a few moments before she realized why. It was a sign of the old order giving way to the new. Josiah Carson had been around as long as Corinne could remember. It was difficult to imagine the clinic without him.

She stepped inside the waiting room, and was relieved to see Marion Perkins sitting at the desk, working on the books. Marion, at least, was still going to be here, smoothing the transition between Dr. Carson and Dr. Pendleton. As the little bell attached to the door jangled softly, Marion looked up.

"Corinne!" Her expression as she recognized the teacher was one of welcome mixed with concern and a little surprise. "You know, I had a feeling you might be by today. It's strange—well, maybe not so strange, really, all things considered. Nearly everybody's been here today, wanting to talk about Susan Peterson." The nurse clucked her tongue sympathetically. "Isn't it terrible? Such a loss for Henry and Estelle. And of course everyone seems to think that little Michelle Pendleton had something to do with it." She leaned forward slightly and lowered her voice to a confidential whisper. "Frankly, some of the things that people have been saying, I wouldn't want to repeat."

"Then don't," Corinne said, tempering the shortness of her words with a friendly grin. "Is Uncle Joe here?"

Suddenly abashed at her near indiscretion, Marion reached for the phone. "Let me buzz him, and see if he's busy." She pressed the intercom. "Dr. Joe? A surprise for you—Corinne Hatcher's out here."

A moment later, the inner door opened, and Josiah Carson appeared, his arms extended, a wide smile wreathing his face, though for a moment Corinne thought she saw something else in his eyes. A sadness? Whenever one of his patients died, particularly a child, Josiah Carson took it hard. Since his own daughter had died, long before Corinne was even born, Carson had lavished his paternal instincts on the children of Paradise Point. But today there was something beyond sadness in his eyes. Something she couldn't quite identify.

He took Corinne in his arms in a massive bear hug.

"What brings you down here?" he said. "You feeling all right?"

Corinne wriggled herself loose. "I'm fine. I guess—well, I guess I was just worried about you. I know how you get when something happens to one of your children."

Carson nodded. "It's never easy," he said. "Come on into the office, and I'll buy you a drink."

Carson gestured her to a chair and closed the door. He produced the bottle of bourbon from the bottom drawer of his desk, and poured each of them a generous shot, eyeing Corinne carefully.

"All right," he said, sipping his drink. "What's up?"

Corinne tasted the bourbon, made a face, and set it aside. Then she met Carson's eyes.

"Michelle Pendleton," she said.

Carson nodded. "Doesn't surprise me. As a matter of fact, I thought you'd be here sooner. Things getting worse?"

"I'm not sure," Corinne said. "Today must have been horrible for her—none of the children would have anything to do with her. Until yesterday, I thought it was just her limp. But now—well, you know how this town can be. People get blamed for things, even when they aren't to blame, and nobody ever forgets." She picked up her drink, sipped at it, then set it aside once again. "Uncle Joe," she said suddenly, "is Michelle all right?"

"It depends on what you mean. You're talking about her mind, aren't you?"

Corinne shifted in her chair. "I'm not sure," she said. "In fact, I didn't really know I was coming down here until I found myself out in front. But I guess my subconscious was trying to tell me something." She paused for a moment, and suddenly drained half of her drink. "Have you heard about Michelle's imaginary friend?" she asked as casually as she could.

Carson frowned. "Imaginary friend?" he repeated, as if the words had no meaning to him. "You mean the kind of thing very small children do?"

"Exactly," Corinne said. "Apparently it all started with a doll. I'm not sure exactly what kind, but Mrs. Pendleton told me that it's old—very old. Michelle found it in the bedroom closet when they moved in."

Carson scratched his head as if puzzled, then nodded. "I know what it looks like," he said smoothly. "It *is* old. Porcelain face, old-fashioned clothes, a little bonnet. She had it on the bed with her when I saw her right after the accident. You mean she's decided it's real?"

Corinne nodded soberly. "Apparently. And guess what she's named it?"

"She told me she named it Amanda."

"Amanda," Corinne repeated. "Doesn't that mean anything to you?" She finished her drink and held her glass out. "Am I old enough for a second drink?"

Wordlessly, Carson refilled her glass and his own. "Well," he said abruptly. "Apparently she's heard some stories about the Point."

Corinne shook her head. "That's what I thought. But June told me she named the doll as soon as she found it. The very day they arrived."

"I see," Carson said. "Then it was just a coincidence."

"Was it?" Corinne said softly. "Uncle Joe, who was Amanda? I mean, was she real? Or are they just stories?"

Carson leaned back in his chair. He'd never talked

about Amanda, and didn't want to start now. But apparently the talk had already started, as he'd known it must. The thing to do was to direct it.

"She was my great-aunt, actually, or would have been if she'd lived," he said carefully.

"And what happened to her?" Corinne asked.

"Who knows? She was blind, and she stumbled off the bluff one day. As far as anyone knows, that's all there was to it." But there was something in his voice —a hesitation perhaps?—that made Corinne wonder if there wasn't something more.

"You sound as though you know more than that." When Carson made no response, she pushed him again. "Do you?"

"You mean, do I believe in the ghost story?"

"No. Do you believe that's all there was to it?"

"I don't know. My grandfather, who was Amanda's brother, believed there was more to it."

Corinne said nothing.

Carson leaned back in his chair and turned to look out the window.

"You know," he said slowly, "when the Carsons named this town Paradise Point, they didn't really have the setting in mind. It was more an idea, I guess you could call it. An idea of paradise, right here on earth." His voice was filled with an irony that Corinne couldn't miss.

"I knew the Carsons were ministers," she said.

Josiah nodded. "Fundamentalist. The real fire and brimstone variety. My great-grandfather, Lemuel Carson, was the last of them, though."

"What happened?"

"Lots of things, from what Grandfather told me. It started when Amanda lost her sight. Old Lemuel de-

cided it was an act of God, and he tried to pass
Amanda off as a martyr. He always made her dress in
black. Poor little girl. It must have been hard for her
—what with her blindness and all. She must have been
a lonely little thing."

"And she was all alone when she fell off the bluff?"

"Apparently. Grandfather never said. He never
talked about it much. I always got the idea there was
something odd about it, though. Of course, he never
did talk much about the family at all—too many
serpents in Lemuel's paradise."

"Aren't there always?" Corinne observed, but Josiah
didn't seem to hear her.

"It was Lemuel's wife," he went on. "It seems she
had something of a wandering eye. Grandfather always thought it was a reaction to Lemuel's constant
hell and damnation sermonizing."

"You mean your great-grandmother was having an
affair?"

Carson smiled. "She must have been quite a woman.
Grandfather said she was beautiful, but that she never
should have married his father."

"Louise Carson," Corinne whispered, " 'Died in
Sin.' "

"Murdered," Josiah said softly. Corinne's eyes
widened in surprise. "It happened out in that building
June Pendleton uses for a studio. Lemuel found her
out there, with one of her lovers. Both of them were
dead. Stabbed to death."

"My God," Corinne breathed. She could feel her
stomach tighten, and wondered for a moment if she
was going to be sick.

"Of course, everyone sort of assumed Lemuel had
done it," Josiah said, "but he had the whole town

pretty much under his thumb, and in those days an unfaithful wife wasn't particularly highly regarded. They probably thought she'd gotten what she deserved. Lemuel wouldn't even give her a funeral."

"I always figured the inscription on the gravestone must have meant something like that," Corinne said. "When I was a little girl, we used to go out there, and read the headstones."

"And look for the ghost?"

Again, Corinne nodded.

"And did you ever see her?"

Corinne pondered her answer for a long time. Finally, reluctantly, she shook her head.

Carson noted her hesitation. "Are you sure, Corinne?" His voice was very soft.

"I don't know," Corinne replied. Suddenly she felt foolish, but a memory was hanging in her mind, just out of her reach. "There was something," she said. "It happened just once. I was out there in the grave-yard, with a friend—I can't even remember who—and the fog came in. Well, you know how spooky a grave-yard can be in the fog. I don't know—maybe I let my imagination run away with me, but all of a sudden I felt something. Nothing I can put my finger on, really —just a feeling that something was there, close to me. I stood perfectly still, and the longer I stood, the closer whatever it was seemed to come." Her voice trailed off, and she shivered slightly as the memory of that foggy afternoon chilled her.

"And you think it was Amanda?" Carson asked.

"Well, it was *something*," Corinne replied.

"You're right," Carson agreed sourly. "It *was* some-thing. It was your imagination. A little girl in a grave-yard, on a foggy day, and having grown up hearing all those ghost stories. I'm amazed you didn't have a long talk with Amanda! Or did you?"

"Of course not," Corinne said, feeling foolish now. "I didn't even see her."

Carson watched her. "What about your friend? Did she feel the same thing you did?"

"As a matter of fact, yes, she did!" Corinne felt herself getting angry. Not believing her was one thing—mocking her was quite another. "And, if you want to know, we weren't the only ones. A lot of us had the same feeling. And we were all girls, and we were all twelve years old. Just like Amanda. And, in case you didn't know, just like Michelle Pendleton."

Carson's eyes hardened. "Corinne," he said slowly, "do you know what you're saying?"

And suddenly Corinne did. "Yes. I'm saying that maybe the ghost stories are true, and the reason everyone says they aren't is because no one ever actually saw Amanda before. The only ones who even *felt* her were twelve-year-old girls. And who believes what they say? Everyone knows little girls have wild imaginations, right? Uncle Joe, what if it wasn't my imagination? What if some of us really did feel her presence? And what if Michelle not only felt her, but actually saw her?"

The expression on Josiah Carson's face as he watched her told her she had struck a nerve.

"You believe in the ghost, don't you?" she asked.

"Do you?" he countered, and now Corinne was sure he was growing nervous.

"I don't know," Corinne lied. She *did* know! "But it makes sense, doesn't it? I mean, in a strange kind of way? If you can accept that there really is a ghost, and that it's Amanda, who would be more likely to see her than a twelve-year-old girl? A girl just like her?"

"Well, she's had over a hundred years to find someone," Carson said. "Why now? Why Michelle Pendleton?" He leaned forward, resting his elbows on his desk. "Corinne," he said quietly, "I know you're worried about Michelle. I know it seems odd that she'd make up an imaginary friend named Amanda. It seems like quite a coincidence—hell, it *is* quite a coincidence. But that's *all* it is!"

Corinne stood up, truly angry now. "Uncle Joe," she said, her voice tight, "Michelle is one of my students, and I'm worried about her. For that matter, I'm worried about everybody else in my class, too. Susan Peterson is dead, and Michelle is crippled and acting very strangely. I don't want anything else to happen."

Carson stared up at Corinne. She was standing in front of his desk, her back stiff as a ramrod, her expression intense. He began to reach out to her, to comfort her, but before he was halfway out of his chair, she had turned and fled.

Slowly, Josiah sat down. He sat by himself for a long time. It wasn't going right, none of it. He hadn't meant for Susan Peterson to die. It should have been Michelle—it should have been Cal Pendleton's daughter. A life for a life, a child for a child. But not one of *his* children.

All he could do now was wait. Sooner or later, as it always had, the tragedy would come back to the house, and whoever was living there. And when it did, and the house had avenged Alan Hanley for him, it would be over. Then he could go away and forget Paradise Point forever. He poured himself another shot of bourbon and stared out the window. In the distance he could see the churning waters of Devil's Passage. It was, he thought, aptly named. How long had it been since the devil had come to live with the Carsons? And now, after all the years, the last Carson was going to use the devil. It was, Josiah Carson thought, somehow poetic.

He only hoped that not too many of his own children—the village children—would have to die in the process.

Late that afternoon, Michelle made her way to the old graveyard. She lowered herself clumsily to the ground near the odd memorial to Amanda and waited, sure that her friend would come to her. But before the now familiar grayness could close in around her, she felt someone watching her. She turned and recognized Lisa Hartwick standing a few yards away from her, staring at her.

"Are you all right?" Lisa asked.

Michelle nodded, and Lisa took a tentative step toward her.

"I—I was looking for you," Lisa said. She looked almost frightened, and Michelle wondered what was wrong.

"For me? How come?" She started to get up.

"I wanted to talk to you."

Michelle regarded Lisa suspiciously. No one liked Lisa—everyone said she was a brat. What did she want? Was she going to tease her? But Lisa came closer and sat down next to her. Gratefully, Michelle let herself sink back to the soft earth.

"Is it true you're adopted?" Lisa suddenly asked.

"So what?"

"I'm not sure," Lisa replied. Then: "My mother died five years ago."

Now Michelle was puzzled. Why had she said that? Was she trying to make friends with her? Why?

"I don't know what happened to my parents," she ventured. "Maybe they're dead. Or maybe they just didn't want me."

"My father doesn't want me," Lisa said quietly.

"How do you know?" Michelle let herself relax: Lisa wasn't going to tease her.

"He's in love with your teacher. Ever since he met her, he's liked her more than he likes me."

Michelle thought this over. Maybe Lisa was right. Maybe things had happened for her the same way they had happened for Michelle when Jenny had been born. "Sometimes I don't think *any*body likes me," she said.

"I know. Nobody likes me, either."

"Maybe we could be friends," Michelle suggested. Now Lisa's eyes seemed to cloud over.

"I don't know. I—I've heard things about you."

Michelle tensed. "What kind of things?"

"Well, that ever since you fell off the bluff, something's been wrong with you."

"I'm lame," Michelle said. "Everybody knows that."

"That's not what I mean. I heard—well, they say you think you saw the ghost."

Michelle relaxed again. "You mean Amanda? She's not a ghost. She's my friend."

"What do you mean?" Lisa asked. "There isn't anybody around here named Amanda."

"There is, too," Michelle insisted. "She's my friend." Suddenly Lisa stood up and began backing away from Michelle. "Where are you going?"

"I—I have to go home now," Lisa said nervously.

Michelle struggled to her feet, her eyes fixed angrily on Lisa. "You think I'm crazy, don't you?"

Lisa shook her head uncertainly.

Suddenly the fog was starting to close in around Michelle. From far away, she could hear Amanda calling to her.

"I'm not crazy," she said to Lisa, her voice desperate. "Amanda's *real*, and she's coming now. You can meet her!"

But Lisa still backed away from her. Just before the gray mists surrounded her, Michelle saw her turn and begin running.

As Susan Peterson had run.

CHAPTER 21

They held Susan Peterson's funeral on Saturday.

Estelle Peterson sat in the front pew of the Methodist Church, her head bowed, her fingers twisting compulsively at a limp handkerchief. Susan's coffin was only a few feet away, banked with flowers, its lid propped open. Next to Estelle, Henry stared stoically ahead, his eyes fixed on a spot high above the coffin, his face carefully impassive.

A low murmuring began moving slowly through the congregation. Estelle tried to ignore it, but when she heard Constance Benson's voice cut through the unintelligible sounds, she finally turned around.

Michelle Pendleton, wearing a black dress and leaning heavily on her cane, was making her way slowly down the aisle. Behind her were her parents, with June carrying the baby. For a split second, Estelle's eyes met June's. Estelle quickly looked away. Again, she heard Constance Benson's voice.

"Of all the places for them to turn up . . ." she

began, but Bertha Carstairs, sitting next to her, jabbed her with an elbow, and Constance subsided. As the Pendletons seated themselves in a pew halfway between the door and the altar, the service for Susan Peterson began.

Michelle could feel the hostility around her.

It was as if every eye in the church was on her, watching her, accusing her. She wanted to leave, but knew that she wouldn't be able to. If only she weren't crippled—if only she could get up and slip quietly out. But if she tried, things would only be worse. Her cane, tap-tapping along the hardwood floor, would echo through the church, and the minister would stop his prayers, and then they would all stare at her openly. At least while she sat still they tried to pretend they weren't watching her, even though she knew they were.

June, too, had to force herself to sit still, to keep her face impassive, to endure the endless service. It had been a mistake, coming to the funeral. If Cal hadn't insisted, she would never have come. She had argued with him, but it hadn't done any good. He had stonily insisted that Michelle had had nothing to do with Susan's death; therefore, there was no reason for them not to go to the funeral. June had tried to reason with him, had tried to make him see that it would be hard for Michelle, miserably hard, for her to sit in the church, surrounded by all the children who had been her friends, and listen to the service. Couldn't Cal see that? Didn't he understand that it didn't matter that Michelle had done nothing to Susan? It was what people *thought* that counted.

But Cal would not be budged. And so they had come. June had heard Constance Benson, and she was sure that Michelle had heard her, as well. She had seen the look in Estelle Peterson's eyes—the look of hurt, and accusation, and bewilderment.

Finally, the service came to an end. The congregation stood as the casket was borne slowly down the aisle, followed by Estelle and Henry Peterson. As they passed the Pendletons, Henry glared at Cal, his eyes hard and challenging, and Cal felt a tightening in his stomach. *Maybe,* he thought, *June was right—maybe we shouldn't have come.* But then, as the pews began emptying into the aisle, Bertha Carstairs stopped and took his hand.

"I—I just want you to know," she stammered. "My family and I—we're so sorry about all of this. It seems like ever since you came to the Point things have—well. . . ." Her voice trailed off, but she shrugged eloquently.

"Thank you," Cal said softly. "But it's all right. Things are going to be all right now. Accidents happen—"

"Accidents!"

It was Constance Benson, with Jeff's hand gripped tightly in her own. "What happened to Susan Peterson was no accident!" Then, as Cal's face turned deathly pale, she swept out of the church.

Suddenly, the Pendletons were alone. June looked helplessly around, searching for a friendly face, but there was none. Even the Carstairses had disappeared, lost in the crowd around the Petersons.

"Let's go," she said. "Please? We came. We were here. Now can't we go home?"

Next to her, Michelle stood quietly, tears streaming down her face.

Corinne Hatcher had slipped out of the church with Tim and Lisa Hartwick just before the service ended. It hadn't occurred to Corinne Hatcher not to go to the funeral, but it *had* occurred to her that, if she stayed after the service, she might be put in an untenable position. She would be expected—indeed, forced—to recognize that there were many people in Paradise Point who felt that Michelle had "done" something to Susan. Further, she might have to align herself either with the Petersons or the Pendletons. But at last it was over.

"I wonder if Michelle killed Susan," Lisa said from the backseat of Tim's car.

"Don't be silly," Corinne began, but Lisa promptly interrupted her.

"Well, I think she did. I think the kids are right—she's crazy."

"I've told you before, Lisa," Tim said calmly. "Don't talk about things you don't know anything about."

"But I do know about her." Lisa's voice began to take on the familiar whine that so irritated Corinne. She turned to look at Lisa.

"You don't even know her."

"I do too! I talked to her the other day, out at that old cemetery next to her house."

"I thought I told you not to go out there." Tim's voice was mild, but Lisa did not ignore the reprimand.

"I didn't go to her house," she said. "I only went to the graveyard. Can I help it if she was there?"

"And what makes you think she's crazy?" Tim asked.

"Just the way she talked. She thinks the ghost that's supposed to be out there is her friend. She said I could meet her, if I wanted to."

"Meet her?" Corinne frowned. "You mean Michelle thought she was actually there?"

Lisa shrugged. "I don't know. I didn't see anything. But when I told Michelle that Amanda was a ghost, she got real mad." Lisa began to giggle. "She's crazy." She began repeating the word in an odd sing-song voice: "CRAA-zy, CRAA-zy, CRAA-zy!"

Corinne had heard enough. "That's enough, Lisa!" she snapped. As if she'd been struck, Lisa fell silent. Tim glanced at Corinne reproachfully but said nothing until they were in his house and Lisa had gone to her room.

"Corinne," he said when they were alone, "I wish you'd leave the discipline to me."

"She's spoiled," Corinne shot back. "And you know it. If you don't do something about it soon, she's going to wind up in trouble." The sadness in his eyes made her retreat. The subject of Lisa was just too painful to Tim. And right now, there was a subject of more immediate concern. "I want you to talk to Michelle about this imaginary friend of hers," she said.

Tim was thoughtful for a moment, then nodded. "An imaginary friend at her age—wherever it comes from—is certainly abnormal. I don't want to use Lisa's words, but Michelle could be very disturbed."

"Tim," Corinne said slowly. "Suppose Michelle isn't —disturbed, as you put it, and suppose she hasn't really made an imaginary friend? Suppose Amanda really is a ghost?"

Tim stared at her.

"But that's impossible, isn't it." His tone left no room for argument.

Michelle closed her book and set it aside. Try as she would, she couldn't get her mind off the funeral. The way people had stared at her. It had made her feel like a freak. She was tired of feeling like a freak.

She rose awkwardly from her chair, stretched, then limped over to the window. The fall twilight, fading quickly, colored the sea an iron gray, and the sky, its reddish tinge fading to the dark blue of dusk, seemed low tonight. Below her, its outlines blurred in the gathering darkness, was her mother's studio. Michelle stared at it, almost as if she expected something to happen. And yet, what could happen? The studio was empty—she could hear her parents downstairs, their voices low, punctuated occasionally by Jennifer's happy squeals.

Jennifer.

Michelle said the name to herself, and wondered how she could ever have thought it was a pretty name. Then she said it out loud, listening to the syllables. She decided she hated the name. Suddenly, as if her hostility had somehow flowed directly into the baby, Jenny began crying.

Michelle listened to the sounds for a moment, then, as they quieted, picked up her book and stretched out on the bed. She opened it to the passage she had left a few minutes ago and began to read.

Again, she heard Jennifer squall.

Leaving the book on her nightstand, Michelle carefully maneuvered herself off the bed, and, taking her cane, left her room and started toward the stairs.

*   *   *

June looked up from her needlework, listened to the sound of Michelle's cane, then spoke quietly to Cal.

"She's coming down." Cal, who had Jennifer on his lap and was playing with her toes, made no response.

As the tapping of Michelle's cane came steadily closer, June picked up her needlepoint once again. When Michelle appeared at the archway that separated the living room from the entry hall, she feigned surprise.

"Finished with your homework already?" she asked.

Michelle nodded. "I was trying to read, but I couldn't concentrate. I thought maybe Daddy and I could play a game or something."

Cal's face tightened. He remembered the last time they had tried that. "Not now. I'm teaching your sister about her toes." He ignored the hurt in Michelle's eyes, but June could not.

"Don't you think it's time Jenny went to bed?" she suggested. Cal glanced at the clock on the mantel.

"At seven-thirty? She'll be up all night, and so will you."

"She's up all night anyway," June argued. "Cal, I really think you ought to take her upstairs."

She was not going to relent. Cal got to his feet and held the baby high over his head. He looked up into her grinning face and winked at her. "Come on, princess, the queen says it's bedtime." He started out of the room, but Michelle stopped him.

"Can we play a game when you come down?"

Still not looking at her, Cal continued toward the stairs. "I don't know," he said over his shoulder. "I'm pretty tired tonight. Maybe some other night." Because his back was to her, he didn't see the tears well in Michelle's eyes.

June, however, did, and she hastily put her work down. "Come on—why don't we make a batch of cookies?" But it was too late. Michelle was already on her way out of the room.

"I'm not hungry," she said listlessly. "I'll just go back up and read for a while. Night."

"Aren't you going to kiss me?"

Dispiritedly, Michelle went to her mother and kissed her on the cheek. June put her arms around Michelle and tried to draw her close, but felt her daughter stiffen.

"I'm sorry," she said. "He really *is* tired tonight."

"I know." Michelle pulled herself out of her mother's embrace. Feeling helpless, June let her go. Nothing she could say would make Michelle feel better. Only Cal could give her the reassurance she needed, and June was sure that wasn't going to happen. Unless she forced him.

When Cal still hadn't come back downstairs thirty minutes later, June made the rounds of the lower floor, looking up and turning off the lights. Then she mounted the stairs, stuck her head in to wish Michelle a final good night, and went down the hall to the master bedroom. She found Cal already in bed, propped against the pillows, reading a book. Next to him, sleeping peacefully in her bassinet, was Jennifer. For a moment, June found the scene disarming, but she quickly realized what Cal was doing.

"You aren't that tired," she announced. Cal looked at her blankly.

"What?"

"I said you aren't that tired. Don't pretend you didn't hear me." Her voice was quivering with anger, but Cal still only stared at her in puzzlement.

"I heard you. I just don't know what you meant."

"It's simple," June said coldly. "Half an hour ago, when I suggested you bring Jennifer upstairs—so that you could play with Michelle—you seemed to think it was much too early. And here you are, tucked happily in bed."

"June—" Cal began, but she cut him off.

"Oh, come on. Do you really think I don't know what's going on? You came up here to hide. To hide from your own daughter! For God's sake, Cal, don't you know what you're doing to her?"

"I'm not doing anything!" Cal said, almost desperately. "I just—I just . . ."

"You just can't face her. Well, you're going to have to, Cal. What you did down there was cruel. All she wanted to do was play a game with you. Just a simple, little game. My God, if your guilt is weighing on you so much, I'd have thought you'd be dying to play with her, if only so you could let her win. And then calling Jenny 'princess.' Didn't you realize what it would do to Michelle? That's always been your nickname for her!"

"She didn't even notice," Cal said, his voice sullen.

"How would you know? You won't even look at her anymore. Well, let me tell you, Cal, she noticed. She almost started crying. I think the only reason she didn't was that she was afraid no one would care. My God, can't you understand what you're doing to her?"

Her anger suddenly dissolving into frustration, June burst into tears and crumpled onto the bed. Cal gathered her into his arms, rocking her gently, his mind whirling with her accusations.

"Don't, darling," he whispered. "Please, don't."

June forced herself to relax in his arms. He was her husband, and she loved him; what was happening was really no more his fault than Michelle's. It was something that had happened, that's all. Something they would have to get through.

Together.

She sat up and dabbed at her eyes with a Kleenex from the nightstand.

"I've done something," she said. "You aren't going to like it, but we have to do it."

"Done something? What?"

"Corinne Hatcher's friend, the school psychologist. I've asked her to set us up an appointment with him."

"Us? All of us?"

June nodded.

"I see."

The concern that June had seen in his eyes only seconds before faded abruptly, like a curtain being drawn. When he spoke again, his voice was icy.

"Are you sure all of us need to go?" he asked, drawing the covers around himself.

"What do you mean?" June's voice was guarded; she could sense something coming, but wasn't sure what.

"I wish you could have heard yourself a few minutes ago," Cal said smoothly. "You didn't sound quite—well, rational is the word, I think."

June's mouth dropped open in astonishment. For a moment all she could do was stare at him. Was he really saying what she thought he was saying? It didn't seem possible.

"Cal, you can't do this." She could feel her control slipping away from her. Tears were welling up again, and the anger she had thought was dissipated was flooding back.

"I haven't done anything, June," Cal said reasonably. "All I did was bring Jenny up, put her to bed, and then go to bed myself. And the next thing I know, you come in, raving like a maniac, insisting that I'm some kind of monster, and telling me I need to go into therapy. Does that sound rational to you?"

June rose from the bed, her eyes blazing. "How dare you?" she shouted. "Have you completely lost your mind? Are you really going to do this? Are you really going to go on defending yourself, trying to pretend nothing's wrong? Well, you listen to me, Calvin Pendleton. I won't tolerate it. Either you agree, right now, to go with me to see Tim Hartwick, or I swear, I'll take Michelle and Jennifer, and I'll leave you. Right now. Tonight!"

She stood in the middle of the room, waiting for him to speak. For a long time their eyes remained locked in an angry challenge. When finally the moment came, the moment when one of them would have to surrender, it was Cal.

His eyes flickered, then he looked away from her. He seemed to sink into the bed, the tension in his body suddenly released.

"All right," he said softly. "I can't lose you. I can't lose Jennifer. I'll go."

Michelle started back to her room, her hip throbbing, barely able to make her crippled leg function.

She had heard the fight, heard her mother screaming at her father. She had tried not to listen at first, but then, as her mother's shouting suddenly stopped, she had gotten up and crept out into the hall. Still hearing nothing, she had moved painfully down the hall, stopping only when she was right outside their door.

And she had listened.

At first, she had heard only a low murmuring of voices, but couldn't make out the words.

Then her mother was screaming, threatening to leave, telling her father she was going to take them all away.

Michelle, in the hall, had heard nothing then but the sound of her own heart pounding, felt nothing but the excruciating pain in her hip.

Finally she had heard her father. His words echoed in her ears: *I can't lose you. I can't lose Jennifer.*

Nothing about her.

She crept back to her room and got into bed. She pulled the covers up tight around her neck and lay there, her small body shivering, her mind whirling.

It was true. He didn't love her anymore.

Not since that day when she had fallen off the bluff.

That was the day the good things had stopped, and the bad things had started.

All she had left was Amanda.

In all the world, there was only Amanda.

She wished Amanda would come to her, talk to her, tell her everything was going to be all right.

And Amanda came.

Her dark figure, like a shadow in the night, moved out of a corner of the room, drifted toward Michelle, holding out her hand, reaching out, touching her.

The touch felt good. Michelle could feel her friend drawing her close.

"They were fighting, Mandy," she whispered. "They were fighting about me."

"No," Amanda said. "They weren't fighting about you. They don't care about you. They only love Jennifer now."

"No," Michelle protested.

"It's true," Amanda's voice whispered, soft in her ear, but insistent. "It's all happening because of Jennifer. If it weren't for Jennifer, they'd love you. If it weren't for Jennifer, you wouldn't have fallen. Remember how they were teasing you? It was about Jennifer.

"It's Jennifer's fault. All of it."

"Jennifer's fault? But . . . but she's so small . . ."

"It doesn't matter," Amanda whispered. "It will make it easy. Michelle, it will be so easy, and when she's gone—when Jennifer's gone—everything will be like it used to be. Can't you see?"

Michelle turned it over in her mind, listening all the while to Amanda's gentle voice, whispering to her, reassuring her. It all began to make sense.

It *was* Jennifer's fault.

If there were no Jennifer. . . .

Michelle drifted off to sleep with Amanda close to her, crooning to her, whispering to her.

And when she was asleep, Amanda told her what she had to do.

It made sense to Michelle now.

All of it. . . .

CHAPTER 22

As the week dragged by, June became increasingly upset. Several times, she was tempted to ask Tim Hartwick to change his schedule, and see her family sooner. But she resisted the temptation, telling herself she was becoming hysterical.

By the time Friday came, she wondered if it was too late. The Pendletons could hardly be called a family anymore. Michelle had withdrawn even further, going off to school silently each day, then returning home only to disappear into her room.

June found herself pausing in the upstairs hall too often, standing outside Michelle's door, listening.

She would hear Michelle's voice, soft, barely audible, the words undecipherable. There would be pauses, as if Michelle were listening to someone else, but June knew she was alone in her room.

Alone, except for Amanda.

Several times during those days, June tried to bridge the gulf that was widening between her and her husband, but Cal seemed impervious to her overtures. He left for the clinic early each morning and stayed late each evening, coming home only in time to play with Jennifer for a few minutes, then retiring early.

And Jennifer.

It was as if Jennifer sensed the tension in the house. Her laughter, the happy gurgling that June had grown so used to, had completely disappeared. She seldom even cried anymore, as if she were afraid to create any kind of disturbance.

June spent as much time as she could in her studio, trying to paint, but more often than not she merely stared at her empty canvas, not really seeing it. Several times she started to dig through the closet, to find the strange sketch she knew she hadn't done. Something stopped her—fear.

She was afraid that if she looked at it long enough, thought about it hard enough, she would figure out where it had come from. She didn't want to.

When Friday morning finally came, June felt suddenly released. Today, at last, they would see Tim Hartwick. And today, perhaps, things would begin to get better.

For the first time that week, June broke the silence that had lain heavily over the breakfast table.

"I'll pick you up at school today," she told Michelle.

Michelle looked at her questioningly. June tried to make her smile reassuring.

"I'm meeting your father after school today. We're all going to talk to Mr. Hartwick."

"Mr. Hartwick? The psychologist? Why?"

"I just think it would be a good idea, that's all," June said.

* * *

Tim Hartwick smiled at Michelle as she came into his office, and gestured toward a chair. Michelle settled herself into it, then surveyed the room. Tim waited quietly until her eyes finally came back to him.

"I thought my parents were going to be here, too."

"I'm going to talk to them a little later. First, I thought we could get acquainted."

"I'm not crazy," Michelle said. "I don't care what anybody told you."

"No one told me anything," Tim assured her. "But I guess you know what I do here."

Michelle nodded. "Do you think I did something to Susan Peterson?"

Tim was taken aback. "Did you?" he asked.

"No."

"Then why should I think you did?"

"Everybody else does." There was a pause, then: "Except Amanda."

"Amanda?" Tim asked. "Who's Amanda?"

"She's my friend."

"I thought I knew everyone here," Tim said carefully. "But I don't know anybody named Amanda."

"She doesn't go to school," Michelle said. Tim watched her carefully, trying to read her face, but there was nothing to read—as far as he could tell, Michelle was now quite relaxed.

"Why doesn't she go to school?" Tim asked.

"She can't. She's blind."

"Blind?"

Michelle nodded. "She can't see at all, except when she's with me. Her eyes look strange, all milky."

"And where did you meet her?"

Michelle thought for a long time before she answered him. Finally she shrugged. "I'm not sure. I guess I must have met her out by our house. That's where she lives."

Tim decided to drop the subject for a moment. "How's your leg? Does it hurt very badly?"

"It's all right." She paused, then seemed to change her mind. "Well, sometimes it hurts worse than others. And sometimes it hardly hurts at all."

"When is that?"

"When I'm with Amanda. I—I guess she sort of takes my mind off it. I think that's why we're such good friends. She's blind, and I'm crippled."

"Weren't you friends before you fell?" Tim asked, sensing something important.

"No. I saw her a couple of times, but I didn't really get to know her until after the accident. Then she started visiting me."

"Didn't you have a doll named Amanda?" Tim asked suddenly. Michelle only nodded.

"I still do. Except that it isn't really my doll. Actually, it was Mandy's doll, but now we share it."

"I see."

"I'm glad *some*one does," Michelle said.

"You mean some people don't?"

"Mom doesn't. She thinks I made Amanda up. I guess she thinks that because they have the same name. Amanda and the doll, I mean."

"Well, it could get confusing."

"I guess," Michelle agreed. "Actually, at first *I* thought they were the same, too. But they're not. Amanda's real, and the doll's not."

"What do you and Amanda do together?"

"Talk, mostly. But sometimes we go for walks together."

"What do you talk about?"

"All kinds of things."

Tim decided to try a shot in the dark. "Was Amanda with you the day Susan Peterson fell off the bluff?"

Michelle nodded.

"Were you in the graveyard?"

"Yes. Susan was saying mean things to me, but Mandy made her stop."

"How did she do that?"

"She chased her away."

"You mean she chased her off the bluff?"

"I don't know," Michelle said slowly. The thought had never occurred to her before. "Maybe so. I couldn't see—it was foggy that day. . . . Mom said it wasn't, but it was."

Tim leaned forward, and his face grew serious. "Michelle, is it always foggy when Amanda is with you?"

Michelle thought a moment, then shook her head. "No. Sometimes it is, but not all the time."

Tim nodded. "What about your other friends? Do they know Amanda?"

"I don't have any other friends."

"None?"

Michelle's voice dropped. Her eyes seemed to cloud over. "Ever since I fell off the bluff, nobody wants to be my friend."

"What about your sister?" Tim asked. "Isn't your sister your friend?"

"She's just a baby." There was a long silence, but Tim was reluctant to break it, sure that Michelle was about to say something. He was right.

"Besides," Michelle added, her voice little more than a whisper, "she's not really my sister."

"She isn't?"

"I'm adopted. Jenny's not."

"Does that bother you?"

"I don't know," Michelle hedged. "Amanda says . . ."

"What does Amanda say?" Tim urged her.

"Amanda says that ever since Jenny was born, Mom and Dad don't love me anymore."

"And do you believe her?"

Michelle's face took on a belligerent quality. "Well, why shouldn't I? Daddy hardly even talks to me anymore, and Mommy spends all her time taking care of Jenny, and—and—" Her voice trailed off, and a tear slid down her cheek.

"Michelle," Tim asked gently. "Do you wish Jenny had never been born?"

"I—I don't know."

"It's all right if you do," Tim told her. "I know how mad I was when my little sister was born. It just didn't seem fair. I'd had my parents all to myself for so long, and then all of a sudden there was someone else. But I found out my parents loved me just as much as they ever did."

"But you weren't adopted," Michelle countered. "It's not the same." She stood up. "May I go now?"

"Don't you want to talk to me anymore?"

"No. At least, not right now. And not about Jenny. I hate Jenny!"

"All right," Tim said soothingly. "We won't talk about Jenny anymore."

"I don't want to talk about anything anymore!" Michelle glared at him, her face set stubbornly.

"What *do* you want to do?"

"I want to go home," Michelle said. "I want to go home, and find Amanda!"

"All right," Tim said. "I'll tell you what—I have to

talk to your parents for a few minutes. Let's get you a Coke, and by the time you finish it, I should be done with your father and mother. How does that sound?"

Michelle seemed about to argue with him, but suddenly her anger dissipated, and she shrugged. "Okay, I guess."

Tim opened his office door for her and smiled encouragingly at June and Cal. "We're going to get Michelle a Coke," he told them. "You can go in—I'll be right back."

"Thank you," June murmured. Cal made no response at all.

They were waiting when he got back, June sitting nervously in the chair Michelle had occupied a few minutes earlier, Cal standing at the window, his back stiff. Even though his back was to him, Tim could sense Cal glaring. He sat down in his chair and fingered Michelle's file.

"What happened?" June asked.

"We had quite a conversation."

"And do you agree with my wife? Do you think Michelle's crazy?"

"Cal, I never said that," June protested.

"But it's what you think." He faced Tim. "My wife thinks both Michelle and I are crazy."

The expression on June's face, a combination of exasperation and pity, told Tim everything he needed to know.

"Mr. Hartwick—" June began. Then she floundered.

Tim came to her rescue. "Why don't you call me Tim? It makes things easier. Dr. Pendleton? Can I offer you a chair?"

"I'll stand," Cal said stiffly, maintaining his position

at the window. June shrugged, her face lifted to his, and Tim understood the gesture immediately. He decided, for the moment, not to press Cal.

"We talked about this friend of hers—Amanda," he told June.

"And?"

"Well, as far as I can tell, she seems to think Amanda is real. Not necessarily physically real, but definitely a person other than herself. A person who exists independently of her."

"Is that—is that normal?"

"In a small child, say a three-year-old, it's not that unusual."

"I see . . ." June said. "But not for Michelle. Am I right?"

"It may not be all that serious," Tim began, but Cal had turned away from the window and interrupted him.

"It isn't serious at all!" he said sharply. "All she's done is dream up a friend to get her through a rough time. Frankly, I don't see what all the fuss is about."

"I wish I could agree with you, Dr. Pendleton," Tim said quietly. "But I'm afraid I can't. Your daughter is in the midst of some very serious problems, and unless you're willing to face them, I don't really see how you can help her."

"Problems," June repeated. "You said problems. You mean more than her adjusting to her—her condition?"

Tim nodded. "I'm not even sure her leg is the main problem. In fact, I'm almost sure it's not. It's her sister."

"Jenny?" Cal asked.

"Oh, God, I was afraid of that," June moaned. She

turned on Cal. "I told you. I've been telling you for weeks, but you wouldn't believe me!"

"Dr. Pendleton, Michelle doesn't think you love her anymore. She thinks that, because she's adopted, you stopped loving her when you had a baby of your own."

"That's ridiculous," Cal said.

"Is it?" June asked, her voice hollow. "Is it really?"

"It seems her friend Amanda told her so," Tim said.

June stared at him blankly. "I'm not sure I understand."

Tim leaned back in his chair. "Well, it's not really all that difficult to put together. Michelle is having some thoughts and feelings right now that are totally foreign to her. She doesn't like them. In fact, they're tearing her apart. So she's invented Amanda. Amanda, essentially, is the dark side of Michelle's personality, and Michelle simply transfers all her—how shall I say it? Uglier? I guess that's a good enough word—she transfers all her uglier thoughts and impulses—the ones she can't even bear to take responsibility for—onto Amanda."

"Isn't that what they call projecting?" Cal asked, his voice filled with a hostility that Tim chose to ignore.

"As a matter of fact, yes, it is. Except that this is a particularly extreme form. The term *projecting* usually implies the projection of one's own problems onto someone else, but the someone else is usually quite real. A good example would be the faithless husband who constantly feels that his wife is cheating on him."

"I'm aware of the definition," Cal said.

Tim decided he'd had enough. "Dr. Pendleton, I get the feeling you'd rather not be hearing any of this. Am I right?"

"I'm here because my wife demanded it of me. But I think we're wasting our time."

"Maybe we are," Tim agreed. He folded his hands placidly and waited. He didn't have to wait long.

"You see?" Cal asked June. "Even he says we may be wasting our time. If you want to go on with this, you'll have to do it alone. I've heard enough." He started toward the door, then turned back. "Are you coming?"

June met his gaze, and when she spoke, her voice was calm. "No, Cal, I'm not. I can't make you listen, but I'm going to. If you want, you can wait for me. Otherwise, you can take Michelle, and I can walk home."

Tim, who had been watching Cal carefully, was sure he saw Cal flinch slightly at the mention of Michelle, but he said nothing, waiting to see what Cal would do.

"I'll wait," Cal said. He left the office, closing the door behind him. When he was gone, June turned back to Tim.

"I'm sorry," she said. "He—well, he just can't seem to face any of this. It's been terrible."

Tim was silent for a moment, allowing her her anguish. Then he said, very softly, "I think I can help Michelle. She's under a lot of pressure—her physical condition, for one thing. It isn't easy for a child suddenly to become a cripple. On top of that, there's the whole thing with Jennifer. And, of course, the whipped cream on the cake is her father's attitude. All together, it's putting Michelle under a lot of pressure, and things are coming loose."

"Then I was right," June breathed. It was as if a weight was being lifted from her shoulders. "Why does that make me feel so much better?"

"It's always better," Tim assured her, "to understand a problem. It's when you don't know what's going on that you feel completely lost. And at least, with Michelle, we know what's going on."

Michelle sat in the teachers' lounge for a few minutes, sipping at her Coke. She liked Mr. Hartwick—he listened to her, and believed her when she told him about Amanda. He didn't tell her Amanda was a ghost, or not real, or anything like that. Idly, she wondered what he was telling her parents. Not that it would make any difference. No matter what he said to them, they wouldn't love her anymore.

She wandered out of the teachers' lounge and onto the back stairs of the school. Billy Evans was sitting on a swing, kicking at the ground, trying to get the swing going. He was all alone, and when he saw Michelle, he waved to her, beckoning to her. She threw away the empty Coke cup and started down the stairs, leaning heavily on her cane.

"Hi," Billy said. "Will you push me?"

"Okay."

She began pushing him. He laughed happily and began begging her to push him harder.

"It's too high," Michelle said. "You shouldn't even be on these swings. You should be on the little ones."

"I'm big enough," Billy replied. "I can even walk the backstop."

Michelle glanced out to the baseball diamond, where a makeshift backstop had been constructed from two-by-fours and some wire mesh. It stood about eight feet tall and was some twenty feet long. Michelle had seen some of the older boys, the boys her age, scrambling up it, then walking its length. But the younger boys, the boys Billy's age, never dared.

"I never saw you," Michelle said.

"You never looked. Let the swing die down, and I'll show you."

Michelle stopped pushing, and Billy let the swing go through its arc once. Then, as it reached its forward peak, he jumped off, landing on his feet and running out toward the baseball field.

"Come on!" he called over his shoulder. Michelle started after him, moving as fast as she could, but by the time she reached him, he was already scrambling up the wire.

"Be careful," she warned him.

"It's easy," Billy scoffed. He reached the top and straddled the two-by-four, grinning down at her.

"Come on up," he said.

"I can't," Michelle said. "You know that."

Billy pulled one foot up, then the other. Slowly, balancing himself with his hands, he managed a crouching position. Then, wobbling all the way, he rose carefully until he was standing upright, his arms held straight out.

"See?"

Michelle could see him swaying. She was sure he was going to fall.

"Billy, you come down from there. You'll fall and hurt yourself, and I won't be able to help you."

"I won't fall! Watch me!"

He took a tentative step, nearly lost his footing, then regained his balance and took another.

"Please, Billy?" Michelle pleaded.

Billy was moving steadily away from her, inching

carefully along the two-by-four, his balance improving with each step.

"I won't fall," he insisted. Then, realizing that Michelle was about to insist that he come down, he decided to tease her. "You're just mad, because you can't do it. If you weren't a cripple, you could. But you are, so you can't!"

And he began to laugh.

Michelle stared at him for a second, his laughter echoing in her ears.

He sounded like Susan Peterson, and all the rest of them.

The fog started closing around her, the cold mists that she knew would bring Amanda with them. Billy Evans, his face grinning at her, faded from her vision, but his voice, still laughing, cut through the fog like a knife.

And then Amanda was there, standing behind her, whispering to her.

"Don't let him do that, Michelle," Mandy said softly. "He's laughing at you. Don't let him laugh at you. Don't ever let any of them laugh at you again."

Michelle hesitated. Once more, she heard Billy's mocking laugh, and his taunt.

"You could do it! If you weren't crippled!"

"Make him stop!" Mandy hissed in her ear.

"I don't know how," Michelle wailed. She looked around desperately, searching for Amanda.

"I'll show you," Mandy whispered. "Let me show you . . ."

The laughter, the mocking laughter, suddenly stopped, and was replaced by a scream of terror.

* * *

Billy tried to jump, but it was too late—beneath his feet, the backstop was moving.

He lost his balance, tried to regain it, failed. Then his arms were flailing in the air. He was falling.

A second later there was a silence in the schoolyard, a silence broken for Michelle only by the sound of Amanda's voice.

"You see? See how easy it is? Now you can make them all stop laughing . . ."

Her voice trailed off, and she was gone. The fog began to disperse. Michelle waited for a moment, waited for it all to be gone, then she looked.

Billy Evans, his head twisted around so that his empty eyes were staring at her, lay on the ground a few feet away.

Michelle knew he would never laugh at her again.

CHAPTER 23

Michelle stared at Billy Evans's tiny body, lying still on the ground, his face pale and lifeless. Tentatively, reluctantly, she took a step toward him.

"Billy?" Her voice was unsteady, questioning. "Billy? Are you all right?"

But even as she asked the question, she knew he was dead. She took one more step toward him, then changed her mind.

Help. She had to get help.

She braced herself against the backstop and leaned carefully over to pick up her cane. Then, after one more quick look at Billy, she started toward the school building. There was no one left in the yard—no one to come to her aid, no one to do something for Billy Evans.

No one to tell her what had happened.

For Michelle could not remember.

She could remember Billy climbing up the mesh, balancing himself on top.

She could remember him starting to walk, and she could remember telling him to be careful.

And he had laughed.

Then the fog had closed in on her, and Amanda had come.

But then what happened?

Her mind was blank.

She started up the back steps of the school.

"Help!" she called. "Oh, please, can't anyone hear me?"

She was very close to the top when she saw the door open, and her father appeared.

"Michelle? What's happened? Are you all right?"

"It's Billy!" Michelle cried. "Billy Evans! He fell, Daddy! He was trying to walk the backstop, and he fell!"

"Oh, my God." The words were barely audible, strangling in his throat. The visions came back to him, children's faces flashing in his mind, their eyes accusing him. He began to feel dizzy, but forced himself to look at the playground. Even from here he could see the little boy, motionless, lying in a crumpled heap next to the backstop.

By then, Michelle had reached the top of the steps, and was holding on to him, clinging to him, her eyes brimming with tears.

"He fell, Daddy. I think—I think he's dead."

He had to think. He had to *act*. But it was nearly impossible. "Come inside," he mumbled. "Come inside, and your mother will take care of you." He disentangled himself from Michelle and led her inside to the office, where June and Tim Hartwick were still talking. Both of them looked at him in surprise, then, by the expression on his face, knew that something was wrong.

"Call an ambulance," he said. "There's been an accident. A little boy fell off the backstop. I—I've got to take care of him." His voice faded. "I've got to. . . ." He turned and shambled out of the office.

As Tim picked up the phone and began dialing, Michelle suddenly spoke.

"Mom?" Her voice sounded dazed, and June took her in her arms.

"It's all right, honey," June whispered to her. "Daddy's taking care of it, and an ambulance will be here soon. What happened?"

Michelle buried her face against her mother and sobbed uncontrollably. As June listened to Tim talking on the phone, she tried to soothe her daughter. Slowly, Michelle regained herself.

Tim Hartwick hung up the phone as Michelle started to recite the tale. He listened intently, observing Michelle as she talked, trying to read the truth of her words in her face. When she was done, June took her once more in her arms.

"How terrible," she said softly. "But don't worry— he'll probably be fine."

"No, he won't," Michelle said hollowly. "He's dead. I know he's dead."

It was like a recurring nightmare.

Cal crossed the schoolyard in a daze, as though his feet were dragging him back, even as he tried to run. The seconds it took him to reach Billy Evans seemed like hours, and his mind was flooded with the sure foreknowledge of what he would find.

He reached Billy at last and knelt by the boy's limp

body. He glanced at Billy's face, noted the broken neck, then automatically took the child's wrist between his fingers.

There was a pulse.

Cal thought he was imagining it at first, but a moment later he knew: Billy Evans was still alive.

Why can't he be dead? Cal silently asked. *Why does he have to depend on me?*

He leaned over Billy reluctantly, forcing himself to examine him.

He was going to have to move the boy.

He hesitated. Only a few weeks earlier he had gathered up his own child. Now she was crippled. Panic rose in him, and for a split second he felt paralyzed. Then, slowly, his mind began to reason.

When the ambulance arrived, the attendants would move Billy. Perhaps he should wait.

But he was a doctor. He *had* to do something.

Besides, if he didn't, he was sure that Billy would be dead by the time the ambulance arrived—he could see the constriction in the boy's neck, see him slowly strangling. If Billy was to survive, Cal had to straighten out his neck.

He began to move Billy's head.

As the flow of air passed more freely into his lungs, Billy's complexion began to change. The blueness faded. Then, as Cal watched, the child began to breathe more easily.

Cal began to let himself relax.

Billy Evans was going to live.

In the distance, the wail of the ambulance started up. To Cal, the sound was a symphony of hope.

* * *

As the sound of the ambulance grew louder, June stood up and went to the window. From where she stood, she could see nothing—only one corner of the backstop, ominously visible, the rest of it blocked from her view by the building.

"I can't stand it," she said. "Tim, go see what's happening. Please?"

Tim Hartwick nodded. He started out of the office, then paused at the door.

"I told Mrs. Evans to come here. You're sure you don't want me to wait with you?" He glanced pointedly at Michelle, who was sitting on a straight-backed chair, her gaze fixed in midair, her face frozen in an expression of shock.

"If she gets here before you get back, I'll handle it," June insisted. "Just find out—find out if he's alive."

Half an hour later, only Michelle, June, and Tim were left at the school. The ambulance, with Billy and Cal in the rear, had departed for the clinic, and Billy's mother had followed, insisting she could drive herself once she was assured that her son was still alive. The small crowd that had gathered in the schoolyard had quickly dispersed, the people leaving in small groups, whispering among themselves, and occasionally glancing back toward the school, where they knew Michelle Pendleton was still sitting in Tim Hartwick's office.

Tim signaled June to join him in the hall for a moment. When they were alone, he told her that he would like to talk to Michelle.

"So soon?" June asked. "But—she's too upset!"

"We have to find out what happened. I think if I talk to her now, before she's had much of a chance to really think about it, I'll get the closest thing to the truth."

June's maternal instincts leaped to her daughter's defense. "You mean before she's had a chance to make up a story?"

"That's not what I said, and it's not what I meant," Tim said quickly. "I want to talk to her before her mind has had a chance to make whatever happened seem logical to her. And I want to find out why she was so sure Billy was dead."

"All right," June said at last, reluctantly. "But don't push her. Please?"

"I never would," Tim said gently. He left June alone in the hall while he returned to Michelle.

"Why did you think Billy was dead?" Tim asked gently. It had taken him ten minutes to convince Michelle that her friend hadn't died, and he still wasn't sure she believed him. "He didn't fall very far—just a few feet, really."

"I just knew it," Michelle replied. "You can tell."

"You can? How?"

"Just—just by—things. You know."

Tim waited a moment, but when Michelle didn't go on, he decided to ask her to tell him again what had happened. He listened without interrupting while she recited the story again.

"And that's all?" he asked when she was finished.

Michelle nodded.

"Now I want you to think very carefully," Tim said. "I want you to go over it all once more, and try to remember if you left anything out."

Michelle began going over the story again. This

time Tim stopped her occasionally, trying to prod her memory for detail.

"Now, when Billy started walking along the top of the backstop, where were you standing?"

"At the end of it, right where he climbed up it."

"Were you touching it? Leaning on it?"

Michelle frowned a little, trying to remember. "No. I was using my cane. I was leaning on my cane."

"All right," Tim said. "Now, tell me again what happened while Billy was walking the rail."

She told it exactly as she had before.

"I was watching him," Michelle said. "I was telling him to be careful, because I was afraid he might fall. And then he tripped—he just tripped, and fell. I tried to catch him, but I couldn't—he was too far away, and I—well, I can't move very fast anymore."

"But what did he trip on?" Tim asked.

"I don't know—I couldn't see."

"You couldn't see? Why not?" A thought occurred to him. "Was it foggy? Did it get foggy?"

For a split second there was a flicker in Michelle's eyes, but then she shook her head.

"No. I couldn't see because I'm not tall enough. Maybe—maybe there was a nail sticking up."

"Maybe so," Tim agreed. Then: "What about Amanda? Was she there?"

Again, for just a split second, there was that flicker in Michelle's eyes. But, again, she shook her head.

"No."

"You're sure?" Tim urged her. "It could be very important."

Now Michelle shook her head more definitely.

"No!" she exclaimed. "There was no fog, and

Amanda wasn't with me. Billy tripped! That's all, he just tripped. Don't you believe me?"

Tim could see that she was on the verge of tears.

"Of course I do," he said, smiling at her. "You like Billy Evans, don't you?"

"Yes."

"Did he ever tease you?"

"Tease me?"

"You know—the way Susan Peterson did, and some of the other kids."

"No." Again, Tim thought he noticed a hesitation.

There was more to the story than Michelle was telling him, but he wasn't sure that he would be able to get it out of her. Something was holding her back. It was as if she was protecting something. He thought he knew what it was.

Amanda.

Amanda, the dark side of Michelle, had done something, and Michelle was protecting her. Tim knew it would be a long time before he would be able to convince Michelle to abandon her "friend."

As he was wondering what to say next, Michelle suddenly met his eyes.

"He's going to die," she said softly. Tim stared at her, not sure he had heard her right. Then, her voice still soft, but very definite, Michelle repeated the words.

"I know Billy's going to die."

June drove slowly, Cal beside her in the front seat, Michelle in the back. Each of them was in his own private world, although both Cal and June were thinking about Billy Evans, lying in a coma in the clinic. Josiah Carson had done as much for the boy as he could,

and had given Cal a light sedative. Tomorrow a neurologist would come from Boston. But Cal and Josiah
were both sure that the specialist's findings would only
verify what they already knew—Billy's strangulation
had gone on too long; there was brain damage. How
extensive the damage was wouldn't be known until
Billy came out of the coma.

If he came out of it.

The silence in the car was beginning to tell on June.
She was relieved when she finally had an excuse to
break it.

"I have to stop at the Bensons' to pick up Jenny."

Cal nodded once, but made no verbal reply. Only
when she had turned in at the Bensons' did he speak.

"I wish you wouldn't leave Jenny like this."

"Well, I couldn't very well bring her with me, could
I?"

"You could have called me. I'd have come out and
driven you both in."

"Frankly, I wasn't sure you'd even be at the school,"
June said. Then she remembered Michelle's silent
presence in the backseat. "Never mind. Next time I'll
either call you or bring Jenny with me." She opened
the car door and got out, then held the back door for
Michelle. Cal was already on the Bensons' porch as
June and Michelle started up the steps.

Constance Benson must have been waiting for them,
for the door opened just as Cal was about to knock.
June thought she saw the woman's lips tighten as she
glanced at Michelle. When she said nothing, June decided to wait until they were inside to explain what
had happened. But it soon became apparent that Constance Benson had already heard. "I just talked to
Estelle Peterson," she said. "A terrible thing—terrible."

Again, she glanced at Michelle. This time, June was sure there was hostility in her eyes.

"It was an accident," June said quickly. "Billy was trying to walk the backstop, and he fell. Michelle tried to catch him."

"Did she?" Constance Benson's voice was carefully neutral, but June was sure she could hear a hint of sarcasm in it. "I'll get the baby. She's upstairs, asleep."

"I can't thank you enough for taking care of her," June said gratefully. Constance was already on the stairs, but she turned back to face June as she spoke.

"Babies aren't any trouble at all," she said. "It's only when they start growing up that the problems come."

Michelle was standing just inside the door. She took a step toward her father.

"She thinks I did something, doesn't she?" she asked, when Constance continued up the stairs.

Cal shook his head but said nothing. Michelle turned to her mother.

"Doesn't she?" she repeated.

"Of course not," June replied. She went to Michelle, and slipped an arm protectively around her daughter's shoulders. When Constance reappeared a moment later with Jennifer cradled in her arms, she paused, as if unwilling to deliver the baby to June while she was so close to Michelle. There was a silence, broken at last by Michelle.

"I didn't hurt Billy," she said. "It was an accident."

"What happened to Susan Peterson was an accident, too," Constance replied. "But I wouldn't want to try to convince her mother of it."

June felt herself becoming angry, and decided, quite consciously, not to suppress it.

"That's a cruel thing to say, Mrs. Benson. You saw what happened to Susan Peterson, and you know perfectly well that Michelle had nothing to do with it. And today, she tried to help Billy Evans. If she could move faster, she would have."

"Well, all I know is that 'accidents' don't just happen. Something causes them, and you can't tell me any different!" She handed Jennifer to June, but her eyes suddenly moved to Michelle.

"If I were you, I'd be careful with this baby," she said. She was still staring at Michelle. "It doesn't take much of a fall to kill a child this age."

June's mouth dropped open in astonishment as she realized the implication of what Constance Benson had said. She searched for a suitable reply. When no words came, she simply handed Jenny to Michelle.

"Take her out to the car, will you, darling?" she asked.

Michelle carefully took the baby in one arm while she used the other to balance herself with the cane. June kept her eyes on Constance Benson, as if challenging her to say anything further. Michelle, cradling the baby in her left arm, started shakily toward the door.

"Will you go with her?" June asked Cal. "I don't see how she'll be able to get the car door open, too. But I imagine she could do it if she had to."

Cal, sensing the tension between the two women, quickly followed Michelle out to the porch. Left alone with Constance Benson, June struggled to control her voice.

"Thank you for looking after Jennifer," she said at last. "Now that I've said that, I have to tell you that I think you're the most cruel and ignorant person it has ever been my misfortune to meet. In the future, neither I nor my family will bother you again. I'll find some-one else to sit with Jenny, or do it myself. Good-bye."

She started toward the door but was stopped cold by Constance Benson's voice.

"I won't hold that against you, Mrs. Pendleton," Constance said. "You don't know what's happening. You just don't know."

Michelle started down the steps, holding Jenny tight against her chest while she used the cane to find her footing. She stayed close to the bannister, so that if she slipped she could lean against it. When she got to the bottom she stopped, and slowly released the breath she had been holding as she made her way down from the Bensons' porch. "We made it," she whispered, smiling down at Jenny's little face. Seeming to understand her, Jenny looked up at her, gurgling happily. A tiny trickle of spittle dribbled from one corner of her mouth. Michelle dabbed it away with a corner of the blanket.

And then, suddenly, the fog started closing around her. She glanced up quickly, seeing the mists coming fast, and hearing the first faint whispers of Amanda's voice. She saw her father, standing next to the car, watching her.

"Daddy?"

Cal took a tentative step toward her, but the fog closed in on her then, and he disappeared.

"Daddy! Quick!" Michelle cried.

She was going to drop Jennifer.

She could feel Amanda, next to her, prodding her,

whispering to her, telling her to let go of the baby, to let Jennifer—Jennifer, who had taken her parents away from her—fall to the ground.

As Amanda's voice grew more insistent, Michelle felt herself giving in, felt herself obeying her friend's voice. She wanted to hurt Jenny, wanted to see her fall.

Slowly, she began relaxing her left arm.

"It's all right," she heard her father say. "I've got her now. You can let go."

She felt Jennifer being lifted out of her arms. The fog dispersed as quickly as it had come. Next to her, her father stood holding the baby, watching her.

"What happened?" she heard him ask.

"I—I got tired," Michelle stammered. "I just couldn't hold her any longer. I thought I was going to drop her, Daddy!"

"But you didn't, did you?" Cal said. "It's just like I told your mother. You're just fine. You didn't want to hurt Jenny, did you? You didn't want to drop her." There was desperation in Cal's voice, the sound of a man trying to convince himself of the truth of his own words. Michelle, however, was too lost in her own confusion to hear the pleading in her father's words. When she replied, her own voice was uncertain.

"No. I—I just got tired, that's all," Michelle said. But as she got into the backseat of the car, she thought she could hear Amanda's voice, far away, shouting at her.

Then her mother was in the car, too, and they were driving home. But all the way, Michelle could hear Amanda's voice.

Amanda was angry with her.

She could tell by the way Amanda was shouting at her.

She didn't want Amanda angry at her.

Amanda was the only friend she had.

Whatever happened, she couldn't let Amanda stay angry.

CHAPTER 24

It wasn't until Tim suggested that perhaps Michelle should be institutionalized, if only for observation, that Corinne lost her temper.

"How can you say that?" she demanded. She tucked her feet up under her in an unconsciously defensive gesture and clutched her coffee cup in both hands. Tim poked at the fire and shrugged helplessly.

"There was something in her eyes," he said. How many times had he tried to explain it? "I don't know exactly what it was, but she wasn't telling me everything. I'm sorry, Corinne, but I don't believe that Billy Evans fell off that backstop accidentally."

"You mean you think Michelle Pendleton tried to kill him." Corinne's voice was cold. "You might as well say what you mean."

"I did. You seem to want me to say that I think Michelle Pendleton is a murderer, but I won't. I'm not sure she is. But I *am* sure she had something to do with Billy's fall. And Susan Peterson's, too, for that matter."

"You don't think she's a murderer, but you think she killed Susan? Is that what you're saying?" Without waiting for him to reply, she went right on. "My God, Tim, if you'd talked to her just a few weeks ago, you'd know that couldn't be true. She was the sweetest, nicest child. Things just don't change that fast."

"Don't they? All you have to do is look at her." Tim ran a hand through his hair in an attempt to keep his brown curls from tumbling over his forehead, but it did no good. "Look, Corinne, you have to face the facts. Whatever she is, Michelle isn't the same girl who came to Paradise Point in August. She's changed."

"So you want to lock her up? You just want to put her away where nobody will have to look at her? You sound just like the kids in my class!"

"That's not what I meant, and you know it. Corinne, you have to face up to what's happened. Whatever's causing it, Susan is dead, and Billy might as well be. And both times, Michelle was there. And we know that *something's* happened to her," Tim said tiredly. They'd been going around and around the subject for hours, ever since dinner, and they hadn't gotten anywhere. If only, Tim thought, Michelle had given that damned doll some other name. *Any* other name. It was as if Corinne read his mind.

"You still haven't explained Amanda," she said.

"I've explained it five hundred times."

"Oh, sure! You keep telling me that she only exists in Michelle's imagination. Except you still haven't explained one thing—how come everyone around here has been talking about Amanda for so many years? If she's only Michelle's imaginary friend, why has she been around so much longer than Michelle?"

"Everybody hasn't been talking about Amanda. Only a few impressionable schoolgirls have."

Corinne's eyes narrowed angrily, but before she could begin her argument, Tim held up his hand as if to fend her off.

"Let's not talk about it anymore, all right? Can't we just forget about it for tonight?"

"I don't see how," Corinne replied. "It's like a cloud hanging over us."

The ringing of the telephone interrupted her. Corinne automatically rose to answer it before she remembered that it wasn't her phone. Tim, using the diversion to try to change the mood of the evening, grinned at her. "If you'd just marry me, you could answer the phone here any time you wanted to."

He had just reached for the receiver when it stopped ringing. Both he and Corinne waited expectantly for Lisa to call one of them. Instead there was a silence, then Lisa came downstairs.

"That was Alison. I'm going to go over to her house tomorrow, and we're going to look for the ghost."

"Oh, God," Tim groaned. "Not you, too?"

Lisa rolled her eyes in contempt. "Well, why not? Alison says Sally Carstairs already saw the ghost once, and I think it would be fun. I never get to do anything!"

Tim looked helplessly at Corinne. He was about to give his assent, but Corinne stopped him.

"Tim, don't."

"Why not?"

"Tim, please. Just humor me, all right? Besides, even if I'm wrong, and you're right, do you know where they'll be looking for the ghost? Out near the Pendletons', in the Carsons' old graveyard. That's where Amanda's grave is."

"It isn't a grave," Lisa sneered.

"There's a headstone," Corinne said automatically, but Lisa was paying no attention to her. Instead, she was pleading with her father.

"Can I go, Daddy? Please?"

But Tim decided that Corinne was right. Whatever was happening, he didn't want his daughter near the Pendletons'.

"I don't think it's a good idea, sweetheart," he said. "You tell Alison you'll go some other time, all right?"

"Aw, Dad, you never let me do anything. All you ever do is listen to *her*, and she's as crazy as Michelle Pendleton!" Lisa's words were directed to her father, but she was staring at Corinne, her face pinched with anger, her mouth in a pout. Corinne simply looked the other way. For once, she was going to ignore Lisa's rudeness.

"You can't go, and that's final," Tim said. "Now go up and call Alison, and tell her. Then finish your homework and go to bed."

Lisa silently decided that she would do what she wanted to do, made a face at Corinne, then sulkily left the room. An uncomfortable silence fell in Tim's living room as both he and Corinne tried to pretend that their evening wasn't hopelessly ruined. Finally Corinne stood up.

"Well, it's getting late—"

"You mean you want to go home, don't you?" Tim asked.

Corinne nodded. "I'll call you in the morning." She

started out of the room, intent on gathering her coat and purse, but Tim stopped her.

"Don't I even get a good night kiss?"

Corinne gave him a perfunctory peck on the cheek but resisted his embrace. "Not now, Tim. Please? Not tonight."

Defeated, Tim let her go, standing alone in the living room as she put on her coat. Then she came back in and smiled at him.

"Now I know where Lisa gets her pout—from her father. Come on, Tim, it isn't the end of the world. I'll call you tomorrow, or you call me. Okay?"

Tim nodded.

"Men!"

Corinne said the word out loud, then repeated it, as she drove herself home. Sometimes, she reflected, they could be so damn stubborn. And not just Tim, either. Cal Pendleton wasn't any better. He and Tim should be great friends, she decided. One of them hanging on to the idea that everything was fine, and the other hanging on to the idea that whatever was happening was only happening in Michelle's mind.

But it wasn't. Corinne was sure it wasn't, but she didn't know what to do next. Should she talk to June Pendleton about it? She should. Right now. She pulled the car into a sharp U-turn, and headed toward the Pendletons'. But when she arrived, the house was dark. She sat in her car for a few minutes, debating with herself. Should she wake them up? What for? To tell them a ghost story?

In the end, she simply went home.

But, as she went to sleep that night, Corinne Hatcher had a sense of events closing in, as if whatever was finally going to happen was going to happen soon.

And when it happened, whatever it was, they would all know the truth.

She only hoped that, in the meantime, nobody else would die. . . .

Her hip was exploding with pain. She wanted to stop and rest, but she knew she couldn't.

Behind her, but getting closer, she could hear people calling to her—angry people—people who wanted to hurt her.

She couldn't let them hurt her—she had to get away, far away, where they wouldn't be able to find her.

Amanda would help her.

But where was Amanda?

She called out, begging her friend to come and help her, but there was no answer—only those other voices, screaming at her, frightening her.

She tried to move faster, tried to force her left leg to respond as she wanted it to, but it was useless.

They were going to catch her.

She stopped and turned around.

Yes, there they were, coming toward her.

She couldn't see their faces, not clearly, but she thought she knew the voices.

Mrs. Benson.

That didn't surprise her: Mrs. Benson had always hated her.

But there were others.

Her parents. Well, not her parents, but those two strangers who had pretended to be her parents.

And someone else—someone she thought liked her. It was a man, but who? It didn't matter, really. Whoever he was, he wanted to hurt her, too. Their voices were growing louder, and they were coming closer. If she was going to get away, she would have to run.

She looked around frantically, sure that Amanda would come and help her. But Amanda wasn't there. She would have to get away by herself.

The bluff.

If she could get to the bluff, she would be safe.

She started toward it, her heart pounding, her breath coming in short gasps.

Her left leg was dragging her back. She couldn't run! But she had to run!

And then she was there, poised at the top of the cliff, the sea below her, and behind her those voices, insistent, demanding—hurting. She glanced once more over her shoulder. They were closer now, almost upon her. But they wouldn't catch her.

With a final burst of energy, she threw herself off the bluff.

Falling was so easy.

Time seemed to stand still, and she drifted, relaxed, felt the air rush by her, looked at the sky.

She looked down—and saw the rocks.

Jagged, angry fingers of stone, reaching up to her, ready to tear her apart.

Terror finally engulfed her, and she opened her mouth to scream. But it was too late—she was going to die. . . .

Michelle woke up shivering, her throat constricted with an unuttered scream.

"Daddy?" Her voice was soft, tiny in the night. She knew no one had heard her. No one, except—

"I saved you," Amanda whispered to her. "I didn't
let you die."

"Mandy—?" She *had* come. Michelle sat up in bed,
her fear draining away as she realized that Amanda
was there, helping her, taking care of her. "Mandy?
Where are you?"

"I'm here," Mandy said softly. She emerged from the
shadows of the room, standing near the window, her
black dress glistening eerily in the moonlight. She held
out her hand, and Michelle left her bed.

Amanda, holding her by the hand, led her down the
stairs and out of the house. It wasn't until they had
reached the studio that Michelle realized she had left
her cane behind. But it didn't matter—Amanda was
there for her to lean on.

Besides, her hip didn't hurt at all. Not at all!

They slipped into the studio, and Michelle knew
immediately what to do. It was as if Amanda could
talk to her silently, as if Amanda were truly inside her.

She found a sketch pad and set it up on her mother's
easel. She worked quickly, her strokes bold and sure.
The picture emerged quickly.

Billy Evans, his small body perched on the top of
the backstop, balancing himself precariously. The perspective was strange. He seemed to be very high up,
far above the figure of Michelle herself, who stood on
the ground, her cane forgotten as she stared helplessly upward.

Near her, clutching the support post, was Amanda, a
smile on her face, her empty eyes seeming somehow
alive with excitement as Billy started to fall.

Michelle stared at the picture and, in the dimness
of the studio, she felt Amanda's hand in her own. They
stood together for a moment in silent closeness. Then,

knowing what she must do, Michelle let go of
Amanda's hand, tore the sketch from the pad, and
took it to the closet. She found what she was looking
for easily, though she had turned on no lights. She
took out the canvas, that first canvas she had drawn
for Amanda, and left her new sketch—the sketch of
Billy Evans, with the one of Susan Peterson.

She set the canvas up on the easel, and picked up
June's palette.

Though the dim light washed the colors on the
palette to little more than shades of gray, Michelle
knew where to touch the brush to find the hues she
wanted.

She worked quickly, her face expressionless. Behind
her, watching over her shoulder, her hand lightly resting on her elbow, Michelle could feel Amanda watching in fascination, her milky white eyes fixed on the
picture, her expression eager. The picture was telling
her the story—soon she would see it all. Michelle
would show her everything.

Michelle had no sense of time as she worked. When
she finally set the palette aside and stepped back to
look at the canvas, she wondered why she didn't feel
tired. But she knew, really—it was Amanda, helping
her.

"Is it all right?" she asked shyly.

Amanda nodded, her sightless eyes still fixed on the
picture. After a few seconds, she spoke.

"You could have killed her this afternoon," she said.

Jennifer. Mandy was talking about Jennifer, and she
was angry at Michelle.

"I know," Michelle answered quietly.

"Why didn't you?" Mandy's voice, silken but hard,
caressed Michelle.

"I—I don't know," she whispered.

"You could do it now," Amanda suggested.

"Now?"

"They're asleep. They're all asleep. We could go to the nursery. . . ." Amanda took Michelle's hand and led her out of the studio.

As they crossed the lawn toward the house, a cloud drifted across the moon, and the silvery light faded into darkness. But the darkness didn't matter.

Amanda was leading her.

And the fog was coming in.

The wonderful fog that cuddled Michelle, shutting out the rest of the world, leaving her alone with Amanda. Whatever Amanda wanted, Michelle knew she would do. . . .

June woke up in the darkness, some maternal sixth sense telling her that something was wrong. She listened for a moment.

A cry.

Muffled, but a cry.

It was coming from the nursery. June got out of bed, grabbed her robe, and crossed the bedroom.

The nursery door was closed.

She distinctly remembered leaving it open—she always left it open.

She glanced at Cal, but he was sound asleep, his position unchanged.

Then who had closed the door?

She pulled it open and stepped into the nursery, switching on the light as she passed through the door. Michelle was standing by Jennifer's crib. She looked up, her face puzzled, as the room filled with light.

"Mother?"

"Michelle! What are you doing up?"

"I—I heard Jenny crying, and when I didn't hear you, I came in to see what was wrong."

Michelle carefully tucked the little pillow in her hands under Jennifer's head.

Her crying was muffled!

The thought slashed through June's mind, but she immediately silenced it.

The door was closed, she told herself. *That's why I couldn't hear her. The door was closed!*

"Michelle," she said carefully. "Did you close the door between here and our bedroom?"

"No." Michelle's voice was uncertain. "It must have been closed when I came in. Maybe that's why you didn't hear Jenny."

"Well, I suppose it doesn't matter." But it did matter, and June knew it. Something was happening —something she didn't want to think about. She went over to the crib, and picked Jenny up. The baby was sleeping now, making little mewling sounds. As she picked her up, Jenny coughed a little, then relaxed in her mother's arms. June smiled at Michelle. "See? All it takes is a mother's loving arms." She looked more closely at Michelle. Her eyes were clear, and she didn't look as though she'd been asleep only a few minutes ago."

"Couldn't you sleep, honey?"

"No. I was just talking to Amanda. Then Jenny started crying, so I came in here."

"Well, let me get her settled, then we'll have a little talk, okay?"

Michelle's eyes clouded over. For a moment June was afraid she was going to refuse. But then Michelle shrugged. "Okay."

June tucked Jennifer back into the crib, then offered
Michelle her arm to lean on. "Where's your cane?"

"I left it in my room."

"Well, that's a good sign," June said hopefully. But
as they went down the hall, it seemed to her that
Michelle could barely walk. She said nothing, however, until Michelle was settled in her bed, propped
up against the pillows. "Does it hurt badly?" She
touched Michelle's hip gently.

"Sometimes. Now. But sometimes not. When
Amanda's around, it's better."

"Amanda," June repeated the name softly. "Do you
know who Amanda is?"

"Not really," Michelle said. "But I think she used to
live here."

"When?"

"A long time ago."

"Where does she live now?"

"I'm not sure. I guess she still lives here."

"Michelle—does Amanda want something?"

Michelle nodded her head. "She wants to see something. I'm not sure what it is, but it's something
Amanda has to see. And I can show it to her."

"You? How?"

"I—I don't know. But I know I can help her. And
she's my friend, so I *have* to help her, don't I?"

It sounded to June like a plea for reassurance. "Of
course you do," she said. "If she's truly your friend.
But what if she's not your friend? What if she really
wants to hurt you?"

"But she doesn't," Michelle said. "I know she
doesn't. Amanda would never hurt me. Never." As
June watched, her daughter's eyes closed, and she fell
asleep.

June sat with her for a long time, holding her hand, and watching her sleep. Then, as the first faint light began burning through the darkness, June kissed Michelle lightly and returned to bed.

She tried to sleep, but her thoughts, so carefully banished, came back to haunt her.

She hadn't heard Jenny cry because the door was closed.

But they never closed the door.

And Michelle had been holding a pillow.

June left her bed once again, and went back into the nursery.

Carefully, she locked the door leading to the hall and put the key in the pocket of her robe.

Only then was she able to sleep, and she hated herself for it.

CHAPTER 25

Saturday morning.

On any ordinary Saturday morning, June would have awakened slowly, stretched luxuriously, then rolled over and slid her arms around her husband.

But it had been a long time since she had done that, on Saturday morning or any other morning.

On this Saturday morning, she was wide awake, and tired.

She glanced at the clock—nine thirty.

She turned the other way, to see if Cal was still sleeping.

He was gone.

June lifted herself into a sitting position, about to get up, then let herself lean back against the pillows. Her gaze wandered to the window.

Outside the sky was leaden, and the trees, their remaining leaves having lost their sparkle in the gray light, were beginning to look thin and tired. Soon the leaves would be gone entirely. June shivered a little, anticipating the coming winter.

She began listening for the familiar sounds of morning—Jennifer should be crying, and she should be able to hear Cal, banging around the kitchen, pretending to be fixing his breakfast when he was really only trying to wake her up.

But this morning, there was a silence hanging over the house.

"Hello?" June called tentatively.

There was no answer, so she got out of bed, put on her robe, then went to the nursery.

Jennifer's crib was empty, and the door to the hall stood open. June frowned and went through the nursery to the hall. When she got to the top of the stairs, she called out again, louder.

"Hello! Where is everybody?"

"We're down here!" It was Michelle, and as June heard her, she felt herself relax. It's all right, she told herself. Nothing's happened. It's all right. It was only when she was halfway down the stairs that she realized how worried she had been, how much the silence of the morning had frightened her. Now, as she entered the kitchen, she assured herself that she was being silly. Last night's imaginings fled.

"Hi! Everyone's up so early."

Cal glanced at her, then went back to scrambling a batch of eggs. "You were dead to the world this morning, and someone had to fix breakfast. And Michelle helped me, so it shouldn't be a total loss."

Michelle was setting the table. She looked tired, but as June winked at her she smiled slightly, apparently happy to be doing something with her father, even if it was only setting the table.

"Did you sleep all right, honey?" she asked.

"My hip was hurting pretty bad, but it's all right this morning."

There was a good feeling in the house, and June knew the reason for it—Billy Evans hadn't died. Cal had saved him, not hurt him, and now, she was sure, everything was going to be all right. She wanted to say something, comment on the pleasant atmosphere, but she was afraid that if she did, she would destroy it. Instead, she went to the bassinet where Jennifer was sleeping peacefully.

"Well, at least I wasn't the only one who slept in," she said as she picked the baby up. Jenny opened her eyes and gurgled, then went back to sleep.

"She was up earlier," Cal said. "I gave her a bottle about an hour ago. Do you want these on toast?"

"Fine," June said absently. With Cal making breakfast, Michelle finishing with the table, and Jennifer asleep, she felt suddenly useless. "Do you want me to take over?"

"Too late," Cal said. He served the eggs, added a couple of slices of bacon to each plate, and carried them to the table. As he sat down, he glanced at his watch.

"Do you have to go already?" June asked.

"The neurologist should be in by ten. I really ought to be there."

"May I go in with you?" Michelle asked. Cal frowned, and June immediately shook her head.

"I think you'd better stay here today," she said, carefully avoiding any mention of Billy Evans.

"But why?" Michelle asked. Her face started to cloud over, and June was sure there was going to be an argument. She could feel the comparatively relaxed atmosphere of the morning slipping away. She turned to Cal.

"Cal? What do you think?"

"I don't know. I don't suppose there's any reason why she shouldn't go along, really. But I don't know how long I'll be there," he added, turning to Michelle. "You might get bored."

"I just want to see Billy. Then I could go to the library. Or I could walk home."

"All right," Cal gave in. "But you can't spend the whole day hanging around the clinic. Is that clear?"

"You used to let me," Michelle complained.

Cal's eyes shifted uneasily. "That was—before," he said.

"Before? Before what?"

When he made no answer, Michelle stared at him, then she realized what he meant.

"I didn't do anything to Billy," she said.

"I didn't say—" Cal began, but June interrupted him.

"He didn't mean that," she said. "He meant—"

"I know what he meant," Michelle shouted. "Well, I don't want to go! I don't want to go anywhere near your old clinic!" She stood up from the table, grabbed her cane, and started out of the kitchen. The back door had slammed behind her before either June or Cal had recovered from her outburst. June stood up and started after Michelle, but Cal stopped her.

"Let her go," he said. "She has to learn to deal with things herself. You—you can't protect her from the world."

"But I shouldn't have to protect her from her own father," June said bitterly. "Cal, why do you do things like that? Do you think those things don't hurt her?"

Cal made no reply, and June, knowing whatever pleasantness the morning had promised was now destroyed, picked up the bassinet, and walked out of the kitchen.

Annie Whitmore was sitting on the merry-go-round in the schoolyard when she saw Michelle coming down the street. Michelle was walking slowly, and Annie thought she looked angry. Annie looked around quickly, wondering if anyone else was there. She wanted to play with Michelle, but she knew she wasn't supposed to—her mother had talked to her for a long time last night, warning her that from now on, she wasn't even supposed to speak to Michelle, and if Michelle offered to play with her, she was to come home at once.

But Annie liked Michelle, and since her mother wouldn't tell her why she was supposed to stay away from her, she decided to ignore the order.

Besides, there wasn't anybody around to tell on her if she disobeyed.

"Michelle!"

Michelle didn't respond, so Annie called her again, louder. This time Michelle looked in her direction, and Annie waved.

"Hi! What are you doing?"

"Just walking," Michelle said. She stopped and leaned on the fence. "What are you doing?"

"Playing. But I can't get the merry-go-round to go fast enough. It's too heavy."

"Want me to push it for you?" Michelle offered.

Annie nodded, telling herself that it was all right—she hadn't actually *asked* Michelle to play with her.

Michelle opened the gate and limped into the

schoolyard. Annie waited patiently on the merry-go-round. When Michelle came close to her, she grinned.

"How come you're down here on Saturday?"

"I was just walking," Michelle said.

"How come you're not playing with anybody?"

"I am. I'm playing with you."

"But you weren't. You were all by yourself. Don't you have any friends?"

"Sure. I have you, and there's Amanda, too."

"Amanda? Who's Amanda?"

"She's my special friend," Michelle said. "She helps me."

"Helps you? Helps you what?" Annie kicked at the ground, and the merry-go-round began to move, very slowly. Michelle reached out and gave it a push, and it speeded up a little. Annie pulled her feet up and waited until she came around to Michelle before she spoke again. "What does Amanda help you do?"

"Things," Michelle said.

"What kind of things?"

"Never mind," Michelle said, not knowing exactly how to explain Amanda. "Someday maybe you'll meet her."

Annie let the merry-go-round carry her around a few more times, then jumped off.

"How come nobody likes you?" she asked. "I think you're nice."

"And I think you're nice, too," Michelle said, ignoring Annie's question. "What do you want to do now?"

"The swings!" Annie cried. "Will you push me on the swings?"

"Sure," Michelle said. "Come on—I'll race you!"

Annie immediately dashed off in the direction of the swings, and Michelle started after her, moving as quickly as she could and making a great show of panting. When she caught up with Annie, the little girl was giggling happily.

"I won! I won!"

"Just wait," Michelle said. "Someday, I'll learn to run again, and then you'd better watch out!"

But Annie didn't hear her. She was already on the swings, begging to be pushed. Michelle laid her cane on the ground, and stood behind Annie, a little to one side. Slowly, she began pushing the little girl. . . .

Corinne Hatcher sat at her desk, trying to concentrate on the papers she was grading. Ordinarily, she would have ignored them until Monday, and spent Saturday with Tim, but this morning he hadn't called her, and she had known that even if he had, she would have found some excuse. Probably, she would have used these very tests.

And they *were* only an excuse. She wished she could bring herself to simply call Tim, tell him she wished last night's fight had never happened, and suggest they forget about it. But she knew she wouldn't call until she could pretend it was a matter of business. She even knew she would be deceiving no one but herself, but it didn't matter—she still had to have that excuse, that reason for calling other than to make up.

Disgusted with herself, she set her red pen down and glanced out the window.

And saw Michelle.

Her breath drew in sharply, and she instinctively rose from her chair. Michelle was coming into the schoolyard, and Annie Whitmore was apparently waiting for her.

Corinne watched as Annie climbed onto the merry-go-round, and Michelle began pushing it. She could see the two children talking, but she couldn't hear what they were saying. It didn't matter, though—both of them were smiling and laughing.

Then Annie got off the merry-go-round and started toward the swings, slowly at first, then running. For a moment Corinne was worried, afraid that Annie was mocking Michelle, but then she saw that it was a game, and that Michelle had apparently started it, for she was making a great show of trying to run, flailing her arms, panting madly, while Annie watched and laughed.

Corinne found herself laughing, too.

And there, she realized, was her excuse to call Tim. If he thought Michelle was dangerous, wait till he heard about this—she was actually beginning to parody her own lameness!

She left her room and started down the hall toward the office. But as she started to dial, she had a better idea—it still wasn't noon, and if she knew Tim, he'd still be home, lingering over his coffee.

She wouldn't call him. Instead, she'd go to see him, tell him about Michelle. They could spend the day together. As she left the school, Corinne was smiling; today she could even tolerate Lisa Hartwick. She got into her car and started away. As she passed the playground she saw the two girls at the swings, Annie swinging, and Michelle gently pushing her. It was, Corinne Hatcher decided, a good day after all.

"Push me harder, Michelle!"

Annie leaned back in the swing, kicked her little legs up, and tried her best to pump the swing. But she had it wrong, and instead of moving faster, the swing slowed. Again, she called to Michelle. "Harder! I'm dying down!"

"You're high enough already," Michelle said. "You're doing it wrong—you have to lean back when you go forward, and lean forward when you're going back!"

"I'm trying," Annie squealed. She increased her effort, doing her best to follow Michelle's instructions. "I can't do it. Push me harder! Please?"

"No! The way you're pumping, it's dangerous. When you do it wrong, the chains don't work. See? Every time you get to the top, something happens. They get loose, and you drop a little bit."

"I wouldn't if you pushed harder."

Michelle ignored her, and kept steadily pushing, reaching out with her right hand to give Annie a little shove each time she swung past.

But Annie was getting impatient. She wanted Michelle to push her harder. There had to be a way to make her. Then she had an idea. Even as she thought of it, she knew it was mean. But still, if it would make Michelle push her harder. . . .

"You just *can't* push any harder, that's all. You're crippled, so you can't push!"

Crippled!

The word hit her as it always did, like a hammer. Her stomach turned over, and she felt dizzy. Dizzy, and angry.

The fog crashed in on her this time, coming out of nowhere. She could see nothing—only the gray impenetrable mists swirling around her, blocking her vision.

And Amanda.

Amanda, coming toward her out of the grayness, smiling to her, encouraging her.

"You can push her, Michelle," Amanda was saying. "Show her how hard you can push her."

The pain in Michelle's hip, the constant, nearly unbearable throbbing suddenly cleared up, and she felt that she could move easily, without the help of her cane. And if she needed help, Amanda was there —Amanda would help her.

She stepped behind the swing, and the next time Annie came drifting toward her through the fog, she was ready. She put her hands on Annie's back, and as the little girl reached the apex of her arc, and started backward once more, Michelle prepared to push her.

Annie squealed with delight as she surged forward again, and clung more tightly to the chains. This was better—she'd never been this high before. Valiantly, she tried to pump, but she still didn't have the hang of it.

Back she came, and once more she felt Michelle's hands on her shoulders. "Harder!" she yelled. *"Push harder!"*

Again she shot forward, and her eyes widened as she saw the ground rushing up at her. Then she leveled off, and started the upswing, and the ground was replaced by the sky. What was she supposed to do?

Lean forward?

Kick back?

She leaned back, and as the swing reached its forward peak, she was suddenly unbalanced—the chains, so tight in her hands a moment before, abruptly loosened, and Annie felt herself start to fall.

She screamed, but then it was over—the chains

were tight again, and she was on her way back, the weight at the end of the pendulum.

"Not so hard this time," she said when she felt Michelle's hand on her back again.

But if Michelle heard her, she gave no sign. Annie found herself shooting forward again, higher than ever. Once more, as she reached the top, she leaned the wrong way and the chains went slack in her hands.

"Stop!" she yelled. "Please, Michelle, stop!"

But it was too late.

Back and forth she flew, ever higher, and each time the slack in the chain took longer to tighten again.

And then, inevitably, it happened.

The chain went loose in Annie's hands, and she plunged straight down, her body lying across the seat of the swing, her eyes closed tight in terror.

And then there was no more chain.

As the seat of the swing reached the bottom and the hard links of the chain snapped taut, Annie Whitmore's back broke.

A stab of pain shot through her, but it was over almost before it had begun—her head smashed against the ground, the momentum of her fall crushing her skull. She twitched spasmodically, and her broken body fell in a heap at Michelle's feet.

"See?" Amanda whispered. "You can push as hard as you want. After a while, they'll learn. They'll learn, and then they'll stop laughing."

She took Michelle's hand and began leading her out of the playground.

By the time they reached the street, the fog had lifted.

But Michelle didn't look back.

* * *

Corinne opened the door to Tim's house without knocking and let herself in.

"Tim? Tim!"

"In the kitchen," Tim called.

Corinne hurried through the house and found Tim at the sink, elbow deep in dishwater.

"Guess what?"

Tim looked at her curiously. "Well, it must be something special, or you wouldn't be here. And it must have something to do with Michelle Pendleton, since that's who we were fighting about. You don't look particularly upset, so it can't be anything bad. So, you must have seen Michelle, and she must be better."

Deflated, Corinne poured herself a cup of coffee and sat down. "You know what? You know me too well."

"Then I was right?"

"Mmm-hmm. I saw Michelle today. She was in the schoolyard, playing with Annie Whitmore. And she was actually making fun of her own limp! Tim, you should have seen her. She was dragging her leg along, flapping her arms, panting like crazy, and all just to make Annie Whitmore laugh. What do you think of that?"

"I think it's great," Tim said. "But I don't see what all the excitement's about—it had to start sooner or later."

"But I thought—last night you said—"

Tim dried off his hands and came to sit with her. "Last night I was doing a lot of wild speculating, and I might have said some things I didn't mean. And you might have, too. So, shall we have a truce?"

Corinne threw her arms around him. "Oh, Tim, I love you." She kissed him thoroughly, then grinned.

"But isn't it exciting? About Michelle, I mean? It's the first time I've ever seen her do anything like that. She's usually so self-conscious about her limp, and if anyone tries to talk to her about it, she just clams up. But she was making fun of it!"

"Well, before you declare her a perfectly adjusted child, let's see what happens, shall we?" Tim cautioned her. "It might not have been what you thought it was, and it might have been just a momentary thing." Then he grinned mischievously. "And what about Amanda? Have you forgotten all about the famous Amanda?"

"No. Well, not really. Oh, let's not talk about her," Corinne said. "I'll just get all upset again. I was probably overdoing it last night too, and you're probably right—she probably is only a figment of my imagination."

"Well, in that case, Lisa's going to be pretty upset."

"Lisa?"

Tim nodded. "I'm afraid I changed my mind. I mean, we *did* have a fight, after all. So this morning, when Lisa started in on me, I gave in. She's out hunting ghosts."

Corinne stared at him.

"Oh, Tim, you didn't!"

Tim's smile faded at her expression of consternation.

"Well, why not?" he said irritably. "She's with Alison and Sally. What can possibly happen?"

It was at that moment that Billy Evans died in the Paradise Point Clinic, as Cal Pendleton, Josiah Carson, and the neurologist from Boston looked helplessly on.

If any of them had glanced out the window, they would have seen Michelle, standing outside, staring into the room in which Billy lay, a tear running slowly down her cheek.

Amanda's voice whispered in her ear.

"It's done," the strange voice crooned.

Michelle, knowing what had just happened inside, turned away and continued on her long walk home.

CHAPTER 26

"I still don't think we should be here," Jeff Benson said. He glanced over his shoulder toward his house, half expecting his mother to appear at the kitchen window, calling him home. If he'd had his way, he wouldn't have come into the cemetery in the first place, but when Sally Carstairs, Alison Adams, and Lisa Hartwick had appeared that morning, he'd gone with them, thinking they wanted to go down to the cove.

But they hadn't.

Instead, they'd wanted to go looking for the ghost. Mostly, he realized, it was Alison and Lisa who wanted to find Amanda, even though both of them claimed she didn't exist. It had been Sally's idea to start in the cemetery, and when Jeff had protested, she'd accused him of being scared. Well, he wasn't scared—he wasn't scared of the ghost, if there really was one, and he wasn't scared of the cemetery. But there was still his mother, and Jeff didn't want to get into trouble with her.

"If you ask me, I don't think there's anything here at all!"

Alison Adams nodded her agreement. She stood in the middle of the graveyard, her hands on her hips. "Who cares about an old gravestone anyway? Let's go down to the beach—at least that might be fun!"

The four children started back toward the Bensons', and the trail that would take them down the face of the bluff. It was Lisa who suddenly stopped and pointed at the figure of Michelle, coming slowly toward them on the road.

"Here she comes," Lisa said. "Crazy Michelle!"

"She's not crazy," Sally said. "I wish you'd stop talking like that."

"Well, if she's not crazy, how come nobody's seen the ghost except her?" Lisa demanded.

"Stop saying that!" Sally was getting angry now, and she made no attempt to cover it. "Just because you didn't see the ghost, it doesn't mean there isn't one."

"Well, if there is one, why don't you get Michelle to show it to us?" Lisa taunted.

Sally had had enough. "I can't stand you, Lisa Hartwick! You're worse than Susan ever was!" Sally left the group and started toward Michelle.

"Michelle? Michelle, wait up!" she called.

In the road, Michelle stopped and looked curiously at the four children. What did they want? But as Sally came near her, she heard Jeff Benson's voice.

"Hey, Michelle—who did you kill today?"

Sally stopped dead in her tracks and turned back to stare at Jeff.

Michelle stood still for a moment, trying to understand what he meant. Then she realized.

Susan Peterson.

Billy Evans.

He thought she had killed them. But she hadn't— she *knew* she hadn't.

She felt tears welling up in her eyes, and fought to control them. She wouldn't let them see her cry— she wouldn't! She started along the road again, moving as quickly as she could. Her hip was suddenly throbbing with pain, but she tried to ignore it.

Where was Amanda? Why didn't Amanda come and help her?

And then Sally caught up with her.

"Michelle? Michelle, I'm sorry! I don't know why Jeff said that. He didn't mean it!"

"Yes, he did," Michelle said softly, her voice quavering with the tears she was desperately trying to hold back. "He thinks I killed them. Everybody thinks I killed them! But I didn't!"

"I know. I believe you." Sally paused, unsure what to do. "Why don't you come over to my house?" she suggested. "We don't have to stay here and listen to him."

Michelle shook her head. "I'm going home," she said. "Just leave me alone. I want to go home."

Sally reached out to touch Michelle, but Michelle shrank away from her. "Just leave me alone! Please?" Sally stepped back and wondered what to do. She glanced quickly at the three children who seemed to be waiting for her, then back at Michelle.

"All right," she said. "But I'm going to tell Jeff Benson what I think of him!"

"It won't matter," Michelle said. "It won't change

anything." Without saying good-bye to Sally, she began walking away.

Sally watched her go, then started back toward Jeff and the two girls. When she was a few yards from them, she stopped and planted her hands on her hips.

"That was mean and cruel, Jeff Benson."

"It wasn't either!" Jeff shot back. "My mother says she doesn't understand why they don't lock her up! She's crazy!"

"I don't have to listen to you anymore! I'm going home. Come on, Alison."

Her face set, Sally wheeled around and started back toward the road. Alison hesitated for a minute, then started after her. "Are you coming, Lisa?"

"I want to go down to the cove," Lisa whined.

"Then go to the cove," Alison told her. "I'm going with Sally."

"Who cares?" Lisa shouted to the departing girls. "Who cares what you do? Why don't you go see your crazy friend?"

Ignoring her, Sally and Alison continued on their way. When Lisa saw she wasn't going to get a reaction from them, she shrugged.

"Come on," she said to Jeff. "I'll race you down the trail!"

Michelle hobbled painfully up the front steps and across the porch. She opened the door, stepped into the house, and stood still for a moment, listening.

There was no sound, except for the soft ticking of the clock in the hall.

"Mom?"

When there was no reply, Michelle started up the stairs. In her room, she would be safe.

Safe from Jeff Benson's terrible words.

Safe from his accusations.

Safe from the suspicion she could feel all around her.

That's why her mother hadn't wanted her to go with her father this morning.

Her mother thought the same things Jeff Benson thought.

But it wasn't true—she knew it wasn't true.

She went into her room, closed the door, and moved to the window seat.

She picked up her doll and cradled it in her arms.

"Amanda? Please, Amanda, tell me what's happening. Why do they all hate me?"

"They're telling lies about you," Amanda's voice whispered to her. "They want to take you away, so they're telling lies about you."

"Take me away? Why? Why do they want to take me away?"

"Because of me."

"I—I don't understand."

"Because of me," Amanda repeated. "They always hated me. They don't want me to have any friends. But you're my friend, so now they hate you, too. And they'll take you away."

"I don't care," Michelle said. "I don't like it here anymore. I want to go away."

Michelle could see Amanda now. She was only a few feet from her, and her eyes, pale and shining in the gray light of the overcast day, seemed to be boring into Michelle.

"But if you let them take you away," she heard Amanda saying, "we can't be friends anymore."

"You can come too," Michelle suggested. "If they take me away, you can come with me."

"No!" Amanda's voice was suddenly sharp, and Michelle instinctively stepped backward, clutching the doll close to her chest. Amanda moved toward her, her hand out.

"I can't go with you. I have to stay here." She took Michelle's hand. "Stay with me, Michelle. Stay with me, and we'll make them all stop hating us."

"I don't want to!" Michelle protested. "I don't know what you want. And you always promise to help me, but something always happens. And they blame me for it. It's your fault, but they blame me for it! It isn't fair! Why should they blame me, when it's you?"

"Because we're the same," Amanda said quietly. "Can't you understand that? We're exactly the same."

"But I don't want to be like you," Michelle said. "I want to be like *me*. I want to be like I used to be, before you came."

"Don't say that," Amanda hissed. Her face, furious now, was twisted into an expression of hatred. "If you say that again, I'll kill you." She paused, and her milky eyes seemed to blaze with a light of their own. "I can do it," she said softly. "You know I can."

Michelle shrank away from the black-clad figure, terrified. She wanted to run, but she knew she couldn't. She knew that Amanda was telling her the truth.

If she didn't do what Amanda wanted her to, Amanda would kill her.

"All right," she said. "What do you want me to do?"

As she said the words, the rage seemed to drain from Amanda's face, and she smiled. "Take me out to the bluff," she said. "I want to go out on the bluff, out by the cemetery." She took Michelle's hand once more and started to lead her out of the room.

"This is the last time," she said softly. "After this, it'll all be over, and they won't laugh at me anymore."

Michelle wasn't sure what Amanda was talking about, but it didn't matter. All she knew was that it was almost over.

This is the last time, Amanda had said.

Maybe things were going to be all right after all. Maybe after she'd done whatever Amanda wanted, things would be all right.

She left the house and began walking slowly toward the cemetery.

June stood very still, staring at the canvas on her easel.

How it had gotten there, she didn't know.

Yet there it was, terrifying her. She had been staring at it for a long time—it was as if the picture had trapped her in some kind of hypnotic trance.

It was the same picture she had found in the closet.

Only it was finished now.

She stared at it in utter horror, unable to fully comprehend it.

The sketch was now a complete painting.

There were two people, a man and a woman.

The man's face was still hidden from view, but the woman's face was not.

It was a beautiful face, with high cheekbones, full lips, and a perfect widow's peak at the forehead.

The eyes, green and sparkling, were almond-shaped, and they seemed to be laughing.

It would have been a beautiful picture, except for two things.

The woman was bleeding.

From her breast, and from her throat, blood was gushing, spilling down the woman's body, dripping to the floor. In contrast to the serene expression on the the painted face, the blood had a grotesque quality to it. It was almost as if the woman didn't know she was dying.

And scrawled across the picture, in the same crimson as the blood pouring from the dying woman, was one word: *Whore!*

It was hard for June to look at anything in the picture except for the woman's face, but as she stared at it, trying to fathom it, she began to realize that the background of the picture was familiar.

It was the studio.

The windows were there, and the ocean beyond. The two figures were on a couch. June slowly moved across the studio until her perspective on the windows and the sea was the same as that on the canvas.

She glanced around, trying to place the couch in the picture. It would have been a little to the left, standing out from the wall about five feet.

She realized where it would have been before she really looked.

The stain.

The ancient stain she had tried so hard to clean up.

She forced herself to look at the spot.

"No!"

She screamed the word, then screamed it again.

"Dear God, no! It's not happening!"

Across the floor, from no apparent source, a stain

was spreading. June stood transfixed, unable to tear her eyes from the spot.

It *was* blood.

"No!" She uttered the word once more, then, calling on all her willpower, she fled from the studio.

Jennifer, lying in her bassinet—forgotten by her mother—began to cry. Softly at first, then louder.

At the clinic, Josiah Carson and Cal Pendleton sat quietly in their office, waiting for the neurosurgeon to finish his autopsy.

The moment Billy Evans had died, Cal had taken the responsibility for his death upon himself.

"I moved him. I should have waited."

"You had to move him," Josiah told him. "You were just too late, that's all. If you had only gotten to him sooner—" Carson let his voice trail off, let the words sink into the distraught man across from him, sure that Cal was remembering the panic that had gripped him yesterday. Then, when he was sure Cal understood him, he made his voice soothing. "By the time you got to him, the damage was already done. It's not really your fault, Cal."

Before Cal could make any reply, the phone rang. Carson picked it up. He recognized June Pendleton's voice, knew she was crying.

Something had happened.

She was sobbing, nearly incoherent, but Josiah understood that she wanted them to come out to the house immediately.

"June, calm down," he said. "Cal's right here, with me. We'll get there as soon as we can." He paused, then: "June, is anyone hurt?" He listened for a moment, then told her to stay where she was. Cal stared at him as he replaced the receiver on the hook.

"What's happened? Josiah, what's happened?"

"I'm not sure," Carson replied. "June wants us out at the house, right now. Nobody's hurt, but something's wrong. Come on." He stood up, but Cal hesitated.

"What about—?"

"Billy? He's already dead, Cal. There's nothing we can do for him. Let's go."

Cal reached for his coat.

"She didn't say what was wrong?"

Carson ignored the question and led Cal out of the office.

As they left the clinic, Josiah Carson realized what was happening. It was all about to come together. He didn't know how, but he was sure. June Pendleton had found something.

Something that was going to explain everything.

Or make it worse.

June had just put the telephone down, and was wondering what to do next, when it suddenly began ringing. *He's not coming,* she thought. *It's Cal, and he's not coming. He's going to tell me he's busy, and he can't come. What am I going to do?*

She picked up the phone.

"Cal?"

"June? It's Corinne Hatcher."

"Oh." June's voice faltered. "I'm sorry. I was just talking to Cal. I—I thought maybe he was calling me back."

"I won't keep you long. Look, this may sound crazy, but have you seen Lisa Hartwick today? I'm with Tim, and we're trying to find her. She and some friends—well, it sounds silly, but they were going ghost-hunting."

June had heard nothing except that Corinne was with Tim Hartwick.

"Corinne, can you and Tim come out here?" She tried to keep her voice calm, reasonable. "Something strange has happened."

Corinne was silent for a moment. Then: "Strange? What do you mean?"

"I can't begin to describe it," June said. "Please come."

There was an edge of panic in her voice that made Corinne say, "We'll be right there."

Sally Carstairs and Alison Adams crossed the street and began walking toward the schoolground, intending to take the shortcut across it to Sally's house on the other side.

"We shouldn't have left Lisa," Sally was saying. "When Mom finds out, she'll be mad."

"There isn't anything we could have done about it," Alison replied. "Lisa's like that—she always does whatever she wants to. If you want to do it too, fine, but if you don't, tough!"

"I thought you liked her."

Alison shrugged. "She's okay, I guess. She's just spoiled." They walked along in silence for a moment, then a thought occurred to Alison. "I thought you were her friend."

"Whose?"

"Michelle's. Before she got crippled, I mean."

"I was." Sally smiled, remembering how Michelle had been only a few short weeks ago. "She was nice.

She probably would have been my best friend. But ever since she fell, she's sort of stayed by herself."

"Do you think she's crazy?"

"Of course not," Sally said. "She's just—well, she's just different now."

Alison suddenly stopped short. Her face turned pale. "Sally!" she gasped. "Look!"

They were near the swings, and Sally quickly saw what Alison was pointing at.

Annie Whitmore's body lay twisted in the dirt, one leg still hooked over the seat of the swing.

Jeff Benson's words rang loudly in Sally's ears.

Who did you kill today?

She remembered last week, when Michelle had been playing with Annie Whitmore.

Who did you kill today?

She remembered Michelle, walking along the road, coming from town.

Who did you kill today?

Grabbing Alison's hand, Sally Carstairs began running across the playground—running home, running to tell her mother what had happened.

CHAPTER 27

Michelle walked slowly along the trail at the top of the bluff. A light rain was beginning to fall, and the horizon, indistinct against the steel gray sky, faded away. But Michelle, listening to Amanda's murmurings, was oblivious to the day.

"Further," Amanda said. "It was a little further."

They took a few more steps, and then Amanda stopped, her brow creased, her expression uncertain.

"It's not right. It's all changed." Then: "Over there." She drew Michelle a few yards farther north and stopped near a large boulder that stood precariously balanced above the beach.

"Here," Amanda breathed. "It was right here . . ."

Michelle looked down to the beach below. They were directly above the spot where only a month and a half ago she had picnicked with her friends. At least, they had been her friends at the time.

Now the beach was empty; the tide was out, and

the litter of rocks, worn smooth by centuries of flowing water, lay exposed to the threatening afternoon.

"Look," Amanda whispered. She was pointing to
the far edge of the beach, where the retreating sea
had laid bare the shelf of tidepools. Michelle could
make out two figures, indistinct in the rain.

One of them she recognized at once: Jeff Benson.
And the other one—who was the other one? But suddenly she knew it didn't matter.

Jeff was the one.

It was Jeff Amanda wanted.

Who did you kill today?

His words rang in her ears, and Michelle knew
Amanda was listening to them, too.

"He'll come this way," Amanda purred. "When the
tide comes in, he'll come this way. And then. . . ."
Her voice trailed off, but a smile wreathed her face.
She kept one hand on Michelle's arm, but with the
other she reached out and touched the boulder. . . .

June was still sitting by the telephone when Cal
and Josiah Carson arrived.

She heard them come through the front door, heard
Cal calling to her.

"In here," she replied. "I'm in here."

Her voice was dull, and she was pale. He went to
her, kneeling down by her chair.

"June, what is it? What's wrong?"

"The studio—it's in the studio."

"What is? Has something happened? Where are
the kids?"

June stared at him, her face uncomprehending.
"The kids?" she echoed. Then it hit her. "Jenny! My
God, I left Jenny in the studio!"

Her torpor was gone. She stood up, but a wave of dizziness struck her and she sank back into her chair. "Cal, I can't do it—I can't go out there. Please, go out there, and take Dr. Carson with you. Bring Jenny back with you."

"You can't go out there?" Cal asked. His expression reflected bewilderment. "Why not? What's happened?"

"You'll know. Just go out there, and look. You'll see." The two men started out of the room, but June stopped them. "And Cal? The picture—the picture on the easel: I didn't paint it."

Cal and Josiah exchanged an uncomprehending look, but when June said nothing else, they started for the studio.

They could hear Jenny crying before they were halfway there. Cal broke into a run. He dashed inside, glanced hurriedly around, but ignored everything except his daughter. Scooping the howling baby into his arms, he cradled her against his chest.

"It's all right, princess," he crooned. "Daddy's here, and everything's going to be fine."

He rocked her gently for a moment, and her howling quieted. Only then did he look at the painting on the easel, the painting that June had made such a point of saying she hadn't done.

He stared at it, frowning slightly. At first, it made no sense. And then he realized what it was—a woman, dying in the act of making love, her expression a combination of rapture and—and something else. But what was it?

"I don't get it—" he began, his voice puzzled and uncertain. But then he saw the expression on Josiah Carson's face, and his words faded in his throat.

Carson was staring at the picture, a look of comprehension slowly taking shape on his face.

"So that's it," he whispered. "That's what happened."

Cal stared at the old doctor. "Joe, what is it? Are you all right?" He took a step toward Carson, but the old man waved him aside.

"She's done it," he said. "Amanda finally saw her mother, and she killed her. A hundred years later— she killed her. Now she'll be free. Now we'll all be free." He turned to Cal. "It was right that you came here," he said quietly. "You owed it to us. You killed Alan Hanley, so you owed it to us."

Cal looked wildly from Josiah to the picture, then back to Josiah. "What the hell are you talking about?" he shouted. "What's going on? What is it?"

"The picture," Carson said softly. "It's all in the picture. *That woman is Louise Carson.*"

"I—I don't understand—"

"I'm trying to tell you, Cal," Carson said. His voice was reasonable, but a strange glint shone in his eyes. "That woman—it's Louise Carson. She's buried out in the cemetery. My God, Cal, June went into labor on her grave—don't you remember?"

"But that's not possible," Cal said. "How would June know—" Then he remembered: *I didn't paint it . . .*

Cal moved closer to the painting, studying it carefully. The paint was fresh, barely dry. He stepped back again. Only then did he realize that the setting of the picture was the studio. It gave him an eerie feeling. His gaze left the canvas to sweep over the room. He was vaguely aware of Josiah Carson, behind him, muttering indistinctly.

"She's here," Carson whispered. "Don't you under-stand, Cal? It's Amanda. She's using Michelle. She's here. Can't you feel it? She's *here!*"

He began laughing then, softly at first, then louder and louder until Cal could stand it no longer.

"*Stop that!*" he shouted.

It was as though a spell had been broken. Carson shook himself, then glanced once more at the picture. With an odd expression of victory on his face, he started for the door. "Come on," he said. "We'd better get back to the house. I have a feeling things have just begun."

Cal was about to follow him when he saw the stain on the floor. "Jesus," he whispered.

It was as it had been the day they moved in. Reddish brown, thick, caked with dust, almost un-identifiable. But it had been cleaned up. He remem-bered it clearly, remembered June, on her hands and knees, chipping at it.

And now it was back.

Once more, he looked at the painting. The blood, dripping from Louise Carson's wounded breast, gush-ing from her open throat. . . .

It was as if somehow the past, so clearly depicted on the canvas, was alive again in the studio.

Tim Hartwick and Corinne Hatcher arrived as Cal and Josiah Carson returned to the house. June, still pale, hadn't moved from her chair in the living room. The group gathered around her.

"Did you see it?" June asked Cal. He nodded. "I didn't paint it," June repeated.

"Where did it come from?"

"The closet," June said vacantly. "I found it in the

closet a week or so ago. It—it was only a sketch then. But today, when I went out there, it was on the easel."

"What was?" Tim broke in. "What are you talking about?"

"A picture," June said softly. "It's in the studio. You might as well go look at it—it's what I wanted you to see."

Mystified, Tim and Corinne started out of the room, but paused as the telephone rang. Though June was closest to the phone, she made no move to pick it up, and it was Cal who finally answered.

"Hello?"

"Dr. Pendleton?" The voice at the other end was shaking.

"Yes."

"This is Bertha Carstairs. I—I wonder, is Joe Carson there with you?"

Cal frowned slightly. "Yes, he is." He looked questioningly at Carson, half-expecting him to refuse the call. But Carson seemed to be himself again, as if the strange scene in the studio had never happened. He took the phone.

"This is Dr. Carson."

"It's Bertha Carstairs, Joe. Something terrible has happened. Sally and Alison Adams just came in, and they told me that Annie Whitmore is in the playground. Joe—they think she's dead.

"She's under the swings. Sally said it looked as though she'd fallen off. Like it was an accident or something . . ."

Her voice trailed off, and Carson knew she was holding something back.

"What else, Bertha? There is something else, isn't there?"

Bertha Carstairs hesitated, and when she spoke again, she sounded almost apologetic.

"I'm not sure," she said slowly. "It might not be important—it might not mean anything at all—but, well. . . ." She paused a second, then her words came clearly over the line. "Joe, Sally saw Michelle Pendleton today. She was walking along the road, coming from town. And Sally said that last week Michelle and Annie were playing together quite a bit, and what with Susan Peterson, and Billy Evans—well, I don't know. I hate to say it. . . ." Again, Bertha's voice faded away.

"I understand," Carson said. "It's all right, Bertha."

He hung up the phone and turned to the four people who were watching him. "It's Annie Whitmore," he said. "Something's happened to her." He told them what Bertha Carstairs had said, leaving out nothing.

"Dear God," June moaned when he was done. "Help Michelle. Please help her!" Then her eyes widened and she leaped to her feet.

"But where is she?" she cried. "If Sally saw her coming out this way, she must have been coming home." Her eyes suddenly wild, she ran toward the hall. "Michelle? MICHELLE!"

They heard her repeat her daughter's name as she ran up the stairs. Suddenly there was a silence, then they heard her coming back down again.

"She's not here. Cal, she's not here!"

"It's all right," Cal told her. "We'll find her."

"Lisa!" Tim's voice was choked, but only Corinne knew what he meant.

"She was with Sally and Alison," she said. "Uncle Joe, did Mrs. Carstairs say anything about Lisa?"

Josiah Carson shook his head. Tim grabbed the

phone. "What's her number?" he demanded. "Quick, what's the Carstairses' number?"

Snatching the telephone from him, Corinne dialed. The phone rang once, twice, then twice again before Bertha Carstairs's harried voice came on the line.

"Mrs. Carstairs? This is Corinne Hatcher. What about Lisa Hartwick? Was she with Sally and Alison? Did she come home with them?"

"Why, no," Bertha said. "Just a minute—" There was a silence, then Bertha came back on the line.

"She stayed out at the Bensons'. She and Jeff were going down to the cove. I wish the kids wouldn't play down there—the currents are so dangerous—"

But Corinne cut her off. "Never mind," she said. "I'm out at the Pendletons', and I'm sure we'll find her." She hung up the phone and turned to Tim.

"She's out here somewhere. She and Jeff Benson were going down to the beach."

"It's that doll," June suddenly screamed. "It's that damned doll!" They stared at her, but only Josiah Carson understood what she was saying. "Don't you see it?" she cried. "It all started with that damned doll!" Once again June rushed up the stairs and burst into Michelle's room. She looked around frantically, searching for the doll.

Amanda!

It was all Amanda's fault.

If she could just get rid of the doll!

And then she saw it, propped up on the window seat, its glass eyes staring emptily out toward Devil's Passage. She crossed the room and picked it up. But as she was about to turn away from the window, a flicker of movement caught her eye.

She stared out, trying to see through the rain-blurred glass.

Out by the bluff, north, close to the cemetery.

It was Michelle.

Standing on the bluff, leaning against a boulder, staring down toward the beach.

But she wasn't leaning against the boulder.

What was she doing?

She was pushing it.

"Oh, no," June gasped. Grabbing the doll, she dashed out of the room.

"She's outside," she called. "Michelle's outside! Cal, go get her. Please, go get her!"

The fog was gathering quickly around Michelle, and the beach had disappeared. All she was aware of was Amanda, standing close to her, touching her, whispering to her.

"They're coming. I can see them, Michelle. I can see them! They're coming closer . . . they're almost there. . . . Now! Help me, Michelle. Help me!"

Michelle reached out, touched the rock. It seemed to vibrate under her fingers, as if it were alive.

"Harder," Amanda hissed. "We have to push it harder, before it's too late!"

Again, Michelle felt the rock move, then watched as it teetered. She wanted to pull away from it, but couldn't. She felt it slip, lurch a little, then come free. . . .

It was a low sound, almost lost in the crashing of the surf, but Jeff heard it, and looked up.

Above him.

The sound had come from above him.

Then he saw it, plunging toward him.

He knew the rock was going to hit him, knew he had to move quickly, jump to the side—backward—anywhere. But he couldn't move. His mouth quivered, and his stomach tightened. He was going to die—he knew it.

But he was frozen. Only at the last second did his muscles suddenly obey him. Too late.

The boulder, four feet across, hit him. He buckled to the ground, feeling the crushing weight of it, and he thought he could hear it, grinding him under its mass.

And he could hear something else, too.

Laughter.

It floated over him as he died, and he wondered where it was coming from. It was a little girl, and she was laughing at him. But why? What had he done?

Then Jeff Benson died.

Michelle heard the laughter, too, and knew it was Amanda. Amanda was pleased with her, and that made her happy. But she wasn't sure why Amanda was pleased.

The fog began to clear, and Michelle looked down. She could see the beach again.

There was a girl on the beach, standing still, staring at the fallen rock. It could have hit her, Michelle realized. But it hadn't.

Then why was the girl screaming?

It was the boulder. Something was sticking out from under the boulder. But what was it?

The last traces of the fog drifted away, and Michelle could see clearly.

It was a leg. Someone's leg was sticking out from under the rock.

And Amanda was laughing. Amanda was laughing, and saying something to her. She listened carefully, straining to hear Amanda's words.

"It's done," Amanda was saying. "It's done, all of it, and I can go now. Good-bye, Michelle." She laughed once more, happily, and then the sound of her voice faded away.

There were other voices now. Michelle could hear them. Voices calling to her, shouting at her.

She turned. There were people running toward her, calling her name.

She knew what they wanted.

They wanted to catch her, to punish her, to send her away.

But she hadn't done anything. It was Amanda who did it. All she had done was obey Amanda. How could they blame her? But they would—she knew they would.

It was like her dream.

She had to get away from them. She couldn't let them catch her.

She began running, her lame leg dragging at her, holding her back. Her hip throbbed with pain, but she tried to ignore it.

The voices were getting closer to her—they were catching up with her. She stopped, just as she had in the dream, and looked back.

She recognized her father, and Dr. Carson. And there was her teacher, Miss Hatcher. And that other man—who was he? Oh, yes, Mr. Hartwick. Why was he after her? She had thought he was her friend. But he wasn't, she knew that now. He had been trying to trick her. He hated her too.

Amanda. Only Amanda was her friend.

But Amanda had gone.

Gone where?

She didn't know.

All she knew was that she had to get away, and that she couldn't run.

But in her dream she had gotten away. Desperately, she tried to remember what she had done in her dream.

She had fallen.

That was it.

She had fallen, just like Susan Peterson, and Billy Evans, and Annie Whitmore. And like Jeff Benson, fallen under the rock.

That was the answer.

She would fall, and Amanda would take care of her.

As the voices closed in around her, shouted to her, Michelle Pendleton stepped off the bluff.

But Amanda didn't come to take care of her. Just before she hit the rocks, she knew.

Amanda was never going to come again. The rocks reached out to her, as they had in the dream. Only this time, she didn't scream.

This time, Michelle welcomed their embrace.

There was a quiet in the living room of the Pendletons' house, but the silence offered no peace to the four people who sat stiffly around the fireplace. June seemed almost impassive, her eyes fixed on the fire that she had lit early in the day, lit only so that she could burn the doll. And burn it she had, and then,

as if by unspoken consent, the fire had been kept
alive.

They still didn't know what had happened.

Josiah Carson had gone home, refusing to tell any
of them what he had been talking about in the studio.
Cal had tried to repeat Josiah's garbled mumblings,
but they seemed to make no sense, and finally, sometime in the afternoon, Tim had gone out to the studio.
He had stared at the strange painting for a long time,
then begun searching, not knowing exactly what he
was looking for, but knowing that somewhere there
would be something—something that would give him
an answer.

He had found the sketches and taken them into the
house. They had studied them, and seen with their
own eyes how Susan Peterson had died, and how
Billy Evans had died.

And each of them, at one time or another, had
drifted out to the studio to look once more at the
crimson-streaked painting that still rested on the
easel, a mysterious link with a past they didn't understand.

It was Corinne who first noticed the shadow.

It was indistinct, nearly lost in the vivid violence
of the picture, but once she had pointed it out to
them, they all saw it.

From one corner of the picture, a shadow appeared
to project across the floor toward the dying Louise
Carson.

It was a silhouette, really. A silhouette of a young
girl, wearing an old-fashioned dress, and a bonnet.
One of her arms was raised, and in her hand there
seemed to be some kind of an object.

To each of them it was clear that the object in the child's hand was a knife.

They all knew that Michelle had done the sketches and the painting. Tim insisted that it was the dark side of her personality expressing itself. She must have seen a picture of Louise Carson somewhere, and the image had remained in her mind. And then, as she began to invent "Amanda," she had begun to take the stories of Paradise Point, the legends of that other, long-dead Amanda, and weave them together. For her, the ghost had truly been real. Even though it existed only in her own mind, it had been real.

Lisa Hartwick had been given a sedative and put to bed. When she woke up she felt confused, then remembered where she was.

She was in Michelle Pendleton's bed, in Michelle Pendleton's house.

She got out of bed, and went to the door. She listened, and heard the sound of voices murmuring downstairs. She opened the door and called to her father.

"Daddy?"

A moment later Tim appeared at the foot of the stairs.

"I can't sleep," Lisa complained.

"Well, that's all right. We'll be going home soon, anyway."

"Can we go now?" Lisa asked. "I don't like it here."

"Right away, honey," Tim promised. "You get dressed, then we'll go."

Lisa returned to the bedroom, and began dressing. She knew what they were talking about downstairs.

They were talking about Michelle Pendleton.

Lisa wanted to talk about her too, and tell everyone what she had seen on the beach.

But she was afraid to.

She was sure that if she told them, they would think she was crazy, too.

As she started down the stairs, she decided that she would never tell them what she had seen. Besides, maybe she hadn't really seen it at all.

Maybe there really hadn't been anybody up there with Michelle. Maybe what she'd seen hadn't been a little girl in a black dress, wearing a bonnet.

Maybe it had only been a shadow.

EPILOGUE

It was Jennifer Pendleton's twelfth birthday.

Jenny had grown into a beautiful girl, tall, blond
and blue-eyed like her parents, with a finely chisele[d]
face that belied her youth. People meeting her fo[r]
the first time seldom realized how young she wa[s]
and Jenny enjoyed pretending to be older than he[r]
years. If it worried June and Cal when boys seven o[r]
eight years older than their daughter called Jenn[y]
for dates, they tried not to show it: Jennifer was no[t]
only beautiful, but she was bright, and if she though[t]
she could get away with it, she delighted in watchin[g]
her parents worry about her.

June Pendleton had become something of a[n]
anomaly in Paradise Point. As the years passed, thos[e]
twelve years since the Pendletons had come fro[m]
Boston hoping for a better life and found, instead, [a]
nightmare that had, finally, been beyond their com[-]
prehension, June had turned more and more to he[r]

t. She had found it difficult to make friends in Paradise Point—first because she was a stranger, and later, though it was never said to her face, because certain people in town had never forgiven her for her daughter's madness. Even as Michelle and her strange insanity passed into the lore of the Point, her mother still lived with it, was reminded of it every day.

At first, she had wanted to leave and return to Boston. But Cal had refused. Through it all, his love for the house had never wavered. And, though he never spoke of it, not even to his wife, he had never forgotten Josiah Carson's strange words in the studio that day. Whether Carson had spoken the truth or not, Cal chose to believe him. He was, at last, free of the guilt that had plagued him since the day Alan had died. He hadn't killed Alan—Amanda ne that, as she had killed them all, including m daughter. So he had stayed in Paradise gnored the talk, and thrived.

h Carson had left the Point almost immedi- after Michelle died. Nearly everyone in the had thought that something had gone wrong arson's mind—he had spent his last few days adise Point rambling about the "vengeance of st," but nobody had paid too much attention Instead, Carson's vague mumblings only built hy for Cal. Slowly at first, but inevitably, they gun to accept him as the village doctor. There ter all, no one else.

er Cal nor June ever talked about the events lve years ago, and when they talked of Mi- which was seldom, they talked about Michelle as she had been before they had come to Paradise Point. Those first two months in Paradise Point, the months that had nearly torn their family apart, they preferred to ignore.

June didn't mind; the memories were too painful.

And so the Pendletons lived quietly in the old house above the sea, Cal happily tending to his small practice, and June quietly working in her studio, on her darkly threatening seascapes.

And through it all, Jennifer had grown up, carefully shielded from the tragedies of the first weeks of her life. She heard rumors, of course—it would have been impossible for her not to have. But whenever she had asked her parents about the rumors, they assured her that she mustn't believe everything she heard from her schoolmates. Stories, they told her, had a way of getting exaggerated.

That Jennifer could rarely convince any of her friends to come to her house had stopped bothering her years earlier—she simply attributed it to the fact that she lived too far out of town.

But then, for her twelfth birthday, she had asked if she could have a party.

June had opposed the idea, sure that the mothers of Paradise Point would never allow their children to come out to the house, but Jennifer had, as always, gone to her father. Cal had overruled June, telling her that he thought it was time Jenny began having a social life.

And, when the party actually took place, and all Jennifer's friends showed up, June began to think that maybe she had been wrong—maybe Paradise Point *was* beginning to forget.

* * *

Carrie Peterson looked curiously around the old house. She wondered, for the fourth time, why her parents had argued with her about coming out here. It seemed to her like a perfectly ordinary house. How could anybody believe the stories her parents had told her? Well, they were pretty old, Carrie thought, and old people had all kinds of funny ideas. She thought the house was great.

"Jenny, can I see the upstairs?" she asked. Jenny grinned at her.

"Sure. Come on."

Leaving the party, the two girls climbed to the second floor. Jenny led Carrie down the hall to the large corner room she had moved into a year earlier. "This is my room."

Carrie immediately crossed the room to sit on the window seat. She stared rapturously out at the sea and sighed happily. "I think I could stay in this room forever."

"I know," Jenny agreed. "But my parents didn't want to let me have it. I had to argue, and argue."

"Why?" Carrie asked.

"It was my sister's room," Jenny said.

"Oh." Carrie remembered all the stories she'd heard about Jenny's sister. "She was crazy, wasn't she?" she asked.

"Crazy?" Jenny asked. "What do you mean?"

Carrie looked at her curiously. "Well, Jenny, everybody *knows* your sister killed four people. So she must have been crazy, right? I mean, it's either that, or you have to believe all the ghost stories, and who's going to believe that old stuff?"

Suddenly Jenny realized why her mother hadn't

wanted her to have the party. Her mother had known. She'd known that the kids would come, and they'd look around, and then they'd start asking about Michelle. But Jenny didn't want to talk about Michelle. She didn't know very much about her, and what little she did know had never made very much sense.

"Can't we talk about something else?" she said. But Carrie was not to be put off.

"You know, my mother didn't want me to come out here today. She says this house does things to people. She says as long as it's been here, it's had a reputation, whatever that means. I guess it means this house makes people crazy. Do you think that's possible?"

"It hasn't made me crazy," Jenny said levelly. Carrie's prattle was making her angry, but she was trying not to show it.

"Yes, but you're different," Carrie said. "You were born on a grave. Now, that's what *I* call creepy!"

"I was not born on a grave!" Jennifer said hotly. At least she was sure of this much. "I was born in the clinic, in my father's office. Just because I started to come while my mother was in the cemetery, doesn't mean I was born on a grave."

"Well, it doesn't really matter, does it?" Carrie said. "Even though old Mrs. Benson always said it was a bad omen. And I guess she was right, wasn't she? I mean, with Michelle killing her little boy, and all that?"

Jenny's anger suddenly reached the boiling point. "Carrie Peterson, you take that back! It's a lie, and you know it. You take it back!"

Faced with Jenny's wrath, Carrie's expression

turned stubborn. "I won't," she said. "I won't, and you can't make me."

The two girls glared at each other, but it was Jenny who broke away first. "I want you to go home," she said. "I want you to go home, and take all your friends with you!"

"Well, I wouldn't stay here another minute, anyway," Carrie shot back. "Maybe mother's right—maybe this house does make people crazy!"

She stamped out of the room. Jenny heard her going down the stairs, calling to all her friends. There was a momentary hubbub, and then she heard the front door opening and closing.

And, finally, silence.

Only then did Jennifer go downstairs.

June was standing in the hall, perplexed.

"What happened, sweetheart? Why did everyone leave so suddenly?"

"I asked them to," Jenny said. "It was a crummy party, so I told them all to go home."

June's Bostonian breeding, her sense of propriety, a sense she thought she had left behind her years ago, came flooding back. "You shouldn't have done that," she said sharply. "You were their hostess—if the party wasn't going smoothly, you should have done something to make it right. Now I want you to go to your room, and think about it, then this evening you can call up every one of those children, and apologize. Do I make myself clear?"

Jenny stared at her mother. She'd never talked like this to her before—never in her life. And it hadn't even been her fault—it had been Carrie Peterson's fault! Hurt, Jenny burst into tears and fled up the stairs.

As soon as she got to her room, she saw the package.

It was sitting on her bed, wrapped in silver paper, with an immense blue bow on it.

Jenny frowned.

Why hadn't she seen it before?

Then she figured it out. While her mother had been lecturing her, her father had slipped into her room and left it on the bed—a special surprise.

Jenny was grinning as she opened the package, and as she lifted the gift out of the box, her grin turned into a smile.

It was a beautiful doll—and old! Jenny realized it must be an antique, and wondered where her parents had gotten it. She'd never seen anything like it.

It had a blue dress, all ruffles and lace, and a perfect porcelain face, surrounded by dark curls held in place by a tiny bonnet.

Jenny hugged it close. "You're beautiful," she whispered. "You're so beautiful." Her hurt and anger completely dissipated by the gift, she rushed downstairs.

"Mom? Mom! Where are you?"

"I'm in the kitchen," June called. "What is it?"

Jenny burst into the kitchen, and threw her arms around her mother. "Oh, Mother, thank you! Thank you, thank you, thank you! It's beautiful. Just perfect!"

Puzzled, June disengaged herself from Jenny's arms.

"Well, I'm glad you like it," she laughed. "But would you mind telling me what you're talking about?"

"My doll," Jenny cried. "My beautiful doll." Then,

as June stood looking at her in amazement, Jenny had
an inspiration. "I know what I'm going to name her!
I'll call her Michelle! It's such a beautiful name, and
I've always wished Michelle and I could have been
friends. She was beautiful, wasn't she? With dark
hair, and beautiful brown eyes? I'll bet the doll looks
just like her! So now we *can* be friends. Oh, Mom, it's
just wonderful. Where's Dad? I've got to find Dad,
and thank him!"

And then she was gone, out of the house, searching
for her father.

June stood quite still, trying to put it all together.
A doll? What doll?

What was Jenny talking about?

Slowly, a thought beginning to grow in her mind,
June left the kitchen and headed for the stairs.

It couldn't be true.

She knew it couldn't.

It was quite impossible.

But Jenny was going to name the doll Michelle.

June started up the stairs.

She paused at the door to Jenny's room.

The room she hadn't wanted Jenny to have.

But Jenny had insisted, and she had given in.

She opened the door hesitantly, and stepped inside.

The doll was on the bed, and as she looked at it,
June felt a scream build inside her.

She had burned the doll. She clearly remembered
burning it, twelve years ago.

But it was there, and it was not burned, and its
sightless, glassy eyes stared blindly up at June.

As the beginnings of panic began to grip her mind,
a memory welled up inside her, a memory from her
youth.

It was a bit of poetry, from Milton:

> Comes the blind Fury with th' abhorred shears,
> And slits the thin-spun life.

Very quietly, June Pendleton began to cry.

When the Wind Blows

A chilling novel of occult terror! **John Saul**

author of *Suffer the Children* and *Punish the Sinners*

To the Indians, the ancient mine was a sacred place. To the local residents, it was their source of livelihood.

But the mine contains a deadly secret—and the souls of the town's lost children. Their cries can be heard at night, when the wind blows—and the terror begins.

A DELL BOOK $3.50   (19857-7)